THE NEW ELITE

THE NEW ELITE

EXCEPTIONAL S. BEAUFONT™ BOOK 4

SARAH NOFFKE

MICHAEL ANDERLE

DISRUPTIVE IMAGINATION®

Copyright © 2020 Sarah Noffke & Michael Anderle
Cover by Mihaela Voicu http://www.mihaelavoicu.com/
Cover copyright © LMBPN Publishing
A Michael Anderle Production

LMBPN Publishing
PMB 196, 2540 South Maryland Pkwy
Las Vegas, NV 89109

First US Edition, March 2020
Version 1.03, June 2021
eBook ISBN: 978-1-64202-787-7
Print ISBN: 978-1-64202-788-4

THE NEW ELITE TEAM

Thanks to the JIT Readers

Angel LaVey
Deb Mader
Debi Sateren
Diane L. Smith
Dorothy Lloyd
Jackey Hankard-Brodie
Jeff Eaton
Jeff Goode
Larry Omans
Micky Cocker
Misty Roa
Nicole Emens
Paul Westman
Peter Manis
Veronica Stephan-Miller

If we've missed anyone, please let us know!

Editor
The Skyhunter Editing Team

For Craig F, my favorite gillie.
Thank you for all your help making the Scotland setting come alive.

— Sarah

To Family, Friends and
Those Who Love
to Read.
May We All Enjoy Grace
to Live the Life We Are
Called.

— Michael

CHAPTER ONE

Over one thousand years ago

The undulant waters of the North Sea crashed into Captain Quiet's ship, nearly scuttling it in the stormy seas. He'd never seen a storm like it.

The ship, the *McAfee*, was used to negotiating the trade route but had never done so in a storm of this magnitude. No one else had dared to voyage out when the storm clouds promised torrential downpour, but Quiet had no choice. Their cargo was of supreme importance.

He thought of the families below the deck seeking refuge from a warring nation, unable to live any longer in their home country. The refugees staying on land wasn't an option. They would have been captured again and imprisoned.

Then there would have been no way for Quiet to rescue them. The only options were to leave immediately and voyage across the seas in the deadly storm and hope Mother Nature cut them some slack. Alas, it appeared she wasn't going to take pity on the crew of the *McAfee*.

The howling winds ripped through the mainsail and tore it in two, making the ropes whip out and knocking one of the crew to the deck.

Quiet spun and pointed to the men trying to stabilize the main-mast. One more heavy wind would crack it in half.

Without a word, the Captain of the *McAfee* sent one of the crew members to help the fallen sailor.

Quiet had always been called so by his crew, although it wasn't his real name. They always seemed to understand him, even though he was so soft-spoken. It was just how he was made, and he would have it no other way. When he did speak where others could hear him, people listened, an excellent reason to always be less instead of more. He had never minded being physically smaller than the magicians, elves, and fae on his crew. Size was a relative thing for him.

Right then, his low center of gravity kept him steady as his men stumbled across the deck. The storm was getting worse. The *McAfee* tilted violently to the side, nearly capsizing yet again.

They wouldn't make it through the storm to their destination. None of them would survive the night. Quiet knew that with absolute certainty.

He had one option. It would save the refugees. It would save his crew and the *McAfee.*

But it would, without a doubt, kill him.

CHAPTER TWO

A gnome's magic could be stored for an extended period of time. Unlike magicians, gnomes could vault away power like a savings account, allowing it to build.

Quiet had been doing so for years. He couldn't remember the last time he had used magic, preferring to do things with his hands and his mind instead. This situation was precisely why he had been hoarding his magic.

Maybe subconsciously, he'd known something of this magnitude would happen, or perhaps it was only destiny. Quiet wasn't sure if he believed in such things. Right then, it didn't matter because his voyage had come to an end.

He grabbed the ship's wheel and began to mutter a series of incantations. The crew wouldn't know what had happened until it was too late for them to do anything. The important thing was, they would be safe, and the families would be unharmed. The *McAfee* would land in the calm waters of the Atlantic Ocean, unscathed and ready to sail another day.

The spell he was knotting together wouldn't kill Quiet, but it would make him pass out and where he landed, well, that would ensure an eventual death. He wouldn't be on board the *McAfee* *anymore*, the only place he'd ever thought of as home.

But that was exactly why he had to save it.

The gnome rotated the ship's wheel three turns to the right, managing to remain steady as the crew was thrown back and forth across the deck.

He whipped the wheel the opposite way, two turns, as the main-mast creaked, a dangerous sound that hinted of last moments.

Finally, Quiet stepped backward and bowed his head in a final goodbye, rain splattering his face and covering the tears flowing down his cheeks.

The *McAfee* flickered. Quiet worried the spell hadn't worked. He glanced at his feet that remained on the moving deck. When his ship disappeared around him, he smiled, knowing his spell had worked.

He had transported his ship, its crew, and those they had rescued to calm, safe waters where they could sail on to a better place.

Briefly suspended in mid-air, Quiet said a simple goodbye to the Earth he'd loved all his life and would no longer see again, then he plunged into the unforgiving waters of the North Sea to be swept up in the great storm. He could save an entire ship and its people, but ironically not himself. Not if he was going to funnel all his power into ensuring the spell worked, and there was no reason to do anything unless it was done right.

The exhaustion hit him as soon as he plunged into the freezing cold sea. Waves buried him and carried the gnome away.

CHAPTER THREE

The afterlife tasted like sand.

To Quiet's surprise, his body still hurt after death. He thought he'd feel weightless. Free. Finally, at peace.

But instead, everything in his body screamed for his attention. Especially his lungs.

He rolled over on to his back, and that's when the eruption began. Coughs rocketed from the little gnome's body and made him think he'd choke on his lungs. The idea he still had lungs after drowning in the North Sea was especially perplexing.

Quiet continued to cough, a seemingly unending sound that was especially loud in his ears even though they were clogged with water.

Rolling over once more, Quiet got to his hands and knees and spat out what felt like a gallon of water. It filled his mouth and triggered his gag reflex.

Dying was horrible. He hoped it would be over soon, but something told him it might not. It might have been his gasping for air, even as his chest burned and his face felt hot.

He shook his head, and wet hair spattered across his eyes. All Quiet wanted was for this death thing to be over. It appeared death, like everything in life, was a process. He crawled across the sandy beach, which he fully believed was a part of his hallucination.

He was sinking to the bottom of the North Sea. That was what was happening.

The granules of sand under his fingers was the strangest sensation. The cold wind whipping across his water-soaked body was surreal, and the heaviness of the emotion that he'd never see the world he loved again was the worst heartache he'd ever known.

It all had to be an illusion, he thought to himself. The thought sent him back on his tailbone to sit and look at the choppy sea, feeling as though surrender was a fake breath away. The gnome rocked back and forth, his hands in his lap as he shivered violently. He wasn't sure why he saw whitecaps and a gray sky and a storm in the distance when Quiet knew he was drowning. It was just how death was, he guessed.

He had never done it before, so it made sense it would feel all strange and disorienting. Death, like life, had to be a bit like trickery. One moment you think you're going to win and then it all crashed down. Just like Quiet had thought they'd get away scot-free with the refugees, or like so many times in life when things felt comfortable and then became the hardest thing in the world.

The Captain of the *McAfee* sat staring at the ocean, wondering when clouds and sky and angels would welcome him to the afterlife.

It didn't come.

When hunger and thirst set in after a long hour, something he hadn't expected appeared.

"Hello, dear," a woman's voice sang beside Quiet.

He turned his head and found a creature who looked more like a tree than a person. Her skin was brown and flakey like bark. Her hair flowed like vines, and her eyes were the color of the bluest sky. They blinked at him in a way that made Quiet feel unconditionally loved.

"Who are you?" Quiet asked. He found it strange how he had a voice.

"I'm Mother Nature," the figure said.

"Mother Nature?" he asked. He spoke louder than he usually did. "Is this heaven?"

She shook her head of vines. "Oh, no. You're still alive, but not for long unless I save you, which I intend to do."

"What?" Quiet questioned. He was thoroughly confused. "How can you save me? I died."

"No, not quite. But you're close. And, I'm Mother Nature," she argued. "I can do whatever I like. After your brave sacrifice, I have a proposal for you. It will mean you live an extraordinarily long life."

He looked at the sea he loved so much, at the world he'd cherished all his life. Finally, he stared at the strange woman he felt intimately acquainted with. "What is it? What would you have me do to stay here on this Earth? I'll do whatever it takes, Mother Nature."

"You can start by calling me Mama Jamba," the woman said and laid her bark-covered hands over Quiet's, taking away any pain that remained in his being. "You and I are about to start a friendship that will last a very, very long time."

CHAPTER FOUR

Present day

The groundskeeper for the Gullington spooned sugar onto his bowl of hot porridge, his attention honed on sprinkling it evenly.

"How is Bell?" Sophia asked Mahkah when he entered the dining hall of the Castle. His boots were muddy as he pulled off his gloves, and there was dragon blood on his cloak. He'd obviously been on the Expanse, changing Bell's bandages again.

He nodded, sniffling, his nose red from the cold. Spring was warming up the Gullington, but not by much. "She's better, although only marginally. It's going to be a long healing process for her," Mahkah answered

"Relatively speaking," Evan stated. "A year isn't really a big deal in the scheme of things when you're a dragon."

"You wouldn't want to be down for a year," Sophia said, her lips pursed and a disapproving look on her face.

"Girl, I was down for close to a century, with nothing to do," Evan complained. His eyes flicked to Quiet, spooning more sugar onto his porridge.

"But you could still walk," Sophia argued. She watched as Wilder slipped into the seat across from her, carefully keeping his eyes down and trying to be inconspicuous.

"But you could walk," Evan sang in a high-pitched tone, mocking Sophia.

She didn't pay him any attention as she studied Wilder, who whistled nonchalantly and picked up a scone, not taking a bite out of it.

Ainsley stole everyone's attention as she trudged in from the kitchen, holding a platter of assorted meats and potatoes. "Here's some boring food you've all had a bazillion times. It will taste the same as it always does."

Evan stabbed his fork into a sausage, seizing it before Quiet, who was going for the same one—a plump link perfectly charred on two sides. "Same as always is what I like," Evan said, taking a bite.

Ainsley puffed out a defeated breath, blowing her red hair off her forehead. "I guess if you like the same old same old. No variety. Just the same as what you had and experienced the day before and the day before that..."

Evan took another bite of his sausage, not at all sympathetic to Ainsley's obvious bout of depression.

"You okay?" Sophia asked as she discreetly watched Wilder pocket the scone in his cloak and lean forward, appearing interested.

"Yeah, you seem down," he said to Ainsley, a look of concern plastered on his face. "What's going on?"

Ainsley glanced around the dining hall, lost in thought. "Oh, just contemplating life and the monotony of it all."

"Sounds cheerful," Evan said through a mouthful.

"Oh, you wouldn't get it. You get to leave here. All of you do, but not Quiet and me," Ainsley complained. She picked up his plate, still filled with food, and hurried for the kitchen.

"Hey, I'm not done with that," Evan called to the housekeeper's back, but she didn't answer.

Sophia looked at Quiet, who was still spooning sugar onto his porridge. She knew why Ainsley couldn't leave the Gullington for long—the curse that had erased her memory would finally kill her if she stayed outside the grounds for long. She didn't know why Quiet couldn't leave, according to the shapeshifter, he couldn't leave at all. Not even for an errand like Ainsley could.

"So, you're having porridge with your sugar, are you?" Evan asked, raising a curious eyebrow at the gnome.

Quiet stiffened, the teaspoon of sugar over his bowl. Without looking up, he muttered something that sounded like, "Mind your own business."

Without asking permission, Evan reached over and stole Mahkah's empty plate before loading it up with more meat and potatoes.

"Sophia," Mahkah began, not at all annoyed by Evan's usual rude behavior, "would you like to work on some flying combat this morning?"

Her eyes shifted to Wilder, catching him slipping another scone into his cloak. "Actually, that would be great. Do you want to join us?" she asked him.

Embarrassment crossed Wilder's face briefly before he shook his head, trying to cover hoarding food in his cloak. "I would, but I can't."

"Why can't you?" Evan asked through a mouthful of potatoes.

"Because," Wilder simply answered, picking up another pastry.

Sophia studied him. He'd been secretive since working with Subner on side missions, which she had respected knowing she had her own secrets, but she sensed something was stressing him out more than usual.

"Because he's training with me," Hiker chimed in, striding into the dining hall and joining the conversation like he'd been there the entire time.

Wilder, who had been about to slip another scone into his cloak, brought it rapidly to his mouth and took a bite. "Actually, sir, I need to—"

The look on Hiker's face cut Wilder off and made him go silent.

"Need to what?" Evan asked. He rested his chin on his propped-up hand and leaned forward, batting his eyelashes at the other dragonrider. "Go on then, Wilder. Tell us what you have to do and why you are pocketing scones."

"Is that where they've all been going?" Ainsley asked, coming through the kitchen door with an empty platter. She set it in front of Hiker, a proud smile on her face.

The leader of the Dragon Elite eyed the bare plate before bringing his gaze up to meet Ainsley's. "Alright, I'll bite. What's the deal? Why the empty platter?"

Hiker was noticeably different after stopping his brother and finally getting rid of the evil that had haunted him for centuries. That didn't mean he was happier or lighter. If anything, he seemed burdened in different ways now.

"Well," Ainsley began. "I just figured I'd give you all a sampler platter of what I'm looking forward to today, this week, this year, and the rest of the decade."

Hiker sighed, frustration edging into his face.

The housekeeper pointed to the far right of the platter. "For your starter, we have a pastry of naught, which is filled with long bouts of silence. And over here." She pointed farther to the left. "We have a sandwich of nothingness, which has a rather boring sauce on it with a side of who gives a damn." She directed her finger to the far side. "And for dessert, we have plain cake drenched in 'am I dead yet' syrup."

Hiker pushed the platter away. "I think I'll stick with bacon."

"Have it your own way." Ainsley shrugged and retreated to the kitchen.

"Is she okay?" Sophia whispered.

"Not in the least," Evan answered. "That one is certifiably insane. There was this one time last week I found her setting out a bowl of milk. When I asked her about it, she told me it was for our new pet, a cat named Aristotle or something."

"Do you mean Plato?" Sophia questioned.

Taking another bite, Evan shrugged. "Doesn't really matter. There is no cat, and Ainsley lost her mind a long time ago."

Quiet mumbled something as he held up a fist and shook it vehemently.

"Okay, little guy," Evan said to the gnome. "You simmer down there, sir. We will have no hostility at the table."

The groundskeeper muttered more forcefully, although his words were still inaudible.

"What is he going on about?" Sophia asked Wilder in a hush.

He shook his head. "I don't know. He's been a bit more agitated lately, though."

Sophia had wondered if Plato had entered the Castle in the past. The lynx had hinted at it, and now there were portals that joined the Castle to the House of Fourteen and the Great Library. There were supposedly laws in place to keep anyone not connected to the Dragon Elite from entering the Gullington, but most rules didn't apply to Plato. He came and went from the House of Fourteen, according to Liv, although it should have been impossible.

It seemed to her the staff who cared for the Castle and Gullington had been more agitated lately. She knew why Ainsley was. She was obviously feeling the strain from not being able to venture outside the grounds for long. Maybe Quiet was too. Perhaps it had all started with the big victory, a reason that might seem strange to most but made sense to Sophia.

For centuries, the Dragon Elite had been confined to the Gullington with no real purpose. For Ainsley and Quiet, the confinement had given them purpose—to care for the lost and lonely Dragon Elite.

However, now the dragonriders had a new potential. The world recognized them once more as the world's adjudicators. There were a thousand dragon eggs, and everyone had a renewed sense of purpose —everyone but Quiet and Ainsley. They were still confined.

Sophia was about to ask Quiet a question, one he would answer, even though she wouldn't understand his response. Before she could, Mama Jamba bounced into the dining hall singing *Wide Open Spaces* by the Dixie Chicks. The woman had a beautiful voice. Immediately everyone froze, captivated by the words and melody.

The meaning of the song was strangely timed, Sophia thought, listening to Mother Nature rock into the chorus as she took a seat. She wasn't in her chair for more than a few seconds when Ainsley buzzed back with a platter of blueberry pancakes.

Hiker was obviously frustrated by the special treatment Mama Jamba got, getting what she wanted for breakfast when the rest of them got whatever the housekeeper felt like serving up. Yet no one said anything as Mother Nature continued to sing about a woman needing wide open spaces to feel free and happy.

When she finished, everyone resumed moving around once more, Hiker pouring a cup of coffee and Quiet stirring his mostly bowl of sugar. Mama Jamba glanced at Sophia.

"You have something to ask me, dear." It was a statement rather than a question.

"Oh," Sophia said, shaking her head. "No, nothing really."

"I sense that it's of importance to you," Mama Jamba fired back.

Sophia found her face blushing. "It's only a curiosity."

The woman as old as time cut into her pancakes, took a bite, and relished the sweet fluffiness. When she was done chewing, she wiped the corners of her mouth. "I'd venture to say curiosities are what start great ideas. Always follow them the same way a cat does. The same way one becomes a stray, following a lead and getting lost."

Those statements felt too pointed, but Sophia shook them off. "Well, I was just wondering, why do you take the form of a southern woman from America? Why not something else?"

Mama Jamba took another bite and winked at Sophia. "That's a lovely question, my dear. The truth is, I've been in many different forms over my time. Many at this table can attest to that." Her eyes diverted to Quiet and then Hiker. "I've decided to take on this form because southern women are nurturing and polite. I can't think of anything our Earth needs more right now."

"Even though Thad Reinhart has been killed and his companies disbanded?" Sophia asked.

Mama Jamba took a long sip of water and nodded. "The dangers are never completely gone. Such is life. But yes, I like this form for right now, but who knows what the future will demand? It always depends on the global climate—both literally and figuratively."

"I guess that makes sense," Sophia said. She glanced down at her empty plate and realized she hadn't eaten a thing yet.

"As I was saying," Hiker interjected, looking at Wilder. "I require your help on the Expanse this morning for training."

"Well, sir—"

Hiker held up his hand to cut the dragonrider off. The leader of the Dragon Elite pushed up from the table. "Whatever you have going on with Subner will wait. I'll need you until further notice."

Sophia drew in a breath. "I could actually use your help, Wild—"

"Just he and me," Hiker interrupted. "I need Wilder's help with something…important."

Sophia glanced around the table for clues as to what Hiker could mean. Everyone suddenly seemed busy with their food. Quiet shoveled porridge laced sugar into his mouth. Mama Jamba licked her lips as she drenched more of her pancakes in syrup. Evan stabbed another sausage before plunking it on his plate. Only Wilder seemed to share her curiosity.

"Wilder, five minutes," Hiker ordered. "I'll see you on the Expanse."

"Yes, sir," Wilder replied, a disappointed expression on his face.

When Hiker strode for the hallway, it broke everyone's concentration.

"If it makes you feel better," Mama Jamba said to Wilder without looking up from her meal, "it doesn't matter if those scones go stale. They were never going to work as bait anyway."

"Bait for what?" Evan asked as he leaned across Sophia, a curious expression on his face.

Wilder removed the crumbling pastries from his cloak and rolled his eyes. "For the rats I've been trying to lure to your room."

Sophia knew he was joking, but she desperately wanted to know what Wilder was up to. More than that, she wanted to know what Hiker needed his help with.

CHAPTER FIVE

E ven though spring had arrived in Scotland, the winds howling
across the Expanse held onto the winter chill, unwilling to
accept warmer weather was supposed to be on the way.

"The weather is just being disrespectful at this point," Evan said
bitterly, pulling up his muffler and covering his neck.

Mahkah glanced back toward the Cave. On the Expanse, in front
of the Cave, Bell could be seen surrounded by Simi and Tala. Lunis
and Coral were parked in front of Mahkah, ready to practice.

"Winter retreats when it's ready," Mahkah said in his usual calm
voice. The top portion of his long black hair was pulled up, and the
bottom half draped down his back.

"Well, I wish spring would boot it out of the way," Evan
complained, rubbing his hands and trying to bring warmth into them.

"It can't," Mahkah said simply. "Spring bows to winter, and will not
take the stage until winter has exited. It's every season's right to stick
around until it is done."

Evan shook his head and rolled his eyes. "That's hogwash. You
should write farmer's almanacs because you're as full of bullshit as
those books."

Sophia allowed the two to argue, pretending to pay attention to them but in reality, honing her focus in the direction of Hiker and Wilder on the other side of the Expanse by the Castle. She found if she directed her attention just right, she could listen in on their conversation, but it required she lose the details around her.

Like looking through a telescope, she focused on the leader of the Dragon Elite and the combat expert to try and make out what they were saying. She could see Hiker brandishing a sword, his form awkward as if it was the first time he'd held such a weapon.

"I just don't know how to control it," he explained, his eyes heavy with frustration.

Wilder nodded sympathetically. "Unless you embrace the power you inherited from your twin, it will overpower you."

"That's been the problem," Hiker related. "I crushed my water basin this morning. My bed is in shambles. And I don't even want to tell you the state I left my chest of drawers in when I finally conceded defeat."

A scream from the Castle stole the attention of all the dragon riders on the Expanse.

"Hiker Wallace!" Ainsley's voice rang out from an open window on the second story.

The leader of the Dragon Elite twisted around and caught sight of Evan, Mahkah, and Sophia staring in his direction. "Don't pay attention to that looney woman. Get back to training."

"Okay, let's run some drills," Mahkah encouraged, waving the two forward. "Mount your dragons."

Evan took off for Coral immediately. Lunis, catching the expression in Sophia's eyes, yawned.

You know, the blue dragon began. *I was with Bell all night. Maybe I can sit out for a bit until I rest up?*

Mahkah, who would never refuse a dragon asking for accommodations, nodded. "Yes, I think Sophia observing Evan will be beneficial. Please rest, Lunis."

Sophia came to stand next to the dragon expert as Evan jabbered on about how he was about to show her something amazing. She smiled as she honed her attention back on Hiker.

"This power is a gift," Wilder explained. He held a sword in front of Hiker, ready to spar.

The leader of the Dragon Elite shook his head, his hands around a sword, but his eyes uncertain. "It doesn't feel like it. This is a burden."

"You realize that is a choice," Wilder challenged. He slid his blade across Hiker's and pivoted to the side, bringing his weapon down and stopping it just before it sliced across his opponent's leg. He sighed and took a step back. "You've got to at least try."

Hiker backed up. "Do you know I could slice you in two? I'd end everyone on the Expanse with a simple bad mood. This much power isn't natural."

Undeterred, Wilder shook his head, his chaotic and devilishly handsome hair taking note of the movement. "You're simply not used to it. You can do great things with the power you took from Thad."

"And I can do horrible things too," Hiker argued.

Wilder pointed an arm in Sophia's direction and looked at her. She pulled her gaze away and pretended to be studying Evan as he shot into the air on Coral, demonstrating a flying combat move. "She doesn't use her powers to do horrible things. It's always a choice. We both know your power won't corrupt you, or it already would have. You would have killed long ago for it. But as it was, you took power regretfully, since Thad wouldn't listen to reason and succumb to justice."

Wilder knew Sophia had a twin, she realized.

That had been between her and Hiker prior to everything falling down. She had suspected the truth would come out after the ordeal with Thad and Hiker. She was a part of the example he was obviously following, and he'd enlisted the help of his combat expert to help him figure it out.

Hiker didn't know how to control his power. But that wasn't what was most evident to Sophia. Of more importance was Hiker didn't know how to embrace it, which was worse.

CHAPTER SIX

K *nock, knock,* Lunis said, walking beside Sophia as they made their way across the Expanse toward the Pond.

Sophia remained silent, mulling over what she'd just learned about Hiker.

Knock, knock, he repeated.

"Did you see the 'No soliciting' sign out front?" she asked him dryly.

I'm a dragon. I can't read, Lunis replied.

"Oh, well, way to exacerbate stereotypes about dragons being uncivilized creatures." She gave him a challenging expression. "And that's funny because weren't you just writing a blog last night?"

He shook his head. *I was using voice dictation.*

She shook her head, dismissing him. "Whatever."

Knock, knock, he repeated once more.

"Who. Is. There?" she asked, articulating each word with great boredom. It was the role she was expected to perform when they played the knock, knock game. He didn't like it if she played along.

Interrupting dragon. He snickered to the side like he didn't want her to see him trying to control his laughter.

Sophia sighed. "Oh no…"

I believe you're supposed to say, 'Interrupting dragon who?'

She squinted at him as if she couldn't understand what he was saying. "What am I supposed to say?"

He cleared his throat. *You're supposed to say, 'Interrupting drag—'*

"Roooooar!" Sophia interrupted. She stopped and doubled over with laughter.

Lunis shook his head and continued toward the Pond, swishing his tail back and forth and shaking his head. *You're ridiculous.*

When they came to the cave with the thousand dragon eggs, as Sophia did every time since she'd discovered them—she simply blinked around, frozen. They were calling the place they were keeping the eggs the Nest. It seemed like the best description since that's exactly what it was.

The young dragonrider didn't know what to do for the eggs. Quiet watched after them, or so she thought, as she often saw him retreating from the area when she visited.

She felt like since Mama Jamba had put her in charge of the eggs, she should do something for them. When Lunis was in his egg, she'd made things warmer when he wanted that. She got him a water element when he asked for it. When Liv was too loud, Sophia ensured he had quiet. But she had been able to communicate telepathically with Lunis from the beginning. She didn't have that ability with these dragon eggs, which was probably a good thing because how inundating would it be to have a thousand dragon voices in her head, all making demands as Lunis had in the shell.

Taking a seat on a large boulder at the front of the cave, Sophia glanced around, her eyes running over the many different colored eggs that filled the area. This was the new generation of dragons. Some would magnetize to dragonriders. Some would not. Some would go their own way, and others would want to be part of the Dragon Elite.

Some, according to Mama Jamba, would be pure of heart. Others would be corrupt. Some of the eggs would hatch relatively soon, meaning within the next few years or decades. Others might not hatch for hundreds of years.

There was so much potential before Sophia and so much uncertainty. She'd never been given a task she had absolutely no idea how to manage. Every day she and Lunis visited the eggs and just stared blankly. She wasn't sure if it made her feel any better that Lunis seemed as lost as she was about what to do for the eggs.

I don't think most mothers know what to do until they have to, Lunis offered, sensing Sophia's continued confusion on the matter.

She sighed. "I get you keep calling me that so at some point you can call me the Mother of Dragons. It's not happening."

He chuckled. *That's not it. Okay, it sort of is. How about Mother of dragon eggs? That's more accurate.*

"How about no," she replied.

Sophia, there's nothing to do for them, he said after a moment of silence, his voice serious and full of sympathy.

"I know, but it seems like I should be doing something," Sophia answered with a long sigh. "Like, should I play them music? Make it darker? Lighter? Warmer? Cooler? I simply don't know."

Most of the things we need aren't related to our physical environment, he offered.

She turned and gave her dragon a speculative glare. "I'm not following you."

What do these dragon eggs represent to you? he asked.

She knew this was a leading question but decided to play along. "A new beginning."

And what would you do to protect that? he continued to question.

"I would sacrifice anything. Even my own life."

He nodded. *Because...?*

"Because, as crazy as it sounds, without knowing these dragons..." Sophia paused, looking for the right words. They were so simple and yet saying them felt strange. "I guess I love these dragons. I love what they represent. I love that they give us hope. I love that it means justice will be upheld."

A knowing smile crossed her dragon's face. *The most important thing in the world is love. Just offer them that, and I think it will be enough.*

Sophia returned the smile. She knew Lunis was right. Even though

Sophia didn't know these dragons and could never love them like Lunis, she did have an unwavering affection for them. She was scared, though, because she had never had so much responsibility. A set of words from her father's book rang in her head. *"The more whom we love, the more responsibility we have, for we should be ready to protect them with our hearts and souls."*

She didn't know what that would entail, but Sophia was ready to protect these eggs with her heart and soul. She knew Lunis would do the same. One day they'd hatch, one by one, and that's when she thought the real acts of love would be required.

CHAPTER SEVEN

The Viking's boots thundered across his office as he paced, irritation heavy in his every move. Sophia cut her eyes to Mama Jamba, a question in her gaze.

"Go on, dear," the old woman urged. "Hiker, please pay attention."

He threw up his hands and halted in front of his large desk where Sophia sat. It felt strange to be seated behind the leader of the Dragon Elite's desk, but she'd been asked to do so to show him how to use a computer.

"I just don't think this is necessary," Hiker complained.

"Okay, so you're going to address world leaders and announce you're the world adjudicators," Mama Jamba began, crossing her arms in front of her chest. "Now, how are they supposed to communicate with you about issues that arise?"

He sighed. "Letters have worked fine for ages."

"And how are mortals supposed to send you these letters?" Mama Jamba challenged. "Are you going to get a post box at the nearest town since they can't send letters through the Barrier into the Gullington?"

"I don't know," he said, shaking his head. "We could set something up."

She shook her head. "No, you need something modern and fast. You are learning how to use a computer."

Like a child on the verge of a tantrum, he stomped his boot on the floor. "But I don't—"

"I don't care that you don't want to use technology," Mama Jamba interrupted, fisting her hands on her hips and suddenly appearing larger. "You're going to do as I say, and you're going to like it."

Sophia had a tough time hiding her laughter. Hiker must have sensed this because he glared at her before directing his gaze back to Mother Nature.

"Why do I have to do this?" he asked, a growl in his voice.

"Because I said so," she replied definitively.

He huffed. "That's a lousy reply."

"It's the one you're getting," she fired back. "Son, you will do as I say, or you can leave the Gullington for good."

Hiker's eyes widened with shock. He was the one who usually kicked people out of the Castle, firing Ainsley every other day and booting Sophia out on the off days. The challenging expression on Mama Jamba's face wasn't to be messed with, and by the way he gulped, Hiker knew it.

"Okay, tell me what I need to do, Sophia," he said, coming to stand behind her.

She began click-clacking on the keys, pulling up the right website. "Well, you have to check in on your email. I've set you up an account. This is Gmail, and here's your inbox."

He grunted. "I don't understand any of the words you just used."

She cleared her throat. "It's fairly simple. This is electronic mail. Just go in here, and you'll see your messages."

He squinted at the screen. "What's a Bogo? And what's Nutrisystem?"

Mama Jamba snickered as she took a seat on the couch and appeared thoroughly amused.

"That's an advertisement," Sophia explained. "You'll want to ignore those. Oh, and spam. Just delete it."

"What is spam?" he questioned.

"It's junk."

Hiker rolled his eyes. "There's junk in electronic form? Do mortals have nothing better to do?"

"They really don't," Mama Jamba chimed in, a nail file appearing in her hands. "There's this one GIF of this lady yelling and an impassive cat going around on the interwebs. I won't even tell you how many hundreds of hours of productivity have been lost because of that one."

Hiker looked up. "What are you talking about? What's a GIF?"

"You'll see once we set you up a Facebook account," she answered, starting to file the hot pink nails that matched her velour tracksuit.

"What's a Facebook?" Hiker questioned.

"I'm not sure if he's ready for all that," Sophia argued, giving Mama Jamba a careful expression.

"I want the Dragon Elite to have a new image," Mama countered. "That means branding. You aren't the old dragonriders of the past. You are the new Dragon Elite. When he's ready, Hiker will have a Facebook account just like any modern-day official."

"Okay," he growled. "But no phones. Especially not for the men. I put my foot down there. I'll get into electronics, but I won't have my men's heads clouded with such things."

Sophia glanced up and batted her eyelashes at him. "But it's okay for me to have my head clouded, sir?"

He waved her off. "You were tainted from the beginning. There's no helping that."

"Thanks, sir," Sophia said. "I've set up your username as angryold-viking. I hope that works."

Mama Jamba gave her a punishing look.

Sophia sighed. "I'm kidding. You're HikerWallace. I didn't know what your middle initial was, sir. Is it G for Grumpy-McGrumpisons? I can make you HikerGWallace."

He shook his head. "It's Alexander."

"The young dragonrider is kidding you," Mama Jamba offered.

"Oh, one of those sarcastic jokes again." Hiker scowled at Sophia. "You know I don't get those and appreciate them even less."

"But sarcasm feeds my soul," Sophia argued.

"You don't want her soul to starve, do you?" Mama Jamba asked, pretending to be interested in his reply.

"I think if it dimmed her feisty spirit a bit, that would work well enough," Hiker said, returning his attention to the screen. "Now, how do I know what spam is?"

Sophia giggled. "Well, if it's trying to sell you something, it's considered spam."

"Fair enough," he agreed, nodding like he got it. Sophia suspected he didn't.

"Anyway, from there, you just click on the messages and read them."

Sophia demonstrated and showed the five-hundred-year-old giant how to answer his email. It felt like she was teaching trigonometry to a monkey, but it was progress.

Hiker continued to nod. "Okay, I've got this. You said for today, at the press conference, I need to look at the round things when being interviewed."

"Cameras," she corrected. "And yes. That's how they record you. You want to have your chin up and exude confidence."

Hiker bolstered his chest, appearing proud. "I can do that."

"And you shouldn't answer any questions about technology or the modern world," Mama Jamba cut in. "Have those sent to your email."

"Who will answer those?" he asked.

"Sophia, of course," Mama Jamba answered.

Hiker nodded with caution. "You're headed to the House of Fourteen to manage that situation?"

Sophia smiled. "Yes, don't worry. I'll have them eating out of the palm of our hands by the end."

Hiker grimaced. "Ducks eat out of the palm of your hand. I want them to be like meerkats begging on the far side of the pond for treats."

Sophia sighed. "We need to work on your references, but yes, I get your point."

CHAPTER EIGHT

Mama Jamba thought it would be a good idea to have all the dragonriders accompany Hiker to the press conference. Sophia suspected Mother Nature also sent them as a confidence boost. She'd actually pulled her aside as they were leaving and whispered, "Don't let him look like a fool. Tell him to stand up straight when you see him slouching."

Sophia dutifully nodded and watched the men file out of the Castle.

Mama Jamba ushered her to the door and then pulled her back. "Oh, and don't let Evan speak to anyone if you can manage it."

"Okay," Sophia replied and turned back for the exit.

"Tell Wilder not to smile at ladies because they'll think he's flirting," Mama Jamba called.

Sophia paused. "I'm not telling him that."

"Fine, fine," Mama Jamba sang. "Oh, and Sophia."

She turned around yet again, expecting the old woman to say something silly. "Study the audience. I suspect this press conference will bring out the Dragon Elite's enemies."

Sophia tilted her head to the side. She sensed there was something

Mama Jamba wasn't saying. "Enemies. I thought with Thad Reinhart gone, our enemies were too."

Mama shook her head. "He was our most immediate threat. Thad knew about the Dragon Elite. There will be others who are highly curious about its return. The Dragon Elite doesn't bode well for their selfish desires."

"Do you know of anything specific I need to look out for?" Sophia asked.

Mama Jamba's head jerked to the side, looking at the dining hall. "What's that, Ainsley? You need help? I'll be right there."

"I didn't hear her," Sophia accused, her brow furrowing.

"Because she didn't call out, but she obviously needs my help if she's thinking of putting raisins in the banana bread." Mama Jamba hurried off, her slippers scratching on the stone floor. "Not so fast, my dear! Raisins go in the trash. Not in baked goods."

Sophia shook her head. No one would believe Mother Nature was such an eccentric woman whose favorite foods were pancakes, pickles, and saltine crackers.

Keeping an eye out for enemies was a lot more complicated than merely searching around for sketchy characters in the audience. The press conference, even with strict security, was still full of excited reporters and officials.

It had been decided the dragons would attend in order to really set the stage. What better stage than the front lawn of the White House, the home of the President of the United States.

The four dragonriders stood beside their dragons behind the podium, where Hiker was perched. He hunched over to get closer to the microphone.

"Stand up straight," Sophia whispered, knowing the leader of the Dragon Elite could hear her just fine with his enhanced hearing.

From his back, she saw him shake his head slightly, but he did straighten as he cleared his throat, making the crowd go silent.

"I'm here to inform the world, after a long stint outside our control, the Dragon Elite are back," Hiker began. "As you're aware, the House of Fourteen was instrumental in making magic visible for mortals. During the period prior, the Dragon Elite lived in the dark ages, unable to perform our role for centuries. However, we are and will forever be the adjudicators for this great world. Our rule supersedes those of governments. Our justice is meant to protect. I'm grateful to be able to say the Dragon Elite has taken our rightful place once more. All matters fall under our jurisdiction. Our say is final. We will ensure a peaceful tomorrow for those pure of heart. The rest will be punished for their crimes. There are no exceptions to this. The Dragon Elite is supreme authority reigning over Earth. I'll now be open to questions."

Hands shot up around the large crowd. Sophia tensed. Beside her, Wilder took note. This was the part where the leader of the Dragon Elite either showed their dominance or his lack of knowledge of the modern world. It could go either way.

"Mr. Wallace," a young woman in a navy-blue pantsuit began, "Do I call you mister, or do dragonriders go by a formal title like Rider Wallace?"

He coughed. "Hiker is fine."

Damn it. We need a formal title, Sophia said telepathically to Lunis as she recognized the misstep. *The President of the United States doesn't go by Tricia.*

That would be weird since her name is Lisa, Lunis quipped.

You get my point, Sophia stated. *Why don't we have titles?*

Like King Wallace, Lunis questioned.

No, not like king, she replied.

Like Sir Grumps-A-Lot, Lunis asked.

Again, no.

"What makes your rule supreme?" a reporter asked Hiker, her voice smug.

"We are the Dragon Elite," Hiker declared with confidence. "We have always been the ruling authority over nations and organizations because we are unbiased. We have no interests other than to preserve peace for all."

"Hiker Wallace," yelled another reporter standing in the middle of the crowd. "How is it that you and four other dragonriders are going to manage the world's problems?"

Many eyes in the crowd glanced at the five dragons at Hiker's back, four riders beside them. The dragons had received a fair bit of interest, but not as much as Sophia would have liked. The world was growing weary of magical creatures, not giving them the reverence they deserved.

"You do see the dragons?" Hiker questioned, his voice rising booming over the microphone.

Sophia bit her lip and hoped Hiker kept his temper in check.

"You do know dragons are the most powerful creatures on Earth, and we are their riders, right?" Hiker continued.

"Sir, I get that dragons are strong, but..." The reporter chuckled, "I really don't see how disputes over oil in the Middle East or hostage situations in foreign nations can be resolved by some fire-breathing creatures."

"That is because you are a narrow-minded imbecile who hasn't seen the Dragon Elite operate," Hiker fired back at the reporter.

Oh, man, Sophia thought, lowering her head and wondering how to deescalate this.

"Go, Hiker," Evan said on the other side of her.

Sophia elbowed him hard in the side, earning a murderous glare.

"Mama Jamba said for you to keep your mouth shut," she whispered from the corner of her lips.

"Yeah, well, later my fists are going to have something to say to you," Evan whispered back.

"Can't wait to have that conversation with them," she murmured. "Get the ice pack ready for your knuckles."

"I won't need them, Pink Stuff," he replied, indicating her paisley pink and silver armored top. "But I'll have bandages ready for you."

Sophia had thought about dressing in gray and black like the men for the event. She realized that it would be utterly boring and put on her favorite outfit, both practical and fashionable.

"The coverage on the takedown of Thad Reinhart's facilities was quite impressive," a different reporter in the front row started. "I understand he was single-handedly responsible for instigating many global issues as well, polluting the Earth on a wide scale. Still, that was a single man and a conglomeration of organizations. How are five dragonriders going to preside over the world's affairs?"

Hiker leaned forward, his breathing echoing over the microphone. Sophia held her own breath and hoped he wasn't grimacing at the cameras too much.

"This is why we have decided to take back our official roles," Hiker began, his voice excited. "It is with great honor I disclose to the world at large, after a thousand years, the dragon's population has been restored. The Dragon Elite is now in possession of a new batch of eggs. What we had before was limited and ran out, all the dragons that were ever going to be, having been hatched. We now have a huge crop of dragon eggs and a renewed sense of purpose and hope for the world."

A collective muttering spread across the crowd, silencing Hiker.

"Sir," a reporter called, holding up her hand and trying to get attention over the noise. This one wasn't dressed like the others in pencil skirts and slacks. Instead, she had her shiny black hair pulled back in a ponytail and wore a long black trench coat like she was concealing something. That would be impossible, though. The security for the press conference had been top-notch. And there were four dragonriders at Hiker's back, ready to defend. Anyone who tried anything would have to have a death wish.

"Yes," Hiker said, silencing all the chatter.

The woman stood. There was something different about her face. It almost moved mechanically. And her hair. It was too shiny like it was made from metal. As Sophia blinked, the strangeness began to fade, and within seconds, the woman appeared quite ordinary. Sophia thought magic was at play and what she'd seen initially had been real.

"Where are the Dragon Elite located?" the woman asked. Her voice seemed robotic but also not.

"That location can't be found by anyone but us," Hiker answered at once and pointed to another reporter with their hand up. "Next."

"But, sir," the woman cut back in. "How is it that your location is a secret? Shouldn't we have something from you to strengthen our faith in your mission to protect?"

"Our home base is none of the public's concern," Hiker stated with authority, and again pointed to the other reporter.

"Actually, Hiker Wallace," the woman interrupted, her voice firm, "I would argue it is. If you have no public interests, then knowing where you reside could be of importance. For instance, if you're in the United States, what's to stop you from siding with North America if there is a dispute between it and Europe, for example."

This brought another round of collective muttering from the crowd.

Hiker sighed and cursed under his breath. Thankfully, he had pulled away from the microphone, and only the dragonriders could hear it.

"That's a good point," someone yelled. "How do we know you don't have mutual interests you'll side with if push comes to shove?"

Hiker lowered his chin, and Sophia could just picture the seething glare he was giving the crowd. She'd seen it all too often. "Because as the Dragon Elite, we are free from bias. We were chosen for our non-partisan behavior."

"By who?" a different reporter asked.

"Mother Nature," Hiker said at once. He pointed again toward the back of the crowd. "Next!"

"But Hiker," the strange woman in the trench coat cut in again, still standing amongst the crowd. "Your location is still of interest. How can you not have a bias based on it?"

"Because we are in Scotland!" he boomed. "We live in an uncharted place in the middle of nowhere in a country that doesn't create problems! Is that good enough for you?"

The woman smiled, a strange spark in her eyes. "Yes, thank you, sir."

She took a seat as questions rang out around her.

Sophia watched the woman and tried to decipher why she appeared so strange, but her attention was soon stolen by the many reporters vying for Hiker's attention. They were acting snotty suddenly, somehow encouraged by the rebellious reporter in the black trench coat. Sophia stepped up closer, encouraging the men to edge in with her. With each question, she suspected Hiker's patience was waning. They'd need to pull him off the stage and deem the press conference over soon. The leader of the Dragon Elite was new to this world, and his tolerance for nagging mortals was low. He'd get better, but it would take time.

Sophia still smiled, despite the stressful situation because the Dragon Elite was at a press conference at the United States White House, announcing their role as world adjudicators. Things were shifting. Things were getting better. It was the age of dragonriders, and that was a beautiful thing.

CHAPTER NINE

For five-hundred years or however long it had been, Ainsley had woken in the same bed, in the same room inside the Castle at the Gullington, to the same day ahead of her. To say it got old was a severe understatement.

She wished for the opportunity to venture far outside the borders of the Barrier of the Gullington and see the world. In her distant memories, she remembered her homeland of Ireland. Remembered the way it smelled, the sounds, the familiarity. It was a distant dream.

But there were more to her memories that didn't include Ireland. She remembered exotic lands and strange adventures and entourages and more. There were expensive gowns and diamond-encrusted jewelry and servants.

None of it made sense because Ainsley only owned burlap dresses and plain boots. She remembered her childhood, which was simple and without luxury, and she remembered being at the Gullington, but nothing in between. The memories of adventures and riches were like dreams, and they faded almost at once, slipping from her mind like slimy seaweed through fingers in the ocean.

Ainsley's mother once told her that trusting your memory was like trusting a cat. "You can't make it do what you want, so it does what it wants." The old shapeshifter's voice echoed in Ainsley's mind as she ventured across the Expanse, toward the Barrier on her weekly errands.

Her mother, like Ainsley, had been an elfin shapeshifter. They were more than rare. Most never came out about it because they were then pursued and punished for what they were.

The only thing worse was to be a seer. Magicians, elves, giants, gnomes, and the like all feared shapeshifters because of the deception a shapeshifter could pull if they so desired. But Ainsley had been raised by a good woman, and her mother taught her never to use her talent for selfish gain. For pranks, yes. That was encouraged. Always. But no nefarious deeds should be done with her shapeshifting gifts.

The thing that always got Ainsley was that she remembered her mother, her wise words, and her dying. Yet everything in between was somehow murky. Her mother had been right. Memories were a fickle thing. After five-hundred years, why should Ainsley expect to remember anything clearly? It was all bound to run together eventually.

She tortured herself like she had done something wrong, not remembering, but when she was logical about it, it was hard to remember what she ate for breakie that day. It was better when she put it all into perspective instead of tormenting herself.

The village where Ainsley bought the goods for the Castle wasn't far outside the Barrier, but she never lingered. The reason wasn't that she wanted to return to the monotony of cleaning floors and making meals for ungrateful dragonriders, S. Beaufont being the exception, of course.

The reason was that after an hour outside of the Gullington, Ainsley often felt fatigued and on the verge of catching a bad cold. She couldn't remember the last time she'd been sick. The Castle kept most ailments away. She figured being outside its protection probably brought all the mortal germs into her system. She usually returned quickly after buying her wares so the Castle could fix her up.

Ainsley always bought the same things at the market. Meat, a lot of meat. More meat. Then a side of meat. She also got regular things like potatoes, onions, and spices. The men liked the same dishes and never seemed to mind that it bored Ainsley to make the same thing over and over again for centuries.

One might think the men would get tired of the same fare, but they never seemed to. Maybe it was because they got to venture outside the Gullington. She knew they'd been trapped with her for several centuries, but the option of leaving had always been there for them, unlike for her.

The thought made her wonder why.

Why can't I leave the Gullington, she wondered as she browsed a stall full of root vegetables. That idea led to another and then another, and all of a sudden, she felt the urge to rush back to the Castle and check on a pot of boiling water she'd forgotten about and left simmering.

Ainsley nearly dropped her packages and ran for the Gullington, the urge all-encompassing, but someone reached out for her and grabbed her wrist to stop her.

"Miss." An old woman, her brown face draped in wrinkles, smiled up at the housekeeper. "Would you like to try my herbs?"

Ainsley smiled back and held up her bag of goods, forgetting the nonexistent pot of boiling water. "Oh, no. But thank you. I've already purchased my goods for the day."

"I see that," the woman began, "but these herbs aren't from around here. They are for those looking for something different...something unique, exotic even."

"Oh," Ainsley turned about and gave the woman her full attention. There was never anything different at the market, just the same old vendors with the same products for sale. "That sounds intriguing. I have been looking for a way to kick my cooking up a notch."

The woman waved a wrinkled hand toward her stall. "Then you should look no further. This will bring a new zest to your cooking, and I daresay, to your life."

Ainsley's smile faltered. "Oh, I'd like to try them, but it will have to wait. I'm out of cash, having bought all my supplies with my budget."

A kind smile crossed the vendor's mouth. "Oh, don't worry. The first one is free. Then I suspect you'll be back for more, so good are my herbs."

The woman held out a small pouch of spices. Something strange flickered in her smile, but it evaporated almost immediately, and Ainsley decided to ignore it. There were so few occasions the housekeeper spoke to people outside the Gullington, and even fewer when strangers were nice to her for no apparent reason.

Ainsley took the herbs and smiled. "Well, thank you. I'll look forward to using these and returning to purchase more if we like them."

"I look forward to that as well," the old woman sang and ushered Ainsley into the crowd as if she were trying to get her away.

She turned to wave, but the merchant was bustling off. Stranger, the old woman's appearance seemed to be melting as she retreated, like she was disappearing.

The shapeshifter shook her head, assuming she was seeing things. Being outside the Gullington for too long always did that to her. She turned for the exit to the market and headed back to the Castle with her wares and exotic spices in tow.

CHAPTER TEN

The winds were so fierce in the Gullington they cut through the closed windows, adding a cold chill to Sophia's otherwise warm bedroom, heated by the roaring fire. She flipped through an *Incomplete History of Dragonriders*, feeling distracted.

She couldn't shake the feeling lately they were on the precipice of something. Hiker had made his announcement to the world, labeling them as world adjudicators. Cases were starting to come in, but nothing she'd been assigned to yet. The thousand dragon eggs were "incubating." Everything was going along smoothly, too smoothly.

Sophia was a born optimist, but even she recognized how strange the lack of drama in her life was after it had been filled with unending adventures in the last several months. Flipping a page without reading it, she cringed as the largest gust yet pushed the windows open and sent a violent gust through her room, scattering the notes on her desk and sending her hair off her shoulders.

Pushing the giant volume off her lap, she scrambled to close the window with magic as she grabbed for the papers spiraling through the air by the chaotic wind with her hands. The archaic set of notes she'd had stacked on her desk was a challenge set out by Hiker. Since he had to start using a computer, he'd challenged Sophia to use paper and pen for recording notes or correspondence. He seemed to think he was making a point, so she agreed. She knew there wouldn't be anyone she'd need to send a physical letter to in the twenty-first century.

When she had the papers corralled in her hands, she glanced down and thought how ironic her life was. Just like that, she was about to eat her words.

On the top of the stack of papers was one not written in her handwriting. It was a letter addressed to her from the librarian for the Great Library, Trinity. Somehow, it had magically appeared in her room as things often did, no doubt delivered by the Castle.

Dear Sophia,

I have finished reviewing The Complete History of Dragonriders. *Thank you so much for allowing me to peruse the only copy in existence. As I suspected, the volume doesn't allow for duplication, but now I understand why, so dense it is with secrets.*

I'm happy for you to retrieve your book at this point, however, although I'm at the Great Library at all times, I ask that you return this letter with an appointment time so I'll know when to expect you. I have put a lock on the portal door that connects the Great Library to the Castle after some things came to light while reading The Complete History of Dragonriders, *therefore you'll need to let me know when to expect you so I can remove the lock.*

Sincerely,
Trinity
Librarian for the Great Library

She turned the letter over, expecting there would be something else written on the back like:

P.S. Just kidding. Come to the magical library whenever. Or I'll send the book I took from you back so you don't have to worry about going on an errand when you're obviously busy. Or text me the time you'd like to stop by.

Alas, the page was blank.

Sophia sighed and trudged over to her desk, where she laid the stack of papers down and retrieved a pen from the drawer.

"Letter," she muttered to herself. "I've got to write a letter. Cool."

She scribbled onto the piece of parchment and arranged a time for after dinner, curious about several things. Chiefly, she wanted to know why Trinity would put a lock on the door to the portal to the Castle. That seemed like something she'd need to get more information about. And all the secrets. But she'd be getting the book back soon and then she could read the *Complete History of Dragonriders* for herself, not that she suspected it would be light reading or something she could finish in one night or even a fortnight. The complete volume had to be much longer than the incomplete version, and she hadn't even scratched the surface of that book.

Signing her name to the piece of paper, she stood back and wondered how exactly she was to get the letter to Trinity. Did she need to take it to the portal? Then what was the point of arranging a time? The door would be locked, wouldn't it? Just as her mind was trailing over these complications, the note began to fade until it disappeared entirely.

Sophia sighed. Of course, the Castle would take care of the delivery for her. It was crafty like that. The Castle could do all sorts of weird things that were unexplainable, even when she used magic as part of the clarification.

Sophia hoped the book shone some light onto the sentient building. There were few things she wanted to understand as much as the strange building designed by the thoughts of its inhabitants and fueled by an unseen force.

CHAPTER ELEVEN

"There's the one responsible for this atrocious wind," Mama Jamba said, pointing in Sophia's direction as she entered the dining hall.

Sophia turned around, expecting to see someone else behind her. Maybe Hiker or Quiet or anyone who wasn't her.

There was no one standing at her back, only the empty entrance hall.

Spinning back around, Sophia gave Mother Nature a confused expression. "Say what?"

"You, dear," Mama Jamba stated and shook her head. She combed her hands through her big, silver hair. "I can't even keep my strands in place. Would you settle down, already?"

Wilder glanced up from the table, a curious expression on his face that made his double dimples surface. "You think Sophia is responsible for the crazy winds we're having?"

Mama Jamba shook her head. "Oh, no. I know." The old woman patted the spot next to her. "Come sit and tell me what's going on."

Sophia stayed frozen. "Nothing. And I'm not responsible for this wind. How would that even be possible?"

Mama Jamba smiled politely at Sophia, but the expression sort of had a "Bless your heart" quality. In other words, the ancient woman was thinking, "Gosh, you're dense."

"Sophia, what elemental force do magicians control?" she asked her.

"The wind," Wilder answered and tilted his head to the side.

Ainsley sped through the kitchen door carrying a covered disk that gave off a spicy scent. It tickled Sophia's nose as the steam wafted by. "I don't believe your name is S. Beaufont, is it Wilder?" the housekeeper asked as if she'd been a part of the conversation all along and hadn't just buzzed into the room.

"It might be," he teased, eyeing the covered disk with skepticism. "What's that?"

"Food," Ainsley answered and hurried back to the kitchen.

"Please stop with the lengthy explanations," Wilder called to her back. "I don't have time for all that."

Mama Jamba glared at the dish before bringing her attention to Sophia again. "Magicians do control the elemental force of wind. And some magicians..." She gave Sophia a very pointed look. "Well, their emotions and internal turbulence can be so great they quite literally influence the weather conditions when they aren't aware of their feelings."

Mahkah, who had been sitting quietly at the table, glanced up. "Is Sophia influencing things because she's so powerful or because she's not harnessing her powers correctly?"

Mama Jamba shook her head. "Neither, dear. It's because she has an internal state she's not aware of, and it's manifesting outwardly as the wind."

Sophia grimaced. "I don't think so. I'm fully aware of everything going on inside my head."

"What about your heart?" Mama Jamba challenged.

Both guys whipped their heads around and waited for Sophia's response.

"What about my heart?" Sophia asked, wishing they were having this conversation in private.

"Well, I think safe to say the tumultuous winds are a result of some emotions in your heart you're conflicted over but aren't even aware of," Mama Jamba imparted.

Sophia shook her head. "I don't think so. I'm fairly aware of my emotional state and have no heartache."

Mama Jamba held up a finger. "Oh, but I didn't say heartache. That would be a different weather pattern altogether. Possibly rain if you were an elf. I think you have feelings you're unaware of and don't know what to do with."

Wilder gave her a serious expression, clasping his hands together in front of him on the table. "What are these feelings, Soph?"

She shook her head at him as she took a seat. "I don't have feelings."

Wilder whipped around to face Mahkah, a mock expression of surprise on his face. "She's a robot! I knew it."

Ignoring him, Mahkah said, "I won't comment on the feelings, which are none of my business—"

"Thank you!" Sophia exclaimed.

"However," Mahkah continued politely, "I will say the dragons are having difficulty negotiating through the air during training due to these high winds."

"So, Soph needs to figure things out, is what you're saying," Wilder declared.

"Sophia needs to do whatever she likes," Mahkah replied. "I'm simply stating a fact."

Mother Nature ran her hands over her hair again. "I vote for some meditation and therapy."

Wilder looked at Mama Jamba. "Can't you do something about the winds if it's bothering you?"

She gave him an offended expression. "That would be a gross misuse of my magic, dear. I created this Earth and the elements upon it and much else. You don't see me trying to live life for you too, do you?"

Wilder's eyes slid to the side with indecision. "No..."

"That's because a mother creates, but she doesn't dictate," Mama

Jamba instructed. "If I intervened every time one of my children took over the weather patterns, well, I'd never get my beauty rest."

Evan came into the dining hall, whistling casually. Stopping a few paces from the table, he pointed at the covered dish. "What's that?"

"Food," Ainsley answered, bustling back through the kitchen door and carrying a large bowl of white rice.

"It doesn't smell right," Evan whined, taking a seat with a skeptical expression.

"You don't smell right, but you don't see me pointing it out," Ainsley fired back.

Evan rolled his eyes. "I believe you just did."

Hiker wore the same cautious expression when he entered and took his usual seat at the head of the long table. The riders all nestled at one end together, leaving the other twenty-some-odd seats empty.

Sophia couldn't imagine the dining room table full of dragonriders. She wondered if it would happen in her lifetime. It was hard to say since it was unknown when the dragon eggs would hatch or if they'd have riders. So many unknowns. She wondered if that was what was silently affecting her heart.

"I need you to review an email I got to see if it's spam or not," Hiker told Sophia as Ainsley hurried back from the kitchen with a tray of flatbread.

"I can do that," Sophia answered, happy the old Viking was using the computer and checking his email.

"What's spam?" Wilder asked.

"Things we don't want," Hiker answered.

"Like Evan?" he joked at once, winking at the other rider.

Evan shook his head. "I get no respect."

"Why do you think it's spam?" Mahkah inquired.

"Well, I'm not sure," Hiker began. "There's just something off about it, but it's from this Nigerian prince."

"It's spam," Sophia said at once.

"You haven't even looked at the email yet," Hiker argued.

"It's spam," she repeated.

"But it—"

"Spam," she interrupted. "Don't reply. Don't give him your account information. Just delete."

Hiker shook his head. "How do you know these things?"

"I get out," she replied. "And I was born in the last century."

Evan was the first to lift the lid off the mystery dish to eye the contents. "What is this?"

"Food," Ainsley replied once more.

Hiker gave her his usual annoyed expression. "Would you care to elaborate?"

"It's a curry dish," she answered. "I thought it would be fun to mix it up a bit."

"I don't like things mixed up," the leader of the Dragon Elite seethed, already unhappy about the meal before even taking a bite.

"No, you like the same boring food prepared the same way for hundreds of years," Ainsley pointed out, her hands on her hips and her voice full of frustration.

"I think a bit of change is great," Mama Jamba sang as she ladled the curried meat onto her rice.

"Thank you," Ainsley said, curtsying and holding out her brown dress to the side with both hands. "I got the spices from a new vendor at the market. I thought I'd experiment with them."

Evan fanned steam from his face as he peered down at the plate he'd prepared. "Is it a bad sign it's burning my nose before I've even taken a bite?"

"It might be a tad bit spicy," Ainsley admitted.

The fork clattering to Hiker's plate made everyone's heads jerk up. "A tad?" He grabbed for the water goblet and drained it.

Sophia dipped the tines of her fork into the sauce and licked it. Immediately she copied Hiker, grabbing for her own water to quell the fire in her mouth.

The others, including Mama Jamba, pushed their plates away.

"What is your problem?" Ainsley asked, her voice shrill. "It's perfectly good."

"It's inedible," Hiker complained.

The shapeshifter pointed to the gnome, who was shoveling the

49

curry into his mouth. Sophia didn't remember seeing him come in, but he was small and strangely stealthy. "Quiet likes it!"

"Quiet has an iron stomach and breathes fire," Evan said, his eyes wide as he watched the groundskeeper finish off a plate of the food and go for seconds.

"Oh, well." Mama Jamba tapped her plate and made the food disappear. "I guess I'll just eat rice and bread. It will humble us."

"I don't want to be humbled," Hiker grumbled. "I want meat and potatoes."

Ainsley pointed to the kitchen. "Then, by all means, go make yourself something to eat."

"That's your job," Hiker growled.

Mama Jamba smiled and tore a piece of bread in two. "Oh, this reminds me of the beginning before spices had crossed over from other regions. We often ate plain rice and bread."

"When was that?" Wilder asked as he chewed on his own piece of plain bread.

"Before you were born," Mama Jamba answered. "Well, before any of you were born. Simpler times then."

"I live in the present and would like the food of this century," Hiker said with a seething stare directed at Ainsley.

The housekeeper looked at Sophia. "Then ask her to get you some Taco Bell from Uber Eats." She hurried for the kitchen, her nose high in the air.

"You're fired, Ainsley," Hiker called after her.

"Thank you, sir," she called from the door. "Would you like chicken or lamb for dinner tomorrow?"

"Lamb would be fine," he answered at once, not missing a beat.

CHAPTER TWELVE

Sophia tightened her cloak around her neck as she walked through the Castle. She wasn't used to wearing the garment inside, but it was quite drafty with the high winds outside whistling through the walls.

"Can't you shut up the cracks, Castle?" Sophia asked, holding the collar of her cloak around her neck and shivering. Nothing got into her bones more than the chill of the wind.

The Castle could install electronics inside of itself even though it didn't have electricity, it could redecorate on a whim to play pranks on Evan and even hide an entire fifth story, and yet it couldn't seal up the cracks.

"Figures," Sophia muttered to herself as she found the door for the portal to the Great Library.

She pulled out her phone and checked the time. She was a little early for the appointment she'd set up with Trinity, which gave her an extra moment to consider the wind business again. She shook her head. That was the last thing she wanted to think about. Her gaze fell on the closet door on the other side of the hallway, the one that led to the House of Fourteen, where she was headed after getting the book from Trinity.

Unfortunately, after finally getting the *Complete History of Drag-onriders* back, she wouldn't have an opportunity to sit down and read it. She'd promised Hiker she'd visit the House and make an announcement from the Dragon Elite to the Council. She was grateful she had the role of diplomat to the House of Fourteen, but it was a strange burden for her. She didn't think the Councilors would ever see her as anything but little Sophia Beaufont. They didn't see her as a fierce rider who adjudicated over worldly affairs but as the small girl who used to play ball in the hallways a few years ago.

"Maybe that's what is weighing on my heart and creating the wind," she wondered aloud to herself.

"That isn't it," Ainsley said, appearing out of nowhere.

"What?" Sophia asked as the housekeeper breezed by without stopping. "What are you talking about?"

"The wind." Ainsley turned about to face Sophia and walked backward. "You're causing it, but not because you're conflicted over how those who used to know you see you now."

"What? Well, then what is it? And how do you know?" Sophia asked. She was accustomed to taking advice about her life from those who shouldn't know anything about her.

"Because the Castle told me," Ainsley explained, still walking backward and getting farther away. "It's more about how the new people in your life see you, and how you see them. How you feel about it all."

"What?" Sophia asked and followed the shapeshifter. "Can you explain?"

Ainsley halted and threw her hands down, annoyed. "If I have to explain to you what's in your heart, then you have much bigger issues. Sit, think, and feel on it. You'll figure it out." She turned and then spun right back around. "Or, here's an idea. Go on an adventure. All things come to light when you're risking your life for something."

Sophia grimaced at the housekeeper. "Thanks, Ains. I think I'll just go and hang out with a skeleton and collect the rarest book in the world instead."

Ainsley shrugged. "Suit yourself. You're so boring and predictable."

CHAPTER THIRTEEN

The door on the other side of the portal clicked right on time, signaling it was unlocked so Sophia could enter the Great Library.

She pulled back the door in the dark closet and was assaulted by the stream of light that fell on her from the library. The long banks of windows, filled with Tanzanian sunlight, ran the length of the room and seemed to go on for miles. It would take someone years to explore every inch of the Great Library. The only one she was aware of who had read all its books was Trinity, the librarian, and he was an immortal being who was literally just bones.

"Welllll, hellllo," the skeleton said.

Sophia smiled at the librarian who looked like he'd jumped out of a Halloween movie with his skeleton smile and whimsical style. He always seemed on the verge of doing a tap dance, his clackity bones making a pitter-patter sound.

"Hi, Trinity. How are you?"

He clapped his boney hands together. "It's another fun day in the Great Library. Thousands of books were added to the library today, so I will be kept up all night reading."

Sophia couldn't help but laugh at his enthusiasm. It was infectious. "Do you really read every single book that comes in here?"

He nodded, his neck making a low squeaking sound as the joints ground together.

"Every single book written comes to the Great Library?" she inquired, still astounded by how incredible the Library was.

"Yes, the very moment it's completed," he answered.

"But what about editing?" she asked.

He began to walk, a silent cue for her to follow. "Oh, all updated versions are automatically incorporated into the book. It's magic, obviously!"

Sophia giggled. "Obviously. Do you have any favorites?"

The skeleton threw his arms wide to the shelves towering all around them. The Great Library was two stories filled with endless volumes of books. The windows showed the sunlight on either side of the arched ceiling as it reflected off the crystal blue waters of the ocean.

"I have so many favorites," he began. "It depends on the genre. Fantasy, science fiction, thrillers! Oh, and then there's non-fiction! The best stories can be found there." He stopped abruptly and turned as a podium rose from the floor. Sitting on top of it was a large book she recognized and had only seen once.

Trinity held out his hand. "Like in your book, *The Complete History of Dragonriders*. I found quite a few tales in there. Things fiction authors would love to steal for their own riveting stories."

"You mentioned in your letter you put the lock on the portal between the Great Library and the Castle because of something you learned in the book," Sophia began. "Can you tell me what it is?"

Trinity didn't launch into his answer right away. Instead, he tapped his phalanges against his jaw as he thought. "I guess you'll find out soon enough when you get to the middle part of the volume."

Sophia eyed the huge book with doubt. "I wouldn't bet on it. I really don't have a ton of reading time, to be honest. Any information you can give me will be appreciated."

He glanced over his shoulder to where the portal door was located and the lock hanging off the side, unlatched. "Actually, this whole thing reminds me you shouldn't stay long. I need to lock up things. It really is for the best. Just in case."

"Just in case of what?" Sophia inquired.

"Well, I've suspected this for a long time. When the Castle is connected to other things, it is influenced by them," he started and then paused for effect. "Do you know what that means?"

"Does it mean the Great Library will take on sentient aspects too, responding to the thoughts and whims of its patrons?" she questioned.

He shook his head. "Good guess. Think of the Castle as a major organ in the human body. The things it is connected to, like the Great Library, are other less vital parts of this system. If something were to happen to the Castle, it would affect the things it's connected to, as a heart affects the blood and smaller organs in humans."

"And vice versa?" Sophia asked.

"No, actually," Trinity disagreed. "You would think, but that's what surprised me. The Castle is stronger than the Great Library and the House of Fourteen, which I now understand it must be connected to as well."

"Why do you suspect that?" Sophia asked, curiously and then added, "Although you're absolutely correct."

"Because in order to open a portal to the Great Library, the first one must be established at the House of Fourteen," Trinity explained. "It's a network of systems, like a section of highways. You can't get here without taking the interstate from the House of Fourteen. Does that make sense?"

"Not at all," Sophia grumbled, feeling overwhelmed.

"Well, then take my word for it," Trinity said with a laugh. "The book explains it much more succinctly than I did, but it is also much more complex. I've studied all the world's sciences and magical laws, and this one is quite intricate. Like a combination of quantum physics and advanced magical theory. I've never heard of anything like it."

"Which is why it's in a giant book that can't be duplicated and went missing for a long period of time, I'm guessing," Sophia mused.

"Right you are, S. Beaufont!"

"What you're saying in essence is, the portal to the Great Library couldn't be opened until the one to the House of Fourteen was established, right?"

"Correct," Trinity chirped.

"Are there other portals that could be opened from the Castle?" she asked.

"Quite possibly," he agreed, rocking forward on his feet and back again.

"Can you elaborate on this whole Castle being the vital organ business and why that would cause you to put a lock on the portal door between here and there?" she questioned.

"Yes," he affirmed. "It's really just a precaution. Although I don't have any reason to suspect, I concluded that if something happened to the Castle, it could infect things it is connected to."

"What would happen to the Castle?" Sophia worried.

"Nothing and possibly everything," Trinity stated matter-of-factly. "As I said, it's just a precaution. But the Dragon Elite are in a pivotal time. It's a great time for you all to take back your rightful roles and reign. I'm excited as anyone, but I fear enemies will come out of the woodwork if you will allow me to use such a cliché."

"Allowed," Sophia said dryly as worry started to build in her.

"Once I learned how influential the Castle could be to that which it is connected to, and I started to understand what the Dragon Elite was doing, I thought it might be smart to guard things," Trinity explained. "I'm not saying anything will happen, but I am saying if something infected the Castle, it could take us all down with it."

Sophia swallowed. Her head swam with dizziness. It was hard for her to believe she was a part of something so powerful.

She didn't understand the Castle or the Gullington, but she'd spent enough time there to know, it was quite possibly the most powerful place on Earth.

Which made sense since it was where Mother Nature had chosen to reside after returning to the modern world.

CHAPTER FOURTEEN

Sophia left the *Complete History of Dragonriders* in her room before heading off for the House of Fourteen. The information Trinity had given her was brewing in her mind, but there was nothing she could do with it.

She could be cautious and aware. The Castle was connected to everything, and according to Trinity, the Castle and Gullington were the connecting force, the artery that had to be isolated from Trinity's perspective.

Sophia stepped into the closet portal and sucked in a breath. She heard the wind batter the walls around the Castle and remembered there must be something bothering her. She didn't know what it was but wondered as she traveled through the portal if it could possibly be that she didn't feel adequate when she was at the House of Fourteen.

It still didn't seem like the most plausible explanation. Yes, it was true she got tired of being looked at like she was still a child, but at the end of the day, she didn't really care what others thought of her. She was a dragonrider for the Elite. What did it matter if a bunch of magicians didn't take her seriously? Her word was law. They didn't have anything close to her when it came to influence.

The howling wind stopped when Sophia stepped through the

portal door in the House of Fourteen. She didn't understand why. If she was to be blamed for the high winds, why wouldn't they follow her from location to location? Maybe because the House of Fourteen had better insulation than the old Castle.

Sophia knew that was wishful thinking. The Castle was just as strong if not more so than the House if she'd learned anything from Trinity.

She'd heard wind whistle through the House of Fourteen many times before. It used to keep her up at night when she was a child. Reese, her sister, would crawl into her bed and comb her hair off her forehead. Her sister would tell her stories about a three-toed gnome she met at Roya Lane that day who sold her essence of the beach or some other weird adventure her sister had been on. Before long, the wind subsided, and Sophia would drift off to sleep.

It never happened in reverse, where Sophia fell asleep and forgot about the wind. Just like the past, she couldn't sleep or concentrate when the winds were tumultuous. Sophia allowed her mind to trail back in her memory, to figure out what was needling at her brain, making her chest feel heavy, telling her to pay attention.

When Sophia was young, and the winds would pick up, she remembered being sad. Not just sad, more like confused. For Sophia, belonging had always been a bit of an issue. She never felt like she belonged at the House of Fourteen, mostly because she had to hide her magic since children weren't supposed to possess it. Her siblings were always busy working, and when they weren't, Sophia felt their loss over their parents and sister. Clark mentioned Liv often and how much he missed her.

Sophia sucked in a breath. Smelling the scents of her childhood as she progressed down the long corridor in the House of Fourteen, she wondered if it was possible that all those years ago, Sophia herself had created the high winds with her emotions? Did her confusion over belonging and her inability to take away her sibling's pain cause tumultuous emotions inside of her that stirred the wind? If so, why weren't the winds up now when she was at the House of Fourteen like they were when she was at the Castle?

As often happened, Sophia strode on in autopilot mode, her feet taking her down paths she'd walked all her young life. Lost in thought, Sophia ran into something she at first thought was a wall.

Halting, she looked and found herself staring straight up Rory Lauren's nose.

"Oh, I'm sorry," she said, not taking a step back and unsure why as the giant was pressed up against her.

Unflustered, Rory gazed down at her with his usually calm expression. "Are you okay?"

She nodded, and her chin brushed against the fabric of his plaid shirt. For some reason, she wanted to wrap her arms around the big guy and hug him. Rory was really Liv's friend, who liked to call him her "little sidekick," which he didn't find amusing. That was Rory and Liv's dynamic. He pretended to tolerate her but was secretly very fond of her, Sophia suspected.

Sophia had spent a lot of time with the giant since he'd kept Lunis' egg before he hatched, but she didn't know him all that well. Yet, more than anything, she really wanted to hug him right then.

"I'm fine," Sophia replied, her voice cracking.

"Is that why you're pressed up against me?" he asked, still staring down at her.

She managed a smile. "You haven't moved either."

"I was here first," he replied.

"Do you normally stand in the middle of hallways, blocking the path?" Sophia asked, her voice amused even though she didn't feel that way at all.

"I was drawn to this spot," he answered.

"Oh?" she queried. She didn't feel as awkward as she thought she should about continuing to stand so close to the giant. "By what?"

His eyes fluttered with annoyance. *There* was the Rory Laurens, who so often rolled his eyes at Liv. "By you, of course."

Sophia took a step back then and immediately wished she hadn't. She felt much colder a foot from the giant. "Me? I drew you to this spot and made you be a wall?"

The giant really was blocking the wide corridor with his large frame. Sophia could have squeezed by, but not easily.

"I'm not a wall," he argued. "I'm a person, but I see that in your sister's absence, you've borrowed her humor."

"Said like a true writer," Sophia mused, remembering Rory had recently quit his accounting job to follow his dream of being a novelist.

"We're not talking about me right now," he challenged.

"How did I draw you to this spot?" Sophia asked.

"Elemental forces related to the Earth," he explained. "I'm guessing you were creating quite a few windy conditions at your last location."

Sophia took another step back and peered sideways at Rory. "How do you know that? And yes. Why am I not creating wind here?"

"Because I'm a giant. And I thought so. You're not creating wind here for multiple reasons. Chiefly because I'm here and giants neutralize, which is why you want to hug me right now."

"I don't either," Sophia argued, her face flushing.

"Anyway, regardless, when giants are present, it calms the wind because we own the elemental force of the Earth," Rory continued. "Also, I suspect whatever was really bothering you before isn't as much on your mind when you're in the House of Fourteen."

Sophia thought about this. She put herself back in the Castle and felt something stir inside of her. Was there something about the Gullington creating conflicting emotions? It had to be the dragon eggs. Being in charge of them was a huge responsibility. She was reminded of why she was at the House of Fourteen.

"Are you headed to the Chamber of the Tree?" Sophia questioned, changing the subject.

"When you are ready," he stated stoically.

"Well, I'm ready, but you're going to have to move for me to get by," she joked.

He held his hands out noncommittally. "Do you want a hug?"

"Will you judge me poorly if I say yes?" Sophia asked sheepishly.

"Judge you?" Rory questioned. "Yes. Poorly. No."

"You will?"

"We judge everything no matter what," he explained. "It's impossible not to. From the moment we wake up each day, we're judging. That's part of what makes us conscious beings."

"You can be quite literal, can't you?" she teased.

With his hands still held out, he said, "I am in the business of words."

CHAPTER FIFTEEN

The hug made Sophia feel lighter. Then it made her blush and feel totally embarrassed. Rory didn't seem to feel anything about it. His face just remained neutral.

Sophia followed the giant to the Chamber of the Tree in silence. When he passed through the Door of Reflection, she sucked in a breath and prepared herself.

She reminded herself she was delivering good news. Her job as a diplomat to the House of Fourteen was an honor, and she demanded the respect of the Council. Still, inside she felt like the small little girl who used to wear frilly dresses and have her head patted by the older magicians she was about to present to.

"You can do this," she whispered to herself.

"Or you can't," murmured a familiar voice at Sophia's back.

She smiled to herself and turned around to find Plato the lynx casually standing in the middle of the hallway. "Thanks for the vote of confidence."

"It's important to maintain a balanced perspective," the magical creature answered. "Many think they are optimistic by telling themselves they can do something, but those could also be considered unrealistic dreams of grandeur."

Sophia sighed. "Liv has the strangest friends."

"Your best friend breathes fire and plays Sudoku," Plato replied.

"It helps him to fall asleep," she fired back. "And how do you know about that? He does that in the Cave, and I only know about it because we share thoughts."

"I know things," the lynx said, a familiar air of mystery in his voice.

Sophia rolled her eyes. "You've been in the Gullington, haven't you?"

"Like a circus flea, I've been everywhere," the black and white cat answered.

She shook her head. "I don't know how you've managed to get into the Gullington." She peered around the hallway. "But of course, I don't know how you get into the House of Fourteen either since you're not one of the Fourteen. You're so strange. But onto topics we haven't discussed, why are you here?"

"Because I have to be somewhere," he informed her matter-of-factly, his black tail with the white tip flicking in the air.

Sophia sighed. She should have upped her dose of patience before this visit. "No, I mean, specifically, why are you here interrupting me with realistic missives to crush my dreams of grandeur? You only show up when you have some cryptic message for me."

"Maybe this time is different," he offered.

She stuck her hands on her hips. "Is it?"

Plato shook his head. "No, but I didn't think you wanted to just hang out with me for high tea."

"Yeah, you're Liv's cup of tea."

"Ha-ha," he said with no humor. "You're going to tell the Council about the dragon eggs, are you?"

"Well, they already know since Hiker told the world," she reasoned.

"Yes, but you want to tell them more details," Plato teased, a hint of mischief in his voice.

"I was planning on filling them in on Thad Reinhart and the eggs, yes. Why? Do you think I shouldn't?"

"I think there are some details you should share because they make

64

you look good." He teetered his head back and forth in thought. "But there are other details you shouldn't share because they don't make *others* look so good."

Sophia thought for a moment as she tried to decipher what the lynx was trying to say. "Do you mean the fact Thad Reinhart was a dragonrider?"

"It goes to reason if the Council, and specifically certain magicians with agendas, found out the enemy who nearly destroyed the Earth was one of your own, it may reflect poorly on the Dragon Elite," Plato explained.

"But a magician's biggest enemy is usually magicians," Sophia reasoned. "I mean, the Great War was instigated by one of our own founders from the House of Fourteen."

"I understand that. I firmly believe our enemies are usually our own. Dissension is often the strongest," Plato said, "inside families, nations, and races. You're playing a political game here as a diplomat for the Dragon Elite. Your job is to make dragonriders the supreme rulers, and most of that will revolve around perception. It's not all a cakewalk even if you have a thousand dragon eggs."

"I won't ask how you know we have a thousand since that wasn't public record," Sophia complained, irritation in her voice.

"Let's go with it was a good guess, and you just confirmed it."

"Did you actually guess?" Sophia asked.

"Sort of," he answered. "I mean, I couldn't count all of the eggs in that cave you're calling the Nest. I'm no Rain Man."

She shook her head. "I totally don't get you."

"Well, Rain Man is a reference to a movie about—"

"That's not what I meant, although I didn't get that reference either." Sophia sighed. "So I should lie and tell them Thad Reinhart was just an evil man slash magician or something?"

Plato frowned at her. "Beaufonts don't lie."

"Fine, but you're the one who is telling me to alter the truth."

He shook his head. "No, I'm telling you to omit details that aren't necessary. Anyway, Jude and Diabolos would call you out for lying in the Chamber of the Tree."

Jude and Diabolos were the two regulators who oversaw all proceedings for the Council. Jude was a white tiger and Diabolos, a black crow. Whatever fueled them and made them eternal and sensors of truth and deception was ancient and mysterious magic.

"Okay, so I won't tell the Council Thad Reinhart was a dragonrider," Sophia promised. "Is there anything else?"

"Yes. Bianca Mantovani has a cavity in her back right molar," Plato said.

Sophia's face contorted with confusion. "What? How do you… Why is that important?"

She never got her answer to the question because as he often did, Plato disappeared, leaving her alone outside of the Chamber of the Tree.

CHAPTER SIXTEEN

S ophia hadn't anticipated the pressure that assaulted her chest when she entered the Chamber of the Tree and remembered this was the place founded by her ancestors.

The domed room appeared as it had centuries prior when the founding families created the House of Fourteen. The names of the seven magical families and seven mortal ones were engraved on the tree on the wall behind the bench where the Council sat. Overhead, lights twinkled to represent the magicians all over the world. Standing in a half arc around the room were the seven warriors—all of them present on this rare occasion.

They didn't turn to look at Sophia as she walked into the dim space, lit by firelight. Sophia took the center spot in the Chamber and waited in silence for the Council to acknowledge her.

They all had their heads down, studying their tablets filled with the day's cases.

She waited and she tensed, telling herself the perception of the Council didn't matter and Plato was wrong. She told herself she shouldn't care if they saw her as a ruling force.

But it did.

Before, Sophia had wanted to be seen as equal to the royals of the

House of Fourteen. Now, she wanted, needed to be seen as more powerful than them.

The problem was she didn't feel like it.

Sophia stood with her hands tight together. She knew her sister was at her back, and her brother was at her front. It made her feel marginally better, although when Clark glanced up, he looked at her like she was anybody else. That was always the way with the Councilor. He rarely broke character and acted indifferent as though they hadn't been raised together and bonded by blood. Liv was the opposite. When Sophia glanced over her shoulder to her sister, the Warrior flashed her a smile and winked.

The Council droned on about unregistered magicians for a full minute before Sophia realized their discussion could go on for a long time. That wouldn't work. A Dragon Elite representative who was trying to exert power shouldn't wait around for their turn. They should demand it.

Even though she was trembling inside, Sophia remained steady as she took a step forward and cleared her throat. "I must interrupt to offer the Dragon Elite update to the House of Fourteen."

All heads jerked in her direction, many wearing disapproving expressions.

"Ms. Beaufont, it is not your turn," Lorenzo Rosario scolded.

"I understand that," she remarked, her chin high. "But my time is limited."

"As is the Council's," Bianca Mantovani stated, looking around smugly. "Now, where were we before we were interrupted."

"Talking about the same thing you've all droned on about for ages," Liv said at Sophia's back.

Bianca shot her a murderous stare. "The issue of registering magicians is an important topic that has presented many challenges."

"None of which you are going to resolve today," Liv argued. "I say we have Dragonrider Beaufont give her update."

The scowl on Bianca's face deepened. "I don't believe how the Council conducts its meetings are any of your concern, Olivia."

Sophia glanced over in time to see her sister turn like someone was standing at her back. She shrugged. "No Olivia here. But my name is Liv since you've obviously forgotten."

"Your name is Olivia, according to the records," Bianca contended, belaboring the point.

"I believe we've gotten off-topic here," Haro Takahashi interjected.

"Yes, we were discussing registering magicians," Bianca stated.

"I must insist on giving my update, or I'll have to leave without doing so," Sophia insisted with confidence.

"Then you'll have to leave, Ms. Beaufont," Bianca snapped at Clark beside her. "What new information do you have on the negotiations?"

He narrowed his eyes at the other councilor. "That discussion can wait, and you will refer to our guest by formal title, Dragonrider Beaufont. Please show her the respect she deserves."

Sophia wanted to jump up and down but was certain that would detract from the whole "mature and respected" thing she was going for. Clark was sticking up for her! She was thrilled.

"Really, this is not a meeting run by the Beaufont clan," Bianca maintained.

"No, it certainly isn't," Raina Ludwig said. "And I quite agree that you Councilor Mantovani must show the delegate from the Dragon Elite the respect she deserves."

Bianca's face flushed pink. She opened her mouth, no doubt to say something oozing with condescension but was cut off before she could reply.

"Dragonrider Beaufont, you have an update from the Elite?" Hester DeVries asked from the bench of the Council.

"I absolutely do," Sophia declared, finding her voice hard to come by. It was scratchy and felt unused. She cleared her throat and continued. "I'm here to report the Dragon Elite have ended one of the worst evils, making things safer for the mortal world again."

The Council, as it was prone to doing, stirred.

"Please explain, Sophia Beaufont," Bianca Mantovani demanded.

Wishing she felt stronger, Sophia stood straighter. "Well, the Dragon Elite took down Thad Reinhart, ending what could have been a brutal reign. Then we went on to—"

"Can you please elaborate on the Thad part," Hester asked.

"I can't," Sophia answered. "It's not worth my time or attention. Instead, we will talk about what's coming."

Jude flicked his long white tail, his green eyes shining with curiosity. She wasn't lying. She simply was glossing over the facts. Plato was right. If she had gone into details about Thad Reinhart and his cyborg dragon, it would have just come back to haunt the Dragon Elite's reputation. It was a good thing the only places to document Thad Reinhart as a dragonrider was in *The Complete History of Dragonriders* and the Forgotten Archives, and there was no way anyone in the House of Fourteen was getting their hands on those. Sophia was also quite confident Trinity wouldn't disclose the secret.

Over the next several minutes, Sophia explained to the Council about the new crop of dragon eggs and the future of the Elite as world adjudicators.

"Well." Hester leaned back. "It certainly seems the Dragon Elite have recovered and will reign once more."

Sophia nodded proudly. "Yes, although the timeline is unclear, I'm confident our numbers will recover fully."

Bianca and Lorenzo's faces had grown with anger as Sophia explained how mortals were accepting the Dragon Elite, and governments worldwide were making requests of them. This wouldn't work for their master plan to turn mortals against the dragonriders.

Lorenzo sighed and sounded bored. "I don't see how having a bunch of dragon eggs will change much. It could be centuries before they hatch."

"Or it could be an hour," Sophia argued. "It isn't like a basket full of Easter eggs. We have a sizable crop."

"And what caused this new spawn of dragon eggs?" Raina inquired.

"I did," Sophia said simply.

"You?" Hester questioned, her interest piqued.

"Yes, the first batch was spawned by the first male dragonrider," Sophia explained.

"And this is the second, sparked by the first female dragonrider," Haro speculated, appearing impressed.

"Gives a whole new take to which came first, the dragon or the egg," Liv joked.

Sophia resisted the urge to laugh. "Yes, apparently there was a set of dragons before the first batch of eggs. Who knows how they came about? I'd guess Mother Nature knows. Anyway, a rider magnetized to one of the dragons and caused the first batch."

"And now we have a second," Clark declared with pride.

"And with it, a chance for the Dragon Elite to preside over justice as we have done for centuries," Sophia explained.

"With all due respect," Bianca began.

"Don't use that phrase unless you mean it," Liv interrupted.

The councilor flashed Liv a repugnant stare before turning her gaze back on Sophia. "I don't see how you can know this will change the political climate. We are in a time of great conflict with the mortal world. They can see magic now, and they distrust the various magical races. Problems with them are increasing."

"That is to be expected," chimed John Carraway, one of the Mortal Seven. "I think the return of the Dragon Elite is exactly what we need to win the mortal world's trust again. They need an impartial authority to turn to since the House of Fourteen has a reputation for deception."

"I agree," Sophia said, grateful to have his support as he smiled down at her subtly. "This is our rightful role as given to us by Mother Nature."

"Really." Bianca sighed. "There is no way for us to know that is the truth. You all simply have dragons and therefore appear entitled to declare you're judge and jury for the world, but to me, it seems like a self-elected position."

"That's true," Lorenzo agreed. "Since the history was lost and rewritten, much of the dragonrider's past is murky at best."

Bianca nodded, a smile forming on her flat mouth. "Really, without testimony from Mother Nature, it is just Hiker Wallace's word the Dragon Elite are the ruling authority over mortal affairs."

"I'm not going to parade Mother Nature in front of you to make my case," Sophia said, her eyes fluttering with annoyance.

"Well, then without any proof, how are we to know what you say is the truth?" Bianca fired back.

Sophia shrugged. "True authorities don't have to prove anything. You can watch as we rule the world."

Bianca's bottom jaw moved to the side as she narrowed her eyes. "This is really ridiculous. Just because you say something doesn't make it true."

"Oh, but it does," Sophia disagreed casually. "For instance, if I said you had a cavity in your back right molar, that would become true."

"What?" Bianca questioned. "What are you talking about?"

"You," Sophia stated boldly. "You have a cavity in your back right molar. You know that, right? You should get it checked out."

Bianca's hand flew to her cheek. "No, I don't."

Hester pointed to the white tiger. "I'm afraid you do, Councilor Mantovani. Dragonrider Beaufont isn't lying, or Jude would have flagged it."

Sophia smiled, grateful for the strange information Plato had given her. It was silly to her something so trivial had proven her point, yet things often happened that way.

"Well, it appears the Dragon Elite are back," Raina began. "A supreme source of power and information. The House of Fourteen will look forward to seeing you all manage the incredible responsibility you've been given."

Clark smiled at his sister. "I think I can confidently say it's good to have the Dragon Elite back with a promising future to do good for centuries to come."

CHAPTER SEVENTEEN

F eeling rather satisfied with how things turned out at the House of Fourteen, Sophia stepped back through the portal and into the Castle to find a startling surprise. The place she'd left only an hour before was starkly different from how it had been.

The walls of the Castle were crumbling.

Sophia wondered if she'd messed up the portal somehow and came through to a different time like when she opened a portal using the save point.

The tapestry lining the wall opposite the portal door wasn't in pristine condition as she remembered. It was stained and fraying. The suit of armor beside it was rusted and looked ready to fall over from a gentle breeze. The floors were all broken, and none of the flames were burning in the torches on the wall.

Twice Sophia stepped into the portal and then back out, but each time was the same. Something was majorly wrong with the Castle.

A high-pitched scream from the downstairs stole Sophia's attention and sent her sprinting. Further investigation using the portal would have to wait.

As she progressed toward the stairs, Sophia found more evidence of problems in the Castle. Half of the staircase was missing, and Sophia had to leap over a giant hole to make it down to the landing.

She nearly ran into Wilder, who sped out of the weapon's room, his face grief-stricken.

"The Castle," she told him.

He nodded.

Another scream made their gazes jerk in the direction of the kitchen.

"Ainsley," Sophia said and ran toward the sound of the scream, Wilder on her heels.

She rushed past the dining room table, which had caved in, and hopped over broken chairs. Sophia wondered what had happened to the Castle while she was gone. It didn't seem like a fight had broken out. More like the Castle had suddenly aged a few hundred years.

Sophia busted through the kitchen door to find the housekeeper standing in front of the large center island gawking at a mound of rotten food. Ainsley took no notice of Sophia and Wilder but instead whipped around and pulled a box from the pantry behind her.

"It's all rotten. All of it!" she yelled, pulling moldy oranges from the box and tossing them on the pile in front of her.

"What's going on?" Sophia asked, finally earning Ainsley's attention.

The housekeeper shook her head. "I don't know. I went to go make dinner and found my pantry full of rotten food." Holding up a bag of potatoes covered in sprouts, she grimaced. "I can't do anything with this."

"But the Castle," Wilder said as he looked around the kitchen in the same state of disrepair as the other areas.

Ainsley narrowed her green eyes. "The Castle won't answer me! I've been hollering at it since I discovered all this. It's just silent like the joke is on me."

"Maybe something is wrong with the Castle," Sophia argued. "And that's why it looks like this." She indicated the cabinet doors that were hanging half off.

Ainsley waved her off. "Oh, no. The Castle is just being a drama queen. But it is responsible for the rotten food. I bet it's mad because I said the décor could use some modern flare."

"I don't understand," Wilder asked, peering around the kitchen.

"Well, you see, when S. Beaufont sleeps, I steal her phone because our esteemed leader won't let me have my own," Ainsley explained. "I've been watching Home and Garden TV. There's this great show where they do complete redesigns on houses over a long weekend. It gave me some ideas for some modern interior design we could do to the Castle. I mentioned it and bam! The cranky old building throws a fit."

Wilder shook his head. "No, I don't mean that. I think something is really wrong with the Castle. In the almost two-hundred years I've been here, I've never seen anything like this."

Sophia gulped and looked at the dragonrider next to her. It was hard to believe the guy next to her with his windswept dark brown hair and dazzling blue eyes was two-hundred years old. She felt like a toddler next to him even though they appeared to be the same age, thanks to the chi of the dragons.

The winds howled even more violently through the Castle because many of the windows were now broken. Sophia could only imagine what the rest of the Castle looked like based on what she was seeing.

"Oh, I think the Castle is just trying a new way of getting attention," Ainsley disputed. She threw her hands up as she glared at the ceiling. "You have my attention, and you're about to get my wrath."

Sophia stepped forward to lay a comforting hand on the shapeshifter's shoulder. "I can only imagine how stressful this is for you. Why don't I call Uber Eats and order us some dinner?"

Ainsley swallowed as she brought her gaze to meet Sophia's. "Thank you. That will get us through tonight, and then hopefully, the Castle will fix its attitude because I really don't want to sleep on the floor."

Sophia tilted her head to the side. "Why would you have to do that?"

"Oh, you haven't seen your room," Ainsley said with a sigh. "It probably looks worse than mine. My canopy bed has crumpled, and there's zero chance I can sleep on it."

Sophia blew out a breath. "Okay, well, we'll make do." She cast a glance at Wilder, looking for support. "Will you help me fetch food at the Barrier? I'll order extra in case we need leftovers for breakfast."

He nodded solemnly. "Yes, but let's hope things resolve before then."

CHAPTER EIGHTEEN

Sophia's nervous gaze connected with Wilder from across the dining room table. It wasn't the same table they were used to. Ainsley had managed to stabilize a section and find a few chairs that weren't broken and arrange them to give people a place to sit.

Hiker hadn't said a word since coming down from his office to dinner. He was livid, no doubt confused, and definitely frustrated. All evident from his nervous actions, but he wasn't speaking on the matter of the Castle just yet.

Ainsley had grumbled as they set out the food from Uber Eats, and she lit the torches along the wall by hand. It was something the Castle had always taken care of for the housekeeper, and now she had to do it all on her own.

Wilder and Sophia hadn't mentioned their biggest concern as they set out the food, but they both knew the time would come. She'd lost the *ro sham bo* game and had the unfortunate job of delivering the news.

"So my curry is really good," Sophia began, trying to loosen the mood. Instead, she earned an annoyed expression from Ainsley.

"I make it better when I have unspoiled ingredients," the elf said, scowling at her food and unwilling to taste it.

"Right," Sophia agreed. She remembered Ainsley had made the spicy curried dish recently, and she probably should have picked something else for takeout. They had been rushed after learning about the disrepair the Castle was in.

Evan shook his head. "Man, my room is wrecked. I thought it was just after me again until I came downstairs and saw it hadn't singled me out this time. Does anyone know what the Castle's deal is?"

Mahkah offered a gentle smile. "My room is quite disorganized too. And I haven't got a clue what's going on with the Castle."

Everyone looked at Hiker. He hadn't touched his food, only clenched his jaw, his tension obviously elevating with each passing moment.

"I don't get it," he said quietly. "At first, I thought the Castle was simply mad at me again, ransacking my office like before. Then I came down to dinner and found what you all did." He shook his head. "I really don't understand, but I've rarely understood this place we call home. I'm sure it will pass."

"Sir," Sophia began, pushing her plate away. "There's something we discovered when we went to collect the food."

Her gaze pinned on Wilder, she expected him to offer some encouragement. Strangely, the smile he flashed her helped.

"What is it?" Hiker asked, narrowing his eyes at her.

"Well, I'm sure it's nothing, but we thought you should know that the winds, well, you remember, have been crazy lately," Sophia began, her tone careful.

"I do, in fact," he stated.

"We noticed quite a bit of foreign debris around the Expanse when we hiked to the Barrier," Sophia went on.

Hiker stood suddenly, knocking his chair out behind him. "Are you certain?"

She swallowed and nodded then took in a breath. "Yes, sir. There was trash and things we know shouldn't have been inside the Gullington, blown in by the wind."

"Why is that a big deal?" Evan asked as he looked between Sophia and Hiker.

"The Barrier should keep out foreign debris," Wilder explained. "It always has in the past. Nothing, not even objects can pass through it."

"Oh…" Evan said, his face turning grave. "Which means…"

"The Barrier is down," Hiker whispered, his eyes wide and his face pale.

"But we don't have anything to worry about, right?" Evan reasoned. "We are in the middle of Scotland, off a beaten path."

"But we are visible now," Hiker clarified. "Anyone can see us. Enter our grounds."

"And you just got finished telling the world roughly our location," Wilder reminded him, his voice serious.

"The eggs," Sophia said, sucking in a breath.

"We will guard them," Hiker assured her.

"Has that ever happened to the Gullington before?" Sophia asked.

He shook his head. "No, not ever. This means, whatever is happening with the Castle isn't just a stunt on its part. Something is wrong."

CHAPTER NINETEEN

Wilder had thought the Castle was having a real problem when they found the trash on the Expanse. Sophia knew he didn't want to scare her; she'd sensed that instinctively. He'd been unable to hide his stress when they found things that shouldn't have been inside the Barrier, and now Hiker had confirmed it. Something was wrong with the Castle.

Hiker directed his gaze at Ainsley. "What do you make of this?"

The housekeeper, who always seemed on the verge of joking, shook her head, tears in her eyes. "It makes sense and explains why it won't answer me."

"What is with the Castle?" Evan asked.

Ainsley tied her hands in her napkin, real stress surfacing in her every movement. "I don't know. This has never happened."

"Quiet, what are your thoughts on the matter?" Hiker looked around the table to find that for once, the gnome wasn't present. "Where is he?"

"He didn't come in for dinner," Ainsley answered. "I haven't seen him all day."

"He might be trying to repair things on the Expanse," Mahkah offered.

Sophia hadn't remembered seeing the groundskeeper on the Expanse when she and Wilder crossed to the Barrier to get food.

"Well, as soon as someone finds him," Hiker ordered, standing from the table, having not eaten anything, "send him to my office immediately. We need to figure out what is happening here."

"But what about the adjudication cases, sir?" Evan questioned.

Hiker shook his head. "Cases will come after we figure out what's happening. The Castle comes first."

"Are you serious?" Evan challenged. "It's just a building."

Hiker stopped abruptly at the entrance to the dining hall. "The Castle isn't just a building. It is an extension of the Dragon Elite. It is our home and our sanctuary. If something is wrong with the Castle, something is wrong with all of us. Mahkah, I want you and the dragons out on the Expanse, manning the borders."

Sophia's annoyed expression was caught by Hiker immediately.

"Of course, I mean, guarding the borders," Hiker amended. "Evan and Wilder, you need—"

"To go and check on Quiet," Mama Jamba declared, coming around Hiker to stand next to him. She was much shorter than the large man, and she looked funny when she stood so close to him.

Hiker looked down at her, his eyes crinkling with stress. "Where is Quiet?" the Viking asked. "Is he with the dragon eggs?"

She shook her head. "Oh, no. He hasn't left his room all day. Your groundskeeper is quite sick."

Hiker was confused. "Sick? What do you mean?"

"Sick," Mama Jamba said, drawing the word out. "You know that thing mortals get."

"I know what it is," Hiker argued. "But the Castle ensures we don't get sick. Ever."

"Right. And there are obvious problems with the Castle." Her eyes darted to the food on the table. "Is that curry? I could really use some of that in my life."

Hiker snapped at her. "Mama, tell us what's going on?"

She was momentarily distracted by the food before pulling her attention back to Hiker. "Oh, with the Castle?"

"Yes, with the Castle," he barked.

She smiled sweetly. "I can't really say."

"You can't or you won't?" he questioned.

"Oh, let's not quibble words, my dear, especially when I'm hungry and the food smells so good," Mama Jamba asserted.

Ainsley crossed her arms in front of her chest. "I didn't make this."

"But others can make food just as good as yours," Mama Jamba consoled. "It's not a competition, dear."

"Mama," Hiker started, an edge to his voice.

She turned to face him directly. "Son, it appears your groundskeeper has fallen ill because the Castle is ill and can't repair itself or anyone else. And yes, the Barrier is down, and the Expanse is dying. I'm sorry, but those are the cold, hard facts. You've obviously got several problems on your hands. Instead of questioning me, who will give you no answers and only wants to eat curry, why don't you go and fix your problems? Or at least try to."

Hiker sighed, obviously unhappy with her answer, and stormed off. The other riders sped off after their leader, seeking their assignments. Sophia stayed back as she sensed Mama Jamba had something to say to her by the way Mama had looked at her when she took a seat.

"It's a strange thing that's happened to the Castle, isn't it?" the old woman asked casually as if talking about the weather. She spooned chicken makhani onto her plate as Ainsley began to clean up the other dishes.

"Very strange," Sophia said, carefully watching Mama Jamba.

"Although my heart really goes out to the Castle, I feel most for the groundskeeper laid up in bed," Mama Jamba went on, taking in the aromatic scents as the steam wafted up from the plate. "I mean, the men and Ainsley will look after the Castle and the grounds, but who will look after Quiet?"

Sophia didn't answer. Instead, she lowered her chin and regarded the woman in front of her, waiting for more information she was certain she'd soon receive. She was used to playing this game with

Mother Nature. She knew how the woman worked, delivering bits of information and implying things.

"If only there was someone who could find something to help the gnome to feel better," Mama Jamba mused to herself.

"Shouldn't we focus on fixing the Castle, and then it can heal Quiet?" Sophia reasoned.

Mama Jamba took a bite of the curry, closing her eyes as she enjoyed the flavors. "That's a good thought, but who knows how long that could take or if it would work? Meanwhile, poor Quiet is really ill."

"Yeah, I wouldn't want to wait for the Castle to be fixed if I were him."

"Good girl," Mama Jamba commended.

"I'm no expert on healing magic, though," Sophia protested. "Shouldn't I recruit Hester DeVries?"

Mama Jamba considered this for a moment before shaking her head. "Although Hester is very capable, I think you need a different type of expert for this. Someone with specialized knowledge who knows things and is in a unique position to help you. A fairy godmother, if you will." She brought a full fork of food up to her mouth and paused, a sneaky grin on her face. "I only wished you had someone like that you could call on to help you. Because I can't figure out any way to fix things even if the men do everything they think is right." The blue of Mother Nature's eyes when she looked up at Sophia was almost assaulting. "Oh, this is delicious, isn't it? Good thing we can still eat when the Castle is dying…"

CHAPTER TWENTY

Sophia didn't know why Mama Jamba didn't just tell her what she needed to do, but she wasn't going to start doubting the wisdom of the goddess. She needed to go see Mae Ling at the nail salon. Apparently, she'd know what to do for Quiet.

It made her nervous, leaving the Gullington when things were in such chaos. When she'd gone out to the Barrier, the guys had already taken posts at different sides of the Expanse. In less than an hour, things had worsened. Sophia noticed the grass was wilting and turning brown, something that never happened in Scotland where everything was green year-round.

She heard the footsteps before he spoke. "Where are you going?" Wilder called at her back.

The wind whipped through her hair as she turned to face him. She felt breathless. "Mama Jamba sent me on an errand to try and help Quiet."

"But shouldn't we focus on fixing the Gullington, then the Castle will help him?" he questioned.

She nodded. "That was my thought too, but Mama Jamba insisted. Someone has to help Quiet."

"He's very old," Wilder said as he took a step forward, his voice barely audible over the whistling wind. His dark hair was even more chaotic than usual. "Without the aid of the Castle, who knows what could be wrong with him. It might have been keeping him alive for quite some time."

Sophia sucked in a breath, having not considered this. The riders could thank the chi of the dragon for their longevity, but the Castle was the reason Ainsley and Quiet lived as long as they had without aging. "That just means I need to hurry."

"Do you want my help?" Wilder asked.

She did, but Sophia knew she needed to go on this mission alone. Mama Jamba hadn't said she couldn't tell anyone Mae Ling helped her, but it felt like a secret. Girls weren't supposed to tell people they had a fairy godmother, right? She didn't remember Cinderella sharing that information with Prince Charming. As she was prone to doing, Sophia followed her instinct. "No, stay here and help guard the eggs. I'll return as soon as I can."

The reluctant expression on Wilder's face seemed to speak of more than just his stress regarding the current situation. "Okay, well, be careful then. We'll be here."

She backed away, nodding, and swallowed the tension that rose in her throat. Another gust of wind knocked her hair back into her face. "You be careful too," Sophia said before she turned and sprinted for the Barrier.

The huge nail salon was bustling with customers when Sophia arrived. Mae's Beauty Emporium was even busier than the last time she'd been there. Sophia wasn't worried she wouldn't be able to get in to see her fairy godmother. Mae Ling had said she'd always be available, and Sophia didn't need to make an appointment.

Confidently, Sophia squeezed through the crowd of waiting patrons to the reception desk.

"Hi," she called over the loud chatter in the salon. "I'm here to see Mae Ling."

The receptionist didn't look up from her iPhone as she chewed her gum. "Mae is out."

"Oh, but..." Sophia didn't know what to say. She hadn't expected that.

"Do you want to make an appointment with someone else?" the woman asked, her focus still directed at the Instagram feed she was scrolling through.

"No, I only want to see Mae," Sophia said, chewing on her lip and thinking. Her fairy godmother had told her she'd always be able to find her when she needed her help, but it didn't appear that was entirely true. "Is there a way I can get hold of her? A phone number or something?"

The woman shook her head. "Sorry, I can't give that information out to just anyone." She indicated with her head an envelope sitting on the side of the desk. "Unless your name is S. Beaufont."

"Wait," Sophia said, hope fluttering in her chest. "I am S. Beaufont. Is that for me?"

The woman finally glanced up and looked her over. "Why didn't you say so? Yeah, Mae Ling said you'd be by and I should give you this."

Sophia took the letter sealed with a wax emblem. She had no idea how her fairy godmother knew the things she did, but she was grateful. It appeared once again Mae Ling had anticipated her needs. Now Sophia hoped she could help her with the groundskeeper of the Gullington, or she feared he might die as the Castle withered away.

CHAPTER TWENTY-ONE

The note Mae Ling left for Sophia made no sense, which was pretty much status quo for her life.

Dear S. Beaufont,

Currently, I'm away at school. Since you haven't been accepted into our academic institution, you can't portal here directly. Therefore, when ready, simply break the wax seal on the outside of the letter, and it will send you through to my location.

Sincerely,

Mae Ling

Your Fairy Godmother

School, Sophia wondered and furrowed her brow. In the back of her mind, she recalled a faint memory where Bermuda Laurens mentioned fairy godmother college. She had thought the woman was joking, but then remembered giants weren't much for jokes. It seemed fairy godmother school was real, and Sophia was about to see it for herself.

She peeled the wax seal off the envelope, noticing a symbol of a hand on it. Holding her breath, she broke the emblem in two.

The sensation of portaling was much different than she was used to. It felt like someone wrapped a cord around her sternum and yanked her straight up into the air. The wind was deafening, and then everything went black. Her stomach flipped over three times before the portal spit her out on a grassy lawn. Sophia sucked in a breath. The sight in front wasn't something she had expected, though, in hindsight, she should have.

Fairy godmother college didn't look like any academic institution she'd ever seen.

CHAPTER TWENTY-TWO

S ophia didn't know specifically where the fairy godmother college
was located, but she knew the location was miles from anything
because the portal had transported her to the top of a hill where she
could see green rolling hills for miles around.

The breeze wafting across her face wasn't as aggressive as the
winds at the Gullington, and she was grateful. The air didn't smell like
Scotland's, but she didn't know if she was in America, Europe or some
other country.

She guessed that much like the Gullington, the fairy godmother
college location was meant to stay secret from outsiders. She was
appreciative she'd gotten a pass and would get to see the mysterious
place people trained to become fairy godmothers. She had so many
questions. Like was it only women? Was that sexist? What if a man
wanted to be a fairy godmother?

As the first female dragonrider in history, she resented any organization that closed their doors to someone because of their gender, but
she did find the idea of guys as fairy godmothers strange. There were
so many other questions about magical races who qualified.

Sophia wondered how people were chosen for the position? Did
they get a letter from a snowy owl inviting them to the special school?

How long was the education? A year? A few? It seemed to Sophia if a mortal's bachelor's degree took four years to complete and medical degrees at least eight years, fairy godmothers who would be in charge of directing someone's path should take a significant length of time.

At the bottom of the hill, there was a winding path that led to a building Sophia would have expected to find on any ivy league campus. It was a large two-story brick building with arched windows and a set of pink double doors. Running from the doors to the start of the path was a long rainbow striped rug. The bright colors were such a strange contrast to the rich green grass and brown building. Sophia felt like someone had sprinkled a bit of the circus onto a stuffy brick and mortar building.

She took note of several details around the building as she hiked down to the college. The grounds of the fairy godmother college were similar to mortal campuses, with stretched out lawns and trees with large canopies that created shade for the students lounging about or chatting on benches.

These students didn't look out of the ordinary. They didn't have large fairy wings like the fae did when not glamoured, nor did they have large colorful hair, as Sophia had imagined. They certainly weren't wearing ball gowns and carrying around wands.

Much like Mae Ling, they all looked quite normal. Most were wearing a school uniform, which included a pleated skirt with the same rainbow colors as the rug runner and starched button-up shirts the same pink of the doors at the entrance to the school. As far as Sophia could tell, all of them were women.

She didn't know where to actually look to find Mae Ling but suspected she'd be led to the strange woman, or there would be a message waiting at the front office.

When Sophia opened the front door to the school, she was overwhelmed by the scent of sugar in the air. It was as if she'd entered a candy store where fresh fudge sat on the countertop and bins of ice cream waited to be scooped for hungry children.

The interior of the school was just as perplexing as the outside. The rainbow-striped rug ran the length of the long hallway and disappeared at the far side at another set of pink double doors. Other doors lined the hall and were the same boring brick as the exterior. Sophia had never been to a place so normal with so many elements of whimsy.

Bustling through the halls were students, Sophia guessed and realized almost immediately why she was getting strange looks. She wasn't wearing the school uniform but her silver and blue armor and carrying a sword. The sword always got her curious looks with a bit of caution.

A group of girls turned to gawk at Sophia, whispering to each other as they pointed, and disregarding any manners. Sophia knew she looked out of place. She obviously was. It would have been nice if the girls had acknowledged her and asked if she needed directions instead of pointing and gossiping.

She knew it shouldn't matter. She was the outsider and should expect to be treated as such, but the experience reminded her of when she was young, and the kids at the House of Fourteen school had made her an outcast because she was different. Her sister Reese had reminded her they treated her that way because she *was* different, but that didn't make her feel better then or now.

"They aren't staring at you because you look different," an unfamiliar voice said at Sophia's shoulder.

She hadn't noticed the person who came up beside her, which was unusual since her reflexes and enhanced senses made it nearly impossible for anyone to sneak up on her.

A woman stood next to her, wearing a serene smile with an air of authority about it. Unlike the students, she wasn't dressed in the school uniform. Instead, she had a high-waisted blue satin dress that puffed out as though it was supported underneath with a puffy petticoat. Her long brown hair framed her face, and her brown eyes seemed to have an actual spark about them. She had the reddest lips, which perfectly matched her large dangling earrings.

"Why are they staring at me?" Sophia finally asked, finding her voice.

The woman batted her long eyelashes. "Because you're S. Beaufont. It's not every day we get a celebrity here." She laughed politely. "Honestly, it's not every day we get a visitor, but Professor Ling made a special request, and I honored it."

Sophia blushed, not knowing where to start with what the woman had said. "Oh, I'm not a celebrity."

The woman shook her head. "A child born to Guinevere and Theodore Beaufont, one of the youngest to receive her magic, first female dragonrider, and sister to Warrior Liv Beaufont, and you don't think you're a celebrity?"

Sophia released a frustrated breath. "Oh, well, those are all things I happen to be, but they aren't of my doing. You can't choose what family you're born into, and I only had my magic so early because my twin died."

The woman smiled, but it wasn't a sweet one this time. It seemed to say, "Drop the act. I don't like it."

"Oh, well, I guess I should have also included you're our best chance of avoiding a second Great War," the woman stated matter-of-factly.

"Wait. What?" Sophia questioned, thrown off by this statement.

Instead of answering her question, the woman extended a hand, her fingernails the same aquamarine of her dress. "My name is Willow, and I'm the headmistress for the fairy godmother college, Happily Ever After."

"Oh, it's nice to meet you," Sophia said, taking her hand. "Are you named for the tree?"

Willow took off, her tall heels making a gentle clapping sound as she strode down the hallway lined with the rainbow runner. "Come along, S. Beaufont. I'll show you to Professor Ling. She should be adjourning her class soon." She pulled up her wrist and eyed a large watch that wasn't at all normal. It didn't have a short and a long hand or even numbers but rather strange symbols and glowing lights. "Yes, Samantha is going to dump her confection all over Kimberly's head, ending the lesson early." She pursed her lips and shook her head. "Those two won't get along for another year, and it is really quite the disturbance, but there's no helping it."

"Wait, you know there's going to be a conflict between two students, for the next year?" Sophia craned her neck to look into classrooms as they passed. It looked almost like a craft college. The first room they passed was full of canvases and art supplies and had paint splattered all over the walls. Another room was full of pottery wheels and vases of varying heights. One was filled with looms that had colorful yarn stretched across them and finished rugs and blankets draped in various corners.

"We know all sorts of things…well, we have strong hunches about them," Willow explained. "There's no way to know anything with certainty because free will is always changing the playing field. But we know how our various players usually respond with the bag of tricks their personality loans them and we can infer certain outcomes."

Sophia's stomach rumbled as they progressed to the far end of the hallway. The smell of sweets was so strong it was making her insanely hungry for a giant ice cream sundae or a frosted cupcake or milkshake. "Is there an ice cream parlor somewhere close by?"

Willow smiled, showing perfectly straight teeth that sparkled like a cartoon character's. "There's three on campus, as well as six bakeries, a confection shop, and an assortment of specialty sweet shops."

"Oh, wow," Sophia replied. "If you have that many dessert places, I can't even imagine how many hamburger joints you have."

Quite seriously, Willow said, "None. We have zero places that serve burgers, sandwiches, soups, salads, or the like."

Sophia frowned. "Why is that?"

"We only have desserts," Willow repeated.

"Why?" Sophia asked, curious by this reveal.

"It's just part of the charm of being a fairy godmother." She turned into a room and waved Sophia in with her. "Okay, it looks like the class is finishing up. I'll leave you here until Professor Ling can attend to you." She glanced at her strange watch-like device. "Looks like it will just be another minute."

"Okay, thanks." Sophia studied the classroom. It looked like one of those bakeries on reality television where multiple contestants have to make huge, complex cakes in a ridiculously short amount of time to win a prize. There were several workstations stocked with ingredients and mixers and bowls. At the front of the class, Sophia could hardly see Mae Ling, who was shorter than everyone who surrounded her. They held plates of desserts, apparently presenting them for their professor to judge.

"Oh, and S. Beaufont," Willow called, grabbing Sophia's attention away from the classroom activities.

"Yes?" Sophia inquired.

"I wasn't named after the willow tree," she disclosed as her large red earrings swayed back and forth. "It's the other way around."

CHAPTER TWENTY-THREE

For a full minute, Sophia couldn't get the image of the earrings swaying like branches of a willow tree out of her mind. Even after the headmistress for Happily Ever After left, Sophia saw details of the woman in her mind vividly.

As a magician who grew up in the House of Fourteen, privy to all sorts of things, she still had no idea about this part of the magical world. It was chilling there were fairy godmothers who looked after certain people, and they had a college and only ate desserts. It made her wonder what else was out there she'd yet to learn about.

A disgruntled yell stole Sophia's attention away from her trailing thoughts. She looked up to find a girl dumping a bowl of ingredients onto another girl's head, producing loud gasps from the classmates gathered around them.

Mae Ling clapped her hands to disperse the gawkers. "Okay, we're done for the day. Samantha, you've earned yourself ten hours of math problems."

The grunt that followed was full of frustration. "Ten hours! But math will hamper my creative abilities. I'll have to study twice as hard to counteract its effects."

"Yes, it will," Mae Ling said. "Maybe you'll consider that the next time you attack one of your fellow colleagues."

"But you knew I was going to do it," Samantha complained. "Why couldn't you stop me?"

Mae Ling sighed. "You're in your second year, and you don't know the answer to that?"

"Oh, Professor Ling," a woman with long blonde hair said, holding her arm in the air.

"Yes, Joan. You want to answer this," Mae Ling instructed.

"Yes," Joan answered. "Your job and ours as fairy godmothers isn't to intervene but rather to offer guidance. If we are doing our job, we will never have to stop things but rather provide guard rails."

"That's correct," Mae Ling agreed. She threw her hands in the air, and pink and gold dust sprinkled down on Joan's head. "My compliments."

The woman smiled broadly, relishing the experience of being dusted with pixie dust or whatever it was. "Thank you!"

"Okay, I've got a godchild to deal with," Mae Ling told them, her eyes locating Sophia at the back of the room. "Go on to lunch and try not to fill up on unnecessary stuff again, Megan."

"Sorry," the girl with confections in her hair said. "I'm still trying to get used to the idea I don't need to drink water."

Mae Ling shook her head. "It will just dilute your system. Instead, fill it full of sugar, dear."

"Thanks," the girl called as she charged past Sophia. The rest of the students did the same, some giving her curious glances as they passed. She tried not to stare back, but they were all so normal looking, despite the colorful uniforms. it was hard to believe they were magical fairy godmothers.

That seemed to be the way of Sophia's strange world. Nothing fit into any preconceived notion. What she saw was unbelievable, and what she didn't see was even stranger.

CHAPTER TWENTY-FOUR

When all of the students had filed out of the room, Sophia smiled as Mae Ling approached, appearing much the same way she was at the nail salon. She was wearing a smock like usual, although this one was bright pink like that of the doors and uniforms. The old Asian woman's face was smooth, and her black hair hung to her chin.

"You look very tired, dear," Mae Ling said, studying her. "What have you had to eat today?"

Sophia had to think. "Not much. Some vegetables. Chicken. Maybe some rice."

Mae Ling shook her head. "There's part of the problem." She went to a workstation filled with pastries and glanced around for something specific. "Oh, this will do nicely."

Gingerly, she picked up a tray of assorted colored macaroons and carried it over to a high bar. "Please come have a seat and snack, and we'll talk."

Sophia did as she was told, even if there were a hundred questions running through her head, making her move at less than her normal speed.

"Go on then," Mae Ling encouraged and waved her forward.

"Oh, thanks." Sophia eyed the dessert.

"I do mean for you to eat these," Mae Ling teased. "But I was referring to your budding questions. Ask away."

Sophia giggled and picked up a pink macaroon. "Well, this school—"

"Happily Ever After," Mae Ling interrupted.

"Yes, Happily Ever After, it's quite interesting," Sophia said.

"I figured you'd get a kick out of it." Mae Ling spoke proudly as she took a seat at the bar opposite of Sophia.

"You teach baking?" Sophia inquired. She bit into the cookie and immediately wondered why there weren't trumpets to signal the moment she tasted the best thing in the world.

Mae Ling smiled at Sophia's wide-eyed expression. "They are good, aren't they?"

"Yes!" Sophia exclaimed and stuffed the rest of the macaroon in her mouth.

"I teach Baking 101, a skill all godmothers need to be exemplary at in order to fuel their magic and stay on top of their game," Mae Ling explained.

"Wow, I never would have guessed," Sophia said and took another macaroon, a mint green one this time.

"Well, you know well enough a magician's magic is fueled by calories," Mae Ling offered. "When you do a complex spell, it depletes your reserves. That's why we are encouraged to load up on calorie-dense foods. It works well for godmothers."

"What else do you teach?" Sophia asked and licked her fingertips, not wanting a single crumb to get away.

"I teach Beauty 101, 102, and 202," Mae Ling answered. "We cover nails, skin, and hair in all of those classes."

"Oh, the curriculum here is…different," Sophia commented and hoped she didn't sound offensive. She expected colleges to teach science, literature, and math, but she reasoned she'd never been to a school for fairies.

"We specialize in the creative arts as the main mode of business for our fairy godmothers," Mae Ling explained. "All of our alumni must have a profession upon leaving. I chose to go into beauty, but each godmother gets to make their own choice."

"So, being a fairy godmother isn't your profession?" Sophia asked.

"Well, that would hardly pay the bills," Mae Ling remarked with a laugh. "That's more of a calling and has its own rewards. But I have to eat, and expensive chocolate requires money, so we teach our students how to be successful following creative endeavors. They become writers, artists, stylists, designers, bakers. You get the point."

"And math is a punishment?" Sophia inquired. "Don't you need math to run a business?"

"No, not if you have magic." The old woman winked at her. "But yes, for our students, who are not allowed to use magic to complete their first few years of work, math is a punishment because it drains their creative vault, making their other studies much more difficult to complete."

This was all too much for Sophia. She felt like she lived in an upside-down world, where you ate ice cream for breakfast and math was toxic, and creative pursuits were valued over practical ones. She liked that world very much. Alas, she hadn't been elected to be a fairy godmother, but rather a dragonrider—which thankfully didn't call for much math either.

"How is one chosen to be a fairy godmother?" Sophia asked.

"Willow makes those assignments," Mae Ling explained. "It's complex and probably along the lines of how dragonriders are chosen. I can't really indulge much on that one, my dear."

"Wow, that's really fascinating." Sophia took another macaroon.

"Yes, and Willow assigns fairy godmothers to their children, which was how I got you," Mae Ling proclaimed. "And you've come to me today for help on a very special matter. So go on, dear."

Sophia stopped chewing. "Wait, you don't know why I'm here?"

"Of course I do, but it's in the asking that the magic of our relationship begins," Mae Ling told her. "That's taught in Happily Ever After 101."

Sophia grinned. "I haven't taken that course."

"Nor will you ever," Mae Ling hummed.

Sophia finished her bite and wanted something to wash it down. Not a second later, a cold glass of milk materialized beside her plate of cookies. "Thank you," she said, taking a sip and washing down all the delicious bits. She wiped her mouth and glanced up at the woman before her. "The reason I'm here is about Quiet."

Mae Ling nodded immediately and held up her hand, pausing her. "To save Quiet, you must go to where silence is the most plentiful."

Sophia shook her head. "No, I didn't actually mean quiet as in the adjective. I meant as in the—"

"I understand," Mae Ling cut in. "But your answer still has a riddle to it because otherwise, I get bored. I like to spice things up a bit."

"Oh," Sophia said, deflating. She loathed riddles.

Mae Ling waved her off. "Fine, no riddles. Go to Antarctica. It's freaking cold there, and it's quiet, and if you follow my directions, you'll find an ice fortress. Fight your way through the elements and earn the loyalty of the queen within, and she will give you a magical herb. It will heal your friend Quiet."

Sophia's eyes darted one way and then the other. "Um, thanks, but can you just tell me how to fix the Castle so it can heal Quiet? That seems a bit easier than fighting a bunch of bad guys, which don't get me wrong, is totally a normal Thursday for me and not something I'm shying away from. It's just I'm not sure how long Quiet has and—"

Mae Ling touched her hand and interrupted Sophia. "Quiet has until you return with the antidote."

"What?" Sophia questioned. "Antidote?"

"Why yes," she answered. "The groundskeeper for the Gullington was poisoned."

"By who?" Sophia asked.

"By those who want things," Mae Ling responded simply.

Sophia shook her head. "I don't understand."

"Well, you might not for some time," Mae Ling pronounced. She looked off like she saw something in the distance. "Yes, you definitely won't understand for quite some time, you must still follow my directions to the letter. The Gullington will experience threats, but that shouldn't be your concern. Stay and defend it, and things will get worse. Instead, you need to go and get the antidote to fix the problems. Never band-aid them."

"How is fixing Quiet the solution?" Sophia asked. "Shouldn't I fix the Gullington?"

Mae Ling released a long breath, suddenly looking tired. "I'm afraid there is no way to save the Gullington. You can only hope to help the groundskeeper. Then you can go from there. Maybe you relocate. Maybe you don't. That's yet to be seen."

"I'm really confused." Sophia scratched her head and then looked up. "But as you said, I'm going to remain confused for some time."

Mae Ling smiled. "You're starting to get it, my dear. That will make everything easier." She held out her hand and a folded piece of paper appeared. "This has the coordinates for the ice fortress. The Queen will know why you're there, but she won't give you what you desire until you prove you're worthy."

Sophia took the piece of paper. Her stomach was uneasy, probably from all the sugar. "This queen, what does she rule over?"

"Wish I could tell you, but you've overstayed your welcome," Mae Ling told her and snapped her fingers, sending Sophia through a portal back to the Gullington.

CHAPTER TWENTY-FIVE

Given no warning about her departure from Happily Ever After, Sophia felt like she was waking from a dream when she fell through the portal into the area outside the Barrier. The grass crunched under her feet from the hard landing and her knees buckled, sending her face-first to the ground.

The abrupt landing was disorienting. When she'd regained her composure, she was still confused as she entered the Gullington, crossing through where the Barrier used to be.

Dragons streaked through the dark sky, fire streaming from their mouths and screams echoed from all over. Sophia spied figures running across the Expanse, their actions reeking of violence.

Sophia's heart pounded in her chest. She took off toward the Pond on the other side of the Castle, where it seemed most of the action was. She didn't understand what was happening in the Gullington. Yes, the Barrier was down, but she'd only left an hour prior. How could so much have changed already?

Mae Ling's words came back to her in a rush. Someone had poisoned Quiet, but that didn't make any sense. They lived in a literal bubble inside the Gullington. Aside from when she got them Uber Eats, they didn't eat out, and the last time had been some time ago.

Sophia started to wonder as she ran if Quiet had somehow gotten outside the Barrier, but she remembered what Ainsley had told her about the groundskeeper.

While the shapeshifter couldn't leave the Gullington for long periods of time because of what happened during the battle with Thad Reinhart —which she didn't remember—Quiet couldn't leave at all. He could venture to the perimeter but not too close according to the house-keeper, so it seemed unlikely he left and was poisoned. Sophia could automatically cross off the list that anyone inside the Gullington had poisoned the gnome. She might not know everything about her fellow dragonriders, but she knew they were good through and through.

Then it came back to Sophia. The dinner Ainsley had served to the group earlier that week had been too spicy for everyone but Quiet. What had the housekeeper told them?

"I got the spices from a new vendor at the market. I thought I'd experiment around with them," Ainsley had said.

Was it possible a potential enemy of the Dragon Elite had given the spices to Ainsley? It was the only thing that made sense. But that wasn't all Mae Ling had said of importance, Sophia thought as she doubled over in exhaustion still far from the fight. She didn't know the last time she slept, and crossing the Expanse took time. It was miles wide, and her dragon was far. She would have to call him to her, but first, she had to remember what her fairy godmother had told her.

She thought back until she could practically taste the macaroons and smell the sweet aroma in the classroom at Happily Ever After College. Slowly the words she had just heard came back to her, and she stiffened. More than anything, she wanted to join the fight and help her friends to defend her home from whoever was attacking it. She wanted to protect her eggs. But she was told to trust Mae Ling for a reason, and her fairy godmother had been very clear:

"Yes," Mae Ling had declared with confidence, "you definitely won't understand for quite some time, but that still means you must follow my directions to the letter. The Gullington will experience threats, but that shouldn't be your concern. Stay and defend it, and things will get worse. Instead, you need to go and get the antidote to fix the problems. Never band-aid them."

Sophia gulped and fisted her hands. She pressed her lips together, unable to believe what she was about to do. With her mind, she reached out to her dragon.

Lunis, are you there? she asked.

Soph, you're back, he said, relief flooding his voice.

What's going on? she asked, wanting to rush but staying still.

In her head, she felt Lunis' confusion. He didn't know why she wasn't helping, but it wouldn't be long before she filled in all the gaps for him. He'd been busy fighting and hadn't heard her conversation with Mae Ling and preoccupied with the fight he hadn't caught up on her thoughts.

There are thieves, he explained. *They crossed through the Barrier a bit ago and are hunting for something. We're guessing the eggs.*

Oh no, Sophia screamed in her mind.

Don't worry, he soothed. *Hiker and Bell won't move from the entrance to the Nest. They are strong. Stronger than ever before. It will take a great force to get through.*

And the others? she questioned.

They are putting up a good fight, but I will be honest, he said and paused, reluctance in his voice. *Whoever this is that came after us, they were ready. They have numbers and strength. I think they've been waiting for an opportunity.*

I think they made their opportunity, Sophia confessed. *I don't know how, but I'm certain they poisoned Quiet. I don't know how they brought down the Barrier or hurt the Gullington.*

I'm not sure either, Lunis agreed. *There's something mysterious at play here none of us can see. The dragons are clear on that one.*

Okay, well, I need you to come to me, Sophia requested.

So I can bring you to the fight? he inquired.

Sophia shook her head, already regretting what she had to say, but knowing she had to. *No, you and I must go.*

What do you mean? he asked, his voice screaming with disbelief.

I know it sounds crazy, but Mae Ling said we can't stay and fight, she explained. *We have to go and get an antidote for Quiet.*

Lunis focused on her thoughts for a moment, and it all became clear.

Things were so much easier when someone could spy your thoughts, Sophia reflected.

I'll be right there, Lunis stated. *I just need to relay the information to the others so they don't worry.*

Sophia agreed with a nod. She would have to wait on the other side of the Expanse, forced to watch the streaks of fire and outlines of fighting figures instead of helping. It all seemed so wrong and made her feel like a coward. She reminded herself she was leaving to seek another solution. The wind cut through her and reminded her there were other things her heart was wrestling with she had to deal with.

"You're leaving," Wilder said at Sophia's back. A rush of wind chilled her to the bone again. This time when she felt that familiar rush, she knew it was caused by the sweeping motion of a dragon's wings.

She turned to find Wilder sliding off his dragon, Simi, and hurrying over to her.

"I didn't have time to get all the details, but Lunis told Simi you're going to get an antidote for Quiet," he explained as he rushed over only to stop inches away. His hands reached out but halted short of touching her.

Sophia nodded. "I've learned there's more treachery hurting the Dragon Elite than just these invaders. I need to follow this lead and get the antidote, or Quiet will suffer." She held out the piece of paper Mae Ling had given her.

Wilder's eyes fell to it, hesitation heavy in his eyes. "I'll go with you. We can do it faster together than if you go alone."

Sophia felt the warmth of her dragon when he landed at her back, the way it always felt when Lunis was near.

She backed up and shook her head. "No, you should stay here and guard the Gullington. Nothing can happen to those dragon eggs."

Wilder made up the distance, this time reaching for Sophia and grabbing her hand.

She sucked in a breath and looked up at his wide eyes.

"But what about you?" he asked. "Where are you going? How long will you be?"

She shook her head. "I really don't know. I only know I have to do this, or I'd stay. You have to know, if I had that option, I wouldn't leave you or the Gullington."

He didn't look convinced. She worried he thought she was a coward by running away, but he surprised her by taking a step backward and releasing her hand.

"Soph, I don't know what's going on, but if you have to go, you have my full support." He glanced at Lunis. "You two stay safe and return to us as quickly as you can."

Sophia didn't say another word because anything she could say seemed cheap. Instead, she turned and ran for her dragon, jumped onto his outstretched wing, and slid into the saddle. Giving Wilder one last look before grabbing the reins and taking off into the air, she flew straight out of the Barrier and away from the only place she'd felt at home. She prayed it would stay safe until she returned, hopefully with a way to save its groundskeeper.

CHAPTER TWENTY-SIX

A nt-freaking-arctica. That's where Mae Ling had sent Sophia and Lunis, and it was cold. Really freaking cold. The sun was up, which was something at least, providing them with light to see their surroundings, which were unsurprisingly not that diverse. It consisted of snow, ice, glaciers, freezing cold water, and a clear blue sky.

I guess it makes sense this is where an ice queen would live, Lunis reasoned, landing in the snow and looking out at the miles of white.

It was so bright it made Sophia's eyes water, and the air was so biting it hurt her bones.

"I still don't understand what this queen rules over," Sophia mused, looking around and wondering where the fortress was. She should have asked Mae Ling more questions, not that there had been time for such things.

Snow, Lunis offered. *Maybe cold. Or silence.*

That piqued Sophia's interest. "Actually, that's what Mae Ling said when I asked her how to help Quiet. She said I should go to a place that's plentiful with silence."

Lunis glanced around at a iceberg peacefully floating in the distance on the blue water and the miles of ice that stretched out around them. *I think this is the quietest place I've ever heard of.*

"Ha-ha," Sophia said and shook her head at her dragon. "That was by far the worst joke you've ever made."

Really? The worst? he questioned. *I'm sure I can beat that. I'll borrow one of your sister's jokes.*

"Hey," Sophia argued. "Liv's jokes are funny."

They are punny, which counts for negative credit, he stated.

"You know, at some point, you two are going to have to try and get along."

Why? he asked his tone serious.

"For my sake," she begged.

Why else.

She pursed her lips at him and slid off his back.

What? Lunis questioned. *I need a little extra motivation is all. I mean, I want to do things for you like save your life and help you fight battles and save people. But do I really have to get along with your sister? She calls me Stanley and Clifford and treats me like I'm a big dog.*

"You sort of are," Sophia said with a laugh.

It's true, but don't ever tell her that, Lunis teased, joining in her laughter.

It felt wrong they were having a good banter when she knew her friends were battling mysterious bad guys at the Gullington. She reasoned they were bolstering their spirits before the battle began.

Mae Ling had said they'd have to fight villains and win the queen's allegiance to get the antidote. There were still so many questions. Who was this queen, and why was she in the middle of a place uninhabitable to most? What did she rule over? What was this antidote?

Maybe it's a piece of a glacier? Lunis reasoned.

"Well, I'm not sure that will work since I've got to get it back to the Gullington."

Yeah, and then there's the question of who poisoned Quiet, Lunis added seriously.

"I still feel like I should be fixing the Castle." Sophia had the strongest urge to abandon the mission and go on her way, but that wasn't what her instinct told her. Wanting to run away came from the fear in the pit of her stomach. Between instinct and fear, she knew which one to trust. Always her instinct.

No, Mama Jamba had told her to go to Mae Ling rather than fight, and her fairy godmother had told her to find this ice queen rather than fight. That was what she was going to do.

"Okay, which way do you think is the castle?" Sophia asked and looked around. "The directions said something about finding a staircase of sorts."

Well, if I was a queen with an ice fortress, I'd definitely enchant it so others couldn't find me, Lunis rationalized.

"Good point," Sophia agreed. "So how do we pull down the glamour and knock at the drawbridge or whatever the ice lady has blocking the courtyard?"

I'm not sure, but look at that. Lunis indicated something in front of them with his head.

Having to squint from the brightness combined with the angle of the sun directly in front of them, Sophia glanced in the direction he had pointed out. She couldn't figure out what he was referring to until she noticed a black shape. It was gliding across the ice and then plopped into the crystal blue waters with a splash.

Sophia yanked Inexorabilis from its sheath to be prepared for whatever danger they were about to face. A brief look at Lunis told her whatever it was wasn't a threat. He acted like a puppy dog about to charge, his tongue hanging slightly out of his mouth, and his blue eyes wide with excitement.

She turned her attention back and saw another black shape gliding on the same trajectory and plopping into the water. Her gaze followed until she found a mound of snow and saw a penguin standing at the top. It held out its wings proudly, like an Olympic diver about to perform. Then like the other two before it, the bird ran and jumped off the peak, diving onto the ice and sliding across it before landing in the water with a splash.

"Oh wow, that's the cutest thing I've ever seen," Sophia said, wanting to clap at the awesome performance the little birds were giving them, whether they meant to or not. Sophia and Lunis were happy to witness such a fun sight. It took Sophia's mind off the fact she was freezing her tail off, even with the fur-lined cloak she'd summoned.

Another penguin took the spot on the top of the peak. It unfolded its wings and did a sort of salute. Sophia and Lunis watched as it lifted its chest proudly, about to take off. It looked at them with brightness in its eyes as if it was looking forward to impressing them, and then the ground under their feet began to shake.

The penguin's expression changed. Fear filled its eyes, and it dove back in the opposite direction, disappearing. Sophia looked to Lunis, wondering if he'd seen something she hadn't. His expression was confused.

A moment later, their questions were answered when a giant abominable snowman rose up from behind the peak. Its long arms reached toward the sky as a ferocious roar ripped from its mouth and shook the ice under their feet.

CHAPTER TWENTY-SEVEN

The monster was easily the height of a two-story house and as wide too, especially with its arms extended. Long white fur covered the creature's body. A gray beard hung from its chin, and its eyes were bright blue surrounded by red veins like it had an extra-long night of partying. The abominable snowman would have been beautiful if it hadn't had a murderous expression on its face.

Again the monster opened its mouth and roared, its sharp canines reminding Sophia of a deranged werewolf.

"Um, I think we are going to have to fight that thing," Sophia said beside Lunis, her hands tight around her sword.

Well, I wasn't about to make it a friendship bracelet, her dragon replied.

"What should be our strategy?" she asked, bracing herself as the beast threw its fist onto the peak where the penguins had been jumping off and smashing it into snowy bits. The ground rumbled, making Sophia's teeth clatter together.

Apparently, behind the peak was where many of the penguins were hiding. A dozen of the little birds scattered, waddling for other snowbanks or the water's edge. The angry monster grabbed up one of the penguins. It screamed in terror, its little feet kicked on the other side of the beast's hand, and its head bulged from the pressure of being held so tightly.

"You have to rescue the penguins," Sophia urged to Lunis.

What? he questioned. *They are the perfect distraction. I say we use it to get away and follow Mae Ling's directions. Didn't you say something about a staircase?*

"No!" Sophia argued. "You have to save that one!" She pointed at the bird who was doing an excellent job of wiggling free but was still partially pinned in the snowman's hand. The monster opened its mouth, and it's pink tongue fell out as it brought the penguin up like it was going to pop it into its mouth like a bonbon.

If the monster wasn't eating the penguin, I would be doing that exact same thing, Lunis reasoned. *Those birds make delicious snacks.*

"Lunis!" Sophia complained.

If I get that one free, there are a dozen more the snowman will go after. He swept his neck to the side, indicating the birds still scattering in different directions.

The penguins would take refuge behind a snowbank and then scurry in another direction. They obviously weren't the smartest animals, but that didn't matter. Sophia wasn't going to allow them to be murdered on her watch, and she wouldn't allow Lunis to eat them. They were too cute and had put on a fun show for them.

"You're going to rescue them all, Lunis."

Is that a demand, he asked, lowering his head and looking her straight in the eyes. Lunis had once told her that in their lifetime together, she would make three demands of him. So far, she'd already made two. They were like her genie wishes, and she was down to her last one. Although she wanted to save the penguins who were still frantically scurrying around under the abominable snowman's feet, she wasn't going to use her last demand on them. Sophia realized the penguins were trying to attack the monster to free their friend, who was moments away from being eaten.

"Lunis, I'm not making a demand of you. I'm making a request. Those guys are caring enough they are trying to save their friend.

They could easily be fleeing, but they aren't. Creatures like that are worth saving."

He sighed. *Fine. I'll save the dumb bird. But you should take the opportunity to kill that monster.*

Sophia tightened her hand around Inexorabilis, the heat of the battle about to ensue rising in her eyes.

CHAPTER TWENTY-EIGHT

L unis took off and flew in a spiral around the snowman, confusing it. Even as big as Lunis was, the monster was still sizable in comparison. Sophia wished the moon was full so he could do his 747 trick and triple his size.

The monster, who Sophia nicknamed Gilbert, swiped through the air with its fist to try to knock Lunis out. He slid out of the trajectory of the monster's hand just in time.

Gilbert, really, Lunis questioned. *Why Gilbert?*

Sophia ran for the monster as she tried to figure out the best way to attack. She also had to be careful not to run over penguins who were still scurrying around the beast's feet.

He looks like a Gilbert to me, she said, pushing a penguin out of the way just as the snowman lifted its giant leg and slammed its foot down, sending snow exploding all over. Sophia felt like she was in a bizarre snow globe as her vision was momentarily obstructed.

She brought her sword across, expecting to meet the dense flesh and bone of the monster's leg. Instead, the sword went through smoothly as if she was slicing through snow.

More snow exploded as the bottom part of the beast's leg disappeared. The creature fell to the side, suddenly off-balance.

I don't think he looks like a Gilbert, Lunis disagreed as the monster dropped the penguin from its grasp, to catch itself before it fell on its face.

The dragon dove and caught the penguin before it landed on the ice, a fall that would have been fatal. The bird landed on Lunis' wing and bounced before finding its feet with a surprised expression.

Around Sophia, the penguins jumped and yelped in relief.

Gilbert fell on all fours, several penguins pinned underneath. Sophia brought her sword up with both hands and stabbed the monster in the other leg. The bottom part of the leg exploded into snow that rocketed up into the air and sprinkled down to cover Sophia's head and shoulders.

Shaking her head free of the snow, she had a new confidence, as she thought it would be rather easy to kill the beast if each attack made the body turn into snow.

Watch out, Lunis yelled in Sophia's head.

Gilbert's large hand swung through the air, rocketing in Sophia's direction faster than she could react. It knocked straight into her like a wall of ice and swept her feet out from under her. Sending her through the air, she landed hard on her back a dozen yards away.

She couldn't breathe for a moment, her lungs freezing as she swallowed a handful of snow. She pushed up to her feet quickly and rolled to the side as another hand zoomed in her direction. Even without feet, the monster had plenty of mobility as it crawled toward her. Its long arms reached out and nearly connected with Sophia.

She sprinted for freedom and saw Lunis busy rescuing penguins who were close to being crushed under Gilbert. He now had a few of the birds on his wings as he swooped through the air, avoiding the monster's claws.

Use your fire, Sophia yelled mentally as she discovered she'd dropped her sword. Finding it in the snow seemed unlikely to happen in a timely manner.

The bright fire that rocketed from Lunis' mouth was a stark contrast to the snow. As soon as it connected with Gilbert, the monster writhed in pain and began to instantly turn into a huge puddle, with hair, teeth, and claws.

Sophia couldn't believe how easy that was. She let out a breath of relief and watched her dragon swoop around, penguins jumping onto his back so he could use his wings more.

I think we call him Dead Gilbert, Lunis said in her mind.

Well, that was a piece of cake, Sophia replied.

A flurry of snow spiraled like a cyclone around the puddle that had been Gilbert and obscured the area.

Sophia narrowed her eyes and tried to figure out what was happening as something rose into the air.

Not the piece of cake I usually like, and I don't think this was as easy as you thought.

Sophia saw what he meant as the flurry of snow cleared and revealed another, slightly smaller, Gilbert. The monster had reassembled itself, and the fight was far from over.

CHAPTER TWENTY-NINE

Gilbert Number Two was just as beautiful as his prior form, and thankfully he was now the size of a one-story house. The penguins scurrying around were still in danger as he swung his arms, trying to catch the birds. It stomped and shook the ground, sending many of the penguins on their sides and stomachs.

Okay, no to using fire, Sophia said to Lunis as he flew in her direction, penguins still on his back.

I agree, he replied. *He can just regenerate. I think we have to rely on you cutting the beast down.*

The only problem with that is I don't have my sword, Sophia divulged, her chest vibrating with anxiety.

That is a problem, Lunis agreed as he cut around Gilbert, trying to steal its attention from Sophia. The monster stomped as he swung about, nearly crushing several penguins.

Why don't they get out of here, Sophia asked Lunis.

I think they are guarding something, he suggested.

I hope it's an ice fortress with a queen who wants to give me the antidote, she said.

I don't speak penguin, but I think it's a bunch of eggs, he revealed.

How do you know then? she queried as she searched through the snow for her sword, her hands freezing.

Well, from up here, I can see a bunch of eggs on that peak. He indicated an ice tower just behind the snowbank.

Oh hell, Sophia muttered. *Well, keep Gilbert away from snacking on the eggs.*

Right now, I'm trying to keep Gilbert Two from snacking on you.

Thanks. Sophia tried a summoning spell to draw Inexorabilis to her. As she suspected, it didn't work because Wilder had put a spell on the sword to keep it from being summoned. It was supposed to help her from losing it to an enemy in battle, but in hindsight, maybe it hadn't been the best idea.

The ice shook under Sophia as a loud sound echoed overhead. On her hands and knees frantically searching through the snow-covered ground, she watched a crack split the ice and ran straight under her.

Well, that doesn't seem like a good thing, she commented to her dragon and rolled on her back to put distance between her and the spreading chasm as the crack deepened.

Oops, Lunis said in her head.

She turned to find Gilbert Two throwing his fist repeatedly on the ice and making the ground vibrate violently.

What happened, she asked, still searching for her sword.

I didn't do anything, Lunis protested. *Olaf has a nasty temper. When he doesn't get his way, he throws a tantrum.*

Well, his tantrum is making it nearly impossible to find my sword, Sophia complained, her vision vibrating as she rode the ice. It felt like she was on an amusement park ride.

I'd ask him to stop, but I don't speak abominable snowman nor penguin, Lunis joked.

Speaking of the penguins. Sophia nearly ran into one of the birds as she crawled across the ice, trying to put distance from the crack that probably led to frigid waters.

"You're in my way," she grumbled to the birds waddling in front of her, blocking the path to where she thought her sword might be.

I think they are trying to help, Lunis offered.

Why is that? Sophia inquired as she pushed up to a standing position.

Because that one on the other side of you seems to have found something, he said coyly.

Sophia swung around to find one of the penguins straining to pick up something, its face contorted.

"Inexorabilis!" Sophia rejoiced, diving for the hilt she could see peeking out of the snow.

She grabbed the sword and pulled it up as the birds scattered. "Okay, penguins. It's time to kick some snowman butt."

The little birds congregated around her, excitement making their eyes dazzle. They seemed ready for battle.

I don't know if snowmen have butts, Lunis joked with a laugh.

Sophia shook her head as the penguins rallied around her. "You guys distract Gilbert Two. Lunis, you save any who get too close to danger." She brandished her sword, feeling reenergized. "I'm going to make an ice sculpture."

CHAPTER THIRTY

L ike little warrior penguins charging into battle, the birds swung around and raced in the direction of Gilbert Two. They even howled a piercing battle cry.

I didn't know penguins made that noise, Sophia marveled as she marched after the birds.

I'm learning more about them than I ever wanted to know, Lunis said, gliding through the air and distracting Gilbert Two as the penguins took positions around the monster on the ice. Lunis still had quite a few of the birds on his back, which was cute and also strange. It made him look like a cartoon version of himself.

Whatever you do, don't tell the other dragons about this penguin business, he ordered.

Your secret is safe with me. Sophia snuck up behind Gilbert Two as he swung a fist through the air and actually caught the side of Lunis' wing. Lunis was knocked to the side, and the penguins spilled off the side of his back.

No, Sophia screamed as Lunis tilted dangerously to the side and nearly careened into the ice peak with the eggs. He recovered just in time and raced toward the ground to swoop up the falling penguins before they hit the ice.

One disaster was averted, but as Gilbert Two swung around, Sophia recognized a new one had presented itself.

The monster leaned forward, his blue and red eyes narrowed at her. He roared, and the air rushing out of his mouth blew her hair back and instantly made her ears ache from the volume.

The penguins went to work, quickly darting around Gilbert Two's legs, trying to distract him and giving Sophia a moment to consider her plan of attack.

All I have to do is slice the beast in half, and it will be done, she said mostly to herself.

Easy as pie. Lunis dropped his penguins at the top of a snowbank where they would be safe, then dove back in her direction, his eyes focused on Gilbert Two.

The only problem with the plan of slicing the monster in two was he was as large as a house. Sophia couldn't figure out how to get an attack in with its long arms spread on either side of its body.

Lunis, sensing her issue, flew at Gilbert Two's back and scratched across it with his claws. Sophia expected that part of the creature to turn to snow and make her next move much easier. Nothing happened except Gilbert Two got even more pissed, swinging around to face the dragon who was swooping higher up in the air.

It must be Inexorabilis that cuts through the monster, Lunis reasoned as he pulled up his wing as Gilbert Two jumped, trying to knock the dragon out of the sky.

Well, keep his attention then, Sophia instructed, powering up her sword using magic. It was her only hope of making the next attack the last one. She had one chance to get this right.

Behind her, the crack in the ice was widening. The cold was making her ache all over, and Lunis hadn't said it, but she knew he'd hurt his wing when he'd been hit. The penguins were showing signs of exhaustion, and one would get trampled or eaten soon.

Sophia had to make this attack count, or they were all toast!

CHAPTER THIRTY-ONE

I nexorabilis shook in Sophia's hand as she powered up the sword. The combat spell grew in intensity, making her chest burn. She had to plan the attack right to save them all, and she had to do it quickly. She also had to wait until the spell was complete, or the assault might not be strong enough to do the trick.

Sophia feared a misplaced attack would just anger Gilbert Two more. Then he'd throw another tantrum, and they might all fall through the ice into the freezing cold water.

Her hands sweltered from the heat building in the blade. As her palms began to sweat, Sophia worked to keep her grip on the hilt.

The penguins were doing their job of distracting Gilbert Two, and any time he was close to swinging around, Lunis swiped at him with his claws to keep the monster's back to Sophia.

She only needed a few more seconds.

I don't think we can hold him much longer, Lunis said nervously.

He was growing weak from the cold, she knew.

Yes, you can, Sophia encouraged.

Sometimes the best things in battle weren't weapons or strength, but words of encouragement. It could get a warrior through when defeat felt inevitable.

I don't think I can, Lunis stated.

She noticed that his wing was locking up. The cold was getting to him, and the injury wasn't helping. Each time Gilbert Two rocketed his hand through the air, it was getting closer to knocking the blue dragon out of the sky.

Sophia let out a deep breath and reminded herself and Lunis of words by JM Storm that had gotten them through a lot of tough situations.

Magic happens when you don't give up, even though you want to, she told her dragon. *The universe always falls in love with a stubborn heart.*

Maybe it was the encouraging words or the desire to never be defeated or that the penguins bought Lunis a moment by distracting the monster on the ground. Whatever the reason, he pulled into a fantastic spiral move that made Gilbert Two raise both his hands into the air and cover his face as if he were afraid he was about to get punched in the teeth.

The long gangly arms had been a part of the problem. Sophia hadn't known how she would attack with them in the way and blocking Gilbert Two's torso.

Now they were covering the monster's head, and a second later, the combat spell was complete. Sophia didn't waste another moment. She swung the sword, a bright beam of light streaking behind it as it progressed.

She brought Inexorabilis through the air so fast it made a high-pitched wailing sound that got the beast's attention. It went to turn for her, but she was too fast. With a force unlike she'd ever had to use before she pulled the blade cleanly through the abominable snowman's body, slicing it in two.

The result was instantaneous. Snow blasted from the two severed halves and launched Sophia up and back from the explosion.

This time she held tight to her sword as she flew and landed inches from the chasm Gilbert Two had created. In a rush, she rolled over, her face hanging over the side before she pushed away to safety.

The brief glimpse into the crack had been of blackness. The mysterious feeling of foreboding she'd felt in that split second she'd glared into the darkness was unexplainable and didn't make any sense.

She pushed away from the crack as she stood, whirling snow blowing across her face as whatever had made up Gilbert Two drifted off with the wind. Sophia wasn't sure what the monster was, but she was grateful to see it was gone this time.

The penguins all waddled in her direction, relief and joy evident on their cute faces. Lunis landed at the top of the snowbank near the other penguins. Their eggs were safe on the ice peak at their backs.

Sophia looked up at him and smiled. *Good job*, she complimented her dragon.

Same to you, Sophia.

She let out a breath of relief. The cold made her cheeks feel numb.

Hey, Sophia, Lunis said, an edge of mischief in his tone.

Yes, she answered in her mind.

Do you want to build a snowman, Lunis sang.

She narrowed her eyes at him. *No, Ana. Hell no.*

CHAPTER THIRTY-TWO

Sophia pulled in a full breath and immediately regretted it. Her insides felt like they'd just been covered in ice from the frigid air.

They'd defeated a monster, perhaps one of the many tasks Mae Ling told her she'd have to pass to win the queen's allegiance.

Sophia just wanted another minute to relax before they found the next deadly beast they had to defeat. She had put a warming spell on her and Lunis, but it was wearing off fast.

Reaching into her pocket, she pulled out a bag of macaroons Mae Ling had sent her with and took a bite of one. She felt her magic reserves slowly fill up, and with them, her body heat rose.

Thanks, Lunis said, flying down from the snowbank. He'd left the penguins up there, and now they were sliding down the slope one at a time, jumping onto their stomachs to the ice and skidding all the way across the slick surface until they launched into the water.

"Cute little guys," Sophia observed, entertained by their playful display.

Tasty guys, I'm sure. Lunis landed beside her, the rush of wind from his wings chilling Sophia.

She looked him over. "Your wing?"

It will be fine, he replied dismissively. *The chi of the dragon is already working to repair it. Another hour and it will be completely back to normal.*

"And you're warm enough?" she inquired.

I have fire in my belly, he answered with a wink.

He was acting strong. Sophia knew he had magical scales to protect his outsides and fire inside that kept him warm, but he had still been so cold it had slowed him down earlier. She took another bite of the cookie and hoped whatever they faced next wasn't a blizzard. After this adventure, it would be fine with her if she never saw snow again .

On the heels of this thought, the last penguin slid down the snowbank. Something rumbled on the other side of the embankment.

Lunis and Sophia exchanged nervous expressions.

Their next enemy was approaching, and by the way the ground was quaking under their feet, it was large.

The roar that filled the air told them a bit more about the creature about to materialize. A few images sped through Sophia's mind of what they would possibly have to face.

Maybe a deranged ice moose, Lunis offered.

Maybe, she answered.

Or an evil penguin, he continued.

I'd let you eat that, she replied.

Good, because I'm hungry and those little guys are starting to look mighty tasty, Lunis said, indicating the penguins still waddling around them like lost little sheep.

They aren't sheep, Lunis, Sophia told her dragon. *You get to eat sheep and other dumb animals but not sweet little penguins who helped us survive.*

He sighed as a puff of snow shot up from the embankment. Something big was approaching from the other side.

Fine, let's hope this is an ice sheep because I could use a snack, the blue dragon grumbled.

Sophia offered him a macaroon, her focus still on the top of the embankment framed by the blue sky.

Lunis shook his head. *No thanks. I don't eat things that didn't once have a face.*

Sophia couldn't help the laugh that spilled from her mouth. *You're like the opposite of a vegan.*

I'm the anti-vegan, he stated humorlessly. *I don't remind others of what I don't eat all the time. I don't have an agenda I'm constantly forcing down people's throats. And at parties, I'm not constantly questioning what ingredients were used in the dip.*

Where are these parties you go to and have dip? Sophia questioned as another puff of snow shot up from the top of the hill.

I go to parties, he argued smugly. *I just don't tell you about them because it would be hashtag awkward since you aren't invited.*

Sophia gave her dragon an amused expression. *That's fine,* she replied. *I wouldn't want to share dip with you anyway. I'm certain you double-dip.*

I don't, actually, he said as the embankment began to rumble more violently. *I eat it all in one bite, not leaving any for the other guests because I'm a dragon, and we don't share.*

Sophia shook her head at him. *You're hashtag weird.*

If Lunis had a reply, it was interrupted as the largest bear Sophia had ever seen rose from the top of the embankment. It stared down at them, a strange expression in its dark eyes.

CHAPTER THIRTY-THREE

Sophia felt like she was looking down into the chasm again. The blackness of the bear's eyes was so reminiscent of what she'd seen when she looked over the edge earlier. Unlike before, she didn't feel that mysterious feeling of foreboding, although she thought maybe she should since this creature was huge. Its rippling muscles were evident even with its thick fur and strange silver armor that covered its body.

This wasn't a normal bear.

I'm not sure it even is a bear, Lunis said to Sophia.

It's definitely not wild, wearing that armor, Sophia mused as she ran her eyes over the intricate covering wrapped around the bear's shoulders, head, and back.

The armor was made of a strange metal that didn't appear to be either silver or gold. The bright sun reflected off it and cast a bluish-green shimmer that reminded Sophia of music as if the light created a magical musical note that could be seen in the air as vibrations.

Have the dragons ever seen anything like this? Sophia asked, watching as the bear regarded them from up high, studying them. She flexed her fingers by her side, Inexorabilis in her other hand, ready to battle again.

There's nothing in the collective consciousness of the dragon I can find, Lunis answered, *which doesn't mean much since it's as vast as the Great Library. I might just not be using the right search terms.*

Sophia shook her head, always surprised by the things her dragon said like he was a hipster millennial. She figured in a way he was, being the first of the new generation of dragons.

The eyes of the bear were similar to Lunis'. They appeared full of ancient wisdom. The black she'd seen in the chasm had felt as though it was more than just darkness—like something of great power resided there. She witnessed the same thing in the bear's eyes.

Sophia didn't know if they should make the first move since the creature was merely looking at them.

Should we introduce ourselves? she asked. One of the many benefits of the chi of the dragon was the Dragon Elite could speak the language of any race or culture. As world adjudicators, it was crucial they could communicate with everyone.

I'm not sure, Lunis responded. *I get the impression he wants to both eat you and help.*

Why does he have to be a "he?" Sophia questioned.

Lunis sighed. *Because there's no pink on his armor. Is that the answer you're looking for, Sophia?*

She shook her head. *You and your stereotypes. Just because someone is female doesn't mean they like girly stuff or the color pink.*

A loud roar spilled from the bear's mouth, his canines dangerously long. The sound filled the air and made the snow on the hill where he stood vibrate.

I think we should discuss gender stereotypes later, Lunis suggested, tensing beside Sophia.

She nodded. *Good call. I think introductions are about to happen, but I'm not sure if they will include a cordial hello or just a bunch of claws and teeth.*

Let's prepare for both, Lunis said as the bear charged in their direction.

The light was nearly blinding as it spilled across the bear's armor as it progressed down the embankment, snow flying up from his giant paws. The armor made a clanking sound that reminded Sophia of ancient battles she'd never been a part of.

She tightened her grip on Inexorabilis, but something told her not to raise her weapon.

Listen to that, Lunis encouraged at her side.

You don't think we should fight, she questioned, watching as the bear made incredible progress. It would be on them any second.

In battle, there is a time to fight and there is a time to stand down, he offered. *As an adjudicator, you have to know the difference. What does your instinct say?*

It was hard for her to hone in on her instinct with a massive beast racing toward her with teeth bared and black eyes staring them down, but under the rising fear was a small voice telling her, "Stand down."

To Sophia's own surprise, she sheathed her weapon on her hip, not something she would normally do if a giant dragon wasn't by her side, but she felt her actions would send a message to this bear she sensed was beyond sophisticated.

The magical bear seemed like it was going to barrel straight into them, not having slowed at all. The momentum of sprinting down the hillside had made the bear move so fast it had been a blur for a moment.

Hold your position, Lunis encouraged. *Don't even blink.*

Sophia didn't think that would be a problem since she wasn't even breathing. She stayed stone-still as the bear ran, a beautiful grace in each of its movements. It sped past the penguins and straight in their direction.

Sophia had forgotten about the birds who were waddling in various areas, her attention on the beast speeding in their direction.

The bear showed zero signs of slowing down, and the sound of its armor clanging together grew louder. The fierce expression in its eyes deepened. Seconds from careening into the dragon and rider, the large white bear skidded to a halt and sent a barrage of snow onto Sophia and Lunis, drenching them completely.

CHAPTER THIRTY-FOUR

Not moving, Sophia and Lunis stared at the huge bear that stood in front of them. She didn't even shake off the snow covering her shoulders and head. Lunis also stayed immobile, facing off with the bear.

The bear wasn't as large as Lunis, but it was close. Sophia knew without a doubt if they fought with the warrior-like bear, it would be a deadly battle. This was a creature built to fight. It was wearing a special armor that no doubt would protect it from Lunis' fire and Sophia's magic.

As the beast watched them from across the short distance, Sophia couldn't tell whether it was leaning toward a cordial introduction or a battle to the death.

She assumed when it had just charged in their direction, it was a test of sorts. Did it want to see if they'd fight? Did it think they'd flee? Lunis could fly, a definite advantage over the bear.

Sophia didn't want Lunis to fly until his wing was repaired, and what he'd said about knowing when to fight really struck a chord in her. It was part of her strategy as a new dragonrider. The other men were always quick to pull their swords and use force, asking questions after. Sophia preferred to rely on strategy and talk things out, not assume every conflict had to result in violence.

Sophia studied the peculiar creature and took in the beautiful design of its armor. Now that it was closer, she saw there was a large medallion hanging around its neck. A beautiful blue stone sat in the center of the talisman, and symbols she didn't recognize running around the edge. She wished the chi of the dragon gave her the ability to read any language too. Since it was more of an automatic thing, the skill didn't lend itself to writing, only talking.

Sophia desperately wanted a clue about whether this strange bear was a potential friend or foe. She reasoned it was intelligent based on what it had done so far, and it was wearing advanced armor and a medal around its neck.

If Bermuda Laurens was there right now, she might know about this bear. A strange time to remind herself she should have read *Magical Creatures* cover to cover already.

"You put away your sword," the bear said, his voice deep and carrying a peculiar weight to it. A talking bear shouldn't have surprised Sophia. She had spoken to talking cats, crocodiles, and of course dragons, but there was something different about this beast.

Sophia didn't respond right away. Instead, she took the opportunity to brush snow off her shoulders and shake out her hair. Lunis stayed still, however, the snow framing his shoulders and contrasting with his blue scales.

"I do not wish to fight you," Sophia finally answered, pinning her hands behind her back and holding her chin high.

"But you are human," the bear argued.

"Which means?" she questioned. Penguins were waddling around in the background, many of them making their way over.

"Humans choose to defend even when there is nothing at stake," the bear declared. "It is a point of pride for them."

"And bears are known for being aggressive and irrationally violent," Sophia claimed. "We should probably throw out our preconceived notions about one another and start fresh."

He tilted his head to the side to view her from a different angle like it might help him see any lies. "I am Ickhart, protector of the queen mother, the ice fortress, and the great defender of Kalisbell."

Sophia went on one knee and bowed her head to the massive bear. "An honor to meet you, Ickhart." When she stood, the creature relaxed slightly, although still ready to fight if necessary. "I am Sophia Beaufont, a rider for the Dragon Elite."

"And?" Ickhart asked as if this information wasn't enough.

"And what?" she queried and held out a hand to indicate Lunis. "Do you mean my dragon. His name is Lunis."

Ickhart shook his head. "No, what else are you, Sophia Beaufont? Who do you protect? What do you defend?"

"People," she said simply.

"Which people?" he questioned as the penguins gathered around them, curiosity evident on their little faces as they looked between the two parties.

"Those who need someone to fight for justice," she explained. "Who is the queen mother?"

His gaze darted to Lunis before returning to Sophia. "I'm not at liberty to say."

"Can you tell me where the ice fortress is?"

"Not yet, I can't," he answered.

Sophia assumed this queen was the one she needed to see to get the antidote for Quiet. She also thought the ice fortress was where she needed to go. This bear Ickhart was the perfect creature to lead the way, but the reluctance in his gaze and tone was palpable. She hadn't won his favor yet and hoped it wouldn't be done with a fight.

"And what is Kalisbell?" she asked. "Is that where the ice fortress is located?"

He shook his head. "It is the great kingdom to the north of here. It is my homeland and constantly warring with the Vaskit to the east."

"The Vaskit?" Sophia questioned. "Are they like you...a..."

She didn't know how to put it. What if calling him a bear was offensive? In her world, that's what he was, although she could see he was so much more. Ickhart wasn't like the bears she knew about. He was extremely intelligent. She'd observed that when he had been up on the embankment. His armor was constructed using the finest craftmanship. His voice was full of confidence that only came from a deep knowing. Yes, this creature was beyond intelligent.

"I'm not a bear," he finally said when she'd trailed away. Ickhart must have sensed what she had been thinking, reaffirming her assumption about his intelligence. "Just as a Neanderthal isn't a magician. You might look alike, but there are key differences between the two. My kind are known as the Bruistic."

"And the Vaskit?" Sophia questioned. "What are they like?"

The bear laughed, a sound resembling an abrupt cough. He threw his head to the side and pointed to the area behind them. "You already met one and did me a favor by destroying it, which is why I've spared you and given you this opportunity to use your words instead of forcing you to use your sword."

"The abominable snowman," Sophia guessed. The creature was no longer there, only mounds of snow. "That's the Vaskit?"

He nodded. "Yes, a savage race who have warred with the Bruistic for centuries. The one you killed was an especially horrible beast who had attacked Kalisbell many times." He bowed his head. "We aren't friends. Barely acquaintances, however, you have my gratitude for killing that monster and for saving the penguins."

The birds were gathered around them now, seemingly able to understand the conversation transpiring as they glanced between Sophia and Ickhart.

She was about to explain they were simply trying to survive when Lunis encouraged her silently not to.

Make a demand, her dragon suggested. *This is not a creature who will be endeared to your humility. Saying "you're welcome" and smiling about the matter will get us nowhere.*

That had been exactly what Sophia was about to do, but she knew Lunis was right. She had to use this to their advantage.

"We're looking for this ice fortress and its queen," Sophia said. "Since we have done you a great favor, will you return it?"

Ickhart considered her, his expression not giving anything away. "What do you want with the queen?"

"I have a request for her," Sophia explained.

"As do many," Ickhart responded, his eyes narrowed. "How did you know where to find her?"

"My fairy godmother," she answered, unsure if it was the right answer. She still didn't know who or what this woman was the queen of. The only things out there were ice and snow and cold. This wasn't a land with great exports of fine foods or exotic spices.

Her answer got Ickhart's attention. "You have a fairy godmother?"

"Yes," Sophia replied. "And she told me in order to save Quiet, I must find this queen for the antidote." It seemed logical to just come out with it all. Ickhart was the barrier between her and the queen. She needed him to want to help her.

He didn't respond. Instead, her ears were met by a thunderous sound as the ground shook under their feet, a sensation Sophia was growing used to since coming to the Antarctic.

In unison, Sophia and Lunis turned to find the crack formed by the angry Vaskit was growing in width. The crevice wasn't getting closer to them, making Sophia fear she'd fall into the black chasm. Instead, it was pushing them out, like they were on a sliding floor. A door opened beside them.

"What is happening?" Sophia asked, turning her attention back to Ickhart.

The Bruistic smiled, an expression of surprise on his face. "It appears the queen has heard your request and granted you entry into the ice fortress."

CHAPTER THIRTY-FIVE

When the rumbling had stopped, Ickhart led them to a spot next to the chasm's edge, where a staircase descended into the blackness.

"The ice fortress is down there?" Sophia asked.

Ickhart shook his massive head. "The ice fortress is all around you. You are already in it without realizing that. But to have it revealed, then yes, you must descend."

The staircase disappearing into the strange darkness didn't seem especially safe. For one, it was made of ice, which Sophia thought was not the best material for such things given it was so slippery. Also, there were no guard rails on the side, a safety precaution someone had overlooked. The bottom of the staircase ended abruptly, total blackness meeting the edge.

Swallowing down her hesitation, Sophia said, "Is this safe?"

The question was mostly a joke, so Ickhart's answer surprised her. "It absolutely isn't. One misstep will send those seeking the queen mother to eternal doom. Only those with sure feet and a pure heart can make the journey." He addressed Lunis. "You will be automatically transported inside the fortress if your rider makes it to the bottom of the staircase."

"And if I don't?" Sophia asked.

"Then he will perish," Ickhart replied plainly. "As will you."

"There's no soft landing on the other side of the blackness, I'm guessing," she joked and peered over the side, trying to get any further clues.

"The blackness never ends, Sophia Beaufont," Ickhart explained.

"Cool, cool." She tried to sound casual and gave Lunis a tentative expression. "So I just venture down this staircase and when I get—"

"*If* you get to the bottom," Ickhart corrected.

"Right." Sophia drew out the word. "*If* I get to the bottom, then you'll join me. Sound good?"

She half hoped Lunis told her no, and they should find another way that didn't have such drastic repercussions, but her dragon nodded his head. *Yeah, go for it but take it slow and follow your instinct.*

She forced a smile, trying to act as though this was no big deal.

I'm going down a slick ice staircase into the middle of who knows where and if I fall, I never stop. No biggie.

Sophia reminded herself this was all so she could meet a mysterious queen protected by a race of creatures she didn't even know existed and who had battled snowmen for ages. The world was a strange and vast place, and there were so many things she had to learn about it.

Sophia desperately hoped she would get the chance to do so as she took her first step down the giant staircase.

CHAPTER THIRTY-SIX

To say the first step was slippery would be a severe understatement. For a moment, it felt like she was trying to walk down a waterfall.

Her hand went for the wall next to the one side of the staircase but pulled it back with a yelp. It was as if the cold ice wall had bit her fingertips.

"There are no accommodations to assist you down," Ickhart said at her back.

Sophia knew turning her attention to the Bruistic would put her off balance, and probably end her at the top of the staircase, so she simply nodded. She had a feeling the task before her might be impossible.

She had planned to hug the edge of the staircase next to the wall, but even being close to it gave her a pinching feeling. No, it was better if she stayed in the center of the staircase.

The blackness on the other side of the stairs was oddly mesmerizing, calling her attention, but she guessed it was a trick and she'd get sucked into a hypnotic display.

She needed to keep her attention straight ahead on the next step. The only problem was she could hardly make out the next bluish step, let alone the three after. There was only enough light to see a short distance.

Descending into a dark chasm that had given her a sense of foreboding, when she couldn't see where she was headed, might have been the most intimidating thing she'd ever done. But there was no turning back now. Quiet needed her. The Gullington was relying on her. She silently sent positive thoughts to the men defending their home, hoping they were holding their own. She wished she was there fighting alongside Wilder and Mahkah, but her journey had taken her away.

"To a mysterious and deadly staircase I have to descend on my own," she said, talking to herself. She thought the sound of her own voice would make her feel better, but it echoed off the ice walls and made her feel like she was surrounded by a howling ghost as her words repeated over and over.

Consumed with fearful thoughts, Sophia had forgotten how cold she was. Her teeth chattered as she took another step, her footing never so intentional. The next couple of stairs illuminated. The whole thing reminded her of the Martin Luther King quote:

"You don't have to see the whole staircase, just take the first step."

It seemed like a good description of how her life had been going lately. She could hardly see much past the proverbial headlights, but she could see enough to keep moving forward, as she was now.

Faith was a tricky thing for Sophia. One had to wholeheartedly believe in something to have it, and yet, the first plunge into it was often done blindly.

"Just take the next step," Sophia whispered to herself.

The whispered voice echoing back at her was a chorus of encouragement, surprisingly helping her to progress.

"Just take the next step."

"Just take the next step."

"Just take the next step."

Sophia found herself smiling. Had she figured this out? It was a game of confidence, and she had self-soothed by using her words and her voice.

"You got this," she said a bit louder, feeling like she was walking on water as she progressed down the next few stairs.

"You got this."

"You got this."

"You got this."

Her words bounced back at her and bolstered her spirit, making her move with greater ease.

She was now so deep down the chasm the light from the top was hardly enough to illuminate the next stair.

"Talk about blind faith," Sophia remarked, reaching out into the darkness in front of her. It was instinct for someone to extend their hands when suddenly blinded, but Sophia could see the area right in front of her and above. Reaching a few inches in front of her made her hands disappear. It was the oddest thing like the cold was trying to eat her up.

"Faith."

"Faith."

"Faith."

The words she's spoken moments earlier echoed all around her, much louder than when she'd voiced them. The one word was a strange choice on the part of the darkness, which she now held responsible for the weird experience.

Sophia dared to look up again, even though directing her gaze anywhere but in front of her felt like a risk.

Between the two ice walls, the blue sky could be seen overhead. Lunis' head was over the edge, and he was staring at her with trepidation, although she assumed he couldn't really see her. She would have disappeared into the darkness. Sophia mused on how strange it was that she could see clearly up to where she'd started, but what was high couldn't see her.

There was something to be said about standing in the darkness and being able to see the light, but the reverse not always being true.

Sophia was intrigued by the philosophical idea she had observed on this voyage when her words echoed back at her again, seemingly out of nowhere.

"Faith."

"Faith."

"Faith."

"Yeah, faith," she remarked, talking to herself again. "I get it."

Sophia expected her own words to echo back at her. Instead, they were someone else's.

"Do you?"

"Do you?"

"Do you?"

She halted and looked around as if she might find the person the voice belonged to, although all she saw was blackness, the ice stairs, and the walls above her. The walls began to shake and Sophia watched as the chasm above her began to close, the walls pushing in together and about to trap her between them.

CHAPTER THIRTY-SEVEN

"Oh, hell!" Sophia yelled as the walls closed in on her. Now her fear wasn't about falling into the blackness or breaking her neck as she tumbled down the never-ending staircase. She'd be crushed between two ice walls.

Strangely her voice didn't echo back at her. She didn't give herself a chance to wonder why.

Stopping, she glanced up the staircase. It was too far to make it back to the top at the rate the walls were closing. She'd be crushed before she made it.

Looking down the staircase, Sophia realized continuing on was the only way, but if she went at her current speed, well, it was hard to say if she'd make it since she didn't know how much farther she had to go.

On her next step, Sophia felt she'd lost her vision. Not only could she not see what was in front of her, but the light above and behind her had been completely blotted out.

What hadn't changed were the walls closing in on her. She could hear the crushing sound as the crack sealed up, forcing her to the side as stairs were eaten up by the wall.

She couldn't see the next step to take. Sophia couldn't see anything at all. The fear bounding out of her chest urged her to freeze and not move and instead let the crushing anxiety paralyze her.

There was another voice in her head, the one she wanted to believe was connected to instinct or maybe faith.

It reasoned she had made it this far on the staircase. Why did Sophia need to see the next step to progress? Couldn't she simply continue down the staircase the same way she'd been doing? It was the same motion, and she had mastered it on the way down.

So that's what Sophia did, moving faster than before.

She put one foot down and then met it with the other one, moving at an even pace. The thundering noise of the walls closing in was the only thing louder than her ragged breath.

For a long time, Sophia moved down the staircase and wondered why the walls hadn't closed in and crushed her. She didn't allow herself to think about it much because all her attention was centered on taking the next step. And the next. And the next.

Once or twice she got distracted and felt her boot slip on the slick ice, but caught herself before falling.

Sophia was prepared to continue to climb down the stairs for as long as it took. The darkness she'd feared didn't bother her as much anymore, and the thundering sound of the walls closing didn't fill her with the same fear. Either she'd die or she wouldn't, but what she wouldn't do was give up.

On the heels of that thought, a bright light shone everywhere, and she stepped onto a firm surface.

CHAPTER THIRTY-EIGHT

Somehow Sophia had gone from the darkest place in the world to the brightest.

She shielded her eyes from the light, not knowing where the source was as her eyes adjusted. Her other senses had kicked into overdrive with her vision cut off.

Sophia heard the gentle trickling of water. She felt a crispness in the air, reminiscent of the first day of winter, and the air smelled fresh and clean. It filled her with a unique idea of purity.

When her eyes adjusted, Sophia lowered her arm to a sight unlike anything she'd ever witnessed. She knew at once she hadn't fallen into the blackness. She'd been victorious and had safely descended the staircase to the ice fortress.

An intimidating force rose up from the ice, exuding power and danger.

It was so beautiful simply looking at it hurt.

CHAPTER THIRTY-NINE

Sophia stood in front of a magnificent castle made entirely of ice. Several towers rose up on the sides of the structure, each filled with tiny windows that were organically shaped. Some were round, while others were square, and no two were the same size.

The towers rose into the air and ended in sharp tips against the wispy clouds in the blue sky. The front of the castle was a series of archways, each dripping with icicles.

More stunning than the castle itself was the area around it. A wall of waterfalls was at the back of the castle and higher than the four-story building. Cold mist wafted off the waterfalls and hit Sophia gently in the face. The sound of the continuously crashing water wasn't as loud as Sophia thought it would be, then she noticed the water had an almost slushy consistently, like a waterfall made out of crystals.

The water met a large lake that nearly encircled the castle. The only thing to connect the lake to the mountains where the waterfall was a set of rocks beside her, where she found Lunis and Ickhart waiting for her.

"I made it!" Sophia rejoiced, running for her dragon and meeting him on the rocks.

He gave her a proud smile as she closed the space between them. "I knew you would. There was no other option."

"There are many other options," Ickhart said coldly. "Most never make it, especially once the light goes out and walls start pushing in."

"Yeah, that was a rude trick," Sophia joked.

"It is necessary," he declared. "Only those with a brave heart and pure intentions will progress when they can't see and know they are seconds from being crushed. The irony is the ones who embrace these dangers are the only ones who make it. Most go back the way they came, or the fear makes them slip and fall into the darkness."

"See, I just wanted to get one of those Ring doorbell camera things for the front of the Cave, and you said that was over the top," Lunis teased with a playful expression.

It was obvious to Sophia he was relieved she had made it. He might have said he knew she would succeed, but there were no guarantees in life or their adventures, and they both knew it.

"First off, only dragons are allowed in the Cave, so a Ring is unnecessary," Sophia disagreed, shaking her head. "And secondly, you're absolutely ridiculous, Lunis."

"Well, my point was my security measures seem a whole lot less extreme now compared to this queen," Lunis remarked.

"Speaking of the queen," Sophia began and turned her attention to Ickhart. "How do I request an audience with her?"

He blinked at her impassively. "That's not necessary. She's been here all along, and stands at your back presently."

CHAPTER FORTY

S tartled, Sophia whipped around only to find no one was standing
behind her, only the ice castle on the edge of the waterfall, and
the lake spread around it.

She was about to question the Bruistic when sparkling snowflakes
whirled up from the ground in front of Sophia as if caught by a
sudden breeze, twirling around and around and building in intensity.

Like the darkness she'd passed on the staircase, it was mesmerizing and also hinted of an ominous force.

The sparkling snowflakes froze in the air until one by one, they
drew a figure somehow more beautiful than the castle in the distance.

The queen stood taller than Sophia. Long whitish blonde hair
cascaded over her shoulders and reached past her hips. On her head, a
row of crystal beads hung like a crown. She wore a pale blue sleeveless
gown, as though she was attending a summer ball and not standing in
the middle of a frozen fortress. More surprisingly than her startling
blue eyes, porcelain skin, or breathtaking beauty were the angel wings
covered in white feathers that stretched up and back behind her.

Sophia didn't know who this queen was, but she and Lunis both
knew she deserved their respect.

Sophia dropped into a low bow and saw her dragon do the same.

"You may rise, Sophia Beaufont and Lunis," the woman said, her voice the sound of icicles in the wind.

When Sophia stood straight, her eyes watered from the chill in the air. In the excitement, she'd forgotten how cold she was as her warming spell slowly dissipated.

"I can offer you no warmth, dragonrider," the woman informed her. "We will have to make this quick, for I fear your magic will not keep you warm for long."

Sophia felt into her pocket and found the bag of macaroons empty. She nodded. "Yes, this world is very difficult for us."

The queen gave her a knowing smile as her wings fluttered. "You say that, but I've seen few handle it with the grace you have shown."

Sophia returned the smile. "Well, thank you. So you know why I'm here. Can you help me?"

"I'm very curious," the woman said. "You are here because of Quiet, the gnome? Is that right?"

"You know Quiet?" Sophia asked, shocked. She never considered this possibility. She hadn't thought about the possibility that anyone outside of the Gullington would know Quiet. Wilder said he was very old, but she knew he'd spent most of his life inside the Gullington serving the Dragon Elite.

"Of course, I do," she said with fondness in her blue eyes.

Sophia's gaze ran over the queen's wings. "Are you...an angel?"

"I am not," the woman said with great dignity. "But I was created by the angels, very much like you. And when I was made, they marked me with their wings."

"Oh." Sophia's mind spun with questions. She didn't even know where to begin. As her insides started to vibrate with cold, she knew she didn't have much time. Her first assumption had been the queen was an angel, and that could explain how she had known the groundskeeper for the Gullington. But now, Sophia was even more confused.

"The angels created the five main races," the woman continued, sensing Sophia's confusion. "You're aware of that much, correct?"

"Yes, as well as the dragonriders, right?" Sophia asked.

The woman nodded. "Technically no, though you have the blood of Archangel Michael in you through your dragon."

Sophia recalled the legend she'd read in *The Incomplete History of Dragonriders*:

"When the Archangel Michael fell during a battle, his blood seeped into the Earth. It spread, finding the thousand dragon eggs scattered across the planet. The blood of the archangel infiltrated the dragon's eggs, all one thousand of them. It is believed a dragon and their rider share the same blood once magnetized. Therefore, the blood of the Archangel Michael flows in the rider's veins and protects them in ways no other magical creature can be."

"Oh, that's right," Sophia said. She tried to piece things together, but the cold was making it hard to think properly.

The woman pressed a hand to her chest as her wings beat the air, gently fanning cold air in Sophia's direction. "I am known as Queen Mother of the fae because I was created by the angels to be the first of our kind." She humbly bowed her head. "I am Queen Anastasia Crystal, and I was one of the first magical creatures to grace Mother Nature's Earth. I was the very first fae, and I will always be the last. None can live if my heart does not beat. I am the source of my race—the glorious fae."

CHAPTER FORTY-ONE

D   *id you know this?* Sophia thought, instantly curious if Lunis was aware of this information.

Mind-freaking-blown, he said in her head.

Apparently, the dragons weren't privy to this part of the history, she thought.

Remember, the consciousness of the dragon is as vast as the Great Library. It's impossible for me to know all of it.

"You are the mother of the fae," Sophia echoed, a chill running over her from the realization rather from the actual cold.

Queen Anastasia Crystal nodded serenely.

Possibilities began running through Sophia's head. If this woman was the mother of the fae and had been created by the angels, that meant there was a goddess or god of sorts for the other magical races.

It was enchanting and awesome, and Sophia now understood why it was so difficult to get to this queen. Knowing what she reigned over was simply astonishing. She was the lifeblood of the fae.

Sophia looked around at the ice fortress and slushy waterfall, everything starting to make sense. Of course, the Queen Mother of the fae would live in a place such as this since the fae governed the element of ice.

"It can be overwhelming when one learns how things began and their significance," Queen Anastasia Crystal said, an understanding smile on her face. "Remember that we have little time before the cold will do permanent damage to you and your dragon."

"Right," Sophia replied. She tried to catch her breath, suddenly feeling winded. "So how do you know Quiet, and will you please help him? Mae Ling said you could give me the antidote to fix him, although I can't tell you what's wrong with him."

That seemed like an oversight on Sophia's part. She never even thought she should know the diagnosis for the gnome before seeking the solution, but the knowing smile on the queen's face put Sophia's fears to rest.

"I've known Quiet for a very, very long time," Queen Anastasia Crystal began. "Long ago, my people were in grave danger. Many of them were in a warring dispute, and he dared everything to get them to safety. He risked his very life to ensure the ship taking them to safety arrived, and because of him, my people survived what should have killed them. Because of Quiet, my race wasn't wiped out, nearly killing me. I learned a valuable lesson about the beauty of sacrifice from him, and so yes, of course, I will help him."

The Queen Mother of the fae held out her hand, and a glass bottle with a clear blue liquid appeared in her palm. "Give this to one of my oldest friends, the groundskeeper for the Dragon Elite, and he will recover from what ails him."

"Thank you!" Sophia reached for the glass bottle, her hands shaking, but the queen pulled it just out of her reach.

"One important thing," Queen Anastasia Crystal said, a warning in her voice. "This antidote will only work under one condition."

Sophia swallowed and tensed. She waited for the Queen Mother of the fae to continue.

"You must have Quiet reveal his real name to you for this potion to save his life," the queen ordered her voice grave.

Sophia blinked and wrinkled her forehead. "His real name…"

She knew Quiet was the gnome's nickname. He had told her that when she was new to the Gullington. It had been on the first night when Hiker had kicked her out of the Castle. She had thought she was done with the Dragon Elite and was heartbroken, and she'd have to return to the House of Fourteen as a loser who had failed.

In a torrential rainstorm, the groundskeeper had come to her and said that if she didn't leave the Dragon Elite for good, he'd reveal his real name to her one day. Then he had shown her Adam Rivalry's crash site and given Sophia the clues she needed to start the hunt for Thad Reinhart.

Her chest swelled with hope. Quiet had already committed to telling her his real name. All she had to do now was ask for it and then offer him the potion, and then everything would be better, well mostly. The Gullington was still in trouble, but recovering the groundskeeper was evidently part of securing the Dragon Elite's headquarters.

Sophia smiled and felt hopeful as she reached out and took the antidote from Queen Anastasia Crystal.

"Thank you," she said. "I'll get his name."

The queen didn't return the hopeful expression. "If it were going to be easy, I wouldn't assign it to you as a requirement."

"Oh, but he—"

"Quiet will not want you to know who he truly is," Queen Anastasia Crystal interrupted. "He might have once enticed you with the idea, but he never planned to tell you the truth because it will change everything."

"What?" Sophia hiccupped in the cold. "How?"

"Great power is held in one's name," Queen Anastasia explained. "You know that well, S. Beaufont. If you discover who Quiet truly is, it could potentially rob him of his power."

"But wouldn't he prefer that over death?" Sophia questioned.

The glorious queen smiled, and her angel wings flapped slightly. "I am not the right person to ask, for I live alone in my fortress so as to protect the power of my race."

Sophia nodded, realizing this was much more complicated than life and death.

"I can't say what will happen to Quiet if his name is known, but I know he'd rather no one knew his truth," Queen Anastasia Crystal went on. "And yet, if you don't find out his name, he will most assuredly perish and with him, a legacy as old as the Dragon Elite."

CHAPTER FORTY-TWO

The ominous words of Queen Anastasia Crystal rang in Sophia's head all the way back to the Gullington. She had mistakenly thought learning Quiet's real name would be easy. He had said if she stayed at the Gullington, he'd tell her what it was. Evidently, there were conditions on that arrangement.

Maybe he thought she'd forget or he figured he'd tell her in a few centuries. Whatever the reason, she had to learn his name. His very life depended on it.

So no pressure, Lunis said to her as they made their way toward the Barrier.

The chill breeze sweeping across the hills of Scotland was like a summer wind compared to the cold they'd experienced at the Queen Mother's fortress. Sophia's head was still reeling from everything she'd learned.

They had met the first fae, the Queen Mother, who protected an entire race. The whole idea was so new Sophia didn't even know where to start.

"Like why is Rudolf Sweetwater the king of the fae if there is a Queen Mother?" Sophia asked her dragon, the two having mused over the revelations all the way back to the Gullington.

Well, I think he's more of a political figurehead, Lunis answered. *Also, it seems Queen Anastasia Crystal can't really be out where others have access to her. For one, if anything happens to her, it would kill the entire race.*

"Talk about pressure." Sophia sighed.

She seems like she's more about the longevity of the race, Lunis continued. *Where Rudolf has leadership over them, ensuring they don't seduce too many mortals or take advantage of their beauty by stealing all the modeling contracts in Hollywood.*

"Good point," Sophia agreed. She chewed on the inside of her cheek as she considered everything.

And now you're wondering who the King Father or Queen Mother of the magicians is, Lunis said as more of a statement rather than a question. He knew what was in her brain.

Sophia nodded. "It's just so weird. I never thought about how it all started, and when I've asked Mama Jamba about it before she said it was confusing. She created the Earth and most of us, but she works for the angels."

I believe her words were, 'the managerial structure is a bit strange,' Lunis told her with a laugh.

"Yeah, it makes me think I need to spend a lot more time reading *The Complete History of Dragonriders* when I have a chance."

I think the key phrase is 'when you have time' which we both know is limited and with all the drama maybe even more so than usual, Lunis stated.

Sophia nodded. "Yeah, so the angels created the five major races by, I'm assuming, creating these individuals, Queen Anastasia Crystal being one of them."

And they created the dragonriders in a way, Lunis added.

"So, is there someone out there in charge of magicians, elves, gnomes, and giants?" Sophia asked.

It goes to reason, Lunis answered.

"But they would be as vulnerable and powerful as Queen Anastasia Crystal," Sophia argued.

I think with great power comes great vulnerability, Lunis replied.

"I just never really thought about how incredible it was when this world was set up. It's beautiful and complex and overwhelming all at the same time."

Before you got this inside experience, having chats with goddesses like Mama Jamba and others, you just thought it was like 'poof,' and everything was created. Now there's a structure and people connected to it all.

"Real people too," Sophia said. "Like Mama Jamba and Papa Creola are actual people with personalities and quirky traits."

And yet, they are the most powerful people slash gods in the world, Lunis told her. I think that's the real irony to this, but it makes perfect sense. The most powerful entities are real and strange and flawed. So much of what has been and what will be rests on their shoulders. It just proves you can't ever discount a person. The power of this world resides in the hands of those who would be underestimated by most passing them on the street. That's one of many reasons everyone deserves our respect.

"Yeah," Sophia said, breathless from the realization.

Well, except that one guy who cut me off today, Lunis joked.

"That was a plane," Sophia teased with a laugh. "I don't know the etiquette of plane crossings and whatnot, but I think he had the right-of-way."

I breathe fire, Lunis argued. I always have the right-of-way.

Sophia chuckled again as they crossed through where the Barrier of the Gullington used to be. Her lightheartedness immediately fell away at the devastating sight in the distance.

CHAPTER FORTY-THREE

Night still covered the Gullington in darkness, but a fire streaking through the sky made it appear as though it could be sunset.

The Castle was dark and appeared abandoned. Sophia had never seen it like that. There were always torch lights flickering in the windows, and the flames of the lanterns marking the entrance.

Even if it wasn't lit, the Castle always felt alive, more of a feeling than anything else. However, Sophia felt she was looking at a dying figure, and her heart ached with a brutal force she'd never known before. Having lost her siblings, she knew what death felt like, and the Castle was close, her instincts screamed.

The real danger was by the Pond where the dragon Cave was and the cave that held the eggs. Sophia saw figures sprint across the Expanse in the distance, fighting.

She couldn't make out which were Dragon Elite and which ones were the trespassers by their appearance, but she could by their actions. She knew the dark figure next to the Cave was Wilder because of the way he fought with seamless grace. He was fighting multiple thieves at once and keeping them back with a speed she'd never witnessed him use before.

Behind him, closer to the Pond, Sophia made out a figure who had to be Mahkah, throwing radiant green spells at a set of villains closing in on him. Three dragons flew, torching the grounds, trying to push the trespassers past the Barrier. But what was the point if they could just get back in? They needed the Gullington to recover and the Barrier back up, but Sophia had no idea how to do that.

She turned the potion bottle Queen Anastasia Crystal had given her over in her hands. Like before, she wanted to run to the fight, to help the men and to find Hiker who wasn't in view as far as she could tell, which worried her.

"They've been fighting all night," Sophia said, her voice vibrating.

And somehow they are losing, Lunis observed.

"How?" Sophia questioned. "We're the Dragon Elite." It was a point of pride for her. They were the adjudicators for the world, not some magicians that anyone could easily defeat.

We'll have to find out, Lunis confirmed. *They are holding their own, though. I'm going to help.* He unfolded his wings, about to take off.

Sophia wanted to climb onto his back and join him, but her eyes went to the Castle in the distance. She had to help Quiet. That's what Mama Jamba had said, and Mae Ling had echoed.

She shook her head at Lunis. "Give them hell. Torch every single one of those thieves. Don't let them near our eggs."

Lunis nodded, nobility in his ancient gaze. *I will make you proud. Do what you must.*

She wanted to say more, but there was no time, and they both knew it.

The battle wouldn't last much longer, which meant one side was about to lose and the other win.

Sophia needed the winners to be the Dragon Elite, but the side victory fell on didn't depend on her. She clenched the antidote for Quiet in her hand and took off at a sprint for the Castle.

CHAPTER FORTY-FOUR

The Castle door was locked!

It was never locked. She tried again, frustrated that after everything, a stupid door would get in the way of her doing what needed to be done.

"Oh no, you don't," she said, stepping back to try an unlocking spell on the door.

To her shock, it didn't work.

"Are you serious?" She groaned and tried another spell.

She half hoped it meant the Castle was doing better. Maybe it was recovering if it was able to lock the front door. It had a way of keeping the residents of the Gullington in places it desired. If the Castle locked a door, it meant no one was getting in until it so desired.

Sophia had to get into the Castle. Queen Anastasia Crystal had said Quiet would most assuredly perish and with him, a legacy as old as the Dragon Elite if Sophia didn't save him.

She banged on the front door. The stained glass window with an angel on it vibrated from her force. "Let me in, Castle! I need to get in there!"

Sophia expected to hear the lock click and the Castle would acquiesce to her demand, but nothing happened.

Pulling back her boot, Sophia kicked the door hard, more out of frustration than to break it down. "I defeated a freaking abominable snowman! Open up!"

She stepped back and pointed her hand at the Castle. She didn't expect the spell to work. If the Castle didn't want to open up, she was subject to its whims, but she had to try, and with each passing moment, the screams from the Expanse were tearing at her resolve not to join the fight. If the Castle door didn't open, she'd have no choice but to abandon helping Quiet and help the dragons and their riders, her friends.

About to fire a spell at the Castle that would take all of her magical reserves, it never left her as the door swung backward, and the tired and frantic face of Ainsley swam into view on the threshold.

"S. Beaufont!" the housekeeper yelled, waving her forward. "Get in here!"

Sophia sprinted through the front door, ready to charge past the shapeshifter and up to Quiet's room, although she realized she didn't know where it was.

"Ains," she said breathless and halted next to the woman whose red hair was falling into her pale face. "Where is—"

"Did Hiker order you to stay in here too?" Ainsley asked, interrupting her.

Sophia tilted her head to the side. She hadn't expected that question. It made sense, Ainsley wasn't trained to fight, and Hiker had already cost her so much the last time she entered a fight. Sophia was sure Hiker didn't want anything to happen to the elf again on his watch.

She shook her head. "No, I have the cure for Quiet. I need to get to his room. Show me the way?"

Ainsley's face brightened, but only slightly. It was hard to make out her expression in the darkness of the Castle. "Yes, I can do that. Follow me, S. Beaufont. And mind your steps. The Castle is quickly falling apart. One misstep will send you through the floor into the dungeon below."

Sophia trailed the housekeeper, igniting an orb of light in her hand to help her navigate up the stairs. The chandelier had fallen and was in pieces all over the place. Broken candles lined the path up to the second story.

Sophia's heart ached to see the large painting of Adam Rivalry and Kay-Rye lying on its side on the floor. The canvas had been slashed from falling on a nearby structure. Everywhere Sophia looked was devastation, the Castle even worse than when she'd left for Happily Ever After College. It wouldn't be long before the roof caved in, and the whole building was a pile of rubble.

"What is happening here?" Sophia asked in a hush, following Ainsley as she veered off a hallway Sophia hadn't noticed.

She stopped and doubled back to study a tapestry of a unicorn and knight on the wall next to an arched hallway. She was certain it had never been there before.

Ainsley turned, a knowing look in her eyes. "This area used to be hidden. It's the servant's wing. Only we were allowed down this area, but of course, with the Castle in its current state, nothing is closed off. All security measures are down." She sniffed, tears brimming in her eyes. "Which is why those repugnant thieves are pillaging our grounds."

Sophia nodded in understanding. All the secrets of the Castle were revealed, and all she wanted was the curtain of mystery back up. She didn't want to know the secrets of the Castle or see what had been previously hidden, even if she'd been curious before.

This area of the Castle was decorated much more simply than other areas. There were no elaborate display cases with crown jewels and heirlooms. Instead, the hallways were bare and lacked windows.

Sophia was sad. Ainsley and Quiet deserved to have their spaces decorated with shiny armor and beautiful paintings too. She'd address that later when, if the Castle recovered and they survived the plague of doom that had befallen the Dragon Elite.

"I don't know what's happened," Ainsley cried. She shook her head wildly, her disheveled red hair hitting her in the face. "This has never happened before. Not in all my years serving the Dragon Elite."

"And Quiet?" Sophia asked, not knowing what to be more concerned about.

Ainsley's face contorted with more pain. "I've never seen him like this either. He's sick in the worst way. He only wakes up for short spells, and those are growing less frequent. I can't get him to eat or drink. I'm glad you sought a cure."

"Thank Mama Jamba," Sophia said, unwilling to take credit for the old woman's plan.

"I think before the night is over, we'll have more to thank Mother Nature for," Ainsley replied.

"Do you think Quiet is sick because the Castle was keeping him alive?" Sophia nearly passed a small passageway when Ainsley made a quick turn in that direction.

The corridor was so narrow Sophia had to turn her shoulders to the side to navigate through. It seemed logical this would lead to the gnome's chambers since he would have little trouble getting through the passageway. None of the men would have been able to get through. It was a chore for Ainsley and Sophia, who had an even smaller build than the elf.

"I don't know what to think, honestly, S. Beaufont," Ainsley said, worry in her voice. She covered her head, seeming confused.

"Ains, are you okay?" Sophia asked when she stopped, almost running into her in the tight space.

"No, I've been getting these headaches," Ainsley answered, pressing her eyelids shut. "I keep forgetting where I am...who I am."

Sophia laid a hand on her shoulder. The Castle had kept Ainsley alive after Thad Reinhart attacked her. Either the Castle's energy was enough presently to sustain the housekeeper or something else was at play. There was too much going on for Sophia to focus on one thing.

She desperately hoped they figured out whatever was happening to the Castle and the Gullington, or it looked like more than just the Dragon Elite and Quiet's lives would be at stake. Not until that moment had Sophia realized how important the Castle was to them.

"I want you to go find Mama Jamba after you lead me to Quiet," Sophia ordered Ainsley.

The housekeeper blinked up at her in confusion. "Mama Jamba?" she asked as though she had never heard the name before.

Sophia nodded. "Yes, ask her to help you."

"Help me with what?" Ainsley swayed a bit in the narrow passageway.

"She will know," Sophia answered. "But it's imperative you find her. Get her help."

"For the men?" Ainsley queried. "I seem to remember something about them having trouble." She looked off as if trying to recall a distant memory. Her eyes found the crumbling bricks of the walls enclosing them in the tight space together. "This place is in shambles. Someone should really fix it up, don't you think, Sophia?"

She nodded. The housekeeper was losing it, moment by moment. Ainsley couldn't remember the present and wasn't acting like herself. Whatever had held them all together was dissipating, and it filled Sophia with fear.

"Now, take me to Quiet and hurry," Sophia urged. She would have slid around Ainsley and gone the rest of the way on her own, but there was no getting around the housekeeper. The passageway was too narrow.

"Quiet?" Ainsley asked, her brow scrunching with uncertainty.

"Just move forward," Sophia encouraged, tears catching in her throat. This wasn't the time to grieve. They would fix things, and this would simply be a record in *The Complete History of Dragonriders*.

Sophia desperately hoped this wouldn't be the very last chapter recorded in that book.

CHAPTER FORTY-FIVE

The moon was only half full as the blue dragon flew across the Expanse, headed for the Pond.

Lunis always hungered for a fight but never had one been so personal. Unlike Sophia, he wasn't prone to sentimentality, a human emotion dragons didn't experience readily.

Lunis sometimes caught himself having slightly mushy thoughts after spying Sophia's emotions. That was the influence a rider had on their dragon. As a female, Sophia was more sentimental than the men, which meant Lunis was different from the other dragons, something to be expected because of their newness, generation, and circumstances.

Lunis knew the other dragons were experiencing sentimentality right then, the same as him. He could feel Simi's fierce need to protect her home of two centuries. Tala would rather die than allow the thieves outnumbering them to take over the Gullington. Coral had never been more offended than she was at that moment. But it was Bell who was in a rare state. The oldest dragon on Earth was enraged, taking the current events at the Gullington personally. There were few things that scared Lunis, but being on the other side of the red dragon's fury was one of them. Thankfully for him, he wasn't.

As he dove into the battle being waged across the Expanse, he felt a renewed sense of belonging with his ancestors. A chorus of voices filled his head as he swung around a bolt of magic launched by a trespasser. The words were from dragons long passed, but their knowledge was timeless.

Fight, protect, and don't let them take what is ours, the voices of ghost dragons sang in his head.

He maneuvered around, fueled by the chanting, and sent a wave of fire at the offender, turning the magician into barbeque. Killing humans wasn't something Lunis enjoyed. Dragons who bonded to riders weren't savages like their rogue counterparts who had little interest in the human world, a key difference between dragons who magnetized to a magician and those who didn't. He valued human life. Lunis always wanted to be a part of solutions, and not be controlled by his savage whims.

And yet, killing the trespasser had filled him with a satisfaction he rarely felt.

Energized by the kill, Lunis shot forward and sprung into the battle. The Dragon Elite was losing after hours of fighting, and tiring after dealing with the constant influx of thieves who had just kept coming over the borders.

The blue dragon opened his mouth and torched the area where the Barrier should have been, blocking a new set of pirates waving swords and intent on entering their borders.

Not on my watch, Lunis said and plunged through the air. His long tail swung around and batted a thief on the ground, rocketing the man back across the border.

The man screamed a guttural sound as he flew back, his eyes full of fear as his sword tumbled to the ground.

Lunis didn't wait to see where the magician landed but took off for Simi, who was currently deflecting spells from several attacks on the ground.

CHAPTER FORTY-SIX

The smell of must and gunpowder was strong when Sophia entered the groundskeeper's room. Ainsley seemed even more lost once they were there, but Sophia traded places with her and urged her to go back the way they'd come.

"Go and find Mama Jamba," she instructed the housekeeper, ushering out the door and back into the narrow passageway.

"Mama," Ainsley said, shaking her head. "It's been so long since I've seen my mum. I wonder if she'd make me a cup of tea." She clasped her hands around her arms and shook slightly. "I've got the chills coming on. Probably because I didn't wear my mittens to school again."

"Go Ains," Sophia encouraged. She didn't know how much longer the shapeshifter had before she lost her mind completely. Hiker would know. Quiet might even, but neither could help her now. The only hope Sophia could think of was to send Ainsley to Mama Jamba, even though she knew it was a long shot.

Deep down, Sophia knew Mother Nature wanted to help, but sometimes felt it wasn't her place. She'd once remarked that her job was to put everything into place, not to move the pieces. That's why when Thad Reinhart was working hard on world destruction, Mama

Jamba had to sit by and watch. Sophia hoped this time Mama Jamba broke her own rule. Someone had to save Ainsley before it was too late.

And Quiet...

Sophia turned to find a modest room with few furnishings. The gnome was lying in his bed covers pulled up to his chin and his mouth wide as he snored loudly. Sweat covered his forehead and drenched his pillow.

The only decoration in the room was a dark painting that hung over Quiet's bed. Sophia had to get close to make out the image. She'd seen many old paintings in the Castle and the House of Fourteen, but this one seemed extremely ancient for some reason.

It was a scene of a large, majestic ship sailing on choppy waters. Sophia remembered what Queen Anastasia Crystal had said about the gnome and why she would help him.

Sophia ran her eyes over the painting and wondered if it was the ship the Queen Mother of the fae had been referring to. It was strange it was the only personal effect in the bedroom. She looked around, using the orb to light her way as she studied the space.

There was no wardrobe, bathroom, or washing basins like in the other bedrooms, just a bed, a painting, and a sleeping gnome.

Sophia didn't want to wake Quiet. She wished she could just know his real name and give him the antidote, but that wouldn't work.

Carefully she leaned over the bed. "Quiet, it's Sophia. Please wake up."

He muttered in his sleep, words she couldn't make out because they were so muffled.

Reaching out, she shook the gnome's shoulders. "Quiet, I need you to wake up. I have something that will cure you."

This roused the small man, and he opened his eyes, an action that looked as if it was excruciatingly difficult.

He startled at the sight of her and pushed up to a sitting position, pulling the covers with him to cover his chest as though he were afraid of being indecent. She had only seen him in work clothes before and spied that he was wearing a sweaty white dressing gown.

Of course, she had no idea where he kept his other clothes since there was no furniture in the small room.

"Hi," she said, suddenly nervous as she looked into the gnome's red eyes. "I'm sorry to wake you. But I have something I think will cure you."

She held up the bottle of blue liquid Queen Anastasia Crystal had given her. "I don't know what's making you sick, but the Queen Mother of the fae gave this to me. She said it would cure you."

Quiet began muttering fast, his head toggling back and forth, and excitement evident on his face. He reached for the bottle, nodding.

She pushed the bottle into his hand and watched as he struggled to pull the cork off the top. His fat fingers fumbled several times, and he nearly dropped the vial.

"Here, let me help you," she offered, taking the bottle with a sheepish expression.

She would have to reveal the other part of the cure to him, but she sensed she needed to play this just right. Queen Anastasia Crystal had said Quiet wouldn't want to give up his name. Hopefully, he wanted the cure more than the need to keep his secret.

The cork resisted Sophia's first attempts to loosen it, but she was able to pull it free on the second. She handed it to the gnome, watching as his outstretched hand shook as he reached for the bottle.

"Queen Anastasia Crystal did say that for the spell to work, you had to tell me one thing," Sophia said and paused, watching as the gnome's face stiffened with tension.

He shook his head as if in response to the question she hadn't asked yet.

"It's easy," Sophia encouraged. "You once told me you'd tell me. All I need you to do is—"

Incessant muttering cut Sophia off. For being sick, the gnome seemed to have a lot more energy as he shook his head while mumbling erratically.

Sophia continued to hold out the potion. "Look," she began loudly, talking over him, which wasn't difficult. "Just tell me what your real name is."

To her surprise, he thrust her hand with the potion bottle back at her, nearly making her spill it.

She tilted her head and gave him a furious expression. "This is ridiculous. Queen Anastasia Crystal says you'll die without this."

He crossed his arms in front of his chest and continued to grumble to himself, his volume too low for even her enhanced hearing to make out. That was always the way with the gnome, which wasn't surprising, no more than him being so stubborn.

"Really?" she barked. "You're just going to die rather than tell me what your name is?"

Very deliberately, he nodded, the one action she understood fully.

"Fine, what if I guess it?" she proposed.

He shrugged and slouched back down in his bed like he was going to fall back to sleep, even with her standing in front of him.

"Bob, Billy, Jean, Roy, Kyle, Tom, Frank," she said, listing every name she could think of in quick succession.

His eyelids fluttered shut.

Sophia sighed, recognizing this approach was haphazard at best. There was a battle going on in the Gullington. She needed to be there, helping her friends. Sophia didn't have time for this nonsense, trying to save someone who apparently didn't want to be saved.

"Quiet, you have to tell me your name," she tried again. She attempted making her voice sound patient even though she was close to putting a spell on him. Sophia didn't really think it would work, or she would have gone straight to that solution.

Stubbornly he shook his head and urged her from the room, waving her toward the door.

Sophia narrowed her eyes when her gaze caught writing on the painting over his bed. The name of the ship was barely legible, but she could read it. "McAfee," she drawled slowly.

He stiffened.

Sophia's face brightened. "Is that it? Is your name McAfee?"

The gnome smiled and mouthed one word. "No."

Sophia nearly stomped. "Damn it! Why do you have to be so difficult? What can be so important about your name?"

"Everything," Mama Jamba said at Sophia's back.

She swung around, surprised to find the old woman there.

"If you know his name, it will change everything for him," Mama Jamba continued. "He would rather die, I see now, than the alternative."

"But you sent me to get the antidote," Sophia argued. She was furious with the gnome for being so secretive and frustrated at Mother Nature for sending them on a wild goose chase when they could have been saving the Castle and helping the others.

"I didn't know it would require Quiet to disclose his name, now did I?" Mama Jamba asked.

"Well, without his name, the antidote won't work," Sophia said, holding out the bottle of blue liquid.

Mama Jamba looked past Sophia at the gnome. "Then I guess the antidote won't work."

Sophia did stomp now. "This is ridiculous."

"Oh, dear, it certainly is, but don't waste any more time here," Mama Jamba encouraged, stepping to the side and holding an arm to the narrow passageway out of Quiet's room. "Go help the others."

"But what about Quiet?"

Mama Jamba blinked impassively. "Why don't you let me talk to him."

"Can you get him to change his mind?" Sophia demanded, her heart ready to beat out of her chest.

Mother Nature shook her head. "I very much doubt it, but I might be able to buy you all some time. At least a little while."

"How?" Sophia asked.

"Oh, my dear, I can't reveal all my secrets," she answered.

"You haven't revealed any of them!"

Mama Jamba giggled. "Right you are. Still, I need you out on the Expanse, or I think the others will lose this battle sooner rather than later."

Sophia was beyond furious. Mama Jamba had sent her away from the Gullington, and now she was sending her to fight with the warning if she didn't get out to help, they would lose. What if she'd been out there all this time? Maybe they wouldn't be in this position. She simply sighed with frustration before saying, "What about Ainsley? Did she find you?"

Mama Jamba nodded. "You were right to send her to me. I've given her something to help her sleep."

"Sleep?" Sophia questioned. "Will she continue to be confused? Forget who she is and what's going on? Is she in danger of dying like Quiet?"

Mama Jamba pursed her lips. "We're all in danger of dying. That's just the way this world was set up. Believe me, I know. I helped to make the rules. But Ainsley will be okay for a little longer."

"We have to fix the Castle," Sophia said urgently. "That's the only way to save Ainsley and Quiet, to seal the Barrier and stop this madness."

"You're correct," Mama Jamba replied calmly and clasped her hands in front of her. "But I see now other things will have to happen first. You'll have to help the men protect the eggs. You'll have to set out on other adventures." She nodded as if making her mind up about something. "Yes, the events are happening all out of order, but that's no matter. There's time for everything."

"Are you sure?" Sophia asked, looking between Mama Jamba and Quiet, who had fallen asleep during their conversation. "They'll be okay?"

"For the night," Mama Jamba answered. "I can help you through the night."

"And then what?" Sophia wasn't sure she really wanted the answer.

"And then, you'll have to figure out what to do on your own," Mama Jamba stated. "But you and I will have one last conversation, and I dare say, I'll have great advice for you then."

"Why don't you give it to me now!" Sophia yelled, her face flushed.

Mama Jamba just smiled, unflustered by Sophia's outburst. "Because timing is everything."

CHAPTER FORTY-SEVEN

What was happening on the Gullington was personal. As Sophia ran down the steps of the Castle, she felt engulfed in the battle before she was even close. She didn't know who these thieves were or how they had taken down the Barrier and found the Gullington, but she knew they had to be stopped.

The sun was close to rising over the mountains east of the Cave. Morning light peaked up over the hills, giving off a faint glow.

The idea that a new day was dawning didn't bring Sophia hope as she sprinted across the Expanse, finding signs everywhere of the battle that had ensued all night.

The grass that was always lush was dying and scorched by fire. In the distance, dragons were flying along the northern and southern sides of the Barrier, blasting fire and sending the thieves back. Evan and Mahkah were to the east, battling a few rogue thieves who appeared to have climbed down from the mountains. By the cave next to the Pond, Sophia saw Hiker and Wilder defending the Nest where the dragon eggs were stored.

She picked up her speed to cross the space. Like a mother desperate to rescue her children, Sophia felt a draw to the Nest and an unmistakable need to protect.

Briefly, she glanced up and saw her dragon streak across the sky in her direction, and then passing over her.

What's happening, Sophia asked him.

For some reason, they can't enter through the Barrier anymore, Lunis explained. *So we're trying to push them out of the border or kill them on the spot.*

Sophia hurdled over a body she didn't recognize. As she progressed, she saw more. The battle that had been waged all night had many casualties. She only hoped none were the Dragon Elite.

All are safe, Lunis said in her head, sensing her thoughts. *Evan's been stabbed badly in the abdomen, and Mahkah lost a finger, but otherwise, everyone is okay.*

Sophia didn't allow empathy to well up in her. Sadly, she knew when this battle was over, there would be more problems without the Castle to repair them.

I wonder what put the Barrier back up, she mused, hopeful. *Maybe the Castle is back.*

She felt Lunis hesitate before he spoke. *I don't think so*, he finally said. *I think we have to count our small victories. The Barrier is up, but we still have more fights left. The fiercest thieves have made it close to the dragon eggs and the Nest.*

Sophia chanced a look over her shoulder and saw Mahkah and Evan were outnumbered as they attempted to push the trespassers back by the Cave.

Go and help them, she encouraged her dragon. *I'll go to the cave and assist the others.*

He didn't have to affirm for her to know he'd turned around, doing as she asked. Sophia pulled her sword as she ran, making quick progress over the Expanse. She had wanted to join this fight since it started, and now was her chance.

She was weary and worn out like the others, having not slept or eaten in a long time, but she was charged up and ready to make these thieves pay.

No one came into Sophia's territory and hurt her friends without having to answer to her.

CHAPTER FORTY-EIGHT

"Sophia!" Wilder yelled as she neared, relief flooding his voice. He had a cut down one side of his cheek, and his eyes were heavy with exhaustion, but it was evident he was grateful to see her even as he battled two men.

As Sophia approached, running all the way, she noted these thieves had a unique appearance. Maybe she expected masked men or more traditional magicians in long cloaks or some other disenfranchised hoodlum type. These men were cyborgs, and they were dressed like steampunk pirates.

The observation hardly computed in Sophia's brain, but that seemed the right term for them as she watched Wilder slash at one. His opponent jumped back from his attack, bowing his chest to avoid the blade.

The guy had large bug-like goggles strapped around his forehead and short spikey black hair poking up around the glasses. He wore a vest and slung diagonally across his mid-section were some sort of artillery shells. Strapped around his waist were several belts with multiple strange devices locked into various compartments. The weirdest part was the sound he made when he pivoted to avoid Wilder's attacks.

Sophia caught the distinct sound of hydraulics. If that wasn't clue enough that he wasn't totally human when he turned to look at her as she approached, his eyes flipped like a lens on a telescope before it started glowing bright green.

"Move!" Wilder yelled, abandoning his position and diving in Sophia's direction and knocking her out of the way as something streaked through the air straight at them.

Wilder's body covered and wrapped around hers as they hit the grass and rolled away from the blast. The heat hit Sophia's face at once but dissipated as they continued to roll. Wilder didn't let her go until they were a safe distance from the attack.

He jumped up and directed a hand at the young man, sending his own assault, a stunning spell that slammed straight into the pirate's chest. Even though Sophia was accustomed to seeing Wilder use weapons and combat magic in battle, she was momentarily stunned to witness this incredible display.

The man was knocked off his feet and flew back several yards before landing on his back. He jumped up almost immediately but didn't run for them like she would have expected. Instead, he sprinted for the northern border.

Sophia was about to charge off to the Nest when Wilder pulled her back. She spun around, her breathing loud and her thoughts racing.

"Are you okay?" he asked, looking her over.

She pulled her wrist from his grasp. "Yes, but we've got to help."

He kept searching her face as if she was lying about not having any injuries. "That one," he said, indicating the pirate streaking off for the border. "He shoots a strange toxic substance. Are you sure you're okay?"

She nodded and checked in with her various parts to ensure adrenaline wasn't masking some injury. "Yeah, they are all..."

"Cyborg," he stated, finishing her statement. "Why do you think they've given us such trouble? Otherwise, we would have defeated them hours ago."

She nodded and looked around the Expanse, observing the battles still going on. Thankfully many seemed to be dying down, the pirates retreating in many cases. The dragons appeared to have secured the border. With the Barrier back up, they only had to defeat the half a dozen or so still trespassing.

Wilder continued. "They just kept coming. Every time I'd defeat one, five more would replace it, streaking across the hills. They are like clones. I don't know where they all came from."

"There will be time for that later," Sophia said, She knew Wilder needed to process. So much had happened. For someone like Wilder who had the sanctuary of the Gullington for two centuries, it must be incredibly confusing to have his home invaded.

She turned around to face the Nest. Hiker stood at the front of it, a force she couldn't imagine anyone willingly confronting. Even so, there were three pirates approaching him from different sides.

Surveying the area behind them, Sophia was relieved to see Mahkah and Evan, along with the dragons, pushing the pirates beyond the Barrier.

I'm scouting the area for any lone trespassers who could be hiding, Lunis said in Sophia's head.

Good idea, she agreed.

That left only one area to protect, the most important of all. She turned her attention to the Nest.

CHAPTER FORTY-NINE

"The Pond." Sophia narrowed her eyes at the placid water as the sun rose over the mountains.

"It should be secure," Wilder said at her side. "Hiker says the waters aren't passable by boat. The sea creature that inhabits it makes it impossible for foreign ships to navigate across."

Sophia nodded, remembering when Wilder had dived into those waters to get Devon's bow at the bottom and had nearly met his end. The creature was huge and fierce and vicious. She imagined any foreign vessel that tried to cross would meet their doom.

She let out her first breath of relief all day as she saw the Gullington was almost secure. The last three cyborg pirates were currently making their attempt to close in on the leader of the Dragon Elite.

In contrast to the strange trespassers who were wearing long velvet coats and pirate hats, Hiker wore his usual wool kilt and sword. His beard hid part of his face, and his light-colored hair marked the wind that was ever-present on the Expanse.

Sophia hesitated before jumping into action. She wanted to be a part of the fight, obviously, but she also knew Hiker Wallace would be able to defeat five times that many opponents, whether they were magicians or cyborgs, or like these guys, a combination of both.

Over their coats and armor, they had electrical cords wrapped around their chests and round eye patches that flashed bright colors. They all wore knee-high boots and sinister expressions as they crouched, trying to figure out which one of them was going to pounce on the ancient dragonrider first.

"Come on," Wilder encouraged in a whisper at Sophia's side.

She wondered what he was talking about until she turned and saw he had his gaze centered on Hiker.

"Use your power," Wilder continued, talking to himself.

"What's going on?" she asked.

He shook his head, frustration evident in his eyes as he watched the leader of the Dragon Elite. "He won't use his full power."

Sophia nodded. She remembered Hiker had been struggling with embracing his new inherited power after the battle with his twin brother, Thad Reinhart.

Defeating his twin had given Hiker double the strength he had before. Losing her twin was the reason Sophia had been so strong from a young age. But for Hiker, the power was a curse and a reminder of what he'd had to do to win, kill his own brother. He was allowing the guilt to eat him up. Without using the power, he was going to get himself killed, and then what would be the point?

"He can do this," Sophia whispered.

The glint in Wilder's eyes told her he wasn't certain she was right. He had been on the Expanse with Hiker all night. He must have witnessed things that gave him the reluctant expression he was currently wearing.

"Well, then, let's spring into action and help," she suggested and started forward.

For the second time, Wilder reached out and grabbed her arm to pull her back.

She turned, ready to knock him out for stopping her again. "Look, there's three of them, one for each of us. You take the little one. I'll let

Hiker have the one in the middle, and I get the huge one with an ugly face and a ton of scars. I'm dying to kick some ass."

He shook his head with a serious expression. "Let him try. The only way he will embrace his power is if he absolutely has to and a battle is best for those things."

Sophia huffed in frustration. "Really? Right now is when you want to have a teaching moment?"

He seemed to understand but didn't back down. "If he doesn't embrace his power, it could very well eat him up from the inside out. We've contained the borders for the most part. The others are pushing the pirates out. The dragons are doing surveillance, and we're right here to spring into action if necessary. Let's just give him this chance to do what needs to be done."

Sophia considered for a moment and then finally nodded. She trusted Wilder's judgment and didn't want anything to happen to Hiker. She firmly believed he could defeat these three enemies without the extra power. There were few warriors she wouldn't want to face in this world, and Hiker Wallace was one of them.

She turned her attention to the fight about to ensue and sucked in a breath. Sophia hoped the leader of the Dragon Elite wouldn't allow the past to hold him back.

CHAPTER FIFTY

The first pirate, a man with long dreadlocks strung with gold beads, ran for Hiker, a short sword in his hand as he screamed.

Sophia tensed and held her breath. The leader of the Dragon Elite raised his own weapon, a sword made for the very first rider, Alexander Conerly. It had a long blade almost as tall as Sophia, and its hilt was adorned with gems mined by the gnomes. The gold came from the Isle of Man and was crafted by the giants. The blade itself had been forged by the elves. Most importantly, the magic imbued in it was from magicians.

Almost casually, like he was bored by the attempt on his life, Hiker lifted the weapon and brought it up and across, striking blades with the pirate and sending him back down the hill, rolling end over end.

That was progress, Sophia thought.

A quick glance at Wilder told her this wasn't actual progress. He was chewing on his lip, a tight expression in his denim blue eyes.

The second pirate chuckled as he watched his comrade tumble down the hill. He lifted one arm, and Sophia saw strapped to his forearm was a large gun.

She wanted to run and help stop what was about to happen, but she stayed her ground.

Something green, like when the pirate attacked her and Wilder, fired from the weapon straight in Hiker's direction. He didn't even blink as he threw up his free arm, creating a reflective surface for a moment.

The attack, a magical missile of sorts, hit the shield and bounced off, ricocheting back in the shooter's direction. It didn't hit him because, like the coward he was, he took off, retreating down the hill. He tripped over his boots and, like his comrade, tumbled, after one of his legs came off. Sophia realized it was a prosthetic as the guy turned and crawled back to retrieve his limb.

She was impressed Hiker was defending the Nest without so much as breaking a sweat. Again, she spied the disappointment on Wilder's face.

"He can do so much more," Wilder explained in a hush when she gave him a questioning look.

"But he's defeating them," Sophia said.

"Now, he is, but he was hardly fighting before when I was by his side," Wilder stated. "It was like he knew I would do it for him, and he didn't want to chance using his power, but he didn't let anyone get by him into the Nest. I assure you of that."

"Which is why you're making me hang back now and watch when I've been on the sidelines all along," she spat.

"You've been gone," he argued through tight lips, his eyes still pinned on their leader. "And by the looks of you, you've faced just as bad as us."

She glanced down at her torn cloak and blistered hands. The cold had not been forgiving to her body, and she was sure her face was red and cracked from the frigid conditions.

The final man rolled his shoulders back, gritting his teeth at the leader of the Dragon Elite. He pulled duel swords from his belt and screamed like a mad man. He had to have been one too to charge like he did, straight up the hill at Hiker.

Like swatting a pest away, Hiker moved his hand, and the man rose off his feet and flew through the air to land in a heap next to his comrades.

Sophia wanted to rejoice and jump up and down to celebrate they were all alive and safe.

Wilder shook his head.

"What?" Sophia questioned him, turning to face the other dragonrider. "What would you have him do? Take their heads off? Throw them to Timbuktu? He defeated them."

"Barely," Wilder said, pivoting to look at her. "That's the power Hiker Wallace had before. He's not tapping into what he really has. If he would have none of this would have happened." He threw his arm wide at the Gullington, which was a mess of destruction, death, and remnants of chaos everywhere.

Sophia grasped that Wilder was bitter. He'd spent the entire night guarding and protecting the Gullington, exhausting himself against sizable enemies, and he believed Hiker could have done it by himself with little effort. He thought the leader of the Dragon Elite refused to embrace his power, his birthright.

She shook her head at Wilder, recognizing he didn't understand.

"It's not as easy as you make it out to be," she argued. "The power he has didn't always belong to him."

"Oh, and you understand that, do you?" he spat back at her. "Because you and your twin were so close?"

She shook her head, wanting to fight him. Sophia had been hungry for a fight and hadn't been given the one she wanted on the Gullington. Maybe she was going to take it out on Wilder. She felt the urge but did her best to shake it off.

"It is difficult to use power when it belonged to someone else is all I'm saying," Sophia said, her chest still vibrating with the intensity of wanting to lash out. "You wouldn't get it."

"How do you know what I'd get?" he fired back.

"What are you two going on about?" Hiker yelled, striding down the hill and throwing a hand at the pirates he had defeated, binding them in ropes.

What he did with such seemingly little effort was quite impressive to Sophia, but her attention was centered on the dragonrider in front of her, challenging her.

She shook her head. "Nothing. Good job up there, sir."

Hiker walked past them. "We have much work to do to secure the borders."

"It's already been done, sir," Sophia replied. "The dragons have pushed the pirates through the Barrier, which is back up, apparently."

He halted, an impassive expression in his eyes. "Good," he said simply before turning back around and stalking for the Castle. "Get those lowlifes and put them in the dungeon. I'll question them after I've spoken to the others."

Sophia nodded obediently, but Wilder rolled his eyes, obviously still put off by how the leader of the Dragon Elite had conducted himself.

She couldn't understand it. They had protected the Gullington. Yes, there was a lot to figure out, a lot to repair, and a new enemy, but Wilder should be grateful they were all still alive instead of splitting hairs over how things were done.

She shook her head at him, a challenging movement as she made for the first pirate wiggling in his binds. Sophia was looking forward to throwing this guy in the dungeon and punishing those who thought they could steal her eggs.

CHAPTER FIFTY-ONE

I *'ve found something,* Lunis said.

She tensed, tired of surprises. *Whatever it is, kill it. Torch it. Get it gone,* she replied.

I'm afraid it's too late for that, he revealed, regret in his tone.

What is it, she asked.

I know how they got into the Gullington, Lunis offered.

Beside crawling over the borders, Sophia questioned.

Once we figured out that was happening, we went to guard those areas. Four dragons are very efficient, he explained.

So what happened, Sophia asked, knowing she wasn't going to like the answer.

We guarded the northern, eastern, and southern border, knowing those were the most likely borders for trespassing, Lunis continued.

Makes sense, only a fish or a seagull would get across the Pond, she agreed, knowing the waters were inhabited by a sea monster who would demolish anything that tried to cross it from the west.

It turns out these pirates have a ship the sea monster left alone, Lunis stated.

Sophia tensed. *How is that possible?*

I don't know, but the ship is empty now, Lunis said. *The boats have been deployed, and I'm guessing they are sailing to land now.*

Find them, Sophia urged.

I will, Lunis promised.

Sophia grunted. She had to remind herself these were pirates. Of course, they'd have a ship that could sail across the Pond. These were people who shouldn't be underestimated, she realized, but hindsight was a very frustrating thing in her life presently. It made her angry she had to pick up pieces she hadn't known were going to drop.

One more thing.

Go on, she encouraged.

I only know this is important since I spied on you to ensure you were okay when you went to give Quiet the antidote at the Castle earlier, he said.

What is it, she groaned.

The ship, he told her, his tone reluctant.

Yes, she urged.

Sophia could feel the regret strong in her dragon before he spoke in her head.

The ship, he began, *the cyborg magician pirates used to cross the Pond is called the* McAfee.

CHAPTER FIFTY-TWO

S ophia didn't know what it meant, but she knew it was bad.
Really bad.

How was the ship she'd seen above Quiet's bed on the Pond? There were so many unanswered questions. One of the biggest was if many of the pirates had come over the borders of the Barrier on the northern, eastern, and southern sides of the Gullington, then where were the ones who had come on the ship?

Something was wrong.

Really wrong.

She hauled up the second pirate absorbed in thought as she tried to figure out what they were missing.

I only found one rowboat, Lunis told her.

Where? she asked as she used her magic to steer the prisoners toward the Castle.

On the shore, he answered.

She shook her head.

They were missing something.

"What is it?" Wilder invited, suddenly at her side.

She turned to him, still mad about the dispute they'd had over Hiker.

"Did you fight any pirates who came across the Pond?" she asked.

He squinted at her like the morning sunlight blinded him. "What? No one came across from that side. I told you that's impossible."

"But what if it wasn't?" she demanded. "What if they had a boat that could sail on the Pond?"

"You aren't listening to me. There isn't a boat that can do that." Irritation flared on his face.

"No, what if someone sailed across the Barrier from the other side of the Pond using a special boat?" Sophia explained and pointed toward the water that seemed to go on forever.

He shook his head. "No, again, they couldn't have. Even if they could get through the Barrier when it was down, the sea monster would have killed them and capsized their boat."

"But what if there was a boat that was different? One the sea monster wouldn't destroy," Sophia argued, furious he wasn't getting it.

He shrugged. "What if unicorns could fly and there were places where the sun never set? What's the point?"

"Those are called Pegasuses. And that's called Alaska," she said sarcastically. "And my point is, Lunis found a ship on the Pond."

Hiker spun. "What did you say?" he asked, having heard them even from the far distance.

"A ship," Sophia replied. "And there was only one rowboat that came from it."

"That's impossible," Hiker protested.

"But what if it's not," she fired back. "What if it was Quiet's ship, and that's why it can sail on these waters?"

CHAPTER FIFTY-THREE

Three things happened in quick succession.

Hiker Wallace's eyes narrowed on something behind Sophia and Wilder.

Feeling a presence at her back, Sophia released the pirates and pulled her sword.

And on the hill where the Nest was located, a single woman appeared, roughly a hundred yards away.

The woman was someone Sophia recognized. Her long curly black hair seemed normal from a distance but moved like snakes and had the appearance of wires. Like the other pirates, she wore a white ruffled shirt with a leather vest and boots. Unlike the men, she was dressed in a long skirt, with several sashes wrapped around her waist. She was absolutely gorgeous and not quite human.

The woman who stood too close to the Nest where all thousand dragon eggs were resting was a cyborg.

Sophia thought the evil grin she flashed was the precursor to her attack, and she took off, sprinting in the direction of the Nest, Wilder on her heels and Hiker screaming.

It all happened so fast. The woman didn't attack. She didn't even move. Instead, she extended her pale arm, and her hand detached and sped into the cave on a long coil.

Sophia got to the hill, climbing while also firing spells at the intruder. For all her efforts, Wilder's, and everything Hiker threw at the woman, it all fell flat against an impenetrable shield.

When the woman's hand retracted back to her body, it was holding a single dragon egg.

She winked before taking off, jumping off the side of the hill to where the cliff ended on the beach around the Pond.

Sophia was certain they'd get her. Lunis would find her. She'd be trapped. There was no way for her to get out before they caught her.

Just after the woman disappeared, she rose back up into the air, holding onto a long chain. Sophia brought her gaze up, following the metal rope to a blimp that appeared just below where she suspected the Barrier was located.

The craft rose fast into the air, taking the woman suspended from the chain up and away, along with one of the prized dragon eggs.

CHAPTER FIFTY-FOUR

E ven the morning light streaming through the windows of the Castle did little to make the Dragon Elite feel any better as they dragged themselves off the Expanse and into the crumbling building.

Wilder took charge of the prisoners, leading them down into the dungeon while Sophia helped Evan to the dining room table.

"Get Ainsley for me, would you?" he asked through sips of breath, the stab wound obviously growing more uncomfortable, even though he had been putting on a tough act.

Sophia had done everything she could to knock down the blimp, as had Hiker and Wilder. Lunis was too far away to help, but it wouldn't have mattered anyway because as soon as the blimp rose up through the Barrier, it portaled away with the pirate woman and the dragon egg.

Sophia set Evan in a chair before looking up at Hiker. "I recognize her from the press conference," she said simply, knowing Hiker knew who she was referring to. Evan and Mahkah didn't know what had happened since they'd been on the other side of the Expanse.

Mahkah hobbled into the dining room, with his hand wrapped up in a large bandage. Debris was strewn everywhere. If anything, the Castle looked way worse than a couple of hours ago when she went up to visit Quiet. She had a lot more questions for the gnome now, but they would have to wait. For one, there were prisoners to interrogate. There were two badly injured dragonriders sitting at the makeshift dining table, and then there was the fact she couldn't remember when she had slept last. At some point, she was going to require answers, and Quiet was going to give them to her, or she was going to toss him out of the Castle—pulling a real Hiker Wallace.

The leader of the Dragon Elite nodded. "I recognized her, too," he said to Sophia.

"Who?" Evan questioned, sucking in a breath as he pressed his hands to his ribs. Usually, the Castle would have started repairing the injured, but seeing as the place was destroyed, Sophia didn't think that was likely to happen. And yet, the Barrier had come back up, so maybe there was still hope.

"The woman who stole one of the dragon eggs," Sophia answered Evan.

"What?" Mahkah asked, leaning forward.

She nodded solemnly. "Yeah, she appeared out of nowhere." Briefly, she explained what had transpired all the way to when the blimp disappeared.

"She was the one in the audience at the press conference who asked about our location," Mahkah stated definitively.

"Yeah, and hindsight tells me I shouldn't have even hinted," Hiker remarked bitterly.

"This has been planned for a long time, I believe," Sophia consoled.

"I agree." Hiker gazed at the floor. "But how, I don't know."

"Someone poisoned Quiet," Sophia said and divulged what she'd learned when getting the antidote for the groundskeeper and learning about the ship. The men stayed quiet and listened to her. Wilder gave her a stoic expression when she finished, having come up from the dungeon.

No one said anything for a long time, all of them too exhausted to do anything more than breathe.

"So, Ainsley..." Evan finally began, pressing his hand to his ribs where blood seeped through his armor.

"I put her to bed," Mama Jamba informed them, walking casually into the dining hall.

"Cool," Evan replied condescendingly. "Well, when she wakes from her beauty sleep, can you tell her I'm bleeding to death?"

"Will do, hun," Mama Jamba answered.

"Without the Castle," Sophia explained, giving Hiker a meaningful look, "Ainsley has fallen ill."

He sucked in a breath. The other men seemed to understand, though none of them knew the full details of what had happened to Ainsley or that the Castle kept her alive.

"If the Castle isn't doing its normal job, how did the Barrier come back up?" Mahkah asked, giving no indication he was in pain even though he'd lost a finger.

"I did it," Mama Jamba stated. "I figured you all could use a break, and it was the least I could do."

"It's about damn time," Hiker muttered bitterly.

She whipped around and stuck her hands on her hips. "I will remind you, Hiker, my job is not to save you. Your job is to save my planet."

"Normally I would be all about doing that, but my home base was attacked, putting all of us on the defensive, and now one of our eggs has been stolen, and most of us are injured," he complained.

"I'm sorry about that," Mama Jamba said matter-of-factly. "Although I don't like my children to suffer, I can't always save you. Considering the seriousness of this situation, I've put up the Barrier, but it won't last. It's only in place long enough for you all to rest and figure out what to do when it comes back down."

"Which will be when?" Evan asked. "One, maybe two decades?"

Sophia was impressed Evan was joking even though he was pale and obviously in a lot of pain as he clutched his side.

"Try more like one to two days," Mama Jamba corrected.

"That gives us time to rest, but what happens to the Gullington is what I want to know," Hiker mused.

Everyone fell silent, no one having any answers.

"Even if we rest up, we have to be ready if those pirates return," Wilder declared.

"When they return," Hiker said. "They were here for a reason. As mentioned, this was planned and probably for quite some time. Whoever is behind this knew what they were doing. What we need are answers."

He turned his attention to Mama Jamba. "Can you help us?"

She shook her head. "I did already. It really isn't my place."

"Mama," he begged.

"Hiker, you know damn well you have everything you need to rise above this," she said gravely. "I refuse to save my children when they are unwilling to save themselves. You wield power that can wipe out an army. You have riders who will die for you. There are so many resources, but you're going to have put yourself out there and ask for help from those you think you don't owe anything to. If you want answers, start looking around."

Mother Nature put Hiker Wallace in his place.

CHAPTER FIFTY-FIVE

Things were far from over, Sophia thought as she hiked out to the Nest.

They were just beginning.

There were more questions than there were answers. Quiet. The *McAfee*. The cyborg steampunk pirates and how they knew so much about the Gullington.

The most heartbreaking part was her lost egg.

She settled down on the grass overlooking the Pond. For some reason, Sophia couldn't bring herself to enter the Nest. She felt like the dragons inside their eggs would all cast judgment on her for losing one of them.

Instead, she glanced out at the Pond, where the *McAfee* floated on the open waters. It was the property of the Gullington for now. The pirates had left it because it had only been a means into the Gullington. Hopefully, it offered some answers. Like where it had come from and why. She'd take time to investigate it. She'd do a lot over the next forty-eight hours before the Barrier came down again, and more attacks ensued.

Sophia wanted to believe the pirates wouldn't be back, but there was no point in disillusioning herself. They knew where the Dragon

Elite was, and they'd be watching. When the Barrier came down, the Gullington would be visible and the borders crossable.

The pirates had come with strong numbers. Not only that, but their strategy had been brilliant. Sophia had to give it to them. They had fought, knowing the Dragon Elite would take a position by the Nest. According to Wilder, they never tried hard to get into the cave. Instead, they let themselves be picked off until the Dragon Elite thought they'd won. At the last moment, the strange woman with wiry hair from the press conference swooped in and stole a dragon egg and then was lifted off by a blimp.

It all made Sophia so angry she couldn't even sleep even though she was exhausted. She couldn't eat, and she couldn't talk to anyone, even Lunis, although her heart sorely wanted comfort.

She turned away from the Pond, tired of looking at the strange ship that seemed to be mocking her.

She caught sight of the Castle. How lonely it looked, broken and dreary in the morning sunlight. She didn't think her heart could break more, and then it did.

Losing the dragon egg had been horrible, but if anything happened to the Castle, to the Gullington or the Dragon Elite, Sophia didn't know how she'd recover.

It all felt so wrong. She'd just regained hope. Hiker had too. The Nest full of a thousand eggs had been the Dragon Elite's saving grace. It had given them so much.

Then a new enemy had reared its head and taken so much away.

"I don't mean to be the bearer of bad news." Mama Jamba's southern drawl cut through the wind howling around Sophia's ears. She'd learned to tune it out, still frustrated by the unrelenting winds on the Gullington and all around.

Sophia hadn't noticed the old woman standing on the other side of her, next to the Nest. There was a lot that could have escaped her right then after days of adventures and no sleep or real nourishment. She blinked at Mother Nature. "What is it?"

"Well, you happen to be sitting in my spot," Mama Jamba said cordially.

Sophia glanced around at the ample green space all around her. She pointed to a patch of earth. "Why don't you take that area?"

Mama Jamba shook her head. "Oh, no. I like where you're sitting, which is why I'm guessing you're sitting there."

Sophia sighed, totally feeling defeated. "Is this a joke because I'm really not in the mood."

Mama Jamba smiled and settled down next to her. "I get that, dear. And yes, you'll have to excuse me. I'm awful at jokes. They really are the strong suit of other gods and goddesses, but not me. I keep trying. Maybe I need to go to clown college."

Sophia couldn't even force a smile, though she sensed Mama Jamba really was trying to cheer her up. The old woman had saved them that day. If she hadn't closed the Barrier, who knows what would have happened. Sophia knew Mama Jamba could always save them, but she respected what the woman had said about her children saving themselves. She guessed it was a sign of being a good parent, raising children who knew how to save themselves.

"That's what I want you to understand most here, sweet Sophia," Mama Jamba said out of the middle of nowhere when they had been silent for a long while.

She hadn't realized she had laid her head on Mama Jamba's shoulder, seeking comfort. "What are you talking about?" Sophia asked, yanking her head up.

Mama Jamba smiled knowingly. "What you said about respecting that my children have to save themselves."

"Mama Jamba, I thought that in my head. I didn't say it."

Mother Nature waved her hand through the air. "Same thing. Anyway, I know it hurts your heart that you've lost a dragon egg." She clicked her tongue and shook her head of silver hair. "I just put you in charge of them, and there you go losing one."

Grief ached in Sophia's throat. "This isn't making me feel any better."

Mama Jamba patted Sophia on the knee. "The thing is, and no mother ever wants to hear this, but sometimes we have to lose our children to understand how much they mean to us."

"That's my lesson?" Sophia couldn't keep the frustration out of her voice.

"No," Mama Jamba stated simply. "Not in its entirety."

"Is it that I'm supposed to allow the dragon egg to miraculously save itself?" Sophia questioned with real attitude in her voice now, exhaustion getting the better of her.

Mama Jamba smiled, not at all offended. "Maybe. More than anything, the lesson is you can do everything to save your children. You can do everything to help them. But at the end of the day, your job is to do the best you can in a world where you control only so much."

"I'm a Dragon Elite," Sophia argued, conviction in her voice. "I am one of the most powerful people on your green Earth. How can I even accept that? How can I let these people get away?"

Mama Jamba winked at her, seemingly satisfied. Then she stood, pushing up like her lower back was bothering her. She groaned slightly. "I think my job is done here."

"Wait, what do you mean?" Sophia asked, looking at the old woman as she hiked down the hill.

"Oh, I should have said, sometimes losing your children is a part of the process," Mother Nature said. "It makes you stronger because you realize how much they mean to you. And what lengths you'll go to get them back."

Sophia sucked in a breath, bowled over by the lesson Mama Jamba had just imparted. No, Sophia didn't want to lose an egg. She didn't want to see the Gullington destroyed and her friends hurting. She understood then how much all of them meant to her, and it was leagues more than she could have ever discovered without this experience.

She went to thank Mother Nature, but it was too late.

Mama Jamba had disappeared. She hadn't faded into the distance as she retreated to the Castle. She did what all mysterious goddesses do and disappeared into the ether to resurface when she saw fit.

Sophia turned her attention back to the Pond, not feeling as sad as she had before.

She was tired. No, she was beyond exhausted.

She was frustrated. No, she was livid.

A fire had been lit in her belly.

If the pirates had come and gone then, the Dragon Elite would have rebuilt. Instead, the pirates had come in and stolen something that belonged to the Dragon Elite and to Sophia Beaufont. She was going to do everything to get back their dragon egg.

She stared out at the ship floating in the open waters of the sea monster-infested Pond and found herself smiling as its sails flapped rebelliously in the wind.

Sophia wanted to know more about that ship, more about these pirates, about Quiet, and the winds on the Gullington that were tangling her hair.

She was going to get answers.

And then she was going to take back her dragon egg and punish a lot of bad people.

CHAPTER FIFTY-SIX

The ragged breathing of the prisoners was the only sound Sophia could hear. She and Evan were trying to figure out how to make them talk. They had been at it for hours and were no closer to getting any answers.

She cut her eyes at Evan and he nodded, knowing he had been tapped into the interrogation.

The dungeon in the Castle of the Gullington would be beautiful if not for the smell of mold and sweat, and if one could forget what happened in such places. It had been ages since this dungeon had held any prisoners, although Evan admitted Hiker had once locked him in the cell where they presently stood for sassing him.

Sophia stepped out, pulling the gate shut as she watched through the bars. The dripping sound at her back reminded her of the techniques Hiker had used on one of the three prisoners.

Sophia had never seen the Viking so angry. The steampunk cyborg pirates weren't intimidated. Evan had wanted to take things further, but Hiker had refused, saying they wouldn't be forced to stoop to immoral levels. Sophia was impressed. It was easy for people to do the right thing when they weren't facing a real challenge. Sticking to ethics when your enemy looked you in the eye and spat in your face was a lot more difficult.

Hiker had simply wiped his face of emotion and left the room, giving the job of interrogation to Evan and Sophia. She had tried to be crafty and trick the prisoners into telling her something about the person or people they worked for.

She'd had seconds to shield herself before the cyborg fired at her through its mechanical eye. After that, Sophia had put a spell on all three of the prisoners, disarming any other defenses they may have. It was a taxing spell but necessary. The Castle would have done it for her if it hadn't been in disrepair and not operating at peak level. The dungeon, according to Hiker, used to automatically disable prisoner's magical powers, keeping them restrained and from attacking.

Whatever Mama Jamba had done to reinforce the Barrier, the Castle seemed to be holding and not crumbling as rapidly as it had been. The protection would only hold for about another day or so, though, and the Dragon Elite would be forced to defend their borders and watch the Castle degrade once more.

Evan picked up the leather belt they had taken off the pirate whose hands were restrained in the rusted chains on the brick wall. All the cyborgs had been smart enough not to carry any identification, but the one they were currently interrogating had a personalized belt, his first and last name engraved into the leather.

Hiker hadn't seemed surprised when Sophia discovered it.

"Idiots love to put their names on things. Like they are going to forget who they are after a night of drinking whiskey," he had explained.

"So," Evan said, drawing out the word as he doubled the belt over and slapped it into his hand. "Rhett Wren. What a horrible name. It was like your parents wanted everyone to stutter your name."

"Rut rho," Sophia muttered, finally saying the joke that had sprung to her mind when she first heard the prisoner's name.

Evan glanced at her, confusion on his face. "What?"

"It's a Scooby Doo reference," Rhett Wren told him dryly, giving Sophia an annoyed expression. "I have heard it before."

"Yet, you were dumb enough to put your stupid name on your belt," Sophia taunted from the other side of the bars.

"I'm proud of my name," he grumbled, his fingers flexing in the restraints.

"The only name I care about, maggot eater, is the person you work for," Evan threatened, pushing his face close to the prisoners, apparently unafraid he would get spit on like Hiker.

Rhett, to Sophia's surprise, didn't launch any saliva onto Evan's dark face, probably because he was slapping the would-be weapon they had taken off the prisoner in his hands.

"I already told you, I don't know their name," Rhett said, his cyborg eye glowing in the dark cell.

"Then tell me how you know her," Evan demanded.

"She recruited me," he replied simply.

Evan grinned and stepped back. He glanced at Sophia. "Now we know Wiry Hair is the leader."

She nodded. It was progress. She had assumed the leader of the band of cyborg pirates was the woman with the retractable hand who had stolen the dragon egg and escaped via blimp, but it was good to get a confirmation.

Rhett narrowed his human eye at Evan. "Oh good, after hours of this, you finally got some information. Feel adequate, dragonrider, since the world hates you."

Evan pulled back the belt, about to lash the pirate.

Sophia jerked up her hand and restrained him using magic. Evan's arm froze in mid-air, the belt suspended after it whipped backward.

Evan glared at Sophia, giving her an expression that spoke acutely of his disapproval of her restricting him from harming the prisoner. "Seriously, girl."

She shook her head. "You heard what Hiker said. We aren't going to inflict violence on them. Use your magic to torture him mentally. Use your words. But you are not going to use force."

Evan sighed. "Fine. Will you release me?"

Sophia did, and Evan's hand shot forward, the belt landing across the man's torso, making a metallic sound. He didn't even flinch but rather grinned at Evan. "Benefits of being made of mostly metal."

Evan shook his head, backing away.

"Evan," Sophia said, a warning in her voice.

"What?" he complained. "I was already wound up. When you released me, there was no stopping the attack."

She opened the cell door and encouraged him to exit. "I don't think you can restrain yourself. Take over disabling their cyborg powers. I want to try something."

Evan stepped out of the cell, belt still in hand. "Okay, but no more talkie-talkie. It's time to graduate to other methods."

Sophia nodded and leaned forward to whisper in Evan's ear so only he could hear her. "Shield yourself as well as restrict them."

Understanding flashed in his eyes.

Sophia felt her magic released when Evan took over for her.

She lowered her chin to her chest and closed her eyes and sent out a signal. Almost immediately, screaming filled the air. All three prisoners were suddenly wailing as if in excruciating pain. They weren't. Sophia wasn't about to disobey Hiker, mostly because she agreed with him. The strong didn't use force to get what they wanted. They used strategy.

Each of the men was being inundated with images that would scare them most, whatever was specific for each of them. The chains rattled violently from the walls as they jerked, writhing as if in physical pain. Rhett's feet dropped out from under him, and he hung awkwardly from his restraints.

"Trin," he groaned, drool running down his chin as his eyes remained closed.

Sophia stopped the spell and stepped close to the bars. "What did you say?"

The prisoner heaved all over the stone floor, instantly filling the air with a putrid smell.

"Oh, man," Evan complained. "Gross."

Sophia gave him an irritated glance. They were making progress.

"Tell me what you said, or I will keep torturing you the same as before," Sophia threatened.

"Trin Currante," one of the other prisoners groaned behind her.

She turned to face the cell holding a cyborg with a busted nose and scratches down his face. He had tumbled down the hill when Hiker fought him, and it had bloodied him badly.

"Trin Currante," Sophia repeated. "What is that?"

"Who," the man sputtered between breaths. "The woman you are looking for. Our boss."

Sophia looked at Evan before redirecting her gaze to the pirate with large black goggles strapped around his head. "Tell me more."

"I-I-I don't know much," he said, shaking his head like he was trying to dispel the images she had forced into his head.

The spell had been extremely taxing to do on all three men at once. Sophia hoped she didn't have to do it again because it probably wouldn't work.

Faking confidence, she pursed her lips at Evan. "Looks like I get to send their worst nightmares back into their head."

"Do it, princess," he encouraged.

"No!" Rhett yelled from his cell. "I will talk. I will tell you what you want to know, but there isn't much. Trin saw to that."

"Go on then," Evan ordered sternly.

"She used the blimp to search Scotland and find this place when the Barrier came down," Rhett explained in a rush. "We were sent in via portal and told to attack you all until she swooped in. That is all I know. I promise."

"I don't know, Pink Princess," Evan complained, shaking his head. "I don't think we can believe him. See if you can jog his memory a bit."

"That is all we know!" the other prisoner behind them yelled. "We weren't given a location. She recruited us and sent us messages about the mission."

"How?" Sophia asked.

"Internal messages," he explained, his breath rattling in his chest as much as the chains binding him. "Us particular cyborgs have visual message centers. It displays information over our cortexes."

"What do you mean, 'Us particular cyborgs'?" Evan questioned, crossing his arms in front of his chest.

"We were made at a specific facility," he answered. "We all have functions."

"Facility?" Sophia questioned. "What are you talking about?"

"It's shut down now," Rhett stated, his voice suddenly sounding tired. "It was called the Saverus. Most of us were abducted and changed."

"You mean, someone kidnapped you all and made you into cyborgs?" Sophia queried.

He nodded roughly.

"By this Trin Currante?" Evan quizzed.

Rhett shook his head. "No, she was one of us. She rescued us. Shut it down. Got rid of the magicians who ran it."

"And then she enlisted you to help her," Sophia said, piecing it all together.

"Well, we had to," Rhett declared. "We owed her. She saved us. We were imprisoned before that."

"Have you gotten more messages from her since being here at the Gullington?" Sophia was grateful they were making progress. After three hours of interrogation, it appeared she had figured out how to get them to talk.

Rhett groaned suddenly in pain. The other two prisoners joined in, both screaming.

"Hey, you didn't have to do the mental torture thing to them again," Evan complained, gripping his bandaged side. "I mean, I'm all up for punishing these guys after one of their mates stabbed me, but they were actually talking, and now, well, they're making a bunch of racket and not talking."

The men's moans of pain had grown in volume, making it hard to hear anything else.

Sophia shook her head. "I didn't do it. I don't know why they are moaning."

"T-T-Trin," Rhett groaned between attempts to breathe.

"What about Trin?" Sophia asked, grabbing the bars of the cell.

"M-m-message," he stuttered. "She just sent a m-m-message."

"What?" Sophia questioned at once, her heart beating fast. "What does it say?"

"Ter-term-terminated," Rhett told them.

Sophia whipped around, her mouth wide open as she gasped at Evan. "What does that mean? 'Terminated.' Is she telling them to terminate us?"

His eyes slid to the side as he thought. He shook his head and pointed to the cell across from Rhett's. "I don't think so. I think she is telling them what is happening to them."

Lying on the cold floor of the cell was the cyborg pirate. The chains were barely long enough to allow him to lay flat. His face was to the side, and a puddle of blood spilled out of his mouth.

"What happened to him? What did he do?" Sophia raced over and grabbed the bars, studying the space. There were no weapons or any way she could see that he could have taken his own life.

Evan shook his head. "I don't think he did anything. Look." He pointed to Rhett, who looked like he was having a seizure, his head jerking back and forth as he foamed at the mouth. A few seconds later, he fell still against the wall, his eyes wide and unblinking. He was dead.

Sophia ran over to the other cell. The last pirate was the same as the others. They were all dead. Something had killed them, and she was assuming it was the person in their head. The Dragon Elite's new enemy—Trin Currante.

CHAPTER FIFTY-SEVEN

Hiker Wallace paced across his office, which looked a lot more like it did back when Sophia had first shown up, and the Castle was punishing the leader of the Dragon Elite. Most of the books were strewn onto the floor or lying sideways on the shelves. The long bank of windows facing the Pond was cracked, and his desk looked ready to fall apart at any moment. When the Castle had fallen, everything inside of it had too, slipping into disrepair.

"Trin Currante," he said for the tenth time, his eyes off in thought.

"Do you know the name?" Sophia asked, looking sideways at Wilder, who sat on the other side of the couch, seemingly distracted through the impromptu meeting.

Hiker shook his head. "I have never heard it."

Sophia glanced at Mama Jamba, who was peering out the window and humming under her breath the Stevie Wonder song, "I Just Called to Say I Love You."

Sophia thought asking Mother Nature about the new villain was probably a long shot. She opened her mouth and was immediately interrupted by the old woman.

"Of course, I know about her, but I can't tell you anything, dear," Mama Jamba said, answering her question before she asked it. "Not anything of use anyway. She was born a normal magician, and as you witnessed, she isn't one anymore. She is a cyborg like the others who invaded the Gullington."

"But they were abducted," Evan stated, shaking his head. His hair was starting to grow out again after his electrocution in the caves to the north, and he was already working to put the coarse black hair into dreads.

Sophia nodded. "It sounds like, to me, that some organization—"

"This Saverus," Mahkah supplied.

"Yeah," she affirmed. "This Saverus organization abducted a bunch of magicians and turned them into cyborgs."

"Probably using that repugnant magitech Thad Reinhart perfected," Hiker said bitterly.

"It looks like we aren't done with Thad yet then," Evan said with a cold laugh.

Hiker paused his pacing, a resentful look on his face. "Not by a long shot. I should have realized my brother's legacy would stretch well after him. Who knows, this Saverus organization might have been one of his."

"That could have been how he figured out how to bring his dragon, Ember back," Sophia offered. "He might have experimented on humans first."

Hiker didn't seem convinced. "It's hard to know. We need more information."

"Well, according to the prisoners, this Trin Currante ended the organization," Sophia explained. "Then she rescued these men and recruited them for this mission to storm into the Gullington."

"There are still so many questions," Mahkah noted, his eyes low and his injured hand in his lap, wrapped in bandages.

If the Castle were its usual self, it would have healed his finger, making it grow back. It would have mended Evan too, so he didn't suck in a sharp breath when he had to twist or move. As it was, they were healing faster than most, but not as fast as the Dragon Elite were accustomed to.

"Yeah, like how did Trin Currante kill all three of the prisoners remotely?" Sophia mused.

"She knew we had them," Hiker pointed out. "She must have hacked into something in their brain set up by the Saverus organization."

Everyone in the room, including Mama Jamba, turned and gawked at Hiker, shocked he would make such an observation and use so many technical terms.

He brought up his shoulders as he tensed from all the attention. "What?"

"Sir, that was quite the observation," Sophia declared.

The leader of the Dragon Elite shrugged. "I have been studying up on things since the Thad business." He pointed at the laptop Sophia had set up for him. "I have been reading things on this thing."

"What you say makes a lot of sense," Sophia began. "It sounds like this Saverus installed something into the cyborgs' brains to send them messages. Trin Currante figured out how to access it after getting rid of the organization. It goes to reason she figured out a lot more, like if there was a 'kill switch' of sorts. I'm guessing she has the main control panel for these cyborgs and can use it to her advantage."

"Okay, now I'm back to being lost," Hiker said. "I didn't understand a lot of what you said."

Sophia nodded sympathetically. He was trying, although Wilder still thought he was holding back a great deal of his strength. Sophia didn't blame him.

"When this Trin Currante realized they were our prisoners," Evan started, "she flipped the kill switch and ended them so they wouldn't give up any information on her."

"Thankfully, I think we figured out most of it before she cut them off," Sophia said, still feeling heavy after witnessing the three men's deaths.

Yes, they had been trespassers who served as a threat to the Dragon Elite, but they were humans. No matter if someone was good or not, witnessing their death should still take a toll on anyone who valued human life. Otherwise, what is the point of having a soul at all?

"Okay, so the first question," Hiker said, his words came slowly as he worked things out in his mind. "We need to find out who this Saverus organization is and what they did."

"They seem like a corrupt organization," Sophia proclaimed.

"Yes, but I think what they created is somehow worse now. Understanding motivation is key, so we need to learn as much about the Saverus as possible." He turned his attention to Wilder. "I want you to go and dig up as much as you can about this place."

Wilder gave him a reluctant expression. "Although I would like to, sir—"

Hiker threw his hands to his head. "Don't tell me you have a mission for Subner. Not now."

Wilder bit his lip as his gaze fell to the floor. "Okay, I won't tell you anything."

"He has to go," Mama Jamba sang, still swaying by the windows and dancing to the music in her head.

Hiker spun to face the woman. "What are you going on about?"

Unhurried, she turned and pointed at Wilder. "He has a mission, and the timing is awful for us. But he must do it."

Hiker glanced between Wilder and Mama Jamba and shook his head. "Our home has been invaded. Nearly destroyed. It's only holding up now because you took pity on us, Mama."

"It wasn't pity," she amended. "I simply did what had to be done to save my riders. At the end of the day, though, you will have to save yourself. I just bought you some time. I get you need every available person for this and you are not working with much. But son, now you are working with less."

"Less?" Hiker questioned. "I have one rider who can hardly move, let alone ride." He pointed at Evan, who grimaced, holding his side.

"I'm good, sir," he said. "I can ride as long there is no wind, and Coral moves slowly. And there are no complications. And I'm heavily drugged."

"You see!" Hiker bellowed, turned back to Mama Jamba. "And there is Mahkah. He lost fingers."

Mama Jamba offered the rider a sympathetic expression. "I'm

sorry about that. But no one ever said you needed all your digits to get a job done."

"I can help, sir," Mahkah offered. "I'm happy to go on a reconnaissance mission for you."

Hiker waved him off, still glaring at Mama Jamba. "I have got to figure out what is wrong with the Castle and fix it, so I can fix my riders. I have to find out everything on this Trin Currante, Saverus, and what their connection is. And then we've got to get back our egg. Not to mention, we've got to guard this place when the Barrier comes down."

Mama Jamba shook her head and clicked her tongue. "You have got your work cut out for you, son. I'm not sure why you are here going on about things when you have so much to do."

"Because," he complained, throwing his arm back in Wilder's direction. "You are telling me it's okay one of my riders has a mission he has to go off on, and I'm certain I can't know a thing about it."

Mama glanced at Wilder before shaking her head. "No, it's better if you don't. If no one does. But yes, you have got to lose your rider for a bit. Adapt, Hiker. Move on."

Sophia drew her gaze to Wilder, studying how he fidgeted nervously and wasn't even listening to Hiker and Mama Jamba's discussion. He had been preoccupied all through the meeting. Now she knew why.

He was setting off on another mission for Subner, the Protector of Weapons. She understood having to keep secrets, as she had to do when recovering the *Complete History of Dragonriders* or digging up information about Hiker, Ainsley, and the Dragon Elite. However, that didn't make it any easier to be kept in the dark.

She wanted to know Wilder's secrets, to be a part of them and help.

"Are you even listening, Sophia?" Hiker called to her.

She jerked her head up, blinking to attention. "What is that?"

He sighed dramatically. "Of course. Now I have another rider who doesn't pay attention. I asked if you would investigate the *McAfee*."

She nodded automatically. "Yes, of course."

"I don't know what is on that ship," he went on. "And even if you are on the *McAfee*, it doesn't mean you will be safe. The Pond is unpredictable."

"What else can you tell me about the *McAfee*?" Sophia asked.

Hiker shook his head. "Nothing. It is apparently a ship that can sail on the Pond, which I have yet to see. This is all brand-new information to me, but it might have been included in the *Complete History of Dragonriders*. I'm not sure."

He gave her a pointed expression, knowing she had possession of the book. Sophia hadn't even had a chance to crack the book open, and she didn't think that would change anytime soon.

"It's a very strange ship," Evan said, looking out the windows at the Pond. "I wonder who it belongs to."

"It was Quiet's ship," Sophia told him. "I know that much."

Hiker lifted his chin and gave her a skeptical expression. "How do you know that?"

"Oh," she said, sucking in a breath and realizing she hadn't filled them in on everything. "Well, I saw a painting above Quiet's bed when I was—"

"How were you in his room?" Hiker asked. "I have never seen it."

"Nor ever even been in the servant's wing," Evan added.

"That area of the Castle is open now. I went to give Quiet the antidote," Sophia explained.

"So, will he be joining us soon?" Hiker demanded.

So much had happened with the battle and Trin Currante and the egg being stolen. Sophia hadn't had time to explain everything she had been up to. She briefly explained about Queen Anastasia Crystal and the antidote and needing to learn Quiet's real name. When she was done, everyone was quiet for a long moment.

Finally, Hiker turned and looked straight at Mama Jamba. "You know what Quiet's name is, don't you?"

"And you know I'm not sharing it," she answered.

He sighed. "Of course, you are not."

"If that man wants to share his name, he will," Mama Jamba

declared. "It's not my job to do so, and doing so will change everything for him."

"How?" Hiker demanded at once.

She wagged a finger at him. "Oh, no. I'm not giving spoilers, you know that."

The Viking rolled his eyes at her. "Fine. So, the *McAfee* is Quiet's ship. How did it get to the Pond, and how can it sail on those waters when I have never seen a ship out there? I didn't think anything could survive. That has always been part of our protection for the northern border."

Sophia glanced out the bank of windows at the bobbing ship. It was a beautiful sight. "Which brings up so many other questions, like how did Trin Currante know that ship could get through the northern border? Or how to find it?"

"All questions Quiet could answer for us if he was coherent," Hiker grumbled.

"Oh, and if we could understand a word he said *ever*," Evan joked.

"Which also begs the question of how Trin Currante found out how to bring down the Barrier or what she did to the Castle and did she do something to Quiet to make him sick," Sophia mused, the different questions streaming through her head rapidly. That morning, she had discussed with Hiker the theory she had about Quiet being poisoned. They had started to put some things into place to ensure it didn't happen to any of the rest of them. The strategy didn't make Hiker comfortable, but he had gone along with it, showing some flexibility.

Hiker chewed on his lip. "There is a lot we don't know for sure. I want answers, and I want them soon. Mahkah, you go and research this Saverus organization. Find out as much as you can about what the company did and what happened to them and how Trin Currante could be controlling the cyborgs they created." Hiker turned his attention to Evan. "I want you to…go and help Ainsley. She is disoriented and trying to care for Quiet and keep this place running, which is still falling apart."

SARAH NOFFKE & MICHAEL ANDERLE

"Sir, really?" Evan mumbled. "Help the housekeeper? You remember I'm a dragonrider, right?"

"Barely. But Ainsley isn't right," Hiker said. "And you can't really leave, can you?"

Evan sighed dramatically. "Fine, but when this flesh wound is healed, I'm going to go on a real mission."

"Your spleen was filleted like a fish," Mama Jamba corrected. "Get rest, dear Evan, or you will rupture and bleed to death."

It was not what the dragonrider wanted to hear, but he nodded reluctantly.

Hiker drew his gaze to Sophia. "You know what to do. Gather clues so we can go after that dragon egg. The longer it remains outside our borders, the further from our grasp it will get."

232

CHAPTER FIFTY-EIGHT

Mama Jamba was waiting for Sophia when she left Hiker's office. She had that look about her when she was up to something, which was almost always.

"Walk with me, dear," the old woman said, making for the stairs.

Since one didn't argue with Mother Nature, unless they were Hiker Wallace, Sophia did as she was told. She had been about to take off for the Pond to investigate the *McAfee*.

Mama Jamba halted at the top of the stairs, which were still missing sections, the cool air from the bottom floor wafting up through the various holes. The others had tried to use renovation magic to fix the stairs or other hazardous areas. They had tried magic wherever they could to fix the Castle, but none of it worked. Before the Castle wouldn't allow them to change things using spells, and even now it needed their help, that rule still seemed to be in place.

Mama Jamba paused and glared down at the broken set of stairs. "Oh, this is simply getting annoying." She waved her withered hand at the old staircase, and it was repaired immediately, looking brand new.

"That is better," Mama Jamba said with a sigh, gliding her hand along the railing as she hurried down. Sophia tested the first stair before following her to the entryway.

The ancient woman swept her hands back and forth as she made her way for the kitchen, repairing furniture and putting the chandelier back on the ceiling. "I mean, I don't like to do everything for my children, but I can only live in squalor for so long."

"Is this when you are going to tell me what is wrong with the Gullington so I can fix it?" Sophia asked, chancing the question although she sensed it was useless.

Right on cue, Mama Jamba gave her a sideways smile and a wink. "Nice try, darling. No, I'm afraid I can't give you any more help than I have."

"Will you at least tell me how to get Quiet to tell me his real name?" Sophia asked. "If he dies while I have the antidote, well, it just seems so ridiculous and unnecessary."

Mama Jamba stopped in front of the kitchen. "Honey, his blood won't be on your hands if he decides to die rather than come out with his truth." She looked out one of the windows running along the side of the dining hall, which looked remarkably better than it had a few moments prior. A fondness crossed over her face as she stared out at the green rolling hills. "Quiet has been a very devoted servant to this place, and I would be sad to lose him. However, a mother's job is to bring children into the world, teach them the best we can, and let them make their own decisions. Nobody should ever be forced into anything. Otherwise, the results will never be what you expected."

Sophia sighed, used to getting this type of advice from Mother Nature. She wasn't sure how it would help her. She had a cure that would fix Quiet, and maybe he could figure out what was wrong with the Gullington and help fix it. He would be able to shine some light on this *McAfee* business. She was scared to board the ship, not knowing what she would find or if the Pond would capsize the boat. Maybe the pirates had used a special spell to get the boat to cooperate on the waters of the Pond. None of her postulating mattered because Quiet was laid up in his bed, being stubborn, not giving away any secrets, and refusing to take the antidote.

"Mama Jamba, I know you won't overstep boundaries in most

cases," Sophia began, deciding to try one more time. "Like you have fixed things here in the Castle for us, don't you think, just this once, you can tell me how to get Quiet to share his name? At least give me a hint?"

Mother Nature's bright periwinkle eyes were piercing when she looked at Sophia. "Oh, I have always liked your persistence. It's one of your best and most irritating qualities. But that is the thing about our children. You know what the poet, Kahlil Gibran said on the subject of children?"

Sophia shook her head, never even having heard the poet's name before.

"He is one of Quiet's favorites," Mama Jamba offered. "One of mine too. I remember when that man was born, a new shade of rose started growing that day. Quite remarkable the things humans do to this Earth in all the right ways, wrong ones too, unfortunately."

Mama Jamba closed her eyes, pulling in a breath. "Anyway, Kahlil wrote a poem on children. It reminds me of you. Of Quiet." She opened her eyes and began reciting the poem from memory:

"You may give them your love but not your thoughts,
For they have their own thoughts.
You may house their bodies but not their souls,
For their souls' dwell in the house of tomorrow, which you cannot visit,
not even in your dreams.
You may strive to be like them but seek not to make them like you.
For life goes not backward nor tarries for yesterday."

"Thanks for that," Sophia said, enjoying the poem without knowing what to do with it.

Mama Jamba gave her a knowing look. "Oh, you are disappointed, aren't you, dear?"

Sophia slumped immediately, defeat tunneling in her mind and heart. She couldn't hide the expression on her face, but even if she could, Mama Jamba would have seen through her façade. "I love poetry. I really do. But I'm not sure how that helps me right now as I try to help Quiet, and the Gullington, and recover the lost egg, not to mention defeat enemies who we know so little about. I guess I just wished you would tell me something specific, but I know you work through love and in mysterious ways."

"Well, like Kahlil Gibran so well said, I can give you my love but not my thoughts. And I can house your body, but not your soul." The old woman directed a finger at the cold, dark fireplace, and flames jumped to life, filling the room with warmth and light. "Now, that is better. There was a chill in the air before. Anyway, I wanted to check on Ainsley and Evan to ensure they are getting along. Do you want to pop into the kitchen with me?"

Sophia wanted to say no and wallow around in her frustration that her greatest assets were the strongest entities in the world, and they refused to directly give her information. Instead, she reluctantly nodded.

Mama Jamba smiled politely. "Well, then follow me. If anything, this will be of great entertainment."

Sophia followed the woman to the swinging door.

Mama Jamba pressed her backside into the door and paused before stepping into the kitchen, a thoughtful expression on her face. "The reason I can't reveal more obviously is that I can't tell you how to think. You have got to figure this out on your own. But also, it wouldn't matter if I did. If you want Quiet to reveal his name, you must find that which houses his soul, and I'm not that, as the poem so accurately explained."

Sophia nodded slowly, putting together all of Mama Jamba's strange words. She recognized Mama had eloquently told her what she was looking for, without doing so. She had done as she always intended and gave her children the information while letting them decide for themselves.

CHAPTER FIFTY-NINE

"That is not where that goes," Ainsley scolded when Mama Jamba and Sophia entered the kitchen.

The housekeeper was seated on a stool in the corner and slumped against the wall, her color pale and her hair dull. Sophia hadn't seen her that day and was shocked at how much she had changed. Whatever spark the Castle had been putting in the shapeshifter to keep her alive had dimmed. Ainsley was alive, though, and that was what mattered most.

Evan lifted a large platter and placed it on a middle shelf. "Here?"

Ainsley shook her head. "You are messing with me now, aren't you, Cracker Jack?"

Hiding a grin, Evan put the platter on the floor. "Oh, I get it. You want it here."

The housekeeper narrowed her eyes at Evan before directing her gaze to the two women standing in the entrance to her kitchen. "He really is insufferable. I think it would be better if you just invite the sheep in off the Expanse to help me."

Mama Jamba shook her head, striding into the kitchen and making straight for a basket of fruit on the center aisle. "Don't be silly, dear

Ainsley. We both know sheep have horrible organizational skills. I wouldn't so much as trust one to fold my socks."

Sophia was about to laugh when she realized the strange old woman wasn't joking.

"Okay, I'm done putting away the clean dishes," Evan said. "What would you have me do next?"

Ainsley appeared so listless it hurt Sophia's heart. The elf leaned her head against the wall and looked ready to pass out at any moment. "Chop up the onion. If you use magic to do it, remember it will burn your eyes a bit more than if you used manual means."

The kitchen was in better shape than Sophia had seen it when she and Wilder first discovered Ainsley screaming about all the rotten food right after everything had happened with the Castle and the Gullington. Quiet had gotten sick, and Ainsley had started to degrade.

Mama Jamba said Ainsley would be okay for a week or so if she didn't exert herself, and she must stay in the Castle no matter what. This meant Evan would be doing all the cooking since Hiker didn't trust any outside food sources.

Since they had discovered Quiet might have been poisoned, all the food would be bought from extra secure sources through the House of Fourteen and prepared in house. That had been the new strategy Sophia got him to try this morning. She hoped it was the beginning of a whole new era for the leader of the Dragon Elite but didn't want to bet on it.

"Onion...onion..." Evan said, looking at the basket of vegetables delivered that morning through the portal connecting the Castle to the House of Fourteen. Sophia had only to send a quick message to her brother to get a crate of supplies. She explained she'd fill him and the others in on more soon, but to keep any information about the Gullington secret. The last thing they needed was Bianca Mantovani and Lorenzo Rosario getting wind of this and making a case that the Dragon Elite was a liability.

"It's the white orb looking thing, dear," Mama Jamba offered, pulling a box of vanilla wafers from the pantry and opening them up. "You should make banana pudding for dessert."

Evan picked up the onion and pulled his sword from his sheath, a dazzling glint in his eyes. "Sure, but first, I have to chop this. Do you want it sliced, diced, or what?"

"First of all," Ainsley said, holding out a hand to Mama Jamba for a vanilla wafer, "if you use a sword in my kitchen to do anything besides slaughter demons or murderous villains I will make your life hell when I recover. Secondly, banana pudding never goes over well when I make it."

"No sword, huh?" Evan asked, sheathing his weapon and looking around. "How do you expect me to chop this?"

Mama Jamba pointed to the cutting board. "Try a knife, dear." She handed Ainsley a handful of cookies. "Maybe Evan will have beginner's luck with his banana pudding."

Ainsley was not happy with this answer as she nibbled on the cookie.

"Can I get you anything, Ains?" Sophia asked. She had never felt so helpless. Ainsley was degrading, Evan was injured, Mahkah missing a body part, and Quiet was in and out of a coma.

The housekeeper pulled an apron from the wall and threw it at Evan. "Put this on and wash your hands, would you?" She directed her attention to Sophia. "No, thank you, S. Beaufont. I mean, if you could make this awful flu or whatever it is go away, that would be welcome. I don't understand why I had to catch this bug at the most inopportune time."

Sophia nodded sympathetically and caught the knowing expression in Mama Jamba's eyes. They both knew Ainsley had fallen ill because the Castle had been keeping her alive all this time, but the housekeeper didn't know. Or if she did, she immediately forgot.

Evan tied the apron around his waist, trying to be a good sport about his new job reassignment. "Okay, chop onions. Then what?"

"Then marinate and braise the lamb chops, knead the bread and start it rising, dice the potatoes, soak the greens, make the banana pudding, and clean up after yourself when you are done," Ainsley listed, sliding off the stool and tottering for the door.

"Wait, what?" Evan called to her. "What did you say after 'marinate the roast?'"

Ainsley gave him an amused expression at the door. "You will figure it out, or you won't. Either way, I will be there to critique your cooking as you have so thoughtfully done for me for one-hundred-long-years. I'm going to go and take a nap if I can figure out where my room is. I sleep in the basement, right?"

Sophia shook her head. "No, that is where we keep the prisoners... if they haven't been killed remotely by their mysterious leader," she said morbidly as she took Ainsley's hand. "I will take you to your room and fetch you before dinner."

"Thanks, S. Beaufont," the elf said, managing a smile before glancing back at Evan. "Oh, and remember the laundry hanging on the line needs to come in, the bedrooms need to be cleaned, and the sheep need to be let out."

"Let out of what?" Evan asked, scratching the side of his head with the tongs of a fork.

Ainsley shrugged. "I'm not sure. That is Quiet's job. But I'm certain he lets the sheep out every day."

"Why? And where to?" Evan questioned.

"Well, maybe so they don't get wet or cold or something," Ainsley said dismissively, obviously trying to get out of there and to bed.

"Dear Ainsley, you do know the sheep are made of wool and can withstand cold and rain, right?" Mama Jamba asked, wrapping up the bag of wafers and putting them on a high shelf like she was trying to keep them out of her reach, so she didn't eat too many at once.

Ainsley seemed to consider this before shrugging again, disinterested. "Whatever. Figure out what Quiet does and do that too, Evan. And know no matter how hard you work and how pure your intentions are to do a great job, it will never meet Hiker Wallace's expectations, and he will grunt and refuse you any gratitude."

Evan sighed, a smile still on his undeterred face. "Thanks for the motivation. That really helps."

CHAPTER SIXTY

After tucking Ainsley into bed, Sophia slid through the narrow passageway that led to Quiet's room. She was hoping she could convince him to give her his real name. When she arrived in his modest room, she found him fast asleep and didn't have the heart to wake him.

How many centuries had he tirelessly cared for the Gullington doing whatever he did? No one seemed to know what that was when they had discussed divvying up tasks at the meeting. Without the groundskeeper and housekeeper, everyone was going to have to pitch in a little bit. Quiet always had dirt on his hands and clothes, and his nose was usually blistering red from being outside, but what he did was a mystery.

"We will be sure to let the sheep out for you," Sophia said in a whisper, that heavy feeling lingering again in her chest.

She glanced around the room, looking for any clues to tell her what his name could be. Maybe like Rhett Wren, he had it embroidered into one of his garments. Sophia almost laughed, thinking of the ridiculousness of such a thing.

Besides, there wasn't anything in the room. Just a bed, a side table, a sleeping gnome, and an old painting of a ship.

The *McAfee*.

Sophia had to go there next to find answers. Hopefully, she'd learned something about Trin Currante and her band of cyborg pirates. More than anything, Sophia hoped she found something to help her convince Quiet to give her his name. What had Mama Jamba said?

"If you want Quiet to reveal his name, you must find that which houses his soul…"

"Yeah, that doesn't seem hard," Sophia muttered to herself as she left the gnome to sleep in peace.

Lunis met Sophia on the Expanse, which was still covered in brown grass. It wasn't dying like before, but it wasn't coming back.

"The dragons really don't know what is happening to the Gullington?" Sophia asked her dragon when he glided down from the Cave to land smoothly beside her.

Lunis folded his wings into his body and stared serenely across the grounds of the Expanse. *Many assume that because we are the most powerful magical creature in the world—predating most others, that we know all the answers to problems.*

"Based on what you just said, I would say that is a pretty astute assumption."

Well, we aren't all-knowing creatures, he corrected, giving her a snotty expression. Sometimes he took on a regal look most of the other dragons in the Cave shared. Sophia knew his real demeanor was closer to a playful teddy bear.

"Okay, well, do you limited-knowing creatures have any ideas?" Sophia asked.

Yes, the Gullington has been cursed.

Sophia threw up her hands, exasperated. "Well, the investigation is over, everyone. We can get back to our lives. The dragons have figured out what we all failed to see. The Gullington has been cursed. Thanks, Lunis."

The critical expression on his face deepened. *Your sarcasm is echoing across the grounds.*

Sophia smirked. "I figured the sheep might enjoy the joke."

He shook his head. *They have zero sense of humor.*

"Wow," Sophia said in mock sympathy. "No organization skills and no humor. Sounds like my algebra tutor growing up."

Why a child with more magical power than a clan of old magicians had to take math is beyond my comprehension, the dragon offered.

"In case this magician thing fell through, I could get an accounting job," Sophia joked.

You would make a horrible accountant.

"Because my math skills are so awful?" she asked, checking the saddle strapped around him and tightening the buckles.

Because you wear color and have funny jokes, he quipped.

"Save your accounting jokes for Rory, the giant," Sophia said. "He will appreciate them."

Even though he is no longer an accountant? Lunis questioned.

"Especially so," she answered.

I was going to make writing jokes about him at our next meeting.

"Oh?" she asked, affectionately running her hands over his blue scales.

What do you get when you cross a writer with a deadline? Lunis asked.

"What?"

A really clean house.

"Ba-dum-THS," Sophia said, not laughing.

I have a lot more where that came from, Lunis told her proudly.

"Although I would love to hear them, I have to go and investigate that mysterious ship over there." Sophia pointed at the *McAfee*.

I suppose you want a lift, then? he pretended to ask.

She patted her dragon, enjoying the warmth that spread over her from their every interaction. They had a spark, which had brought them together and chemistry that would keep them united for all their lives.

It was that elusive thing people look for all their lives, most never finding it because they settled for the practical, the safe and easy, the opposite of what Sophia and Lunis' life was.

"I would never think of you as a simple lift like some Uber driver," Sophia said, stepping onto the wing her dragon extended and climbing into the saddle.

If I were an Uber driver, I would have an exemplary rating and would be charming, asking my fare thoughtful questions to learn more about them.

With the slightest of intentions, Sophia directed Lunis into the air. He took off after a few steps, gracefully gliding off the cliff edge next to the Nest, where the dragon eggs were safe once more. The wind tangled Sophia's hair back as her heart rose in her throat. Lunis took a sharp dive and barreled to the water's surface. He pulled up inches away, gliding along the Pond, almost blending into the blue waters.

"What would you ask?" Sophia questioned, her voice barely audible over the rushing wind.

Well, it depends on where I was taxiing people.

"Fair enough," Sophia said, studying the *McAfee* anchored in the distance. "Let's say you were taking people around Edinburgh."

Oh, good, I'm staying local in Scotland, he began, a hint of mischief in his voice. *I guess I have many questions for the Scots I would like answered.*

"Oh?" she pretended to ask. She knew Lunis could sense her stress about boarding the mysterious ship and was doing everything he could to make her feel better.

Yes, I mean, I obviously want to know what they wear under their kilts.

"You live in a Cave in Scotland with a bunch of dragons who belong to male riders," Sophia replied. "How do you not know that answer, or can't you find out?"

Lunis scoffed. *How uncivilized do you think we are?*

"I once saw you eat a calf without hardly chewing," she fired back.

That is different, he stated. *We mind our boundaries. You wouldn't want me telling them your personal business. Like about that one thing—*

"There is no thing," she interrupted.

There is a thing, he said, knowingness in his voice as he pulled up near the *McAfee*. *The reason for the chaotic winds on the Expanse. But we don't have to discuss it. Just know that I know there is a thing.*

"Anyway," she drew out the word. "Other questions for unsuspecting Scottish people who have chosen to take Dragon Lyft?"

Right, he chirped, circling over the top of the ship and giving Sophia a chance to survey the area around it and the deck. *Well, I want to know why they sound so angry when they talk?*

"That could just be Hiker," she said with a laugh as she scanned the ship for any clues. It was abandoned, she knew that much.

Yeah, Wilder doesn't have that same disgruntled quality to his voice, Lunis offered. *I would also like to know why they are physically incapable of saying the word 'Carl' or the number 'six.'*

"Is that a thing?" Sophia asked, wondering why the *McAfee* appeared in such pristine condition. It was a very old ship, according to the painting on Quiet's wall, if it was his ship, and he had been at the Gullington for several centuries. The ship below them appeared brand new if one ignored the old craftmanship style of the decoration around the outside and balustrades.

Ask them to say those words, he suggested. *You will see. I would also like to know what the deal is with haggis and whether it is a form of currency.*

"I think they use pounds," she replied.

Finally, I want to know if they can introduce me to David Tennant.

"Because…"

Because all Scottish people know each other, right? Lunis laughed at his own joke. *But seriously, like who wouldn't want to meet the tenth Doctor. He is my favorite.*

"You are very strange," she remarked, steering Lunis closer to the ship's deck.

Sophia would have to plan her dismount just right since Lunis couldn't land on the surface of the ship. Once her feet hit the deck, she wanted to be ready to fight or defend herself from whatever magical force was on board or what the Pond might decide to do.

CHAPTER SIXTY-ONE

Sophia tensed as soon as her boots touched the deck of the ship. She paused, crouched down low, and took note of the sounds, smells, and sights around her.

The boat rocked on the choppy waters of the Pond. With the winds up lately, the usually calm waters were full of white caps and made the ship bob from side to side.

Nothing charged out of the water and tried to lob her head off, so she rose slowly, her eyes constantly scanning.

I need to find something that houses Quiet's soul, she said to Lunis in her mind.

His shadow cast over the ship and waters as he flew close by, ready to swoop down and get her if a sea monster sprang out of the water.

I'm not sure if Mama Jamba was being literal when she said that, he offered.

I hope not, Sophia told him. *I mean, we aren't supposed to part from our souls, I thought.*

That is true, usually, but think of it this way, Lunis began. *Parts of your soul can be in things. In the work you do, the ones you love, the places you value most. Maybe you can find a clue on board of what that is for Quiet.*

Sophia thought she should go down to the lower decks first. It seemed the most logical place to find clues.

And you think, Sophia began, taking a few steps and pausing to see if her movement triggered any attacks. *If I find something related to his soul, it might encourage him to share his name?*

I think Mama Jamba told you to find what houses his soul for an important reason, Lunis answered. *Motivation is key, and right now, Quiet would rather die than give up a seemingly simple thing. You need to remind him of what he's got to live for. Find it and show it to him, and make him want to live regardless of whatever circumstances will come about after you learn his name.*

Sophia scratched her head at the stairs that descended below deck.

It's strange that a name could be of such importance, she said to her dragon.

And yet, if you would have called me the wrong one when we first met formally, you couldn't have been my rider, he explained. *A name holds incredible power, as do words in general. I'm guessing whatever Quiet's real one is, it tells his secret and also might be the source of his power. Maybe you knowing it will be his very undoing.*

Then why would Queen Anastasia Crystal make it a requirement for the antidote to work? Sophia asked, taking the first step on the dark staircase.

Good point, Lunis agreed. *She did seem fond of the gnome.*

Well, he saved her people, Sophia said. *A very Quiet-like thing to do.*

Right, so there is another reason she requires that information for the antidote to work, Lunis remarked.

Sophia sighed. *Wouldn't it be great if everyone just told us the intentions behind the riddle-like stuff they do?*

Lunis laughed. *Where would the fun in that be?*

Obviously, that is what this is all about, Sophia answered. *Make everything as confusing and mysterious as possible for the newbie dragonrider, so she gets a headache trying to solve riddle filled missions.*

I'm sure that is the conversation they all secretly have about you, Lunis chuckled.

Sophia was about to respond when she passed a room that stole her attention. She halted in the doorway and braced herself as the boat rocked back and forth. When it calmed, she pulled in a breath, mesmerized.

The room in front of her wasn't *like* one she had seen before. It was a complete duplicate of Hiker Wallace's office.

CHAPTER SIXTY-TWO

Everything before Sophia was the same as in Hiker's office in the Castle when it wasn't in disrepair. The windows lining the side of the ship were the same arched type that faced the Pond, and the large desk sitting on the far-left side of the room was exactly like Hiker's. It even had the same logbook on one corner. Even more surprising than the leather couch and books on one wall, all duplicates of the ones in the Castle, was the globe next to the windows.

Tentatively, Sophia took a step into the room and grasped this would have been the Captain's quarters, Quiet's private space.

Sophia hesitated before running her fingers over the globe. She rotated the orb on the axis, bringing it around until Scotland was in view.

Because everything appeared the same as the Castle, she half expected to find five red dots blinking on the surface indicating the dragonriders located currently at the Gullington. There was only one dot, and it was labeled The *McAfee*.

Sophia studied the globe for a minute longer, thinking she might find other clues on it, but other than the location of the ship, there didn't seem to be anything else magical about it.

Turning her attention to the books, Sophia stepped along the shelves, not searching for anything but allowing her gaze to run over the spines. The volumes on the shelf were old. Really old. Although everything was in pristine condition, it all looked like it was from a millennium ago.

Sophia hoped to find a book of poetry on the shelves, but the clue she was looking for wasn't going to be that obvious.

Going over to the desk, Sophia opened the logbook, eager to find something helpful. Maybe Quiet's name, she thought.

There was one thing different about the gnome's office versus Hiker's. Beside his desk was a display case, and its location seemed to denote its importance. On a stand next to the captain's desk, the box-shaped case was glass on all sides, except the bottom where a red velvet pillow sat. Sitting on the top of the velvet was nothing.

Sophia stared at the empty display case for a whole minute, wondering what could have been held inside the approximately two by two box. There didn't appear to be any foul play. It hadn't been broken open, but whatever had been inside was gone.

Maybe it's invisible, Lunis offered.

Sophia shook her head. *I don't think so, but that is always something to keep in mind.*

For as pristine as everything was on the ship, all the writing in the logbook was blurred as if it had suffered water damage, but the pages weren't warped as if they had gotten wet and dried.

Magic had no doubt been used to blur the writing, which might have given her clues.

She pulled open the desk drawer and rummaged through it, finding several things that could have given her the captain of the *McAfee's* name. An engraved lighter. A set of receipts. A picture of the crew with Quiet standing in the front, all the names written on the back.

On everything, the name that would have belonged to Quiet was blurred.

Sophia sighed. Why did the sweet little gnome have to be so revoltingly annoying about this?

She studied the picture, looking over the faces of the men who stood behind Quiet. They were all magicians or elves. It was a strange picture, with the small gnome standing in command in front of them.

She shouldn't have been surprised to see the groundskeeper hadn't aged a day. It was common for magical races to age slowly. Dragonriders lived the longest and aged very slowly. The Castle was obviously responsible, but the Dragon Elite weren't immune from growing old. Adam Rivalry's portrait in the Gullington was a testament to that, displaying him with a face full of wrinkles and long white hair and beard. At age eight hundred, he looked considerably well.

The fact Quiet hadn't aged at all in one-thousand years was a bit harder to believe. She remembered Ainsley from when she went back to the reset point. She still looked the same too.

There was something about the Castle that kept those two the same.

But how? And why?

Sophia stuck the photo back into the drawer, having found nothing else of interest in the desk.

She was about to give up her search in the Captain's office when she noticed the corner of a piece of parchment peeking out from under a rug.

Sophia bent to retrieve a letter. The flowery handwriting of the note was hard to read at first, like that of old English. After a moment, Sophia's eyes adjusted to the strangeness of the handwriting, and she was able to make out what it said. It was addressed to Quiet. To Sophia's disappointment, it was addressed to him using his nickname.

Sophia guessed he had that nickname from before he joined the Dragon Elite. It appeared even centuries ago the gnome had been soft-spoken.

She pulled in a breath, feeling the first bit of hope since coming aboard the *McAfee* this letter might hold a clue.

The letter read:

Dearest Quiet,

I hope your travels are treating you well. As your mum, I would be proud of you no matter what. Such is the prerogative of a mother. Nothing makes me happier than to know you have followed in your father's footsteps, deciding to sail the Seven Seas on this beautiful Earth.

This would make your father so very proud. I know losing your beloved father has been as difficult on you as it was on me. Each day brings its challenges, but I'm certain you feel this more acutely, looking out at the waters he once sailed himself.

I have decided you should have your father's most prized possession. I think it will steer you in the right direction when you are lost. Not like the compass you hold so dearly shows you the navigational routes of the McAfee.

Sometimes the best way to find a path when we are lost is to listen to our hearts. I have enclosed your father's captain's hat. When you forget your way, forget who you are or why you have taken this path, look at your father's hat. It will remind you of who you are.

The sea was your father's heart and soul. I suspect it will be yours too.

May your father's captain's hat house your soul on the days you need shelter, and on the days you don't, I hope it reminds you of your purpose. We all need a reminder of why we serve, and this one will be yours, son.

With All My Love,

Your Mum

The hat, Sophia thought, jerking her head up to the empty display case.

Houses his soul, Lunis said, having seen everything Sophia had inside the ship. *Just like Mama Jamba said.*

Yeah, she wondered. *That can't be an accident. Quiet's mum had said the hat would house his soul when he needed shelter. That is what I need to give Quiet to remind him of who he is and why he can't give up. If I can give him back his father's captain's hat, I'm certain he will give me his real name.*

Her eyes rested on the empty velvet next to Quiet's desk as Lunis echoed her thoughts.

Now we just have to find out where that hat is and get it back.

CHAPTER SIXTY-THREE

Sophia had more of a pep in her step as she strode into the Castle that evening. A strange aroma that smelled of an odd combination of spices and burned meat hit her nose when she entered the dining hall. Mahkah, who was already seated at the table, seemed to share the skeptical feeling she was having about that night's dinner.

She offered him a tamed smile. "If nothing else, I think I have a stash of protein bars in my room. I will share them with you."

He nodded appreciatively. "Thank you."

"Oh, good," Hiker said, stomping into the dining area. "This place looks a little more normal."

Mama Jamba had fixed quite a bit of the dining area, making it a bit more pleasant than before. Sophia hoped that Mama had taken pity on her and fixed her bed, which wasn't usable in its current form with the canopy having broken down onto the mattress.

"What have you all learned during your investigations?" Hiker asked, taking his normal seat, but testing the chair before putting his full weight into it. When he was certain it wasn't going to break, he relaxed and let out a breath.

"The Saverus organization was shut down by one of its own

subjects," Mahkah started. "I will need more time to research things, but we are definitely on the right track."

Hiker nodded appreciatively to Mahkah as Ainsley walked past the dining hall for the front door.

"And Sophia, what have you—"

The leader of the Dragon Elite paused when the housekeeper turned and ambled the other way again, appearing lost.

"Ainsley," Hiker called.

The elf poked her head around the corner, a perplexed expression on her face. "Who?" she asked.

"Ainsley," he repeated, enunciating her name.

She glanced over her shoulder. "There is no one else out here but me, sir."

"I'm talking to you," he said sternly.

Her mouth popped open. "Oh, I'm Ainsley. That makes sense. I thought I was an Angela or an Ansel, but Ainsley sounds right."

Sophia looked at Hiker. The poor housekeeper was really losing it if she was having trouble remembering her name.

"Sorry to interrupt you all," Ainsley began, curtseying in the doorway. "I'm looking for, well, I'm not sure actually. My stomach has been making weird noises, and I'm certain that means something."

Hiker sighed. "Yes, you are hungry."

"Oh, then I should eat!" Ainsley said, her face brightening.

"Yes, you should," Hiker responded.

"Very well then," Ainsley sang, working her arms back and forth like she was running but staying stuck in place. "That is what I will do."

"Good idea," he remarked as Mama Jamba came into the dining hall, stepping around Ainsley.

"Why are you just standing there?" Hiker asked Ainsley, who was eyeing the back of Mama Jamba's head like she was an alien.

"I don't know where else to stand," Ainsley answered.

Irritation flared on the Viking's face. "You shouldn't stand at all. We sit when we eat."

"Okay," she chirped.

"So, take a seat," Hiker ordered.

"Okay," Ainsley repeated. The housekeeper sat on the floor.

Hiker covered his brow with his hand and shook his head. "No, Ainsley, at the table."

"Oh, right," she said, hurrying to push herself up from the floor. She took a seat at the far end of the table, opposite of the others, roughly twenty seats down.

Hiker rolled his eyes, dropping his chin. "With the rest of us."

"Oh," Ainsley said, sliding out of her seat. She paused before pulling out the chair next to Mama Jamba.

"What is it?" Sophia asked her, reading the sudden tension on her face.

Ainsley cupped her hand to the side of her mouth and whispered loudly. "That is Mother Nature, isn't it?"

Sophia nodded. "Yes, and she is very nice, and you two are friends."

The housekeeper's eyes widened as she mouthed the word "friends."

"Go on there, dear," Mama Jamba encouraged, sliding her napkin into her lap just as Evan entered from the kitchen carrying a platter of roasted lamb chops. Sophia knew what it was supposed to be, but when he proudly laid it on the surface of the table, it was unclear what the hunks of meat were.

"What is that?" Hiker asked, tucking his own napkin into the collar of his shirt.

"Lamb chops!" Evan exclaimed excitedly.

"What was wrong with those lambs?" Hiker demanded.

The smile on Evan's face dropped. "I tried my best, sir. A little appreciation would go a long way." He turned and stormed back in the direction of the kitchen.

"Oh, that is right!" Ainsley yelled, throwing a single finger in the air. "I remember where I am. It's coming back now."

Mama Jamba patted the housekeeper on the shoulder. "I knew it would, dear. It always takes a bit after napping, but you will feel back to normal by dessert."

"There will be dessert?" Hiker didn't sound excited.

"Not if you don't finish all your vegetables," Evan said, buzzing through the swinging door in true Ainsley style. He was carrying a couple of steaming bowls and laid them down in front of Sophia and Mahkah.

The two exchanged tamed expressions of reluctance. Sophia knew what was supposed to be in the bowls, and yet, there was no reason the potatoes should be a bubbling purple paste or the roasted carrots should be moving around like little bugs in an aquarium.

"About your offer," Mahkah whispered at Sophia's shoulder.

She nodded, grateful she had stashed the protein bars for just such an occasion.

With a polite smile, Mama Jamba used a fork to poke one of the lamb chops. It jumped away from her fork, appearing hurt. "Dear Evan, did you by chance use magic to make this meal?"

He crossed his arms in front of his chest, nodding proudly. "Why, yes. Eat up. And if you want seconds, there is a lot more where this came from."

"I don't think that will be necessary," Hiker choked.

"The thing about cooking with magic is the same with any skill," Ainsley lectured, sounding more coherent than before. "You can't do something with magic if you don't know how to do it otherwise. At least you can't do it well."

"Oh," Evan said, his smile fading. "Well, I don't know how to cook real well, but I'm certain this is pretty good anyway."

Hiker pushed away from the table, shaking his head. "I refuse to eat this. Would you fetch the bread?"

Everyone sat and waited.

After a moment, Hiker gave Evan a pointed expression.

The dragonrider pressed his hand to his chest, surprise on his face. "Oh, you mean, me, sir?"

"Of course, I mean you," Hiker roared, his temper flaring.

Evan hurried back to the kitchen, throwing his hands up in the air. "A thank you wouldn't kill you," he grumbled under his breath.

Mama Jamba peered across the table at Sophia. "And so?"

The question hung in the air, catching Hiker's attention.

Sophia smiled. "I found the house..."

Mama Jamba beamed. "Very good. You think you know where to find it?"

Sophia nodded. "I think I know who can tell me where to find it."

Mother Nature's eyes darted to Sophia's hands resting on the table. "Yes, and the timing is perfect. Your nails look like they could use some polish."

"What are you two going on about?" Hiker asked, lack of food making him grumpier than usual.

"Well," Mama Jamba began. "As you know, Sophia is on a mission to fix Quiet. I think she is on the right track. Just a few side trips, and I'm certain she will have the gnome back to his old self."

"Good," Hiker grumbled. "I'm tired of having half my staff missing or incompetent."

Sophia looked around the table and realized Wilder was gone too, obviously on his secret side quest assigned by Subner. It felt weird to be there without him. She had gotten used to him being beside her at most meals.

Evan pushed through the kitchen door carrying a basket of rolls he tried to pass off as bread. When he laid them on the table, Ainsley pushed back in her chair and doubled over with laughter.

Hiker didn't at all appear amused. "What is that?"

"The bread you requested, sir," Evan said dryly, narrowing his eyes at the housekeeper, who was still laughing uncontrollably.

"Why is it burned?" Hiker asked, eyeing the nearly black rolls.

"It's fine," Evan said, picking up one of the rolls along with a knife. "You just scrape off the outside."

Hiker shook his head. "Would you get that out of here. Bring us...I don't know, anything edible."

"'Would You,'" Ainsley said, still laughing. "Someone has inherited my old name! Would You!"

Evan shook his head and grabbed the basket of burned bread. "I slave away for you lot, and this is the thanks I get. You know I don't have to put up with this treatment—"

"Yes, you do," Hiker interrupted.

Evan waved the basket of burned bread around. "I will have you know I'm a dragonrider. There is a good reason I don't know how to do any of this stuff."

"We must all learn to adapt," Hiker commented dryly, looking around the table for something to eat. The only thing remotely close was the centerpiece of flowers, and Sophia wasn't sure they weren't poisonous, which was probably still better than the food Evan had served.

Ainsley continued to laugh as Mama Jamba pushed up from the table. "Well, you know, a little fasting is really good every now and then." She stood and gave Hiker a pointed expression. "But I would like pancakes, so if you would do as I requested, Hiker, that would be for the best."

He sneered, obviously not happy about whatever she was referring to. "I just don't think—"

"What?" Mama Jamba interrupted. "Are you worried about someone breaking into the Gullington then?"

He tightened his fist on the table. "Mama we did discuss this and—"

"And I told you, as the one who is keeping the security up at the Gullington for the time being, that it will be fine," Mama Jamba cut in.

Hiker growled. "But what if they—"

"Steal all your secrets?" she asked, interrupting again. "What if they help you and keep me from starving?"

He sighed. "You are a timeless being who can't be killed."

"That doesn't mean I like going without my chocolate chip pancakes," she fired back. "Now, I'm going to retire for an early night, but I look forward to a full breakfast tomorrow." She turned for the exit. "You know what to do, Hiker, my dear."

He yanked his napkin out of his collar and threw it on the table.

Sophia expected him to also get up from the table and storm off, so she was surprised when he looked at her and said, "I'm going to ask you to do something I never thought I would."

She tilted her head to the side, nervous and intrigued. "Yes, sir?"

He cleared his throat. "I need you to ask your friends at the House of Fourteen for help."

CHAPTER SIXTY-FOUR

Sophia couldn't believe what Hiker had asked her to do as she made her way to the area outside the Barrier. It was not something in a million years she expected to hear from the leader of the Dragon Elite.

Hiker Wallace was asking for help.

From outsiders.

Things had really changed.

It just went to show circumstances affected everything. Hunger affected people's resolve, and when things got difficult, the strong were only as powerful as those they could call on for help. Thanks to Sophia, the Dragon Elite had a few new allies.

She had texted her sister Liv, sending the full request to her. Sophia half expected Liv to call her right away and ask if Hiker had lost his mind or been killed and impersonated by aliens.

Instead, Liv, who had seen many changes through tragedy and hardship, herself included, simply sent a message that read:

"I'm sorry the Dragon Elite has had it so rough. I will need a few hours to put everything into place. Meet me at the House at midnight."

Sophia sent a confirmation as she crossed the Barrier.

The timing was perfect. Sophia had enough time to go and see Mae Ling and return by midnight to the Gullington.

She halted, recognizing an immediate problem. The last time she had visited her fairy godmother, it had been at Happily Ever After, the college for fairy godmothers. Since she hadn't been accepted to the college, she couldn't portal directly to the school, and she had broken the wax seal Mae Ling had sent for her to use last time.

Sophia stared out at the rolling green hills and considered her options. She started to think about returning to the Gullington when something wafted down from the sky.

As quickly as she could, she yanked Inexorabilis from her sheath and brandished the sword, ready to slice whatever it was. Her eyes narrowed on the small red shape. It was a round balloon drifting down to the ground. Attached to it by a string was a small blue bag.

Sophia had been cautioned about grabbing objects sent to her unexpectedly, but something told her this time it was okay. She jumped into the air, gaining more height than any normal magician would have on a good day. Her fingers grabbed the plastic bag and pulled it down with the red balloon.

Excited and nervous, she untied the red balloon from the package and let it drift off into the sky. She pulled a note from the package and opened it first.

Dear Sophia Beaufont,

It's okay you released the balloon. It will pop and biodegrade within minutes.

Since you need a way to Happily Ever After, I have sent these macarons for you to use as portals. Simply take a bite, and it will transport you. I realize you are hungry, but only eat the one cookie since you will need the others for trips you take to see me. Don't worry, I will have food for you when you arrive.

See you soon.

Love,

Mae Ling.

Sophia pulled open the bag, relief filling her as she smelled the sweet scent of the cookies. A much-needed treat and a way to get to her fairy godmother. Of course, Mae Ling knew she needed to see her and had sent a way. Having a fairy godmother who anticipated her needs was the best.

Maybe things were looking up.

She pulled a single blue macaron from the bag and took a bite, entering the strange portal to Happily Ever After College, a place she was more than happy to return to and explore after her last visit.

CHAPTER SIXTY-FIVE

The Happily Ever After College was just as Sophia remembered, bright and colorful with the smell of baked goods and candy strong in the air. It was nighttime at fairy godmother school, wherever it was located.

The main building stood in the distance. The rainbow-striped runner started a few feet from where Sophia had portaled in and ran all the way up to the door. The windows of the building were all lit up, making her wonder if it was late evening, before bedtime.

The wind made the branches of the willow trees rattle and sent bits of pollen drifting on the breeze, looking like bits of cotton. Sophia reached out and ran her fingers through the long wispy branches, appreciating the fact she knew the woman these trees were named for, and she resided at this very school. Sophia liked the irony of her life lately and felt it was going to get even more so as she went on these adventures.

Sophia made for the pink front doors of Happily Ever After, enjoying how peaceful it felt on the grounds. Even the wind wasn't bothersome to her as it tangled her hair.

She found Mae Ling waiting patiently for her when she entered the building. To Sophia's surprise, the school didn't appear to be winding down for the day. Women in their rainbow pleated skirts and pink blouses hustled down the long hallway, chatting excitedly. Many of them gave Sophia curious glances when she met her fairy godmother at the front of the school.

"Wow, you all have night classes?" Sophia asked, noticing most of the students were carrying their books and supplies with them as they moved through the hallway.

Mae Ling kept her eyes on Sophia as she shook her head. "We have classes at all hours of the day."

"Oh, really?" Sophia asked with surprise. The smell of chocolate made her stomach rumble. The cookie had barely tided her over.

"Well, fairy godmothers don't sleep, my dear," Mae Ling explained.

"They don't?" Sophia questioned, not having expected that. Even Mama Jamba slept. Actually, the woman was very strict about getting her beauty rest.

"Heavens no," Mae Ling replied. "You wouldn't want a fairy godmother who slept on the job, would you?"

Sophia considered this. "No, I guess not."

Mae Ling held out her arm and directed Sophia to the back of the hallway. She followed, again studying all the interesting classrooms as she walked. Each was like a different artist paradise. There were different classrooms than before—one for making jewelry, the gemstones scattered on the workstations dazzling.

There was one for candle making, the scents spilling from the room competing with the smell of sweets in the air. The last one they passed before turning into an office was a nursery, with green plants monopolizing the space. Sophia caught sight of several exotic plants she had never seen before.

"Please make yourself comfortable," Mae Ling said, holding out a hand to Sophia and presenting a chair on one side of a desk.

The chair was something Sophia would need to duplicate at some point. It was a large pink armchair with a high back that arched overhead, creating a small roof over the person seated in it. The tufted buttons that decorated the thing were brass, and the arms were round spirals. It was more of an art piece than a place to sit.

Sophia took a quick moment to explore the room and then slipped into the chair, enjoying its soft comfort immediately.

Mae Ling strode to the other side of the desk, which was neat and clean of papers. Only a MacBook sat in the center. The desk was like the rainbow-striped runner that ran down the hallway in front of the college, a menagerie of colors—each of the drawers a different bright hue of pink, pastel green, pale blue, sunshine yellow, and robust orange.

On top of the desk were whimsical images of stick figures and various shapes of hearts and suns. Also written in places were quotes like, "Life is Short" or "It's All About You" or "Be Who You Will" or "Ain't Life Great."

Behind the desk sat a chair identical to the one Sophia was sitting in.

Like the outside of the college and hallway, the office had an interesting dichotomy to it. Whereas the desk was a splash of assorted colors and the chairs bright pink, the walls were plain brick and the floors a neutral shade.

Mae Ling waved her hand at the desk, and a tray of tea and a tower of pastries and confections appeared in front of Sophia.

"Now, please eat up," Mae Ling said, taking a seat. "You have to be back in just a few minutes."

Sophia glanced at her clock. "No, I'm good until midnight."

Mae Ling smiled discreetly. "Someone will show up early from the House of Fourteen. They aren't the best with time."

"Oh, who?" Sophia asked, going through the list of people she had requested Liv to bring. They all were responsible adults she thought had fantastic time management, but Mae Ling was never wrong.

Sophia grabbed a chocolate éclair on the top rack of the assortment of foods. The glaze was so perfectly arranged, the pastry looked more like a work of art than a sweet treat.

Mae Ling clasped her hands on her desk and gave Sophia a calm expression. "Okay, so go ahead and ask your question of me."

This was the way it worked, Sophia had learned. Even if Mae Ling already knew what Sophia was going to ask her and even if she already knew the answer, it was Sophia's job to first ask the question. That was part of the magic.

"I need to find the captain's hat that belonged to Quiet's father," she said in between bites. "Can you tell me where to find it?"

Mae Ling shook her head. "No, but I can tell you who knows where it is."

Sophia nodded, having expected it wouldn't be so easy. She finished the chocolate éclair, pretty much inhaling the pastry.

Mae Ling held up her finger, twirling it, and the teapot rose to pour Sophia a cup.

"You will want to text your sister and ask her to bring King Rudolf Sweetwater with her tonight," Mae Ling instructed, resting her hands on the surface of the desk once more.

Sophia stopped chewing the brownie she had just taken a bite of, her face frozen. "Why?"

Mae Ling smiled slightly. "Because he knows where the hat is, of course."

With an annoyed sigh, Sophia finished chewing. She took a sip of the tea and found it the perfect temperature. "Of course, King Rudolf is involved in this."

"Naturally," Mae Ling said simply.

Doing as she was told, Sophia pulled out her phone and sent a quick message to her sister to give her enough time to coordinate things.

Almost immediately, Liv messaged back. "Are you sure? Ru? Are you mad at Hiker and looking for a good way to punish him?"

Sophia giggled at her phone. "I just need his help with something. Will you tell him to come through the portal with you?"

Liv shot back a confirmation: "I will tell him now. We are having nachos. I warn you, he won't be alone."

Sophia's brow scrunched up. "I wonder what that means?"

Mae Ling appeared amused when Sophia glanced up at her. "It means you will need this." She twirled her hand once more, and a small velvet pouch appeared on the center of the desk.

Sophia gave her a skeptical expression. "What's in that?"

"You will find out when you know exactly when to use it," Mae Ling told her mysteriously.

Cautiously, Sophia grabbed the sack only to find it strangely heavy for its size.

"Okay, well, I guess that is all then," Sophia said, grabbing a truffle and popping it into her mouth.

"Not quite, my dear." Mae Ling tilted her head to the side.

Sophia again stopped chewing mid-bite. "I can't think of anything else I need your help with. Well, unless you want to tell me how to fix the Gullington or how to catch a cyborg pirate. I will take that information."

Mae Ling smiled good-naturedly. "I'm afraid a fairy godmother can only help with so much. What I want to talk to you about is more of a personal nature."

Sophia pulled her mouth to the side, not having expected this. "Personal. Like my personal life or yours?"

This seemed to amuse the woman. "Yours, of course, my dear. I'm afraid I don't have much of a personal life. When is there time for such things?"

Sophia nodded, relating. "Well, same here. I'm a dragonrider, after all."

"You are also a young woman with your own thoughts and feelings," Mae Ling corrected. "Now, for a change, I have a question for you."

Sophia didn't respond as she waited for her fairy godmother to continue.

"Do you remember the story of Cinderella?" Mae Ling asked her.

It was such an unexpected question Sophia was momentarily speechless. "Yeah, of course."

After reflecting, it made sense her fairy godmother would reference this story, although it was still strange when she was used to discussing worldly affairs with the wise woman.

"Now, you are aware you are the reason the winds are restless lately?" It was more of a statement from Mae Ling than anything else.

Sophia tensed. This wasn't a topic she wanted to discuss right then, maybe ever. She hadn't figured out what tumultuous emotions she had rolling around inside of her she was ignoring, although Lunis liked to insinuate she was in denial.

"Yes, Mama Jamba mentioned it," Sophia admitted.

Mae Ling nodded. "Of course, she did."

"Are you going to tell me about these internal feelings?" Sophia asked, relieved and hopeful she would get advice from her fairy godmother on the subject.

To her disappointment, Mae Ling shook her head. "I'm afraid that is not my job, dear. Did Cinderella's fairy godmother tell her how she should feel about Prince Charming or console her on the situation?"

Sophia thought for a moment before saying, "Yeah, I guess not."

"A fairy godmother's job is to prepare their children for what is to come, not to tell them how to deal with it," Mae Ling explained.

"Is this when you stick me in a big dress with glass slippers," Sophia joked.

Mae Ling didn't laugh. "Not today, my dear. But I do plan on helping you prepare in other ways."

Suddenly, Sophia wasn't as hungry. She ran her eyes over the pastries, wishing she could stuff them all in her mouth.

"What most don't get about the story of Cinderella," Mae Ling continued, "is that her curfew was self-imposed. She could have stayed at the ball past midnight."

"But then the prince would have seen her for who she was," Sophia argued at once, for some reason feeling a strong conviction for the story.

Mae Ling flashed her a knowing smile. "That is exactly right. He would have, and what would have happened?"

Sophia considered. "Well, he would have loved her just the same. It was never the dress or the shoes that made him want her. It was who she was deep inside. It was because she was a good person and he saw that. She lit up the room even without the clothes."

Mocking offense, Mae Ling clasped her hands to her chest. "Now, that makes the fairy godmother of this story sound unnecessary."

Sophia, knowing Mae Ling was messing with her, just smiled.

"Of course, the fairy godmother's job was to give Cinderella confidence," Mae Ling went on. "But at the end of the night, she ran because she didn't want to be found. She was afraid of being loved and not just that, she was afraid of being loved for who she was."

Sophia opened her mouth, and the words spilled out. "Because she didn't think anyone could love her because she was different and poor and—"

"Yes, yes," Mae Ling cut in. "Her circumstances made her think she wouldn't be right for the prince. She thought they were incompatible. And yet, even as she ran, she left behind a shoe, because if we are honest, Cinderella in her heart, wanted to be found."

Sophia was more confused than when they started the conversation.

"You see, my dear, sometimes we feel certain ways and think we'd rather avoid certain things," Mae Ling continued. "But we leave behind glass slippers because the heart wants what the heart wants regardless of whether the mind says it will work or is right for us."

Letting out a weighty breath, Sophia looked at her fairy godmother. "I don't understand."

Mae Ling bobbed her head, a knowing look on her face. "And that is why we are having this conversation. You know you are conflicted about something because your mind says it doesn't make sense. That it won't work, but the heart, well, will it leave behind a glass slipper?"

"This is how I make the wind calm down?" Sophia asked.

The woman smiled, standing up from her desk. "The winds are never still, especially for a person like you. But yes, when you deal with this, the breeze will be gentle once more, for a time anyway."

She glanced at the clock on the wall and nodded. "Now, you will want to hurry back to the Castle. Rudolf will be waiting for you."

"Oh," Sophia said. "He is the one who doesn't do well with time. That makes more sense."

Mae Ling ushered her to the door. "All things make sense in hindsight. The key is to try and make them make sense before then."

CHAPTER SIXTY-SIX

The wind that hit Sophia in the face when she stepped through the Barrier into the Gullington was sort of an insult after her conversation with Mae Ling. She didn't have time to think through all that and to feel her way through things right then.

What Mae Ling had said did make sense. The mind put obstacles in place the heart was happy to leap over. The heart often got people into trouble when they ignored their rational side. At some point, Sophia was going to have to figure out things and decide whether she would run from the ball and if she did, would she leave behind the glass slipper?

For the time being, she had a series of meetings to attend and a lot of changes coming to the Gullington. She glanced at her watch and wondered why King Rudolf was going to be early.

As she hurried up to the Castle, she mused at how strange it was going to be to have people who were not Dragon Elite or those who served them in the Gullington. This was a first, except for when a bunch of cyborg pirates broke into the place and stole one of their dragon eggs.

Mama Jamba, who had put the Barrier back up and was maintaining the security field for the Gullington, had made it so the visitors from the House of Fourteen's portal could come through. Otherwise, the portal would have worked the same way it always had. Those in the Castle could pass to the other places like the House of Fourteen or the Great Library, but the outsiders from those places couldn't come into the Gullington.

For the first time ever, members from the House would enter the Castle. Things were really changing. Hiker Wallace was using technology and asking for help from outsiders.

Sophia froze after rounding the corner at the top of the stairs. It appeared the first outsider was already in the Castle. Never would Sophia have expected it to be King Rudolf Sweetwater and his triplets.

"She is like yay high," Rudolf was saying to Ainsley, holding his hand down by his waist. "And she loves horsey rides on my knee and thinks I'm the smartest person she has ever met. I'm like her uncle, you see."

The housekeeper scratched her head. "You will have to excuse me. I have recently fallen ill, but the description of the person you just gave me doesn't ring any bells."

Rudolf, who had one baby strapped in a carrier to his chest and another on his back in between his large wings and the third in a stroller in front of him, waved his hands in front of him. "Okay, let's try another approach. How about you describe the people who live in this Disney castle, and I will tell you if one of them is Sophia."

"Sophia..." Ainsley said, musing on the name. "Yeah, we don't have anyone by that name here. There is Evan, the bane of my existence, and who has apparently grown a tolerance to the poison I lace his food with."

Rudolf shook his head. "That doesn't sound like her because she would probably die from too much poison."

Sophia rolled her eyes but stayed hidden at the far end of the hallway, too entertained by this strange exchange to interrupt it. She had never considered a reality where these two laffy taffies met and had a conversation.

"Okay, and there is Wilder," Ainsley went on. "He has got great hair, piercing blue eyes, and a sharp wit, but he is also totally full of himself and has smelly feet."

"Hm," Rudolf said, combing his hands over his chin. "That description almost fits, but I wouldn't say Soph is overly confident. I mean, there was this one time I wanted to accompany her to this social affair, and she was like, 'No, Rudolf, I'm too embarrassed to be seen with you.'" He laughed. "I mean, poor girl. She has such low confidence she thought she had embarrassed me in front of a bunch of highbrow magicians."

Ainsley nodded. "Okay, well, we have Mahkah, who is Native American and a few hundred years old. He has got long black hair and hardly ever talks."

"What color are his eyes?" Rudolf asked quite seriously.

"Brown."

He shook his head. "No, that is not her."

"Oh, well, the only other dragonrider here at the Gullington is S. Beaufont," Ainsley stated. "She is petite with blonde hair, blue eyes, and quite the sassy disposition. When she sleeps at night, she mumbles the name—"

"I'm here!" Sophia called suddenly, interrupting and hurrying down the hallway.

"Oh, there you are," Rudolf said, his face brightening at the sight of her.

He glanced back at Ainsley and bowed slightly. "Thanks for your help, but I have found her. That S. Beaufont sounded close to my Sophia, though. I will have to meet her at some point."

Ainsley smiled at Sophia. "I'm off to bed. Will you make sure your friend finds a place to put his pets?" She pointed to the babies strapped to the fae and the carriage.

Sophia opened her mouth to correct the shapeshifter but decided against it. Instead, she simply nodded. "Get some rest, Ains."

The housekeeper turned like Sophia was talking to someone else. Then she shrugged. "Sure. But I don't know why you call me that."

Sophia sighed. It was obviously too much to ask for the people she spoke with to be normal or have their wits about them.

"Hey, Rudolf," Sophia greeted him in a low voice, noticing the three babies were all asleep.

"Hey there, Soph!" he exclaimed and wrapped her in a tight hug, pressing one of the babies into her.

She shook her head as she pulled away. "You are early."

"Well, when Liv said you were desperately seeking my counsel, I decided to come right away." He indicated the babies. "I thought it would be good to come while the Captains were asleep. I never know how long it will last."

"Right," Sophia agreed, appreciating how peaceful the children were.

She didn't have long to admire them because they were interrupted by thundering footsteps. Sophia turned to find Hiker Wallace marching in their direction.

"Who is this?" he shouted down the hallway, not just waking the baby in the carriage but also all the dead in the graveyard on the Gullington.

He stopped in front of them and looked Rudolf up and down. "I don't remember asking you to invite a fae into the Castle. The exception was given to—"

"I know," Sophia interrupted. "I asked King Sweetwater to come along with my sister because I need his help on something related to helping Quiet."

"Then where is your sister?" Hiker asked, looking around like Liv might be hiding behind the statue of the suit of armor.

"Oh, she has indigestion from the nachos and had to stop off to get antacids," Rudolf explained. "She will be here shortly because let's be honest. Wherever Liv is, she will be short, just like little Sophia. In the meantime, could I get a vodka soda?"

Hiker stared at the king of the fae with wide eyes.

"Right," Sophia said and stepped between the two men. She thought Hiker might punch Rudolf in the face even if he was wearing two infants. "Actually, Rudolf, this is Hiker Wallace, the leader of the Dragon Elite."

Rudolf gave her an uncertain look like she was playing a joke on him. He pointed at the tall Viking. "This man? Are you sure?"

Sophia nodded and wondered if Hiker would punch her first just to get to Rudolf.

"He is not the butler for this little place?" Rudolf asked.

"We don't have a butler," Hiker said, a low growl in his voice.

"Oh, well, that is too bad," Rudolf consoled. "How very quaint this place is. How did you get it to look so old? It almost looks as real as the Excalibur hotel and casino in Las Vegas."

"It is old," Hiker snarled through clenched teeth.

"Yeah, so is my Excalibur hotel. The fae had it built about thirty years ago if you can believe it. I think it's time it gets a makeover. I would love the name of your contractor."

Hiker's face turned bright red. "This Castle is over one-thousand years old."

"Oh, well, then it's definitely in need of a makeover." Rudolf whistled. "I can give you the name of my guy. He is a bit pricey, and I think he has a gambling addiction, but who doesn't?"

Hiker put his attention firmly on Sophia. "Don't make me regret allowing your people into the Castle."

Right on cue, all three babies started wailing, their cries echoing through the corridor.

Hiker clapped his hands to his ear. "What is that?"

Rudolf looked around, searching for the noise. "I'm not sure, Walker. What are you referring to?"

"I think he is talking about the Captains crying," Sophia explained. "Are they hungry?"

Rudolf thought for a moment. "Oh, probably not. I just fed them." He leaned in and whispered loudly in Sophia's ear. "I think it's his beard. They don't like facial hair."

Hiker pivoted, giving Sophia a murderous glare. "Let's hope your other friends don't make me want to kill them. If they do, you are burying the bodies."

"Copy that, sir," Sophia said, watching the leader of the Dragon Elite stomp back in the direction of his office.

The babies were whining so loudly it made Sophia squint. "Do you need help?"

"With what?" Rudolf asked, looking around.

"With the Captains."

"Oh, well, Captain Morgan doesn't like to be touched, so don't pick her up." He pointed to the baby in the carriage. "Captain Kirk can't stand puns, so don't say any around her. She really can't stand Liv even if she is her godmother." He pointed to the baby on his back. "And here is Captain Silver. She doesn't like to be looked at directly, hence the reason she is on my back."

"Well, besides their dislikes, is there something they do enjoy that will calm them?" Sophia queried over the incessant noise.

Rudolf thought for a moment. "They like the Kardashians. Where's the television?"

Sophia shook her head. "This shouldn't take long. I have a question."

"You what?" Rudolf yelled, having trouble hearing her over the three babies' cries.

"I wanted to know if—"

"What is a whadatif?" Rudolf hollered to be heard over the noise.

Sophia shook her head. "No, I'm trying to ask you if—"

"You are going to have to speak up!"

Mama Jamba stormed out of her room, giving them a dirty look as she approached. The babies all silenced immediately.

"Oh, Mama Jamba, your presence makes the babies quiet," Sophia said with relief.

She shook her head. "No, it makes them scared for their lives. I was trying to take a nap, you know."

"I didn't know," Rudolf introduced himself, smiling wide, his blue eyes twinkling. He held out a hand to her. "I'm King Rudolf Sweetwater, ruler of the fae."

"I'm Mother Nature, creator of this planet," Mama Jamba replied, not taking his hand.

Rudolf elbowed Sophia in the side. "Some people just have to one-up others."

"Mama Jamba," Sophia begged, ignoring Rudolf. "I need you to stay right here while I chat with the king. Can you do that?"

Mama Jamba shook her head. "I'm afraid I can't. I need to wash my hair. It's Thursday."

As the old woman began to walk off, the babies started to whine again.

"But Mama Jamba," Sophia called to her retreating back. "Can you just give us a minute. Maybe hold one of the babies."

Sharply, Mama Jamba turned. "I don't hold babies, dear."

"But you are Mother Nature," Sophia argued.

"Exactly!" Mama Jamba agreed, turning and striding off.

Sophia sighed and grimaced as the babies all cried in different octaves.

"She seems like a lot of fun," Rudolf commented, not bothered by the constant noise. "A bit of a showoff, but I respect that. Now you had a question for me."

"Yeah," Sophia began. "I was hoping you could—"

"Can you speak up?" Rudolf yelled, bouncing up and down and patting Captain Kirk's back.

Feeling rather irritated and ready to kick the fae out of the Castle, Sophia opened her mouth to try again, but then she remembered. Mae Ling had given her a pouch earlier. She dug into her cloak and pulled out the mysterious sack.

She pulled open the drawstrings and yanked out three small pacifiers and a note.

It read:

For little ones whose father is too dimwitted to shush his face so they can sleep peacefully. Give them these, and they will be fast asleep no matter the interruption.

"Brilliant," Sophia said, sticking the note back in the bag before Rudolf could read it.

She popped the pacifiers into each of the children's mouths, and they silenced immediately.

Breathing out a sigh of relief, Sophia allowed herself to enjoy the peace and quiet for a moment before looking at Rudolf.

"Okay," she said, drawing out the word, worried the babies might start back up any moment. "I have a question for you."

"Forty-two," Rudolf said at once.

"No," Sophia barked, her tolerance for his antics dangerously low. "I am looking for something, and I'm not sure why, but I heard you would know where it is."

Rudolf nodded like he knew what she was talking about. "Yeah. The fountain of youth. Your sister destroyed it because she is a real killjoy."

The portal in the closet connected to the House of Fourteen opened, and Warrior Liv Beaufont stepped into the Castle.

She crossed her arms, glaring at Rudolf. "What did you call me? And who is taking care of your babies when I kill you?"

CHAPTER SIXTY-SEVEN

"Well, you naturally," Rudolf exclaimed at the sight of Liv. "You are their godmother. When I die, you will have them."

Liv shook her head at Rudolf. "You have figured out the perfect way to keep me from murdering you. Well played, Ru."

Sophia hugged her sister, having her there so surreal. In the Castle! The one place she had wanted to share with her family. She never thought this moment would come, and here it was.

Liv's eyes widened as she lifted her chin, staring around in awe as she took in the corridor. "This place is amazing. Clark is going to love it. He'll be through shortly."

"Oh!" Sophia said. "Then I only have a bit to ask my question of Rudolf."

"Yeah, this should be good," Liv said, tapping her foot and looking between Sophia and Rudolf. "You need to learn how to get gum out of your hair or a marble out of your nose? Rudolf has learned the answer to both of those questions, and he doesn't even have toddlers yet, so you can guess who he was practicing on."

Rudolf's eyes slid to the side, embarrassed. "The peanut butter made my hair shiny."

Sophia cleared her throat. "Okay, I will make this fast. I need to know where a hat is, and I heard you know, Ru. It belonged to a male gnome who was captain of a ship. I don't know what his name was, and I don't know what his son's name was either…"

Sophia suddenly felt very shortsighted. She had questions but didn't know the most important details to give to obtain the answers. How was she going to get Rudolf to help her if she didn't even know what Quiet or his father's name was? There had to be tons of gnomes who were captains of sailing ships.

"Um…" Sophia stuttered and caught the concerned look in Liv's eyes. "It's a hat that…ugh. Why don't I know his name?"

"Paul, George, Frank," Rudolf said, listing off different names.

"No, it's a gnome's name," Sophia stated.

"Gillian, Ramy, George," Rudolf offered.

"No, that is the thing," Sophia began. "I don't know what his name is. I don't even know what his son's name is, which is what I'm trying to figure out."

Rudolf rubbed his fingers over his stubbled chin, a speculative look in his eyes. "You don't know a name but need to learn it. I think we can narrow this down. How about Graham, Dale, or George?"

Liv shook her head at the fae before offering Sophia a sympathetic expression. "What else can you tell us about this captain?"

"Well, I'm specifically looking for this captain's hat," Sophia explained. "His son sailed a ship called the *McAfee* and apparently, according to the Queen Mother of the fae—"

"OH, DEAR!" Rudolf yelled, his voice echoing loudly in the Castle.

Thankfully, he didn't wake the babies. The magical pacifiers Mae Ling had given Sophia were doing their job.

"What?" Sophia asked, her heart beating fast. "Do you know who I'm talking about?"

He nodded adamantly. "And I know the name of the gnome that sailed the *McAfee*."

"You do?" Sophia nearly jumped up and down. Things were finally coming together. She wouldn't even have to get the hat. Apparently, all she had to do was know about it and ask King Rudolf. Of course, the fae was the key to her learning Quiet's real name. "What is his name?"

Rudolf smiled wide. "It is Captain Quiet."

Sophia deflated at once.

Liv saw her disappointment and shook her head. "No, I don't think that is his real name."

"Really?" Rudolf questioned. "Are you sure? That is what the fae have always called him. He is legendary in our history."

"Because he rescued fae, saving your race," Sophia supplied.

Rudolf nodded. "Yeah, there was that. When his ship sailed my ancestors to safe lands, they were still considered very poor, which is pretty much worse than death. Fae don't do well when they don't have any money."

"Such simple people," Liv said, shaking her head.

"Anyway, word had spread about the gnome who sacrificed himself to save those on the *McAfee*," Rudolf continued. "Captain Quiet became a legend. Although the crew of his ship refused to change a thing about the *McAfee*, they did give Quiet's most prized possession to the leader of the fae at the time, Queen Visa."

Liv shook her head. "More like a witch than a queen, but whatever."

Queen Visa had been the ruler of the fae before Rudolf. He'd had to kill her to take the crown, but that wasn't why he did it. It had been more of an act of self-preservation since the evil queen was trying to kill him and Liv.

Rudolf gave Liv a commiserating expression. "Yeah, but she wasn't always horrible. Back then, Queen Visa was trying to help the fae prosper. She took the captain's hat, Quiet's most prized possession, as a gift from the crew and sold it. The money from that transaction became a pivotal moment in the fae's history. It was the money that started our empire, making us the wealthiest race of all. Since then, we've all looked down on the rest of you impoverished souls with pity while lavishing in our enormous riches."

Liv shook her head, glaring at Rudolf. "Soph, are you over-whelmed by his humility?"

"It's about to bowl me over," Sophia answered before returning her attention to Rudolf. "Are you saying you know where the captain's hat is?"

"Of course, I do," Rudolf exclaimed.

"Can you tell me?" Sophia asked.

"Of course, I can't," he answered.

Sophia lowered her chin, giving him a murderous expression. "Are you serious?"

"Soph, that is the most prized possession of the fae," Rudolf answered. "It's a secret of our race. If others knew, they might want to steal it."

"That is exactly what I want to do," Sophia told him.

He shook his head. "I can't allow you to steal Captain McAfee's hat."

Sophia sighed. "Quiet's father's name was McAfee. That is why he named his boat that."

Liv let out an irritated breath. "Ru, you are going to tell my sister where to get that hat, or I'm going to kill you and raise your children to believe the Earth is round."

A loud gasp fell out of his mouth. "You wouldn't?"

"I would," Liv fired back.

"But everyone knows it's flat," Rudolf argued.

"Impressionable young babies will believe whatever their godmother tells them," Liv warned.

Rudolf seemed to consider this for a moment before resigning. "Fine, I will help you, Sophia, but you can't keep the hat."

She nodded, hopeful once more. "That is fine. I just need to borrow it for a bit. Are you sure you know where it is located?"

Rudolf scoffed at her. "Captain Quiet and his father are legendary to me. I mean, why do you think I named my children after those gnomes?"

Sophia almost burst out with laughter. She hadn't seen that one coming, but it made perfect sense. "You named your girls Captain because Quiet sacrificed himself for your race? That is brilliant."

"Did you hear that, Liv?" Rudolf asked. "Your sister says I'm brilliant."

"I think she was saying the situation was brilliant," Liv argued. "Now, where is this captain's hat?"

"It's in the Fae's National Museum of History," Rudolf told them.

"I have never heard of it," Sophia said.

"You wouldn't have because you are not a fae," Rudolf explained.

"Obviously," Sophia remarked. "Where is it located? How do I get in there?"

"I can't tell you where it is," Rudolf answered. "And you can't get in there because you are not a fae."

Liv let out a long breath as she lowered her chin. "Ru, round Earth education..."

He rolled his eyes at her. "Okay, fine. I can't tell you where it's located though. I will betray my race a little bit but telling you where our National History Museum is would be going too far."

"Okay, but can you at least take me there?" Sophia asked.

"Fine," Rudolf agreed.

"And you will help her get in there too," Liv demanded.

"I don't know how to do that." Rudolf shook his head.

A single murderous glare from Liv was all it took.

"B-B-But I'm sure I can figure something out," Rudolf stammered.

"And you will help her steal the captain's hat," Liv ordered.

Looking quite defeated, Rudolf nodded. "Yeah, I will do all that, but only on one condition..." He batted his eyes at Liv.

"What?" she growled.

"I will need you to watch the Captains while I take your sister on this excursion," Rudolf answered.

Sophia could see the hesitation on Liv's face.

"I don't know," she began. "I have got a lot of cases, and there is that whole not wanting to be around babies thing. How about their mother takes care of them?"

Rudolf shook his head. "No, Serena needs twelve hours of sleep a day and says the Captains don't respect that. The only person I trust them with is you, Liv."

"Please," Sophia said, drawing out the word, her hands clasped together as she begged her sister.

Liv seemed to be wavering before she finally acquiesced. "Fine, only for you, though, Soph."

"Yes!" Sophia exclaimed, grateful to finally be making progress. All she had to do was go on a secret mission with the king of the fae and steal their most prized possession from a museum where she wasn't allowed. What could possibly go wrong?

CHAPTER SIXTY-EIGHT

Sophia and Rudolf didn't have a chance to continue their discussion about their covert mission to steal Captain McAfee's hat because they were interrupted by the portal door to the House of Fourteen opening.

"Clarky!" Sophia yelled when her older brother stepped through into the Castle.

She threw her arms around her brother, grateful to see him. It felt like it had been a long time, although it really hadn't. Sophia had just been through so much since the last time she had been around her sibling.

"Hey, Soph," he said, hugging her before pulling back, looking the Castle over with amazement. "This place is…"

"Falling apart," Sophia supplied when her brother trailed away. "I mean, you can't really tell right now because Mama Jamba has been repairing things, but when she stops protecting it and the Barrier comes back down, well, it will start to degrade again."

"That is why we are here," Liv offered, laying a consoling hand on her sister's shoulder.

Clark's eyes fluttered with annoyance. "Some of us have the illustrious job of protecting and strategizing with the Dragon Elite. And some of us have been recruited to cook."

Sophia couldn't help but giggle. "But that is the most important job of all. Our housekeeper is sort of crazier than usual, which is saying a lot. She can't cook, and the Castle can't help like it usually does. None of the rest of us can so much as boil water. Without you, Clark, we would surely starve, and then we'd really be in trouble."

"Okay, fine. I will be your chef in the interim."

"Thank you," Sophia gushed as the portal door opened again.

Rory Laurens ducked to enter through the doorway without hitting his head. He was carrying a crate of food and wore a curious expression. Behind him, Bermuda Laurens followed into the Castle, her eyes wide as she took in the sights around them. She didn't say a word to Sophia or the others when she entered. Instead, she began furiously writing in a book she held in her hands.

"Oh, this is too much," Bermuda said, scribbling away, her chin high as she took in the details on the high ceiling. She ran her hands over the wall, studying it with a keen eye. "The material isn't anything I have seen before. It appears to be a combination of—"

Sophia never learned what the combination of materials were that comprised the walls of the Castle because the thundering of Hiker Wallace's boots echoing down the corridor interrupted everything. All eyes turned to take in the hulking Viking, who wasn't dwarfed by the two giants standing nearby.

Sophia was about to make introductions, but before she could, Hiker plucked the book from Bermuda's hand, yanking it up to read what she had just written.

A sound of surprise spilled from the giantess's mouth, but Hiker took no notice as he shut the book with a snap. "There will be no notes taken about the Castle, the Gullington, or the Dragon Elite."

Bermuda bowed slightly, showing respect to Hiker Wallace that Sophia had never seen the stern woman show to anyone. The giantess didn't bow to others. Usually, she only cast disapproving glares. "I understand your need to keep your secrets. But you must know the world wants to know—"

"I don't care what the world wants to know," Hiker interrupted. "If you so much as breathe a single detail to the outside world about my Castle, that will be your last one on this Earth."

There was no one Sophia could think of who could silence the giantess like Hiker Wallace had just done. Bermuda looked like she had just eaten a particularly chewy peanut butter sandwich, her jaw locked as her eyes bulged.

Hiker grabbed both ends of the book and quite easily ripped it in two. If Wilder had been there right then, he would be happy to see their leader using more of his strength. That had to be a part of the power he inherited from his twin brother, Thad Reinhart. It appeared Hiker simply needed to be motivated to embrace it.

"Sir," Sophia began. "You have already met my sister, Liv Beaufont."

Hiker didn't appear happy to see the warrior for the House of Fourteen again. He barely glanced in Liv's direction. They had gotten off to a bad start when the leader of the Dragon Elite trespassed into Liv's apartment a while back, demanding information on a new rider. According to Liv, Hiker kept going on about this man he suspected had magnetized to a dragon egg. Sophia's sister didn't feel the need to give up any information since she didn't know of any "man" who had done such a thing.

"And this is my brother, Clark," Sophia said, presenting the councilor for the House of Fourteen.

"You can cook?" Hiker asked, his voice strict.

"Absolutely. And an honor to make your acquaintance." Clark offered a hand, but when Hiker didn't take it, he stepped back awkwardly.

"Rory and Bermuda Laurens have offered to help with securing the Barrier and shielding the Gullington when Mama Jamba's security comes down," Sophia explained.

"Can you do it?" Hiker demanded, glaring up at the giants.

"Well, we were able to shield the Dragon Elite from seeing Lunis and Sophia before they were ready to join you," Bermuda told him.

Hiker's eyes widened with alarm as he rotated to face Sophia. "What is this?"

Sophia's gaze darted to the side. "Oh, about that..."

Bermuda shook her head. "You never told Hiker about that?"

"I was going to," Sophia remarked.

"When?" Hiker insisted.

"Things have just been so busy," Sophia said. "I mean, since the beginning, there hasn't really been a chance to share those unimportant details."

"They seem pretty important to me," Hiker argued.

Thankfully, the angels seemed to be looking out for Sophia because the closet door opened, and the last invited member from the House of Fourteen entered, her windswept gray hair brushed back off her forehead.

Sophia didn't know Hester DeVries very well, but Liv did and had promised the healer for the House of Fourteen could be trusted.

With the confidence to impress, the Councilor walked straight up to Hiker, her chin held high. "You must be the leader of the Dragon Elite."

"And you are?" Hiker asked her.

"I'm the person who is going to heal your riders," Hester answered. "Lead me in the right direction, and I will get straight to work."

Hiker seemed to appreciate the healer's straightforward style. He nodded and pointed down the corridor, explaining where Evan and Mahkah could be found.

Sophia took a moment to appreciate that so many of her friends were at the Castle. She couldn't wait to show Liv her bedroom. Although her sister had a lot of work to do, helping the Dragon Elite to strategize for when the Barrier came down in a day or two, Sophia hoped they had a chance to catch up properly. She had so many things she wanted to tell her, and one thing she needed Liv's advice about.

Sophia was excited to introduce her brother to Ainsley and the others. She was looking forward to having her brother's cooking, which would no doubt bring back a flood of nostalgia.

The giants would be an interesting addition to the Gullington. It was uncertain how effective they would be at securing the Barrier and keeping the Gullington hidden. It was a large piece of land, and there were only two of them. However, if they at least bought them some time, that would be good. The cyborg pirates would probably be back, and they needed a way to secure the borders until they knew how to defend the dragon eggs and protect them from would-be thieves.

"Okay, Sophia," Hiker began, "I need you to—"

"Actually, sir," Sophia dared to interrupt. "King Rudolf is going to take me to get something I think will save Quiet."

While she knew Hiker would want to argue with her, this was one subject he knew he couldn't. Something had to be done to help the groundskeeper.

Reluctantly, he agreed. "Yes, that will be good anyway, because the Castle is no place for babies."

"Actually," Sophia said, grimacing slightly.

She never got a chance to deliver the bad news because all heads turned when Wilder sprinted down the corridor, sliding stealthily between bodies as if he didn't notice the crowd of strangers congregated in the Castle. He ignored everyone, including Hiker, and grabbed Sophia's hand, panic in his eyes.

"Soph, I need your help!" Wilder exclaimed. "And right away! No questions asked!"

CHAPTER SIXTY-NINE

"What is going on here?" Hiker's voice boomed with disapproval.

Rudolf shook his head and clicked his tongue. "I believe the young lad said, 'no questions asked,' Walker."

Hiker narrowed his eyes at the fae before turning to Wilder. "What is going on?"

Wilder finally seemed to notice he was surrounded by strangers, and everyone was regarding him with curious stares. "Oh, hey...um... Sir, I need Sophia's help with something right away. It's really important."

"That mission you abandoned us to do for Subner, is it?" Hiker asked.

Wilder slid his eyes nervously to the group before nodding. "Yes, sir."

"Why do you need Sophia?"

"I-I-I can't say," Wilder replied.

The Viking looked ready to punch a wall. After a long moment, he seemed to get control internally and let out a long breath. "Fine, Sophia, you can go. But I want you to be fast with whatever this secret mission is."

"In the meantime," Rudolf sang, "the Captains and I will be waiting for you for our secret mission."

Hiker had forgotten about the fae standing there with infants strapped to him and resting in the carriage.

He growled, his eyes vibrating with irritation. "Sophia, you better hurry."

Liv and Clark offered her encouraging smiles as Wilder tugged her away, back the way he had come.

"I will see you soon," she called as she was dragged away on a mission with the last person she wanted to be alone with right then.

CHAPTER SEVENTY

"Where are you taking me?" Sophia asked as Wilder held tight to her hand and pulled her across the Expanse toward the mountains in the distance.

He looked over his shoulder at her. "No questions, remember."

Sophia yanked her hand from his grip. "Well, then, no help."

Wilder halted and spun around to face her directly. "Please, Soph. This is important."

"I get that," Sophia replied. "But so is my ability to know what is going on. If you need my help, you are going to have to explain."

Wilder seemed to waver with indecision. "Fine, can I tell you as we go? We don't really have much time, so I can't go into too many details at once."

"Fair enough," Sophia answered. "Start by telling me where we are going."

He pointed in the distance. "Falconer's cave. There is something there I need your help with."

"Do you need to meditate?" she asked, remembering when Hiker dragged her out on a ten-mile hike so she could connect with the universe and hear the voices of the angels.

"Heavens no," Wilder answered. "There is something in the cave I need you to see."

Sophia thought back to the last time she had been in Falconer's cave. She hadn't seen anything out of the ordinary—a lot of rock, some bugs, and dripping water. And a whole lot of darkness.

"Well, fine," she affirmed. "But we aren't hiking ten miles to the cave. That will take forever." She turned toward the Cave where the dragons would be resting. "Call Simi, and I will get Lunis, and we can get there quickly."

The look of regret that crossed Wilder's face was palpable. "The thing is, Simi is not available."

"What do you mean, she's not available?" Sophia demanded.

Wilder slid his hands into his pockets, nervousness exuding from his every movement. "She is sort of being detained..."

Sophia gasped. "By whatever is in Falconer's Cave?"

The look on Wilder's face was all the confirmation she needed.

"Fine." Sophia reached out and called Lunis. Seconds later, the blue dragon poked his head from the Cave and sprang into the air, flapping his long wings and making quick progress in their direction.

"Wait, you are going to take Lunis and make me hike alone?" Wilder sounded offended.

Sophia rolled her eyes at him as her dragon landed before them. "No, we are both going to ride Lunis."

She looked her dragon in the eye, a silent question in her gaze. She didn't need him to answer for her to know he had agreed to taxi both her and Wilder, something he hadn't done before. Only Sophia had ever ridden him, which was common for dragons. There was usually little reason for a dragon to be ridden by anyone but their riders. This seemed to be a desperate situation, though, and Lunis had understood immediately that Simi was in trouble and needed their help.

"But I can't," Wilder argued, as she mounted Lunis, swinging her leg around and sliding into the saddle made for one.

Sophia gave him an annoyed expression. "Seriously, Wild now is not the time for pretenses. I get it's a bit unorthodox, but if I must wait for you to hike ten miles, we are going to lose valuable time.

Decide right now if you want to ride with me on Lunis or risk your dragon by being stubborn."

Apparently, that was the kick in the pants Wilder needed because he nodded. Sophia extended a hand to him he really didn't need. Still, he grabbed her fingers and allowed her assistance as he swung his leg around and slid into the spot behind her. A shock of electricity radiated from their touch, and she yanked her hand away at once. He grabbed onto the saddle to secure his precarious position.

Sophia grabbed the reins and directed Lunis into the air, feeling strange sharing her dragon with someone else, but if she was going to ride through the clouds, it made sense it would be with Wilder.

CHAPTER SEVENTY-ONE

Lunis had a zillion questions for Sophia, but none of them were very relevant.

I don't see why you won't answer me, he said with a laugh as he landed smoothly outside Falconer Cave.

Because I'm a mean and stingy person, she answered. She waited for Wilder to dismount first before sliding down the side of her dragon and landing on the grass.

Wilder had held out a hand to help her down, but she wasn't going to take his assistance in a million years. This was her dragon, and she didn't need help getting down.

Wilder had asked for her help, and she was beyond curious to find out what he needed her to do. She reasoned he had chosen her because he didn't really have any other choice. Evan was still injured and Mahkah was on the reconnaissance mission investigating the Saverus organization. Of course, Hester would fix both dragonriders, and Wilder could call on them in the future when he needed help.

You are not mean, nor are you stingy, Lunis said. *But I would say you are a certain river in Egypt.*

Sinai, she retorted. *Is that the river you are referring to?*

No, I was thinking more along the lines of—

Tanitic? Mendesian? Pelusia? Sophia asked her dragon, cutting him off.

Have fun exploring the dark cave with Wilder, Lunis sang as she made her way up to the opening at the top of the hill.

I'm almost certain whatever the weapons expert has in store for me is going to be anything but fun, Sophia stated.

Oh, well, I think with the right person, just about anything could be fun, Lunis mused with a snicker.

Sophia looked over her shoulder and shook her head at her dragon as they neared Falconer Cave.

"Everything okay?" Wilder asked, noticing her irritated gaze at Lunis.

"Yeah, I was just considering how my dragon would look with a muzzle," Sophia answered.

It wouldn't stop me from talking in your head, Lunis teased.

What? I can't hear you, Lun. What did you say?

I said that—

Can't hear you, she interrupted, unable to hide the grin on her face as she taunted her dragon.

"What are you laughing at?"

"Just playing with Lunis," she answered. "He likes to dish it out, but let's see if he can take it."

Wilder shook his head at her, a small smile lighting up his eyes. "I wouldn't trade Simi for all the riches in the world, but sometimes I wonder what it would be like to have what you do with Lunis."

"A back talking dragon who is obsessed with pop culture and Pringles chips?"

Wilder laughed. "No, I was thinking more along the lines of a dragon that is more your friend. Mahkah and I are the older riders. Evan too, for that matter, but maybe a little less so. We are from the old mindset that dragons are serious and can't indulge in modern things. Hiker, I'm certain, up until recently, absolutely believed technology would corrupt their power. There has never been a rider and dragon like you and Lunis. You two are something new, something amazing."

Sophia coughed nervously. "Anyway, so what are we doing here?"

Wilder's light expression dropped as he stared at the mouth of the cave. "Follow me. I have something to show you."

Sophia's hand went for her sword, but Wilder stopped her.

"You won't need that...yet," he told her.

CHAPTER SEVENTY-TWO

The chill of Falconer Cave and the ominous feeling drifting in the crisp air made Sophia shiver upon entering.

Her eyes scanned, looking for any clues to tell her what this was all about.

"Is this when you tell me what is going on here?" she asked Wilder as they went further into the dark cave, her voice echoing.

He created a light orb to show their path. "It's easier if I show you."

When she had been there with Hiker to meditate, they hadn't ventured too deeply into the cave, but Wilder went past the initial area, and around a bend. The light from the opening disappeared, and Sophia was grateful for the orb Wilder was carrying to help guide their path.

"Is Simi in here somewhere?" Sophia inquired. The cave was large enough to house a dragon, although the area where they were now was a bit narrow. She doubted the white dragon could have made it through.

Wilder shook his head, his jaw flexing.

"But this is the way to get to her?" Sophia wondered what had happened to the dragon connected to the element of wind.

She suddenly felt like she had been hit in the chest. Wind. How had she forgotten wind was the element connected to Wilder's dragon? She shrugged it off. It was just a stupid coincidence. Sophia knew better.

Her father, according to his wise words in the book she had read before giving it to Liv and Clark, had said:

"There is no such thing as a coincidence. Nothing happens at random. All things that are uncanny enough to appear as flukes are simply events begging for your attention. Devote your awareness to them."

Wilder shook his head again. "I don't know where she is."

Sophia was confused. That was impossible. She always knew where Lunis was. The only exception had been when Gordon Burgress, the lone rider, had used magitech to sever the connection between them.

Sophia wondered if Wilder and Simi had been hit with something similar. Her heart hurt for them instantly. She had never known a pain like the one of losing her connection to her dragon. It had been like losing a part of her soul. She wouldn't wish that on anyone in this world.

Sophia was about to ask more questions when Wilder stopped abruptly, holding the light orb out in front of him.

He pointed at a large boulder in the middle of the cave-room where they stood. The ceiling was high, and the sound of water dripping echoed, making it seem like they were in a gentle rainstorm.

At first, Sophia thought he was pointing to a normal boulder. As her eyes adjusted and she was able to take in the details, she noticed protruding from the stone was the hilt of a sword, only a few inches of its blade peeking out.

Sophia sucked in a sudden breath. "No, it can't be."

The sober look in Wilder's eyes confirmed what she thought was impossible. "I assure you, it absolutely is."

CHAPTER SEVENTY-THREE

"That is impossible," Sophia stammered, shaking her head as she studied the large rock with the sword stuck into the top of it.

Wilder huffed, breaking his serious expression to laugh at her. "Are you serious now? You have a dragon and live at a Castle with a bunch of hundred-year-old magicians. Not to mention, I'm certain I just saw two giants, a fae, and three halflings in said Castle. I will definitely be needing a lot more information on that later."

"It's not that interesting of a story," Sophia lied. "And how did you know the triplets were halflings?"

Wilder tilted his head at her. "Wasn't it obvious?"

She shook her head at him. "You were literally there for about half a second, and most of your attention was on trying to get my help. So no, I don't get how that would have been obvious to you."

He pretended to sigh. "Gosh, you just don't pay attention."

"Ha-ha," she said. "Now, do you want to explain to me why I'm standing in front of Excalibur?"

"Because I brought you here," he answered quite seriously.

"Oh, for love of the angels, I'm going to put you in a headlock," she threatened.

His eyes dazzled as he flashed a challenging smile. "I would like to see you try."

"Oh, you will see, and I promise I will mess up your hair when I do," she quipped. "Later we will spar, but for now, tell me why you brought me here."

His smile dropped. "Subner asked me to retrieve this sword."

Sophia's brow tensed. "But you are not King Arthur. There is no way you can pull that sword."

Wilder shook his head. "I don't think the lore we've known is the right one. It's close, and I screwed up, trying to take the sword."

"What do you mean?"

He pointed to a plaque on the ground in front of the boulder. Sophia hadn't noticed it until he shone the light of the orb on it. "Check this out."

She squatted and read the sign:

"Those unworthy who try to take my sword will have something they value taken from them."

Sophia shot back to a standing position. "You lost Simi."

He nodded, a morose expression in his blue eyes. "Yeah, as soon as I tried to take it, I heard her in my head. Soph, it was awful. Something stole her away, and I don't know where she is."

"The other dragons, though," Sophia questioned. "Were they there when she disappeared? Lunis didn't mention anything."

"No," Wilder answered. "She flew me to Falconer Cave and was waiting outside as Lunis is doing for you now."

She nodded. That made sense.

"So, Excalibur or King Arthur or whoever didn't think you were worthy," Sophia said, mostly to herself. "But you work for the Protector of Weapons. Subner sent you here to get the sword. How can you not be worthy? I mean, I get you are not a king, but also, who can pull this sword if it isn't you?"

A crooked smile formed on his mouth. "I think it's you."

CHAPTER SEVENTY-FOUR

"Oh dear, you have lost your mind," Sophia said, shaking her head at Wilder.

He laughed, his voice echoing. "That is true but totally unrelated to what we are talking about right now."

"Why would I be able to pull Excalibur from the infamous stone?" Sophia questioned. "I'm definitely no king. If you haven't noticed, I'm a girl, and we can't be kings. Up until a little while ago, we couldn't even be dragonriders."

"For your information, I have noticed you are a girl," he commented, a sideways smile still on his face.

"Have you considered going back and seeing Subner?" Sophia asked. "He sent you to get this. He would have known something like this was going to happen. Maybe he knows how to fix it."

Wilder growled slightly as she exhaled. "He probably did know this was going to happen. The guy works in weird ways and isn't always forthcoming."

"What?" Sophia pretended to be shocked. "Father Time's assistant isn't forthcoming? I'm so surprised."

A dimple surfaced when Wilder gave her an amused grin. "Yeah, I know, right? But also, he told me not to return to him without the sword. He said he would offer no other help besides what he already had, and I should troubleshoot things on my own."

"Well," Sophia said, drawing out the word. "I still don't know why you think I will have any better luck. And I don't want to lose my dragon, so I think I will just be off. Good luck."

She didn't move from her spot, but she did cross her arms in front of her chest and give him a challenging expression.

"I don't want anything to happen to Lunis either, and I don't think it will," he explained. "I might be reading into things, but based on what we know about the old lore and what the sign says, I think only royalty can pull the sword."

"Cool, well, go and find a king. There have got to be a few of those around here somewhere," Sophia told him. "I will even help you look. Want me to post on Next Door? I have the app for this part of Scotland."

Wilder shook his head. "Why do that when I have royalty right in front of me?"

Sophia lowered her chin. "No, you can't be serious. I'm a Royal for the House of Fourteen. That is not a king or queen or whatever. It's some status created by the founders."

"But the blood that runs in your veins makes you magical royalty," Wilder argued. "The sword and stone won't know the difference. It just wants someone worthy to pull it. I came from nothing. My family were peasant farmers. But you, Soph, you have got the right blood. I believe you can pull the sword."

"And then what?" she challenged.

"And then I can find Simi," Wilder explained.

"How do you know?" Sophia demanded.

Wilder toggled his head back and forth, thinking. "Well, I don't. But I think the first step has to be to get the sword. We know it has incredible power. If something was stolen using the sword, then having it should get it back, or one could reason. Anyway, Soph, you are my only hope."

She leveled her gaze at him. "You are not giving me the 'you are my only hope' line, are you?"

He batted his long eyelashes at her. "I might be."

"What if something happens to Lunis because you are wrong?" she challenged.

"Then, I will do everything within my power to get him back." He held out his hand, a promise in the movement. "We will work together, and we won't stop until we get our dragons back, but we will be together, and I will be indebted to you. No matter what, I will be indebted to you. Please, Soph. You are my best chance. I'm staking my dragon on this. I believe, heart and soul, you can pull Excalibur from the stone. Will you please try?"

Wilder knew what he was asking of her. More than that, Sophia knew what was at stake. She knew he depended on her of all people. She had lost her dragon and knew the pain he was going through. If there was any way she could help him, she had to do it. She'd do it for any of the Dragon Elite and especially for Wilder.

That wasn't the strangest realization for her, though. Sophia wanted to be what fixed everything for him, and be the one who pulled Excalibur from the stone, not because it would make her a legend, although it would.

More importantly, because she wanted to be a part of this story.

She wanted to be a part of Wilder's happy ending.

After a long moment of deliberation, Sophia nodded and extended her hand just as a cool wind wafted through her hair, although it should have been absent in the cave.

"Fine," she said in a low voice. "I will do it. But if I regret this, you will pay."

He smiled wide at her. "If you do, I will spend my life trying to pay you back, I promise."

CHAPTER SEVENTY-FIVE

Sophia's hands were shaking when she extended them toward the hilt of the most famous sword in the world.

Life was about risk. This was a major one. She was gambling on Wilder's hunch.

She nearly closed her eyes as she drew her fingers closer to the sword, each second feeling like a long minute.

Wait, Lunis said in her head, making her tense.

Sophia sucked in a breath as she stiffened.

I shouldn't do it, should I? she asked her dragon.

Do what? he asked with a snicker in his voice.

Sophia rolled her eyes.

Wilder gave her a curious expression.

"My dragon is a playful jerk," she explained. "Do you want him? I will just give you my dragon, and we can forget this whole Excalibur business."

He smiled at this. "Although a thoughtful offer and Lunis is a fine dragon who would do me well, I really must insist on getting my Simi. She is the only dragon for me."

Sophia nodded. "Okay, I'm going to do it."

Hey, Soph, Lunis said mischievously.

Her eyelashes fluttered with annoyance.

It's sort of a bad time, Lun.

That is the thing, he said, his voice trailing away.

What is the thing? she asked.

Well, about the timing, he answered.

What about it?

Did you file our taxes? he questioned.

A laugh spilled out of her mouth, again making Wilder give her a curious expression.

"We don't file taxes," she said out loud. "Because I don't have a social security number, and you are a dragon."

Wilder shook his head, hearing only half of the conversation. "You two have the strangest dialogues."

She nodded. "You have no idea."

Okay, good, Lunis said. *So we are not in jeopardy of getting penalties?*

For what? she questioned. *For being world adjudicators who pretty much work for free solving the world's problems?*

Yeah, I don't really know how it all works, he explained. *I'm a dragon. We don't deal much in tax law.*

Much? Sophia chuckled.

At all, really. A few of my ancestors have eaten accountants. They are very chewy, apparently.

Maybe it's because they are so stingy, Sophia reasoned.

I figured they would be crunchy. The dragon snickered.

Oh, please don't, Sophia begged.

From all the numbers they crunch, Lunis rejoined, full-on laughing now.

Ba-dum-THS, Sophia said, trying not to laugh. She felt immeasurably better than moments prior, though, and knew that had been Lunis' agenda all along, trying to be a pain in her rear end. That was their dynamic, and she absolutely loved it.

Thanks, Lunis.

Anytime, he said affectionately.

Feeling a lot steadier than before, Sophia pulled in a breath.

Her hands wrapped around the cold metal of the hilt. Excalibur warmed under her fingers at once.

Sophia almost expected something to happen right then. For the sword to explode, and send her flying through the cave maybe, or to feel Lunis jerked from her.

To Sophia's surprise, nothing happened.

Her eyes darted to Wilder, tension heavy in his gaze.

"Go on then," he encouraged. "Try to pull the sword. I know you can do it."

Those seemingly simple six words were exactly what Sophia needed to hear: I know you can do it.

She held her breath and made a silent prayer to the angels above before pulling up on the sword, attempting to yank it from the place it had resided for several centuries.

Nothing happened.

Sophia's heart suddenly pounded in her chest.

The blade moved a tiny amount. The sound of scratching met her ears as she continued to pull, feeling a strange easing as Excalibur released from the stone.

Wilder's eyes widened, and a smile lit up his face. He leaned forward as a bright light shone around where King Arthur's sword met the stone. It shot up, cascading on the cave ceiling, and illuminating the area where they stood.

A humming sound drowned out the scratching of the sword as Sophia continued to try to pull Excalibur from the stone.

She couldn't believe it!

Wilder was right! It was working. The sword saw her as worthy.

The process wasn't fast like she would have expected. It wasn't like yanking Inexorabilis from the body of an enemy she had slain. It was like...well, pulling an ancient sword that had been trapped in stone for centuries.

Sophia gritted her teeth as sweat beaded on her forehead. Her arms shook from the force of trying to maintain constant pressure, the most intense game of tug-of-war she had ever played. She felt if she let up a single ounce, it would yank her through a portal to a land from which she may never return. Sophia bit down on her lip and pulled harder, making the blade hiccup out of the stone several inches. It paused when it was almost out and tugged back at her—its last attempt to not be unsheathed from the rock.

"You can do this," Wilder encouraged, his eyes trained intently upon the stone and the blade, the bright light intensifying. Music filled the cave, echoing everywhere. It was the most beautiful sound, but overwhelming, growing so loud it started to hurt Sophia's ears.

She grunted and used all her reserves to pull the sword. It seemed to be throwing in a last-ditch effort, yanking back at her.

The hilt vibrated in her hands and nearly hauled her off her feet.

Wilder noticed and raced behind her, wrapping his arms around her waist and securing her back down to the ground. He pulled on Sophia to give her an extra bit of momentum. That did it.

Sophia might have been there for days trying to pull Excalibur from the stone. Yes, she was worthy by its standards to pull the sword, but doing it was incredibly difficult.

Together she and Wilder had the combination it took to succeed. He held her tightly and yanked at the same time as her, and the sword swept clean of the stone, its tip flying up.

The light that radiated from the blade was blinding, and the force it unearthed when meeting the cave was uncontrollable. It threw both dragonriders back several yards.

Sophia landed on Wilder, but he didn't release her as the humming diminished, and the light dimmed.

Sophia didn't let go of Excalibur as a portal opened in front of them, swallowing both up whole—transporting them to a brand-new location.

CHAPTER SEVENTY-SIX

The world went black before exploding into an array of bright colors, mostly blues and greens. What stole Sophia's attention most was the biting cold.

As they fell through the portal, an icy wind blanketed them in the face, making it impossible for Sophia to open her eyes fully. This wasn't like the portals she was used to. Those were still disorienting, but this was like riding a rollercoaster backward.

Sophia bit her tongue and tasted blood as they continued to fall. She half expected them to hit the ground, which would kill them both. She was sure of it. It would be worse on Wilder since he was underneath her, his arms still wrapped around her waist and pressing her in tightly.

Above them, Excalibur shone brightly. The sword was like a projectile, sending them down at unbelievable speeds. Even on Lunis, Sophia had never traveled so fast.

She willed her eyes to open all the way, taking in the area around them. Sophia immediately wished she hadn't. Surrounding them were walls of ice. It appeared they were falling through a tunnel made of snow, like when she had to descend the staircase in Antarctica to get to Queen Anastasia Crystal's ice fortress.

The wind whipped past them, and the temperature plummeted further. They started slowing down.

The intensity of the cold grabbed Sophia at the same moment they paused in midair. She was about to twist around when they slowly slipped down a few inches and were gently laid on the surface of an ice platform.

CHAPTER SEVENTY-SEVEN

S uddenly the weight of Excalibur was intense. Holding it up with her hands extended seemed to be the most strenuous task she had ever done. Her arms trembled, and for a moment, she thought she would drop the sword on her and Wilder, impaling them.

Instead, she forced the weight of the sword to drag her arms to the side, and with it, Excalibur dropped to land on the ice, her hands still wrapped around the hilt. She released it and rolled off Wilder.

As soon as she was off him, he jumped to his feet, surveying where they had landed. It was a cave made of ice. They were surrounded by thick white walls that glowed with strange blues and greens.

Although Sophia thought they had fallen through a tunnel, when she brought her eyes up, there was a domed ceiling. More disconcerting was that there was no exit.

Sophia spun around and looked at Wilder, who shared her expression of panic. They were trapped. But she had been able to pull the sword.

"I don't understand," she said, her breathing fogging up from the cold. "Where are we?"

He shook his head, turning in a circle as he continued to search the space. There wasn't too much to it. It looked like they were locked inside of an igloo, although Sophia could make out movement on the other side of the ice wall in front of them.

The cold bit at her insides, and Sophia pulled her cloak tighter. When she had left the Antarctic, after defeating the abominable snowman, she had said if she didn't see ice and snow for the rest of her life, that would be okay. It appeared the angels had ignored her request.

Wilder went over to Excalibur, his hand hesitating an inch from the hilt. He looked over his shoulder to Sophia, a question in his eyes. She nodded, encouraging him to pick it up. What could happen now? She had already pulled the sword from the stone. It appeared there was another part of the challenge.

To her relief and surprise, absolutely nothing happened when he picked up the sword. She watched him as he swung the sword.

"Well?" she asked, curious what he felt from the sword that had seen its fair share of battles.

"It's incredibly impressive," he said, testing the balance.

"Can it get us out of here?"

Wilder nodded. "I'm sure it can." He lowered the blade though, distracted. He took a step in her direction, a serious expression on his face. "You did it. I knew you could, and you did, risking your dragon for mine."

Sophia felt something draw her forward, and she took a step in his direction. They stared at each other, both mesmerized.

Wilder lifted his free hand, his mouth twitching to the side. Sophia was sure he was about to touch her face. Just over his shoulder, she saw movement. It was an unmistakable figure, just behind the ice.

"Simi!" Sophia yelled, pointing.

CHAPTER SEVENTY-EIGHT

Wilder whipped around, his eyes widening.

Behind the wall of ice, a shadow moved. At first, it appeared indistinct. Sophia was worried she had mistaken something else for the dragon's figure. But a moment later, it turned, and the clear outline of the dragon could be seen.

It was unmistakably Wilder's dragon.

He dashed forward, throwing his palm flat on the ice wall. "Simi! Can you hear me? I'm here!"

He beat on the ice with his fist.

The outline of the dragon didn't change as Sophia would have expected if she just caught notice of them.

"Can you hear her?" Sophia asked, referring to the telepathic communication Wilder would share with his dragon, the same as Lunis and she.

He shook his head, stepping backward. "No, but that has to be her."

She nodded. "We will get her out."

Sophia glanced around, looking for anything that would clue her in on what they were supposed to do next. This had to be a riddle of some kind. If she could just figure out what the next part of the challenge was, they would be that much closer to rescuing the white dragon and freeing themselves.

Wilder seemed to be doing the same thing, looking for clues, his blue eyes searching the space. There wasn't much, just ice and bright whites, blues, and greens.

Then both of their eyes landed on the sword in Wilder's hand. There was a silent understanding between them when they looked at each other.

"Do you think?" he asked her, his question lingering in the air.

Sophia shrugged. "It makes sense. I think it's worth a try."

"But Excalibur is a trick. You can't just try something with it because it will punish you if you are wrong."

Sophia knew he still felt guilty losing his dragon when he tried to pull the sword. "Do you want me to try wielding it?"

He considered for a moment before nodding. Expertly, he turned the large sword around, offering her the hilt and presenting it over his forearm like a true gentleman.

She gave him a smile and took the sword with two hands. When she lifted Excalibur into the air, she was again amazed by how heavy it was. Sophia was used to carrying Inexorabilis, which was light and sleek.

In contrast, Excalibur had to weigh four times as much and was massive. This wasn't a sword she would have much luck with in battle. Still, she didn't have to fight with the blade. Hopefully, she only had to use it once.

Loosening her freezing chest with a breath, Sophia stood in front of the ice wall where Simi was trapped. She held King Arthur's blade in both hands and prepared for the strike she was about to attempt.

With a look of uncertainty, she glanced at Wilder.

He gave her a confident expression. "Do it."

Sophia swallowed and swung Excalibur, finding it moved much quicker than she would have expected based on its size and weight. The blade connected with the ice wall. Although legend said it could slice through steel like it was wood, the blade just bounced off the ice, not shattering it and freeing Simi, as she and Wilder had assumed.

Her brow furrowed, and she looked at Wilder with confusion. He shared her perplexed expression as he opened his mouth.

She never heard what he was about to say because the ice under their feet and the walls around them began to vibrate violently, creating a cacophony of noise.

CHAPTER SEVENTY-NINE

Sophia rushed forward and pushed the sword into Wilder's hands since he didn't have a weapon. He took it at once, his movements full of urgency. She whipped Inexorabilis from its sheath, preparing for whatever came next.

While Sophia considered they were about to be crushed in the strange igloo, her instinct told her that wasn't what hitting the ice wall with Excalibur had done. As if ready to confirm her assumption, a hole formed directly above them. It was black and about five feet in diameter.

Wilder held out an arm, encouraging her back away from the hole in the middle of the ceiling. It was a good thing too because a moment later, a large, green ogre who smelled as bad as it looked dropped through the hole.

The monster landed with a thud, the large knuckles of its over-sized hands knocking into the ice floor. It was mostly naked to Sophia's horror. Thankfully, the one-eyed monster had a loincloth wrapped around its privates, fashioned of what appeared to be small skulls. Maybe leftovers of its past enemies.

Around its forearms was spiked armor. Strange black tattoos covered the beast's shoulders and bare chest. It had several silver rings in its large ears, and two large horns protruded from either of the ogre's shoulders.

When it saw Sophia and Wilder standing on the far side of the domed igloo, it opened its mouth and screamed—a noise that vibrated the ground under Sophia's boots. The monster had two large bottom fangs that framed a row of smaller but just as lethal teeth. Its one eye blinked at them, a less than welcoming expression in its gaze.

"I don't think it's happy to see us," Sophia said, holding her sword at the ready.

Wilder did the same with Excalibur. "Maybe it just got woken up from its nap."

"Or maybe it just looked in the mirror," Sophia joked.

"Should I take this one, or do you want to?" Wilder asked, giving her an entertained expression.

"Well, 'ladies first' is the rule, I believe."

He waved his arm forward. "Be my guest, dear lady."

Sophia stepped up, but before she could launch an attack at Skull Pants, the black hole opened in the ceiling again.

She jumped back, certain she knew what was going to happen next.

A second later another just as disgusting green ogre dropped through the opening, landing next to its ugly cousin. It was pretty much the same as Skull Pants, but this one was lucky enough to have two eyes.

"Oh, look," Wilder commented, sounding amused. "One for you and one for me."

"No one will feel left out," Sophia agreed.

Under their feet, the ground shook again. The hole in the ceiling hadn't closed yet, and once again, another angry ogre dropped through the hole, landing behind its brethren. This one had three eyes and somehow appeared more peeved than the other two.

"Okay, so one for you," Wilder began. "One for me. And one to grow on."

"Well, first one to finish their ugly ogre gets the third one," Sophia challenged. "I will take Cyclops. You get Two-Eyes McGoo Head."

"Two-Eyes McGoo Head," Wilder said with a laugh. "That was my grandfather's name, I believe."

Cyclops stomped one foot, nearly throwing Sophia to the ground from the vibration that resulted. She shook her head at Wilder. "Save the jokes until after you have slaughtered your ogre. Then we chat."

He nodded, new excitement in his eyes. "Okay, I will race you. The last one to defeat their ogre has to shovel the dragon poo from the Expanse for a month."

"Wait, since when did we have to clean up the dragon droppings?" Sophia asked, aware the ogres were growing restless and about to attack.

"Exactly," Wilder fired back. "Someone has skirted this responsibility for long enough, being the newbie. It's about time you step up, Soph."

She flashed him a defiant expression. "Yeah, not yet, I don't. I don't plan on losing."

CHAPTER EIGHTY

Sophia faced off against Cyclops and gave him a threatening look. "You ready to go down, Mr. Ugly Face?"

The monster screamed, his breath smelling as bad as him.

The three ogres were so huge, they took up over half of the igloo. Sophia knew defeating three at a time in a confined space would be challenging. She made the executive decision to freeze the ogre with three eyes, Mr. Wrinkles as she was affectionately referring to him.

"Oh, are you afraid you can't handle two at a time?" Wilder taunted, aiming Excalibur at Two-Eyes McGoo Head as he charged. He threw up his forearm and the blade hit the spiked armor, bouncing off. The beast yelled in Wilder's face, brushing his hair back from the wind soaring out of its mouth.

"Why don't you focus on your ogre," Sophia ordered, giving Cyclops a challenging expression.

He stomped, his knuckles dragging on the ground.

"You must have horrible back issues," Sophia remarked to the monster. This seemed to make it even angrier.

It put its head down like a bull and raced straight at her. She could have used the Wilder approach and raised her sword at the beast, using its momentum against it, but she didn't do things the same way as Wilder or the other men of the Dragon Elite. Sophia fought smart, not hard.

Cyclops' head rammed straight into the ice wall, and it stumbled backward, nearly stepping on Sophia. She backed up rapidly, accidentally stepping on Mr. Wrinkle's foot. Thankfully the ugly creature was still frozen.

For a moment, Cyclops staggered around like a drunk. It almost looked like it was a cartoon and had been hit with an anvil. Sophia imagined little tweeting birds circling over his head. It fell, landing on its front side.

In a flash, Wilder spun around, slashing Excalibur so quickly it made the same musical sound they had heard when she'd pulled it from the stone. It sliced cleanly through the massive midsection of the beast. Instead of blood and guts spilling out everywhere, the same light that had illuminated the blade and the stone shot out from the cut, spreading out throughout the space, and momentarily blinding them.

Sophia shielded her eyes with her arm, the light so bright it felt like it might burn her skin. Just when she worried the intensity would be too much, the light evaporated and took with it the hulking figure of Two-Eyes McGoo Head.

Perplexed, Sophia lowered her hand. The beast had simply disappeared, but something seemed off. Wilder didn't share her skepticism. Proud of himself, he twirled the large sword in his hand, pressing out his lips.

"That was easy," he said, nodding confidently. He indicated her ogre, still lying face down on his one good eye. "You want me to take care of Cyclops for you?"

Sophia gave him a cautious expression, looking around as she thought. "No, something isn't right here."

He laughed. "What are you talking about? We have King Arthur's sword. When you have the best weapons, things are just easier."

Sophia shook her head. "No, because whoever pulled that sword would have it when battling these ugly brutes. There is something else to this."

"Like it's a riddle?" Wilder asked, not convinced by her skeptical reasoning.

"I don't know," she mused, watching as the muscles on Cyclops' back twitched. He was coming to.

"Well, you lost this round," Wilder informed her. "Do you want to unfreeze Three Eyes and go double or nothing?"

"His name is Mr. Wrinkles," Sophia corrected. "And no, I'm not taking that as a loss."

"But I defeated my guy first," he argued as Cyclops put his hands under his shoulder and pushed up to his knees.

Sophia clapped her boot on the back of his spine and stomped down, combining the effort with a combat spell. The ogre was immediately sent back down to the ice on his face, a muffled grunt spilling from his mouth.

"I'm not sure you did defeat him," Sophia countered. "He disappeared, but that doesn't mean he is gone."

Wilder shook his head at her. "We really should work on your vocabulary. Gone and disappeared are the same thing."

Sophia's mind scanned what she knew so far and ignored Wilder, who was trying to be cool, flashing her a grin and acting like the victor. "We are stuck in an igloo with ogres."

"Yep," Wilder agreed, running his gaze over the area where Simi's shadow could still be seen behind the ice wall.

"And Excalibur should cut through the ice, but it doesn't," Sophia thought out loud.

"Yeah, that is weird." Wilder pulled back the blade, and before Sophia could stop him, he swung it at the wall again.

"NO!" she yelled, but it was too late.

Like a bell being hit, the dome over them rattled, vibrating Sophia's brain from the echoing sound. Again, the blade of Excalibur simply bounced off the ice wall, having no effect on it.

Wilder gave her a confused expression. "Why did you tell me no?"

A moment later, the black hole in the top of the igloo dome opened, and another ogre as angry as the other three, dropped through.

Sophia shook her head, lowering her chin. "That is why."

CHAPTER EIGHTY-ONE

Sophia lifted her sword and brought it straight down into Cyclops' back. Like with Two-Eyes McGoo, light shot out from the place where the blade pierced his skin, nearly blinding them again as the large body disappeared.

The new and energized ogre charged Wilder. This time he didn't strike the beast with Excalibur. Instead, he deflected the monster's attacks, although they sent Wilder straight into the wall at his back. The shadow of Simi moved behind him, the dragon perhaps sensing her rider had just been assaulted.

The ogre grabbed Wilder by the throat and held him up in the air.

"Do I kill him or not?" Wilder asked through sips of breath, his face turning a violent shade of red.

Sophia thought. "I'm not sure, actually."

Wilder's feet kicked, having been hauled up higher off the ground. "I'm going to need you to make a decision sooner rather than later."

She pretended to be put off. "Don't rush me. I'm thinking."

He brought his elbows down, striking the ogre in the place between its neck and shoulder, and making it drop him. Wilder landed with a thud and rolled out of reach as it grabbed for him.

"You killed your ogre, but you don't want me to kill this one? Is that it?" he panted, crouched down low and ducking as Fourths, as Sophia decided to call him, swung its fist. It wasn't that great at fighting, more blindly throwing its wide arms around and hoping to hit something by sheer luck.

"My ogre was keeping me from thinking," Sophia said. "Since we know how to get another one, I think we are okay."

The next attack by Fourths connected with Wilder's chest and threw him across the igloo into the ice wall. He hit with a thud and slid down, Excalibur still in his grasp. Thankfully he only looked badly jarred but not injured.

"Can I kill this one to give me time to think?"

She shook her head. "No, I want to experiment on him."

Wilder dove when Fourths reached for him. He rolled and jumped back to his feet before wheeling around. "Can't we use Mr. Wrinkles? He's still frozen."

"Yeah, but what if we need two at a time," Sophia reasoned. "I mean, the Ice Dome of Doom did give us three, to begin with. There might be something to the number."

"Ice...Dome...of...Doom," he said in between breaths as he jumped away from the attempts on his life from Fourths. "That is what we are calling this place, huh?"

"Well, it has a better ring to it than Ogre Paradise," Sophia remarked, still considering what they had learned about this place. She pulled back her sword and struck the wall, wondering if it would produce another ogre.

With her eyes pinned up high, she waited for the opening to form. It didn't.

"It must be Excalibur that creates the portal for the ogres," Sophia observed.

"Great." Wilder did not sound excited about the information. "I will remember that for when I turn in my report. Now can I kill this guy?"

Wilder ducked to the side just as Fourths rammed his shoulder into the ice wall where his face had been moments prior. The horns on his shoulder stuck in the ice, making cracks spray out around it.

Wilder and Sophia looked at each other, their eyes wide.

The ogre apparently didn't understand they were having a moment and pressed both of his large hands into the wall, pushing off hard and unsticking himself.

"You see what I saw?" Sophia asked.

"I, in fact, did." Wilder brandished a victorious smile. "We can't break the ice."

Sophia stepped up close to Wilder, putting her back to his as she unfroze Mr. Wrinkles. "But they can break it."

"And that is how we are going to release Simi," Wilder said, relief in his voice.

Mr. Wrinkles awoke with a start, shaking his ugly head and looking around for his prey. His eyes landed on Sophia, and just like a cranky baby, he yelled, a long-pointed tongue hanging out of his mouth.

"You take Fourths, and I will take Mr. Wrinkles," Sophia suggested.

"Fourths?" Wilder asked, looking over his shoulder at her. "Do you name all the enemy monsters you fight?"

"Always," she answered, sliding forward under Mr. Wrinkle's arm span as he tried to put her in a bear hug. "Get your guy to hit the wall. I will do the same. But try not to kill this one."

"Why?" Wilder watched as his ogre lumbered in his direction.

Sophia shot a dizzying spell at Mr. Wrinkles, making the ogre instantly disoriented. It began to spin in a circle on the spot like it had just stepped off a merry-go-round.

Fourths whipped around before Wilder could plan his next attack, knocking his legs out from under him and sending him to his back. Excalibur fell out of his hands, rolling to the side.

Sophia spun around and kicked Fourths in the stomach using a combat spell. The ogre shot back, knocking into the wall behind him. One of the horns on the back side of his shoulder stuck into the ice.

Mr. Wrinkles had finally made himself too dizzy to stand, and like a building collapsing, he fell to the side, the wall catching him. Immediately his horn stuck deep into the wall.

Sophia took the opportunity as the two ogres tried to free themselves from the ice to extend a hand to Wilder. "Because I think when we summon more ogres, they get stronger with each new one," she said, answering his question about why they shouldn't kill the ogres unnecessarily.

Wilder popped up to his feet, nodding at her gratefully for her help. "That makes sense because Fourths has a lot more power to his punch than Two-Eyes McGoo Head. How did you figure that out?"

Sophia watched as Fourths worked to try and free himself from the wall. The ice splintered out from the horn, making a cracking sound that sounded like progress. "Because things usually make sense in these scenarios. If we can get unlimited ogres, there must be a reason. They are relatively easy to kill, but it gets harder if you don't use them correctly."

Fourths finally pushed himself off the wall, the hole he left behind sizable. He shook his head, seeming to try to orient himself.

"And we are supposed to use them to break the ice," Wilder stated, retrieving Excalibur.

"Exactly," Sophia said, watching as Mr. Wrinkles struggled to free himself. He was really pinned into the wall. "I think it would be good if you could get Fourths to break down the rest of that area of the wall. I will get Mr. Wrinkles to take care of this section."

Wilder feinted to one side and then the other with the sword, teasing his ogre. "You think we have to destroy the whole dome?"

"I think," Sophia answered, jumping back as Mr. Wrinkles freed himself and nearly fell on her from the momentum of pulling off the wall. "A few well-placed hits and the whole thing will come down."

Wilder lifted Excalibur into the air and spun out of Fourths' grasp like he was a ballerina turning across the stage. This disoriented the dumb creature, making it shake its head as if the spinning caused it to be dizzy. With its focus momentarily distracted, Wilder shot a wind spell at the monster, and it flew back into the same spot as before, both of its shoulders hitting the wall—the horns piercing the ice.

"Seriously, Soph, how do you figure this stuff out?" Wilder questioned as he turned to face her like they were having a casual conversation and not sparring with angry ogres.

"I pay attention," she said and, ironically, caught an ogre fist straight on the chin. It brought her up off her feet and threw her across the air. Thankfully, Fourths' meaty chest broke her landing. She slammed straight into the still-stuck ogre and fell at its feet. Before it could play soccer with her, she rolled out of its reach, her face aching from the last assault.

"You pay attention, do you?" Wilder teased, after checking she was okay.

Sophia wasn't just in pain now. She was freaking angry. Taking off at a sprint, she ran up the side of the arched wall next to Mr. Wrinkles and jumped into the air, throwing a roundhouse kick into his face as she gracefully twisted around and landed on her feet, her sword still in her hand.

The ogre tottered like a tree being chopped down.

Right on cue, Sophia yelled, "Timber."

The ogre tipped over to the side and landed on the ice wall, its horns on its shoulder sticking deep into the ice.

Sophia narrowed her eyes at Wilder. "And yes, I pay attention."

"Do you?" he asked beside her, a grin on his face.

Both of their ogres were working to free themselves from the ice walls where they were stuck by their own horns. The cracking was like music that grew louder with each passing second.

Sophia wasn't paying attention to the ogres or the game of escaping the ice dome. She was locked on Wilder and the strange look he was giving her. There was something his gaze seemed to be saying, and something in her heart that seemed to be trying to say something too.

She felt the urge to run, although there was nowhere to go, trapped inside the igloo.

She remembered the story Mae Ling had told her about Cinderella, and it made more sense than ever.

Cinderella ran when she didn't have to because the logical part of her brain thought it couldn't work. She thought the prince would never accept her for who she was, but because her heart wanted to be found, she left behind the glass slipper.

SARAH NOFFKE & MICHAEL ANDERLE

Sophia tensed, about to say something, but then both ogres yanked out of the ice. The dome shattered from the action, ice raining down on them.

Wilder dove forward, sending Sophia to the ground and covering her head with his own body. She shielded herself, tugging him in closer and hoped he was covering himself properly too.

The crashing was over almost as soon as it began, and both drag-onriders popped to their feet, knowing the fight wasn't quite over. Wilder whipped around to face Fourths. Sophia put her back to his, facing off with Mr. Wrinkles.

In perfect unison, like they had choreographed and performed it a million times, they brought up their swords and swung them, slicing cleanly through the ogres, sending bright light everywhere as the beasts disappeared.

CHAPTER EIGHTY-TWO

For a second time, Sophia ducked, hiding her eyes from the light. She felt Wilder's arms around her, cocooning her from the blinding force as the ogres disappeared into the ether.

When the tension in his arms released, she stood up, pushing him away. He stood next to her, the two trying to right themselves after the series of disorienting events.

They stood on an ice platform, and a strange green land surrounded them.

It went on forever in all directions like they had been dropped into a weird utopia.

Sophia was nervous about taking a step away from where they were, but Wilder sprang away immediately.

"Simi!" he yelled.

Sophia spun to find the white dragon holding up her front leg regally, like a dog about to shake hands. Wilder didn't stop until he was almost underneath her. He looked up at his dragon in awe, his smile and eyes wide.

Sophia gave them a moment to reunite and tried not to watch as the white dragon dipped her head, running it next to Wilder's, enjoying having him close.

Wilder combed his hand over the large dragon's face, closing his eyes and whispering to her as she soaked him in.

Sophia let this go on for as long as she could, but knowing they were in a strange world they would have to leave soon. Otherwise, who knew what other strange magical creatures would join them next.

"Hey there," she said discreetly, walking up to the cuddling dragon and rider.

Simi batted her long eyelashes at Sophia and gave her a look of respect. "Thanks to you, S. Beaufont. You didn't have to risk everything you hold dear to save me, and yet you did."

Sophia shrugged, not knowing what to say. "Well, I only did what anyone else in the Dragon Elite would do for one of their own. If it was Lunis..."

Wilder laughed. "Evan would have told me 'hell no' and Mahkah would have researched the whole thing for too long for my liking."

"Oh, well, I'm more of a woman of action," Sophia said. "Why wait when we can create solutions together?"

Wilder put his arm around her shoulder and pulled her in close, hugging her tightly. "If everyone saw things the way you did, Soph, the world would be a different place."

"Well, we all need a job, so maybe it's good that it's not," she remarked, moving out of Wilder's grasp. "I guess we should get that sword back, huh?"

She pointed to Excalibur, still in his hands.

Wilder glanced down at the sword and tightened his hand on the hilt as he lifted it with pride. "Yes, I think Subner will be happy to see this. Let's return it."

He turned and looked at his dragon with unmistakable affection. "See you soon?"

"Always," she replied.

Sophia understood then something profound and deeply important. Dragons loved their riders unconditionally. The love a rider had for their dragon was comparable to nothing else. Maybe because of the magic that surrounded a dragonrider, it was easy for someone to fall for them without even meaning to.

The whole thing was very confusing.

CHAPTER EIGHTY-THREE

Roya Lane seemed almost balmy compared to the chill of wherever they had just been. Sophia and Wilder still hadn't figured it out by the time they opened a portal and left. They figured it was a strange alternate plane King Arthur had created for the person who pulled the sword.

"He was a dragonrider, you know," Wilder informed Sophia as they strode through Roya Lane.

"I didn't actually," she replied. "But it makes sense."

Sophia made a mental note that she needed to spend some time reading *The Complete History of Dragonriders*. Then she would have known this information, along with a lot of other stuff, although she didn't know what. That was the thing. Sophia didn't know what she didn't know.

"I know we need to get to the Fantastical Armory," Wilder said, walking beside her. "I'm sort of famished after that fight."

Sophia pulled a packet of broken crackers from her cloak. "You want halfsies?"

He shook his head at her. "No, those are all yours, but thanks for offering me a bunch of crumbs."

She laughed. "Hey, if you were really starving, you would beg for these."

"There are a lot of things I would beg for." He pointed at the crumbly bag of crackers. "That is absolutely not one of them."

"It always depends on circumstance, Mr. Thomson."

"Oh," he said, drawing out the word. "Using surnames. I didn't realize we were so formal, Ms. Beaufont."

Sophia waited for a group of gnomes to pass on the street. They never watched where they were going and seemed to think others should watch out for them. That was a contrast to many of the other magical races on the lane who were giving Sophia and Wilder curious glances as they walked by. That might have been because they recognized them as dragonriders. It could also have been because Wilder was carrying a gigantic sword strapped across his back.

"You can fill up on those stale bits of cracker, but I vote we stop in at a bakery I found the last time I was here," Wilder suggested.

"Are you okay with carrying that sword around a bit longer?"

"Well, I'm definitely not worried about anyone messing with me while I have it on my back," he answered. "And yeah, I will be fine. I do need some sugar to refill my reserves after wielding this thing."

"Okay, show me this bakery," Sophia agreed, holding out a hand and inviting him to direct their path. "Maybe I should leave you here to return the sword to Subner on your own. I'm not sure if he'll be happy with you if he finds out I was a part of the mission. He did tell you to keep the whole thing a secret."

Wilder shook his head. "Oh, no, you are going with me and getting all the credit. I will get in trouble if I have to, although I'm not certain how I could have avoided telling someone about it once Simi was taken from me."

Sophia nodded. "Yeah, I'm curious to hear what Subner has to say."

"I'm certain he'll avoid all questions," Wilder joked. "He is good like that." He halted suddenly, making a group of elves veer around them to avoid hitting him. Their faces would have paid for it if they rammed into Excalibur on his back. "But oh, I'm sorry. I totally stole you away for this mission, and I'm sure you have your own thing going on. If you need to bail and not get your gold star from the Protector of Weapons, I understand."

Sophia giggled. "Me? Have something going on? No, I was just welcoming all of my friends and family from my former life into the Castle, where no outsiders have ever been."

"Oh!" Wilder chirped. "So, you are totally free then."

"Yeah, I can only imagine the many ways King Rudolf Sweetwater is giving Hiker a migraine right now," she said with a laugh. "If he isn't, by some rare stroke of luck, my sister is most definitely getting on the Viking's nerves."

Wilder chuckled. "You know Hiker isn't a Viking, right?"

"Of course, but that is what I'm calling him. He loves it. Just like he loves my jokes."

He winked at her. "You do have good jokes. What is going on at the Castle?"

"My friends came to help," she told him, knowing she wasn't really addressing the question.

"Two giants, three magicians, a fae, and three halflings," Wilder stated. "You have a very strange assortment of friends."

"You have no idea. When I was little, I used to enchant my stuffed animals to move and talk, so at least these friends are real."

"You are making progress." He continued to lead the way, directing her to a narrow alleyway she had never ventured down before. Sophia hadn't spent much time on Roya Lane. Before joining the Dragon Elite, Sophia hadn't spent much time out of the House of Fourteen, either. Her brother, Clark, had been very protective of her growing up. It was understandable since she had unregistered magic at a very early age, and Clark had lost most of his family, so for a while, Sophia was all he had.

"Are you really okay with joining me for a *pain au chocolat*?" Wilder asked. "This bakery has the very best I have ever tried."

Sophia nodded. "Yeah, another hour away won't hurt. It's probably better if I force that lot to figure out how to get along on their own. I can't hold their hands through everything."

Wilder's eyes slipped down, looking at Sophia's hand. "And after you mediate things with Hiker and your friends, what is on your agenda?"

"I have to go break into the Fae's National History Museum to steal Quiet's father's hat," she said in a rush of words.

A fake yawn fell out of Wilder's mouth. "Wow, that sounds pretty boring."

"Just a regular Tuesday," Sophia teased.

"Here it is." Wilder pointed to a blue awning that read: The Crying Cat Bakery. In front of the glass door were spiral topiaries.

Just walking past the window displaying many of the pastries made Sophia's mouth salivate. She was about to push through the door when Wilder caught her hand, making her turn around in surprise. Sophia expected there was some sudden danger he was alerting her to. The sneaky grin on his face put those fears at ease immediately.

"About this place…"

"What?" Sophia asked, tilting her head to the side.

"The couple who run this bakery is a little on the eccentric side," he warned.

Sophia lowered her chin. "You really should meet my friends. They make eccentric types appear normal."

"No, I don't think you understand," Wilder argued. "These two are their own brand of weird."

Shrugging, Sophia said, "My sister's sidekick is a talking cat who is as old as Father Time. He day trades and writes novels when he is not helping her save the magical world. I think I can handle a new brand of weird."

Wilder looked impressed. "I must meet this cat."

"You probably already have and just didn't know it," Sophia explained. "I'm pretty certain the lynx has been stalking around the Castle for a while now."

"Maybe since the Barrier came down," Wilder amended.

Sophia shook her head. "Oh, no. I'm sure he has been around way before that."

"No, that would have been impossible," Wilder disagreed.

Sophia winked at him before pushing open the door to the Crying Cat Bakery. "You don't know this cat. Nothing is impossible for Plato."

CHAPTER EIGHTY-FOUR

The bell on the door chimed as the two entered the Crying Cat Bakery. The smell of fresh-baked bread and coffee hit Sophia's nose, making her stomach rumble. She was pretty hungry after battling those ogres.

The bakery was buzzing with fairies, many of them seemed to be working. Some were dusting the decorations, and others were cleaning tables while a few were glazing donuts. The case of baked goods was like an art piece one would find in a museum.

The cinnamon rolls, which were the size of one's face, were so perfectly round they didn't seem real. Small cakes that were expertly decorated lined the bottom row. The flowers made of pastel frosting were enchanted to open and close like they were blooming on a spring day. Above those were cupcakes of almost every flavor Sophia could think of. There was red velvet to lemon coconut and everything in between. There was a sign on the counter that read, *"If we don't have it, then it doesn't exist."*

Sophia chuckled at the sign.

A woman's head popped out from behind a ten-layer chocolate cake on the top of the main display case. "What are you laughing at?"

The woman had short hair and a studious expression in her eyes.

"Oh, hey!" Sophia greeted her. "I just was laughing at the sign."

The woman, who was wearing flour on her cheeks like it was blush, scowled at Sophia. "Why? What is funny about it? We literally have every baked good you could want."

"Well, it's just impossible to have everything," Sophia argued.

"It's limited thinking like which has kept you in that dead-end job of yours," the woman spat.

"I'm a dragonrider for the Elite," Sophia countered, thoroughly amused by the ornery woman.

"And you will stay there for the next thousand years unless you broaden your thinking!" the baker exclaimed.

Sophia looked at Wilder, who was hiding the grin on his face, although not very well.

"Dear, are you harassing the patrons again?" another woman asked, coming in from the back and carrying a large box labeled "Weapons."

The woman pointed at Sophia. "She started it."

"Of course, she did," the other woman said, her French accent strong. She was shorter than the other lady and had cropped red hair. "But we don't point, remember. And we don't say the things we are thinking out loud. Now, where do you want your assassin weapons?"

The first woman threw her hands up in the air. "Well, I will take the knife right now since I'm going to stab you with it." She leaned forward and whispered. "Cat, assassins don't usually broadcast that information to other people."

The woman, who was apparently named Cat, nodded like this all made perfect sense. "Also, Lee, good assassins don't leave their weapons lying around. You know today is when I clean the back room."

"You clean the backroom every day, dear," Lee said, an inflection on the last word. "Morning, noon, night. Oh, I think a speck of dust fell from the rafters just now. Do you need to rush back there and clean it up?"

Cat shook her head of short red hair. "No, I don't." She glanced up at a tiny fairy dusting the ceiling. "Go on then. Go get that speck of dust."

The fairy buzzed off, blurring through the air.

Wilder cleared his throat to get the arguing couple's attention. They both turned their heads and gave him murderous stares.

"What do you want?" Lee asked him.

"Well, shockingly, I was hoping to buy something to eat. Can I please get a chocolate chip cookie," Wilder said.

Lee shook her head. "We don't have any."

He cocked his head to the side and pointed at the sign. "I thought you had everything."

"We did," Lee explained. "But I ate all the cookies this morning."

"I can whip up some more for you," Cat said good-naturedly. "Do you have any food allergies?"

"Because if you do, you can show yourself out," Lee fired. "We don't cater to pansies who can't tolerate gluten or snotty jerks who shove their vegan agendas down our throats. And those with nut allergies can suck it up, Buttercup. I ain't got time for that nonsense."

Wilder smiled. "Don't worry. I'm not picky. Actually, I'm sure I can find something else since you are out of cookies." He pointed to a display case at the end of the row. "What are these about?"

The case of assorted pastries appeared like all the other ones, except there were little red signs in front of each item. They said things like Bittersweet Chocolate Tarts, Shush It Strudel, Cap 'Em Cannoli, and No Lies Lady Fingers.

"Oh, Scotsman, I don't think you are ready for that," Lee told him. "Why don't you stick with the nonmagical baked goods."

"Those are magical?" Wilder asked, ignoring the assassin baker.

"They are," Cat sang, laying her arms on the top of the case and peering down into it proudly. "Give the tart to someone bitter, and they'll become sweet. Give it to someone sweet, and they will become bitter."

"And if you give it to a cantankerous old witch, you get this," Lee said, holding a presenting hand at her wife.

"Oh," Sophia said, intrigued. "The Shush It Strudel will make someone be quiet, then?"

"Yes," Cat affirmed and looked at the woman beside her. "Would you like a slice, my love?"

Lee shook her head. "No, but remember that loose shingle on the roof needs to be fixed. I will hold the ladder for you, dear, if you will get up there and take care of it."

Cat plastered a smile on her face. "I will definitely do that if you will fix the blow dryer. It's hanging next to the sink, which is still leaking. There is water all over the floor in front of it."

Lee flashed her own disingenuous smile. "I'm happy to look into that, right after you sample those Cap 'Em Cannolis. I think they might be too sweet, but why don't you be the judge of that, sweetie?"

"Oh, do the Cap 'Em Cannolis actually...you know?" Sophia asked, afraid she would have to shut down the bakery if it sold murderous pastries.

"Unfortunately, no," Lee said with a sigh. "They only put the eater into a very long nap. But I will get the formula right at some point, and they'll do what they are intended to."

"I'm afraid that is illegal," Wilder commented, raising an eyebrow at the woman.

"'I'm afraid that is illegal,'" Lee said in a high-pitched voice, doing an awful impression of him. She looked at Cat and shook her head. "He is a unicorn rider."

"Dragon, actually," Wilder corrected with an amused glint in his blue eyes.

"Same thing, Scotsman." Lee waved him off. "Okay, well, I have a job to get to, so hurry up and order."

"A catering job?" Cat asked.

Lee cut her eyes at her. "Yes, a catering job. Is my ski mask clean, dear?"

"If you put it in the laundry basket last night, it is," Cat replied.

Lee rolled her eyes. "Fine, I will wear one of the other ones. This side business isn't going to take off unless I'm prepared before each assignment."

"Oh, is *that* the problem?" Cat argued. "I thought it was because you can't shoot someone even if they pull the trigger for you."

"Well, I need more target practice, honey," Lee explained. "If you agree to help, I'm sure I can get better. Let's go out to the shooting range later. I will tell you *exactly* where to stand."

Cat shook her head. "I would, my darling, but I have to clean behind the refrigerator. It's been ages since I have done that. What would I say if someone saw what was back there?"

"What the hell are you doing looking behind my refrigerator, Jerkface?" Lee asked.

"Sorry to interrupt," Sophia cut in. She had said she could spare an hour for this excursion, but this could turn into more like half the day at this rate.

"Then don't interrupt," Lee chimed. "Can't you see adults are talking, Dragonrider?"

"I was just hoping to get an apple turnover," Sophia said, pointing at the case where the triangle pastries were calling to her.

Cat shook her head. "Oh, no. You don't want those. Pick something else."

"But that is what I want," Sophia argued.

Cat patted the side of Lee's arm. "Get her one of those profiteroles."

"Oh, but I—"

Cat gave Sophia a stern expression, cutting off her stuttering. "You will love these. I make mine so sweet it hurts your teeth. You will really enjoy it."

"Sounds great," Sophia replied, not meaning it.

Wilder pointed at a kolache. "And I will have—"

"You will share her profiterole," Cat said in an authoritative voice.

"You don't want us to buy more pastries?" Wilder protested disbelievingly. "You are ordering us to share when we were willing to give you more money?"

Lee shook her head and handed over a white paper bag with the profiterole. "We don't want your money. Just be on your way and don't tell anyone about the bodies in the back."

"What bodies in the back?" Sophia asked, taking the bag.

Cat rounded on her wife, her brow scowling. "If you got blood on the floor again, I'm going to murder you in your sleep."

"You can try again," Lee said with a laugh. "But next time, you have got to really hold the pillow down for a full two to three minutes."

Cat waved her off as she made for the back of the shop. "Oh, who has time for all that? Just clean up after yourself, would you? I'm tired of being the one who has to dispose of the bones."

Lee stormed after her, fists by her side. "You need to stop throwing those away! We bury bones, not chuck them into the trash like some amateurs."

Sophia and Wilder burst out laughing when the couple disappeared into the back.

"Those two are a riot." Sophia opened the small sack and tore the pastry in two. She offered the other half to Wilder.

He held up his hand, pretending he didn't want any. "Oh, no. I don't eat sugar. It's a gateway drug."

CHAPTER EIGHTY-FIVE

Sophia was still giggling when they made their way to the Fantastical Armory. She reasoned it could be from the profiterole, which was so sweet it made her eyes burst open with surprise at the first bite.

Wilder had shared half with her, and it had been perfect for them. There was no way they could have each finished a whole one. Those kooky old women might have been more intuitive than Sophia realized. Although if Lee really was an assassin, she would have to pay the bakers another visit. She thought she might be able to let it slide since they did make an amazing profiterole and were quite entertaining.

Sophia wiped the powdered sugar from her hands and bobbed her head graciously at Wilder as he held the door to the Fantastical Armory open for her.

Subner was waiting for them just inside the shop full of weapons. In contrast to the bakery that smelled of sweet treats and rich coffee, the Fantastical Armory had a masculine scent about it, like a locker room mixed with the musty weapon room at the Castle.

Father Time's assistant was leaning against one of the glass cases, his shoes crossed in front of him. His long stringy hair obscured one eye, and he had his usual serious expression. He wore a tattered t-shirt that said: "War is over, if you want it. – John Lennon."

"Is it weird the Protector of Weapons is wearing an anti-war shirt?" Sophia asked Wilder in a mock whisper, pretending Subner couldn't hear her.

"Yeah, it seems like no war would put him out of business," Wilder said with a wink.

The hippie-looking-elf rolled his eyes. "Don't even get me started. Yesterday I was wearing a shirt that said, 'What if I fall? Oh, but darling, what if I fly?'" He shook his head, looking severely irritated. "Being a hippie in this incarnation is probably going to kill my usually cheery spirit."

Sophia's gaze skirted to Wilder, and they shared a confused expression.

Subner leaned forward and gave them a conspiratorial expression. "Maybe I can hire you two to do me a little favor. Most dangerous job ever and it will probably kill the both of you—"

"You are really selling this," Sophia interrupted with a laugh.

He waved her off. "It's not that bad. I just need you to murder Father Time. He can't really die, not really, but the whole thing would make him regenerate and make me do so as well. Hopefully, I would come back as something less irritating, like a magician or a gnome."

"Or you might be a pretty little fae," Wilder teased.

Subner shivered as if the idea repulsed him. He shook his head. "Actually, forget it. I can't risk becoming a fae again. The last time that happened, I fell in love, and it pretty much made me throw up."

Sophia clasped her hands together beside her chin and batted her eyelashes at the elf. "You are such a romantic."

"I'm not," he told her. "But that reminds me, Wilder, I have a new mission for you involving cupid and getting his bow and arrow. You can't do it until you help Sophia and the Dragon Elite resolve the security problem at the Gullington."

"You know about that?" Sophia asked.

The Protector of Weapons gave her a cold expression. "Yes, as the assistant to Father Time, the most powerful entity in the world, excluding Mother Nature, I happen to be privy to what is going on at the Gullington."

Sophia shook her head and gave Wilder a teasing expression. "I don't think we will be able to pull off Subner's surprise party after all."

"No, you won't," Subner stated matter-of-factly. "Not to mention you don't know when my birthday is since I was technically never born."

"Hatched," Wilder told Sophia, elbowing her in the side. "He was hatched like a dragon."

"They still have birthdays," she argued.

"Which reminds me, tell Liv when she is done helping you, Father Time has a new mission for her," Subner informed Sophia.

"Oh, we definitely want her help, but if she is needed, I will send her here," Sophia offered.

Subner shook his head. "That is not necessary. This mission isn't time-sensitive since it occurs in the past. The events she needs to stop have already happened, but once she is done, it will change quite a bit."

Sophia nodded to Wilder. "That is so typical."

He agreed. "Change important historical events?"

Subner shook his head. "No, just the number of flavors Baskin Robbins has."

"And that is important?" Sophia asked.

"Yes, it changes everything."

"The balance of the world rests on very strange things, doesn't it?" Sophia remarked.

"Indeed, it does," Subner affirmed.

"Okay." The light expression dropped from Wilder's face. "You want me to go on this cupid mission after the mess at the Gullington is over. Will do."

"Actually, I want you and Sophia to go on it together," Subner corrected.

"You do?" Wilder wondered, surprise in his voice.

"Well, naturally," he answered like this should have been obvious to the dragonrider. "Only the one who helped you free Excalibur could help you steal cupid's bow and arrows."

"Isn't it going to mess up things if we take Cupid's weapon of love?"

"No, that out-of-control creature hasn't been spreading love for eons," Subner muttered. "We will get into all of that later."

Sophia had so many questions. She thought Cupid was a myth. She used to think the same thing about dragons, so it just went to show the world was still full of surprises. Before she could ask any of her burning questions, Subner held up his hand.

"So, S. Beaufont, tell me, were you surprised you were able to pull my sword from King Arthur's stone?" Subner asked.

CHAPTER EIGHTY-SIX

"Wait," Wilder cut in. "Did you say it was your sword?"

Subner gave him an irritated expression. "Of course, it was my sword."

"Do you mean because all weapons belong to you?" Sophia asked. She still didn't really understand how the Protector of Weapons worked.

He shook his head. "No, I mean because Excalibur was originally mine, but then that jerk King Arthur stole it and stuck it in the stone in the Gullington. Although I can technically get in there, I respect the rules of the Dragon Elite."

"You needed Wilder to get it for you," Sophia guessed.

Again, Subner shook his head. "No, I needed you to get the sword, but you don't work for me, so I assigned the task to Wilder."

The hippie elf was obviously getting irritated with having to explain everything to the two of them.

Sophia scratched her head. "Okay, you knew Wilder wouldn't be able to pull the sword."

Subner sighed, nodding along. "Yes, and I knew he would come and get you to help him."

"I lost Simi," Wilder complained. "What kind of set up is that?"

"It's a perfectly reasonable one for someone who is privy to the future," Subner dismissed him, unconcerned about Wilder's frustration.

"But there is no set future," Sophia argued, remembering what she had learned about everything on timelines being in flux due to free will and choices. "What if I refused to help Wilder get Excalibur?"

"Then Simi would have stayed stuck in the Round," Subner answered. "And although that is true about the future, I can also factor in what I know about the players involved."

"We are just pawns in this game for Subner," Wilder grumbled, pretending to be irritated.

Ignoring him, Subner went on, "I know Sophia cares more about her family and friends than anything else in this world. Therefore, I made the educated guess that when you, Wilder, lost what you value most, Sophia would help you."

"How did you know I would go to Sophia for help?" Wilder challenged. "I could have gone and gotten the Queen of England to pull the sword."

"Ah, yes, but she isn't a dragonrider and therefore can't get into the Gullington," Subner pointed out.

"Those who are usually disallowed from entering the Gullington can at the moment," Sophia argued.

Subner sighed heavily. "Fine, fine. Good point. I knew when Wilder was in trouble, he would run to you, Sophia." He gave them both a stern expression that felt like a weird reprimand. "You both know why so I wouldn't push me to answer more questions on this unless you want me to say it out loud."

The tension that ran over Wilder's face was palpable. Sophia swallowed down her own sudden nervousness.

"Okay, so you needed us to recover your sword that King Arthur stole," Sophia said, trying to move the discussion along.

Wilder pulled Excalibur off his back and presented it to Subner. "Here you are."

Subner didn't take the sword. Instead, he shook his head. "Great. Thanks. Now put it back."

"What?" Sophia and Wilder exclaimed at the same time.

"Put. It. Back." Subner punctuated each word with a pause.

"You had us go through all that just so you could tell us to put Excalibur back?" Wilder protested, looking irritated at his boss.

"I did."

"But why?" Sophia wondered.

"Because the act of actually pulling the sword and everything the two of you went through was necessary to create other events," Subner explained.

Wilder's annoyed gaze shifted to Sophia. "A pawn, I tell you."

"Yeah, I'm getting pretty used to Mama Jamba and others orchestrating things in my life," she said, thinking of how Mae Ling always seemed to be setting her up, like Subner seemed to be doing.

"Do you at least want to look the sword over or add it to your collection?" Wilder inquired, still holding Excalibur out to the elf.

"No," Subner answered. "For as irritating as it was that King Arthur stole my sword, his hiding place was pretty perfect. He knew I wouldn't be able to pull the blade because I'm not royalty. It is much safer at the Gullington in Falconer's Cave than here on Roya Lane. And that sword in the wrong hands would be very dangerous, so it should go back into the stone."

"But what if someone in the Gullington pulls it?" Sophia questioned. "It's not as safe and secure a place as it once was."

"The likelihood a thief who is royalty breaks into the Gullington is much less than someone breaking into my shop," Subner told her. "Especially if word got out I had Excalibur, the most prized sword in history."

"Yeah." Wilder looked at Sophia. "I think you are the only one at the Gullington who can pull the sword since you are the only royalty inside the area."

"For now, she is," Subner said mysteriously.

Sophia blinked at the Protector of Weapons but decided not to question him on these possible future events where there was another royalty at the Gullington. "You knew Wilder would ask me to pull Excalibur, and you knew I would help him. And you also knew my Royal blood from the House of Fourteen would allow me to retrieve the sword. Correct?"

"They were all educated guesses." Subner sounded bored.

"And now after all this fun guesswork, we get to go put the sword back where it was," Wilder stated dryly.

"We didn't even get a souvenir t-shirt," Sophia complained.

Not amused by their banter, Subner pushed off the counter and walked around behind it. "Actually, S. Beaufont, I do have something for you to repay you for your efforts."

"What about me?" Wilder asked.

Subner glanced up from the case. "What about you?"

"Well, what do I get for losing my dragon for a part of a day and risking my life to get a sword you didn't even really want?" he questioned.

"A good story to tell your children," Subner answered, sorting through different items in the case.

Wilder huffed but didn't respond otherwise.

"Now, where did I put that..." Subner muttered to himself. His face brightened. "Oh, here it is." He pulled a pocketknife from the case. The craftmanship of the knife was striking, even from a distance. Sophia could tell a lot of care had been taken to etch the design of the serpent-looking dragon on the side. Gold inlay was used around the sides to highlight details.

He handed it over to Sophia, giving her a look she couldn't quite make out. It seemed to have a hidden meaning behind it.

She smiled, looking the knife over. "Thank you. It's beautiful."

"And tiny," Wilder observed.

"I made this pocket knife a few decades ago," Subner explained.

"I like it has a dragon in the design," she said, turning the knife over and admiring the details. She had no idea why Subner would give this to her as a gift. It was good to have a knife stashed away in her boot or something though, Sophia reasoned.

"I knew you would," he hinted.

Sophia raised an eyebrow at him. "You knew I would like the design of the dragon, which is why you thought to give it to me?"

He shook his head. "No, when I made it, I knew you would like the dragon design, which was why I chose it."

"You made this knife for Sophia a few decades ago?" Wilder asked. "Like before she was even born?"

"Yeah, I also made you something before you were born," Subner revealed.

"Over two-hundred years ago?" Wilder questioned. "Before you even knew me?"

Subner nodded, not thinking this was weird.

Sophia's eyes trailed away in thought as she was reminded that Wilder was so much older than her. All the guys were, so she wasn't sure why it mattered. Evan was over a hundred years older than Sophia, and based on his behavior, no one would have guessed. Most of the time, Sophia forgot there was an age difference between her and the others, but she had always felt much older than she was.

"Well, what did you make for me?" Wilder asked Subner, looking around the shop expectantly.

"You can't have it yet," Subner told him.

Wilder rolled his eyes. "I should have guessed."

Sophia opened the pocketknife and saw the blade was engraved with two initials. "S.B."

She glanced up. "You really did make this for me?"

Wilder laughed. "Did you think he was just trying to pass it off as something he made for you? Like he was regifting it?"

"I don't know," she answered. "It's just a little weird for someone to make something for you before you are even born that is so personalized. My parents didn't even know they were going to name me Sophia until after I was born."

"Such is the strangeness of the nonlinear timeline," Subner commented, watching her intently as she studied the knife.

She turned the knife over, studying the other side of the blade. There was a strange pattern on that side. It looked like an organic design of swirls, but there was something strange about it. Sophia narrowed her eyes, trying to figure out what the pattern reminded her of. Her vision slightly blurred as she focused, and then she saw it.

Sucking in a breath, she looked up at the Protector of Weapons.

"Is that…" she asked, awe in her voice.

Subner nodded and flashed her a rare smile. "It is."

CHAPTER EIGHTY-SEVEN

Sophia closed the blade and put it away before Wilder could see what she was referring to. Subner hadn't elaborated. Instead, he ushered them to the door, telling them they should run along to the Castle. Apparently, dinner was about to be served, and Sophia would need to "manage" relations among her friends and the Dragon Elite. That is what he said, but she sensed he was just trying to get rid of them.

"What was on the blade of the knife?" Wilder asked her after they stepped through the portal outside the Barrier to the Gullington.

"Things," she said dismissively.

"Why do you always insist on going on and on about things?" he joked.

She ignored him as they passed through the Barrier. "The Castle is still standing, so that is a good sign."

"Meaning whatever is plaguing the Castle isn't getting worse just yet?" he questioned.

Sophia shook her head. "No, meaning Hiker hasn't destroyed it trying to murder King Rudolf or Liv."

"Do you think the giants will be able to help with the Gullington?"

She shrugged. "I don't know. Hopefully, they can secure the

Barrier when Mama Jamba stops protecting things. Whether they will know what is wrong with it is uncertain. Bermuda Laurens is an expert in a lot of things, but I think the Gullington is outside her field of knowledge."

"Well, I hope they figure it out," Wilder said, a longing in his blue eyes as he stared across the Expanse.

"Yeah," Sophia agreed, studying him as he looked out, an undeniable sadness in his gaze. Like her, he often put on a smile and made light of things, but the Gullington had been his home for almost two centuries. As hard as it was for her to see it in trouble, it had to be excruciatingly painful for him.

He sighed. "If nothing else, maybe when you help Quiet feel better, he'll know what is what with the Gullington. Really, if anyone does, it will be him."

Sophia nodded, still watching the other dragonrider. When he turned to face her abruptly, he caught her staring.

"What is up, stalker?" he asked, a teasing quality to his voice.

She jerked her head away, trying to cover her embarrassment. "Nothing. I thought you had something in your teeth."

"Oh, can you see through lips now?" he challenged.

"I think you know I can," Sophia retorted.

"Were you looking at me?"

"No," she lied. "I was looking at Excalibur on your back."

"Right," Wilder said, not sounding convinced. "Do you want to go with me to put it back in the stone in Falconer Cave?"

Sophia shook her head, backing for the Castle in the distance. "I shouldn't. I need to get back and mediate."

He nodded, although there was an unmistakable look of disappointment on his face. "Yeah, I get it. I will be up to the Castle for dinner in a bit. I want to stop by the Cave and see Simi. Make sure she is okay after the whole ordeal."

Sophia would do the same thing in his situation, although she was slightly disappointed he wouldn't be going up to the Castle with her. She was looking forward to introducing Liv, Clark and the others to him.

"What is it?" he asked, seeing the expression she didn't hide fast enough.

"Nothing," she lied again as a wind swept across the Expanse, blowing her hair back from her face and shooting her cloak out behind her.

"You said your brother was cooking dinner for us tonight?" He seemed to be lingering even though they both had other things to do.

Sophia offered a smile, grateful for the question that kept her there. "Yeah, he is a pretty good chef. Much better than Evan."

"That is good," Wilder commented, twisting his tongue in his mouth, working his jaw back and forth like he was weighing some internal indecision.

Sophia took a step backward. "Anyway, I will save you a seat at the table."

He took a step in her direction. "There are over twenty seats in the dining hall."

She laughed as she backed away toward the Castle. "Well, the giants will take up several seats each."

"Good point," he said, his eyes lingering on her.

"Anyway, I have to go." Sophia hesitated. She didn't, but she wanted to run, and put her back to the guy before her and get as far from the strange tension rising between them, that was growing with each of their interactions.

"I know, but wait," Wilder called to her.

She paused and regarded him like he was a painting—unreal but inspired by something quite tangible.

"I don't think I really thanked you earlier," he started.

"You did." She glanced over her shoulder at the Castle.

"No, not well enough, I didn't."

"It's fine, Wild." She walked back several paces.

He made up the distance. "No, it's not. You saved Simi for me. Most may not know how important that is, but you do as another dragonrider."

"We've been through this," Sophia argued. "I just did what you would have done if I was in that position."

367

He laughed like she had told a joke. "I would love to see the situation where Sophia Beaufont actually asked for my help."

"Why would I do that?" she fired back, grateful he was breaking the tension with something that made her laugh.

The wind sent Wilder's hair back. "You probably won't ever. You are not the kind of girl who needs saving. It's one of the things I like about you."

"I got to run," Sophia said, pointing behind her to the Castle.

"I know," he repeated. "But first, I need to properly thank you. Simi is my world. She is my life. And you saved that. If it wasn't for you—"

Sophia's mouth twitched as she shook her head. "It's fine. Thank me with a trip to Bora Bora or something. Right now, I have got to—"

"Run," he finished. "I know. I get it."

She knew he did. They both knew she couldn't stay there one more minute and not just because her presence was needed at the Castle.

Sophia offered Wilder one last timid smile before she turned and ran, the wind propelling her toward the steps of the Castle, sending her cloak and hair out in all directions.

This time, she didn't look back.

But if she had, she would have seen what she had dropped.

CHAPTER EIGHTY-EIGHT

Wilder Thomson was many things.

He was a man of his word, someone who valued friendship over wealth and prestige—and inexplicably taken by the woman who had just run from him.

He watched the wind carry Sophia Beaufont away. Wilder didn't look from her until she disappeared into the Castle. He enjoyed how her cloak and hair whipping around her body made her appear like she was in the sky, riding her dragon.

There was more he wanted to say to Sophia, but she didn't want to hear it. He understood. Things wouldn't be easier for them if he said more to her. If he said all he wanted to.

He didn't blame her for running, but he did wish he knew the way to her heart.

Wilder was about to head in the direction of the Cave and call his dragon down to him. Just as he was turning away from the Castle, a glint of something shiny in the grass caught his attention.

He marched across the Expanse, following the path Sophia had just taken.

In the grass was an object he recognized. For a magician who had always felt and seen the life of a weapon, he didn't get any reading from the pocketknife he retrieved from the grass. It was the one Subner had given to Sophia in thanks for her help retrieving Excalibur.

Maybe he didn't get a reading on the pocketknife because it hadn't had a real life yet, stored at the Fantastical Armory with Subner all this time. Or maybe the Protector of Weapons had put a shield on it, disallowing Wilder from reading anything about the knife. He knew the elf had that ability since Subner was the one who had made it so Wilder could pick up information on weapons.

He studied the exemplary craftsmanship of the knife, the dragon design on the outside, and the gold inlay. Then he opened the knife and found Sophia's initials on one side of the blade.

He turned the blade over and peered at the image on the other side. It was a crisscross of designs that seemed abstract. As he studied it longer, a single object came into view.

He shook his head, not understanding why that object would be on the blade of Sophia's knife.

CHAPTER EIGHTY-NINE

The Castle was buzzing with noise when Sophia entered. At first, she couldn't determine if there was a fight going on in the dining hall or a party. Her head was buzzing after her conversation with Wilder. Not just her head, but that was all she was giving notice to right then, maybe ever.

"All I'm saying is that is not how they like their Beef Wellington," Ainsley yelled from the dining hall.

Sophia snuck to the doorway and peered through to find the housekeeper with her hands in the air and her red hair a wild mess.

Clark was opposite her, a picture of perfect poise as he regarded her with quiet contempt. "And how do the dragonriders like their Beef Wellington?"

"In the trash," Ainsley answered at once. "We don't eat frou-frou food like that around here. Hiker Wallace wants food that sticks to his ribs. Not things rolled in pastry and sprinkled with bits of mushroom. I don't even think he'll eat a mushroom."

Clark shook his head, obviously working to keep his temper in check, although the shapeshifter was challenging him on a new level. "That is not really how Beef Wellington is prepared. I assure you it's very hearty."

371

Ainsley shook her head erratically. "He doesn't want hearty. He wants the same thing he always has every day I have cooked for him."

Clark sighed. "But you can't cook for him. You can't cook for anyone right now, which is why I'm here. Why don't you just relax and let me do what I came here to do?"

"Annoy me?" Ainsley yelled back, getting in Clark's face. Thankfully it didn't provoke him.

He shook his head. "No, I came here to help. I wish you would let me do it."

"Fine!" she exclaimed. "Don't cry when Hiker throws your food across the room and tells you that you are rubbish."

Clark didn't respond as Ainsley fled from the room, not even seeing Sophia by the door as she stormed up the stairs.

She peered around the doorway and waved discreetly at her brother, who was pushing his hands through his hair. "Hey," she said, offering him a sympathetic smile.

"Hey," he replied, his voice more husky than usual.

"Ainsley means well, she just..."

"She just is dealing with a lot," he supplied, nodding with understanding. This was what made Clark a good Councilor for the House of Fourteen. He was more empathic than most, able to read the details of a situation and know what really needed to be done for the best interests of everybody.

"She is," Sophia admitted. "I mean, she is not a ray of sunshine when in normal mode, but she has been taking care of the Castle and the guys for centuries."

"It must be tough to be sick suddenly and have newbies filling up her Castle taking over things."

Sophia was glad Clark understood. "Yeah, I can't even imagine. Thanks again for coming to help."

He offered her a smile. "Of course, Soph. You know I will always be here for you. I mean, not until recently could I be here at the Gullington for you. This is nice." He looked around at the Castle, admiring it. "What a marvelous place you have become a part of. Mom and Dad would be incredibly proud."

A fondness crossed his face, the same expression he always got when he thought of their parents or when he spoke about them. For Sophia, there was little emotion for her at the mention of their dead parents. She used to try and make herself feel something for the people she never really knew, but it was hopeless.

Her siblings adored their parents and spoke about them like they were legends. Everyone who knew Guinevere and Theodore Beaufont were. But for Sophia, it was like idolizing someone in a history book. She could appreciate the cold, hard facts about them, but nothing else because she didn't have her own memories to connect her to those two incredible people.

"Are you settling in?" Sophia asked, changing the subject. "I mean, besides the housekeeper telling you to throw your dinner in the trash and berating you for trying to help."

He chuckled. "Yeah. This is a very comfortable place, although much different from the House of Fourteen."

"You should see the Castle when it's well," Sophia explained. "It anticipates your needs, and if it likes you, supplies what you want. If it doesn't, like with Evan, it deprives you. Very quirky old castle. More personality in this place than most people I have met."

Clark nodded appreciatively. "I can see that. Although the circumstances which brought me here are unfortunate, I'm still grateful I got a chance to see the place you are a part of."

"You won't be staying much longer, so fill up your scrapbook with mental images before you get kicked to the curb," Ainsley said, buzzing back into the dining hall and right past them. She disappeared into the kitchen.

Clark gave Sophia a curious expression. "How does a housekeeper who hardly leaves this place have such a modern vernacular?"

She grinned. "She watches YouTube with me at night."

"Of course, she does. You would obviously be educating the Dragon Elite about the modern world."

"Just wait until I pass along my Amazon addiction," Sophia teased.

The door to the kitchen swung back open, and Ainsley stuck her head through. "Are you going to cook, or are you going to chat all day? When the dragonriders come in, they'll be hungry, and no one likes waiting around while snotty guys in suits take forever to polish the silverware."

Sophia kept the laugh begging to escape her mouth at bay. "I think she is referring to you."

Clark nodded. "Yeah, she is a real name caller." He turned and gave the housekeeper a polite smile. "I will have dinner done on time. I promise."

Ainsley pointed at Clark as he hurried in her direction, looking past him at Sophia. "This guy is a real piece of work. I feel sorry for whoever his family is. Holidays must be a real bore fest."

CHAPTER NINETY

"Are you cold?" Rudolf asked Sophia, walking past her, a baby still strapped to his front and to his back. Both were still quiet, sucking away at the pacifiers Mae Ling had given her.

She arched an eyebrow at him. "No, why?"

"Well, why are you wearing a blanket?" he asked.

Glancing down at her body, she shrugged. "Do you mean my travel cloak? Which I wear because I'm a dragonrider who goes on badass adventures, on my dragon?"

He held up his hands. "I guess. It looks to me like you are wearing a blanket."

"Where is the other baby?" Sophia asked. "Captain Morgan?"

He looked around suddenly, anxious. "Oh, I thought you had her."

"I have been off on a mission," Sophia explained to him. "And you and I need to leave for the Fae Museum of National History right after dinner."

"Because?" he asked, trailing away.

"Because we have to steal that captain's hat," she told him, feeling suddenly tired.

"Because?"

"Because I need it in order to remind Quiet of what he has to live for," Sophia explained.

"Because?"

"Because if I have to keep explaining things to you, then you are going to get murdered," she fired back.

"That is what I keep saying," Liv said, coming into the dining hall pushing the baby carriage. "You left this in the weapons room. Not a place where I think small humans should be."

"But she likes her stroller," Rudolf argued, not getting what Liv was talking about.

She shook her head and looked Sophia over. "Oh, so the mission..."

"It was fine," Sophia replied, waving Liv off.

"That is not what I meant," Liv offered. "Something else happened."

Sophia shook her head. "Nothing happened. Nothing. I recovered Excalibur, fought a bunch of ogres, rescued a dragon, met some assassin baker, and then found out it was all pretty unnecessary to begin with."

Rudolf leaned over, checking on Captain Morgan. "That sounds almost exactly like the day I had."

Liv cut her eyes at him. "You fell asleep on your side with those children strapped to you, and I had to change Captain Morgan's diaper."

"Well, I had a dream that was like Sophia's day," Rudolf protested, looking up at the tall ceiling. "It's something about this place. It's almost like this place is old and has lots of memories or something."

"It's probably one of the oldest buildings still standing," Sophia commented.

Rudolf waved her off. "Right. Just like the Cosmopolitan on the Vegas strip."

"Nope." Liv turned her attention to Sophia. "You and me, we are talking after dinner about this stuff that didn't happen."

"No, Rudolf and I have to go break into a museum."

"I'm always up for breaking into places that have national treasures, but I'm putting down the big sister foot," Liv demanded. "You are exhausted and going to get some rest. You can leave for this mission with Rudolf, which will rob your soul of much joy, first thing in the morning."

"I'm really looking forward to it too," Rudolf chimed, bouncing around as the babies strapped to him started to fuss.

Sophia sighed. "Yeah, fine. We will leave tomorrow."

She had to admit she was exhausted, and having some time to chat with Liv would be good for her spirit. It could also cause her feelings to come out, and that worried her. Still, there was no arguing with Liv when she made up her mind.

CHAPTER NINETY-ONE

"What is that smell?" Evan said, taking in a big inhale when he entered the dining hall.

"Your face," Sophia fired at him.

Liv gave her an appreciative expression. "Good one."

"Ha-ha," he said, walking past Sophia and moving a bit better than she had seen him recently.

"Did Hester fix you up?" Sophia asked him.

"Yeah, it's weird to have to do things the old fashioned way," Evan admitted.

"You mean with an actual healer instead of having a sentient castle heal you while you sleep?" Sophia teased.

"Yeah, totally 'old-school,' as you would say."

Sophia shook her head at Evan. "I guess you have met my sister Liv, and Rudolf and the others."

"Yeah, and I screamed when I saw the giants because no one told me they were going to be here," Evan said.

Liv's eyes fluttered with annoyance. "Yeah, I had to intervene when this dimwit pulled a sword on Rory, trying to fight him."

He held up his hands. "What? The last time I encountered a giant, they tried to knock my head off. They aren't the most pleasant people.

I thought the giant might have broken in through the Barrier and was pillaging the Castle."

"Too bad they didn't succeed in knocking your head off." Sophia let out a tired sigh. "I did tell you, Evan, that the giants would be here."

He shook his head. "We both know I don't listen to you, Soph."

"Isn't he cute?" she asked Liv.

"Like a hairless cat," her sister admitted. "I wonder if Hester can give him back that stab wound."

"We can always ask," Sophia suggested.

Right on cue, the healer entered the dining hall. "Hey, ladies. I've finished with Mahkah and think I should head back to the House of Fourteen now. I don't want anyone to grow suspicious and they might with us all missing at the same time."

"That is a good idea," Liv declared.

"How is Mahkah?" Sophia asked.

"He is as good as new. I was able to regrow the finger. Although if he loses it again or any other parts, there is no hope. Sorry. I can only fix a lost appendage once on a person."

"I'm sure he'll be extra careful," Sophia promised, although since she had known him, Mahkah had bad luck with getting injured. "Were you able to…"

The light expression on Hester's face fell away as she filled in what Sophia hadn't said. "I'm sorry, but for some strange reason, my healing powers don't work on the groundskeeper or the housekeeper."

"Oh." Sophia couldn't keep the disappointment out of her voice.

"I'm sorry, dear, but I think whatever this incredible Castle was doing to keep them healthy and alive is much more powerful than me," Hester explained. "They'll need the Castle back to recover."

Sophia nodded. "I have an antidote for the groundskeeper. I just have to get him to take it, and that is a bit complicated. Hopefully, once he comes to, he'll know how to fix the Castle."

"And then it will fix Ainsley," Evan exclaimed, mock fondness in his voice. "And this place will go back to being a circus once more."

"Don't be a jerk about this place," Sophia warned. "Things might be stable right now, but that may not last."

Liv patted Sophia on the shoulder. "Don't worry. We are here, and we are going to help. We will keep the Gullington as safe as we can until things are back to normal for you."

"Except for me," Hester said, offering a smile. "I must be off."

"Thanks for your help," Sophia said, hugging the healer she had known her entire life. She had always trusted the DeVries. Now she did even more.

"Anything for a Beaufont." Hester touched Sophia's chin slightly as she regarded her with fondness. She looked around at the dining hall, her eyes dazzling with delight. "This place was quite a sight to see. I feel honored. I only wish I could have met Mother Nature while I was here. I hear she is larger than life."

Mama Jamba hustled into the dining hall, her bunny slippers scratching against the stone floor. "Now, where did I leave my hair curlers?" She looked up at Sophia as she passed. "Dear, have you seen my bag of foam curlers? They really are the only way I can get this hair tamed, especially with all that wind you keep kicking up all over the Gullington."

Sophia smiled wide. "You know, Hester. Today is your lucky day."

CHAPTER NINETY-TWO

"Lucky day?" Mama Jamba asked, looking around at the group. "Every day on my green Earth is lucky."

"This is…" Hester's gray eyes widened with shock as she looked between Sophia and the little woman wearing a purple plush hoodie over a T-shirt that read: "Mother Nature is My Pharmacist."

The healer had the same expression of disbelief most did when they met the infamous Mama Jamba. She covered it almost immediately and bowed low to the woman. "It is an honor to make your acquaintance, Mother Nature."

"Call me Mama Jamba," the old southern belle said. "And Bunny, we've known each other all your life. This isn't our first meeting."

Hester blushed. "Bunny. No one has called me that since…"

"Your papa," Mama Jamba supplied. "Where do you think he got your nickname from?"

"From you?" Hester asked.

Mama Jamba nodded. "Indeed. It's a story for another time because a Warrior for the House of Fourteen needs your healing ability."

"Oh, who?" Liv asked, worry suddenly covering her face.

"Not your man," Mama Jamba said, relieving her fears. "It's Maria

Rosario. Minor injuries, but still, it's best if you hurry off now. We will meet again."

"Thank you," Hester told her and offered the group a polite smile as she hurried for the exit, showing herself out.

"Mama Jamba, will you tell me what is going on at my kingdom right now?" Rudolf asked. "How is Serena doing? Is there anything calling for my attention?"

She leveled her gaze at the fae. "As always, the Las Vegas strip you call your kingdom is polluting my Earth with traffic, noise, and debauchery."

He sighed with a relieved expression. "That sounds about right."

Mama Jamba did not appear impressed by his reaction, and her lips pursed. "Serena is taking her afternoon nap, which will later be followed by her evening lounging and capped off with vegging on the sofa and watching children's television, but the jokes are all going over her head so she will be back asleep before it gets too late."

Rudolf nodded. "I hope she doesn't overdo it again."

"It sounds like she will survive," Liv said dryly.

Evan very non-discreetly slid behind Sophia when Rory entered the dining hall. The giant made the oversized entryway appear normal-sized.

"What are you doing?" Sophia asked Evan over her shoulder.

"I'm hiding," he answered, peering over her head at the giant.

From the corner of her mouth, she told him, "I think he can see you."

Evan nodded. "Yeah, but I don't think he'll hit a girl."

Liv laughed. "Rory won't so much as give the wasp nest on his back porch a dirty look. He personifies the term 'gentle giant.'"

Evan gave her an uncertain expression. "Giants hold grudges, though, and I don't think this big guy is going to forget I pulled a sword on him."

Sophia leaned over and talked loudly into Evan's ear. "That giant can hear you."

"Are you sure?" Evan still crouched behind Sophia, although she made a tiny shield.

"Yeah, I believe so," Sophia answered with a laugh.

"He is going to put you in a book and kill you," Liv teased Evan. "That is what writers do with people they don't like, isn't that right, Rory?"

"I have killed approximately a dozen characters who were modeled after Liv here."

She narrowed her eyes at him. "Hey, Rory. Why did the writer cross the road?"

He surveyed the dining hall. "I guess Mum is still with Hiker."

"I'm so glad you asked," Liv said, dismissing the fact the giant was ignoring her question. "Well, the writer was supposed to be finishing her book, so she crossed the road to grab a coffee, do her taxes, and maybe buy a new panini press."

He shook his head. "That joke doesn't make sense. You can't buy a panini press at an accounting firm."

Evan tapped Sophia rapidly in the arm. "Are you serious about these people overseeing magic in the magical world? I think it's more likely they escaped the nutter house."

"You are one to talk," she fired back.

Liv shook her head at the giant. "I feel like you missed the point of the joke. But I get I threw you off by making an accounting reference." She turned her gaze to Evan. "Actuary, Rory used to be an accountant."

"You stop that," Rory said, cringing from the bad pun.

"I can't," Liv argued. "I'm on a payroll."

The giant covered his face, shaking his head.

"Okay, I'm going to go see if Clark needs someone to taste the sauce," Liv declared, striding for the kitchen. "Calc you later!"

That one made Sophia laugh. Lunis and Liv were a lot more alike than either one wanted to admit.

"Hey, Rory," Sophia called. "Did you hear about the writer who jumped out of the window on the fifteenth story?"

His gaze slid up to the ceiling. "Oh, no. Not you too."

"He could have gone to the sixteenth, but that is another story," Sophia said with a laugh.

Ba-dum-tsk, Lunis called proudly in her head.

Mama Jamba clapped her hands excitedly. "Oh, good. We are telling bad jokes over dinner. That is a great way to ensure the conversation keeps moving since Hiker is in a real bad mood."

"Wait, these jokes aren't bad," Sophia argued. "And Hiker in a bad mood? Shocking. Why this time?"

"Yes, those jokes are atrocious," Evan affirmed. "And our fearless leader is probably mad because I discovered Post-It notes and plastered them all over his office, labeling the various things they were placed on."

"You need a job," Sophia said, unimpressed.

"Hey!" Evan argued. "I was out of commission, and no one wanted me to cook."

"Well, now that you are back, you can help with strategy and do stuff that is useful," she told him.

They didn't have to wait to find out why Hiker was angry this time. He thundered into the dining hall, Bermuda Laurens close on his heels.

"But," the giantess said, her tone insistent. "I was simply hoping you could explain how the Gullington isn't on any maps when the Barrier is up and can't be seen by anyone but the Dragon Elite and those who serve them."

"I don't know," Hiker growled, stomping over to his usual seat at the head of the table.

"It's magic, dear Bermuda," Mama Jamba explained, settling into her usual seat.

Bermuda, who for once didn't have an authoritative appearance about her, nodded to Mother Nature. "I understand that. It's just it's an unclassified type of magic."

"And I want it to stay that way," Hiker admonished.

Sophia thought the truth was that Hiker didn't really know how the Gullington worked. If he did, she believed he would know how to figure out what was wrong with it. He couldn't even get the Castle to cooperate when it punished him and redesigned his office. Ainsley probably understood the Castle better than most, and Quiet knew the Gullington, but neither was in any condition to explain anything.

Sophia agreed with Hiker on this one. She knew Bermuda meant well, wanting to record information for her reference guides and books, but it was best if no one knew the secrets of the Gullington. Already they had been punished and put on the defense simply because Hiker revealed the location of the Dragon Elite.

"You say the Castle, when it's acting normal, is able to manifest anything you all desire?" Bermuda inquired, looking between Evan and Sophia as they took their seats.

"Actually, it lavishes Pink Princess with whatever she likes," Evan grumbled. "Some of us don't get that kind of special treatment."

"Only jerks who say bad things about the Castle," Sophia spouted.

"Well, some of us are stuck up little do-gooders who think manners are important," Evan fired back.

"And some of us—"

"Why yes," Hiker interrupted Sophia before she could make her jab, "these are dragonriders who are mature enough to preside over world affairs. I realize you might have mistaken them for children."

"What did the fisherman say to the card magician?" Mama Jamba asked, laying her napkin in her lap and looking around the table.

Hiker rubbed his temples, shaking his head. "Oh, no. Not you now, Mama."

"Pick a cod, any cod," she answered with a laugh.

Both giants exchanged unpleasant expressions.

"What?" Mama Jamba protested, looking at the unlaughing faces. "We said we were going to exchange bad jokes at dinner tonight."

Liv trotted from the kitchen carrying a large silver platter. "Dinner is served."

"Oh, I know who will win the bad joke contest," Bermuda said, looking at Liv as she laid the Beef Wellington on the table.

The warrior offered the giantess an amused grin. "You know you love my jokes."

"I never even get them," Bermuda retorted.

Liv held out her hand, presenting the Beef Wellington. The pastry was the perfect toasted shade of brown, and the savory smell wafting from it made Sophia's stomach grumble with anticipation. "I have been slaving away all day, and now you all can enjoy my efforts."

Clark pushed through the kitchen door, carrying various dishes. He shook his head at his sister as he laid them on the table. "Taking credit for my work again?"

She nodded and tucked into the seat next to Sophia, where Wilder usually sat. He wasn't present though...not that she had noticed as her eyes darted to the entrance.

Ainsley materialized in the doorway right then, a tired expression on her face. "Why does it smell like something died in here?"

Mama Jamba pointed to the Beef Wellington. "It was a cow, and I think it's been dead for a while."

"Ainsley," Hiker said in his commanding tone. "You need to eat. Get in here and take a seat."

"But sir," the housekeeper argued. "I'm certain the magician poisoned the food. I can't eat it in good confidence."

Hiker cut into the Beef Wellington, raising an impressed eyebrow when the knife slipped through easily. "You mean like when you served us all poisoned food that only Quiet ate, making him deathly ill?"

Ainsley scowled at the Beef Wellington like it had offended her simply by existing. "I don't remember any of that happening."

"Oh dear, Clark," Mama Jamba moaned, taking a bite. "These mashed potatoes are the very best thing I have ever tasted. What is that secret ingredient?"

"Salt," Clark said. "Lots and lots of salt."

"It will make your fingers swell," Ainsley warned, crossing her arms stubbornly in front of her chest.

"But it makes food taste better," Clark argued.

"Enough talk about the food," Hiker ordered, although he already polished off half his plate. "What is the update from everyone?"

"I'm feeling much better, sir," Evan said. "Thanks for asking."

The leader of the Dragon Elite rolled his eyes. "I don't care, Evan. I was referring to the work our guests are doing to help us."

Evan scoffed. "Oh, fine. Maybe I will just go work for the House of Fourteen." He gave Liv a meaningful expression. "Do you value the warriors and councilors who work with you?"

She shrugged as she crammed a bit of fresh baked roll into her mouth. "Not really. I mostly berate them and make sarcastic remarks."

Evan threw his arms in the air melodramatically. "Is there no humanity anymore?"

"Be quiet, Evan," Hiker told him, looking directly at Liv. "I think the strategy session went well. Are you comfortable with what we laid out in case of an attack?"

Sophia glanced between Hiker and Liv. She couldn't believe he was talking to her sister like she was a normal human and not grumbling at her as he did with the dragonriders. He said their planning strategy went "well."

"Yeah, I'm good with that," Liv answered, giving herself a second helping of mashed potatoes.

Clark was right about the salt. It was what was missing from most of Ainsley's cooking. The housekeeper wasn't touching any of the food, so she might not taste the difference to be able to compare. Even though Hiker had ordered her to eat, she seemed persistent in refusing. Hiker showing concern about Ainsley eating and keeping up her strength was a first. She was also sitting at the table with the others, which was nice but also different. It seemed right.

Sophia reminded herself that back in the day, before Ainsley's "accident," she had been a regal advisor for the Dragon Elite. Like what Liv had done with Hiker that day, Ainsley used to advise on strategy. That association had led the elf to be front and center in a deadly battle with Thad Reinhart. She had jumped in front of an attack meant for Hiker, and her entire world had changed forever— but she knew nothing of it.

"And you giants?" Hiker asked, looking between Rory and Bermuda, who looked awkward sitting in chairs meant for dragonriders, but they were sturdy and built for bigger people than most furniture since riders sometimes came in larger sizes. Not the current generation, Sophia observed, thinking of Wilder and Mahkah, but Hiker and Evan were larger in size than average magicians.

"Their names are Rory and Bermuda," Rudolf supplied, bouncing beside the table, taking bites of his food as he stood, rather than sat. There was little way he could have sat with Captain Kirk and Captain Silver strapped to his front and back sides. "I have trouble remembering their names too. I get it."

"Bermuda delivered your children," Liv reminded him.

"Who?" Rudolf asked, looking around confused. His gaze landed on the giantess. "Oh, her. Yeah. And great job except Captain Silver's face is still sort of mushy from being extracted."

"Birthed," Bermuda harrumphed.

"You say birthed, Serena says evicted," Rudolf related. "Potato, tomato."

"That is not how the phrase goes," Liv corrected.

"Fine," Rudolf said, rolling his eyes. "Tomato, potato."

Liv shook her head. "Rory, were you able to secure the Gullington?"

He didn't appear confident. "Not entirely. This area is much larger than what we are used to guarding."

"Well," Mama Jamba informed them, licking her spoon clean of mashed potatoes, "you will have to do the best you can because when I go to bed tonight, the security measures I have been using to secure the Gullington will come down."

"Mama, really," Hiker begged, a rare pleading quality to his voice. "Can't you keep them up a bit longer?"

She shook her head. "No, son, I can't. I need my beauty sleep, and holding up the Barrier keeps me from sinking in deep to REM."

"You created this entire planet, yet you can't help out your Dragon Elite for another night?"

She shrugged unaffected. "I created the Dragon Elite to help me, son. Not the other way around. I did take pity on you. I bought you time, and look at you! I never thought it possible, but you brought in help, and I'm sure the giants will be of great use as well as the House of Fourteen. Or you will get them all killed. Who knows?"

390

Hiker shook his head. "You probably."

She toggled her head back and forth. "Maybe. Hard to tell. I'm not really focusing on the future right now since this Beef Wellington is demanding all my attention."

Ainsley let out a frustrated sigh, picking up one of the fresh rolls and angrily tearing into it.

"And what are you still doing still, fae?" Hiker asked, looking at Rudolf.

The king didn't seem to know he was being spoken to directly. He just continued to sway, chewing on his bite as he held his baby to his front and patted its backside.

"Ru," Liv said, prodding her friend.

"What? What?" Rudolf asked.

Wilder and Mahkah both rushed in right then and halted at the sight of all the weird characters gathered around the table.

"Come in and grab a seat." Hiker waved them in. "These are Sophia's...friends. You can do introductions later."

Sophia darted her eyes to Mahkah's finger. There was no way anyone could have been able to tell it had been regrown using magic. She was happy he was back to normal.

"Sorry we are late, sir," Wilder apologized as he took a seat next to Rory, giving him a curious expression.

"No one noticed," Hiker said dismissively.

"Rudolf is here because we are going off on a mission tomorrow first thing," Sophia answered the leader of the Dragon Elite's question.

"Right," he said, drawing out the word. "Then he'll be gone, and no more babies in the Castle."

"Not for a little while," Mama Jamba sang, all her attention on the food she seemed to be thoroughly enjoying.

Clark, intuitively reading the tension on Sophia's face, stood suddenly. "I hope you all saved room for cake. I made chocolate."

Evan threw down his napkin, a wide smile on his face. "About. Damn. Time."

Ainsley cast a rude glare at the dragonrider. "Just remember that when I recover, and I will, you will need to sleep with one eye open. It won't matter, because all my attacks on you will be covert. You will be waiting for me to attack your front, but you will have no idea you are sleeping on sheets washed in poison ivy."

Evan pushed away from the table. "On that note, I'm moving out of the Gullington."

CHAPTER NINETY-THREE

Everyone knew Evan wasn't moving out of the Gullington, even the new friends who had joined to help in the interim. It was obvious Evan wasn't "move out" material. He was a permanent resident of the Gullington, as were all the Dragon Elite riders.

Once the Gullington was secure once more and the housekeeper and groundskeeper recovered, Sophia was going to go after those evil pirates who had stolen one of her dragon eggs. She would make them pay—that was a guarantee. She also had to satisfy the question of why they wanted the dragon egg.

It was common knowledge in the magical world dragon eggs were extremely valuable. When they once had to transport Lunis' egg, poachers had come out of the woodwork to try to steal it. The thieves had a way of locating the eggs, and that had led them to the Gullington when the Barrier went down.

Sophia got the idea there was more to it than just monetary value for Trin Currante. This was a woman who had been altered, escaped the Saverus organization, and then brought it down. Sophia didn't think Trin Currante was after riches. There was a very specific reason she had gone after a dragon egg, and once Sophia had a chance, she was going to figure it out.

SARAH NOFFKE & MICHAEL ANDERLE

For now, there were too many other things calling for her attention, namely the Gullington and keeping it safe and the mission ahead to help Quiet.

Liv ran her hands over the Castle's walls in Sophia's room, taking in the details as the sun set over the Pond through the darkening windows. "I like the rustic feel mixed with the modern flare."

Liv pointed to the television and pink bean bag chair in the oversized bedroom. Those items did seem out of place next to the antique furniture and canopy bed. For now, everything was back to how it was before the Gullington went through whatever happened to it. The furniture had been repaired, and the walls were no longer crumbling, but when Mama Jamba went to sleep that night, her protections would come off the Castle and the Expanse.

It was impossible for any of them to know if what had happened before was a fluke or if it would happen again without the protective wards. It was clear Ainsley wasn't any better, although she wasn't getting any worse, and the whole thing was making her very irritable.

Only time would tell what would happen to the Gullington and its staff when Mama Jamba's protections came off. The giants would help keep things in balance, but their power was nothing compared to Mama Jamba's, obviously. Hiker mostly wanted their help with securing the Barrier. They weren't powerful enough to keep the Gullington hidden when the time came, but if they could hold the Barrier, that would be something at least.

A lot was about to happen, and she was frustrated she wouldn't be there to help. She and Rudolf would be leaving first thing in the morning to retrieve Quiet's father's captain's hat. The timing was awful with Mama Jamba taking her protections off the Gullington, but it had to be done. Quiet was getting worse. No one wanted to say it, but everyone knew the truth, he didn't have long. Sophia needed him to take the antidote, which meant he had to give her his real name.

She shook her head, wishing things didn't have to be so difficult, and he would just tell her his name and be done with it. She also knew if he was being so stubborn about giving up his real name, it was for a good reason. One she longed to understand.

Mother Nature and Mae Ling had been adamant about getting Quiet to take the antidote. Sophia thought the groundskeeper was the only one who knew how to fix things for the Gullington. Or at least he was key to this whole complex situation.

What Sophia had confirmed out of all of this was no one really knew much about the Gullington. The more Bermuda Laurens asked questions, the more Sophia recognized Hiker didn't know how to answer most of them. He pretended he was trying to keep things secret, but she thought he didn't know the answers, even after almost five hundred years. The mysterious Castle that had cared for the dragonriders all these centuries had kept its secrets well.

Mama Jamba was probably the only one who knew the truth about the Gullington, and everyone knew she wasn't talking. Quiet might also know, but even if he could talk, no one would know what he said.

"Do you like it here?" Liv asked, a playful tone in her voice.

Sophia folded a pair of pants, having done her own laundry for a change since Ainsley and the Castle were out of commission.

"Of course, I do," she replied.

She looked around fondly, trying to tame her reaction. This was a diplomatic moment. Sophia wanted to be honest with her sister, who she was closer to than anyone besides Lunis. She wanted to gush about how much she loved the Castle and enjoyed returning to the Gullington after each mission.

She also didn't want to hurt her sister's feelings. Before coming to the Gullington, Sophia had lived with Liv, and it had been fantastic. Liv had provided a great home where Sophia felt safe and could thrive. It wasn't that there had been anything wrong. It was just, the Castle was better for Sophia.

Sophia thought her sister would understand. Liv had to know the House of Fourteen, and Sophia's old life wouldn't fit her anymore. She would never resent Sophia for moving on.

"The Gullington is my home now," Sophia began, holding back her expression and watching her sister carefully.

Liv nodded and swallowed. "Yeah, I figured. It suits you."

"Who would have thought?" Sophia remarked. "Maybe it's the age of the Castle or the history or the fresh air. I don't know."

Liv gave her a suspicious grin. "I have learned it's less about where you live and more about who you live with. That is what makes a place feel like home."

Sophia shook her head. This was what she wanted to avoid. "No, if that were the case then—"

Liv held up her hand. "I love you, Soph. And I know you love me. But you are a dragonrider and being around your own, that is what makes sense for you. They get you, and you have your dragon here. Lunis couldn't live with you when you were with me. This place should be your home. You know the old expression?"

"Home is where your dragon is?" Sophia joked.

Liv laughed. "I was thinking more along the lines of, 'Home is where the heart is.' But yes, 'Home is where your dragon is' works for you too."

"Well, it's true," Sophia lamented. "Having Lunis here changes everything."

"What I don't get is how these guys all survived for centuries without you," Liv wondered.

Sophia gave her a confused expression. "Why would you say that? They did fine without me."

Liv laughed abruptly. "You might think so, but my meeting today with Hiker, well, he let something slip."

Sophia put her clothes away, trying to hide her curiosity. "Oh?"

"Yeah," Liv said, hiding a grin.

"You might have read into things," Sophia offered.

"I might have," Liv agreed. "You be the judge. He said to me today, 'I'm not sure how we got along all this time without Sophia.'"

Sophia dropped the clothes she had been folding. "No. You misheard him."

Liv shook her head. "How often do I mishear people?"

"Well..." Sophia thought. "You don't."

"He realizes what Trudy DeVries, the seer, saw about you long ago," Liv told her, revealing information she'd had yet to share with Sophia.

"Why haven't you told me about this premonition?" Sophia asked, wanting to be angry, but knowing there was no point in it. If Liv had kept something from her, it wasn't for any reason other than she hadn't had a chance to share it with her.

Right on cue, Liv shrugged and reached across the bed to help fold some of her laundry, even though she did a bad job of it. Liv's strong suit had never been household chores. "I just haven't had a chance, Soph. Anyway, Trudy told me you would bring much-needed balance to the Dragon Elite. I think Hiker is starting to feel that. He might have resisted your presence here before because you challenge him on every level, but that is part of what he needs."

"You mean he is not still cursing about the laptop I made him use?" Sophia asked.

Liv laughed. "Oh, he definitely is. By the way, we have to get that guy some typing classes. Watching him put information into the computer today took all the patience I had. It really couldn't have taken any longer."

Sophia laughed. "You should see him searching for something. He literally searches for google, clicks on it, and then googles."

"Hey, guess what the internet's favorite animal is?" Liv had a sneaky grin bouncing around her eyes.

Sophia lowered her chin. "What?"

"A lynx!"

Sophia didn't laugh. "You would be telling that bad joke."

"Yeah, I missed sharing it earlier at dinner," Liv laughed. "Which reminds me."

The look on her sister's face let Sophia know they had gotten to the part of the conversation she had been trying to avoid. It was why Liv had come up there to Sophia's room since it hadn't been to help her with laundry.

Sophia reached across the bed and took the stack Liv had folded, realizing she'd have to redo them all later. "Thanks," she said instead as she put the clothes to the side.

"Do you want to tell me what is going on?"

"Well, Rudolf knows where the captain's hat is," Sophia told her in a rush. "You and Clark will watch the Captains while we—"

"I think you know that is not what I'm talking about," Liv coaxed. "Although watching triplets is something I would only do for you, my love. If they spit up on me, you are doing my laundry."

"Deal. I do appreciate it," Sophia said. "If I could go without Rudolf, you know I would."

Liv tilted her head to the side, a thoughtful expression on her face. "You know, in battle, he is one of the few people I want by my side. He is strange and inappropriate, but there is no one who will show more bravery when facing danger than that fae. Rudolf has gotten me into a fair amount of trouble, but he has got me out of way more. And he has some strange luck."

Sophia nodded, remembering when Rudolf accompanied her on the mission to find the Fierce so she could locate the Great Library. "Yeah, there is something curious about him. He is simultaneously super annoying and incredibly helpful. Like how did it come down to him to help me with this mission? The Captains...they were named after Quiet. What were the odds?"

Liv gave her a fond expression. "Life is kind of beautiful like that."

"Which is what makes all the battles worth fighting," Sophia agreed, feeling restless after she had put all the clothes away. She wanted something to do with her hands.

Liv patted the bed, encouraging Sophia to take a seat. "Come and talk to me. Because you know what, Soph, there is more to life than fighting for justice."

Sophia crawled onto her large bed and felt the exhaustion begin to tunnel in her brain as soon as she rested on the mattress. "Coming from you, that is rather ironic to hear."

Liv settled next to her sister, wrapping her arms around her own legs. "You know, I totally get it. I used to be this head-down, get-the-job-done, no-nonsense kind of gal."

"Then what happened?" Sophia asked, already knowing how this story ended because she had watched it transpire.

A soft smile wrapped itself around Liv's mouth and lit up her eyes. "I fell in love, and I realized there was more to life than fighting bad guys and wearing myself down."

Liv was referring to Stefan Ludwig, another warrior for the House of Fourteen. Battle had brought the two together, but their adoration for each other kept them there. They were a romance for the ages.

"Don't get me wrong," Liv continued, "that is still how my life goes for the most part, but there is a new motivation. I don't always want to work. Not like I used to. I have someone I want to spend time with, someone I crave seeing at the end of the day. Having that changes everything. We go from being these warrior robots who fight for justice, to these feeling beings who fight for love."

"Do you know, I can tell when you are thinking about him because you get this smile on your face?" Sophia observed, having witnessed her sister hiding a private smile many a time, distracted by thoughts of the guy she harbored feelings for.

Liv and Stefan Ludwig had come a long way. It was for that reason, Sophia knew her sister understood better than most. The two warriors for the House of Fourteen hadn't been able to be together for a long time, forbidden by House laws. In true Liv style, she had fought against those laws and changed them. In doing so, she had changed her future, and probably the future of many others in the process. In truth, Sophia knew the world was a better place because Liv Beaufont loved Stefan Ludwig.

That was what a great romance did. It changed the world for the better. Her parents had it. Liv had it, and Sophia didn't want anything less for herself. There was no way she could settle when she had seen what was possible.

Sophia also knew the scariest thing in the world was going after that kind of love and risking everything for it. The fear of rejection, of failure, of heartbreak, was more intimidating than war for her.

"So, tell me what is going on with you?" Liv asked her sister when they had been silent for a long moment. There was a thoughtful expression on Liv's face.

"It's nothing," Sophia lied, trying to keep her face neutral. With Liv, it was impossible. She sighed and decided to be honest with Liv, and with herself. "I rescued Wilder's dragon, and now he is acting like I did something of great importance and looking at me in strange ways. Well, looking at me in strange ways more often than before."

"Everyone knows the way to a man's heart is to save his dragon," Liv joked.

Sophia giggled. "It wasn't that big a deal."

"Oh, so this hasn't been going on for a while?" Liv challenged.

"Since when?" Sophia asked.

"Since a while ago?" Liv asked. "Maybe since the beginning."

Sophia shook her head. "No, why would you ask that?"

Liv seemed to hide the expression on her face. "Just because I know you, Soph. And I know how people react to you."

Sophia ignored her, then remembered the pocketknife Subner had given her at the Fantastical Armory. She popped out of bed and retrieved her cloak lying across the back of the sofa.

"What is up?" Liv asked.

"Subner gave me something curious," she explained.

"A headache with all his riddles?" Liv pretended to question.

Sophia's laugh lacked humor as she checked the various pockets where she could have stuck the knife. It wasn't there.

"What is it?"

She lowered the cloak and shook her head. "It seems without meaning to I dropped something."

Liv didn't seem to think much of it. "Well, that's how it usually happens. We hardly ever drop anything because we mean to."

Sophia nodded, her eyes thoughtful. "Yeah, but what if subconsciously, I actually meant to…"

Liv tilted her head to the side before shaking it. "You are talking riddles like Subner right now."

Sophia stared off without really seeing. She felt like she was living a riddle, and maybe she knew the answer. She didn't want to admit it. She swallowed down the nervous tension in her throat and tried to push away the uncertainty. This wasn't the time for matters of the heart, but she knew she couldn't avoid them forever.

CHAPTER NINETY-FOUR

The sun hadn't risen the next morning over the Gullington when Sophia began going through her weapons, preparing for the mission ahead.

She slid her sword into her sheath and whipped her cloak around her shoulders, tying it tightly, not knowing where they were headed and what kind of weather she should prepare for. Rudolf had refused to tell Sophia where the Fae's National History Museum was located.

The three Captains were all sleeping quietly on the surface of Sophia's made bed. Rudolf had dropped them off a few minutes prior with the promise he would return soon. She gave the babies a fond look as she grabbed the grappling hook lying beside Captain Morgan and fastened it onto her belt.

There was something about a sleeping baby that was very calming to look at. Sophia had never really been around young children, recently having been young herself and the smallest of the Beaufont family.

Sophia looked around her room, feeling like she was missing something but not knowing what.

The pocketknife, she thought.

She wished she had it for this mission but didn't know why.

Sophia reasoned she had probably lost it at the dinner table. It could be hiding under the sofa, having fallen out of her cloak when she threw it off last night. She decided she was going to stop overthinking the whole thing. The fact she had dropped it was not that big of a coincidence. Now, if a certain someone had found it, well, then that might be something she couldn't dismiss so easily.

A soft knock sounded at the door.

Sophia jerked her head up, a little more jumpy than usual. "Yeah?"

Liv poked her head into the bedroom, looking refreshed after a night of sleep at the Castle. It had been nice for Sophia, knowing her siblings were sleeping under the same roof as her for a change.

"Hey, they are sleeping still. Good," Liv said, coming into the room and giving the children a fond expression.

"Yeah, Ru, dropped them off and said he would be back soon," Sophia explained.

"Because?" Liv asked, giving her a cautious expression.

"He said he was grabbing something for the mission," Sophia answered. "Something about looking his best."

Liv hardly waited for Sophia to finish her sentence before she bounded back out the door and sprinted down the corridor of the Castle. When she returned a few minutes later, her face was red and her breathing ragged. "Well, that was a close call. You can thank me later."

Sophia gave her sister a cautious expression. "What just happened?"

"Oh, nothing," she said dismissively. "Rudolf just thinks big missions call for him to wear his big-boy clothes. Believe me, you did not want to see him in those tights. I have taken care of it, and he has agreed to wear his usual flamboyant clothes. While they include bright colors, you won't have your eyes burned out by seeing way too much of what he calls his 'manhood.'"

Sophia shivered. "Thanks. You just saved me."

Liv nodded. "That I did. That I did."

Rudolf knocked at the door. "Are you decent?"

"Ru, we are in here with your babies," Liv grumbled, annoyed.

He pushed open the door. "So that is a no?"

Liv held out her hands in a choking motion. "Okay, let's run through what you need us to do to keep these lovelies alive."

Sophia couldn't help but smile at her sister. She knew for Liv, taking care of babies wasn't an ideal job. In truth, Sophia thought Liv would be pretty good at caring for children. She had an intuitive nature, and others inherently liked her. There was something about Liv Beaufont that was likable. Maybe because she fought for justice or protected the little guy, but Sophia thought there was more to it than that.

Liv teased Rudolf. She outright made fun of Rory, and she got on Bermuda's last nerve. But the truth about this warrior for the House of Fourteen was she allowed those she loved to be who they were, without changing them. There was something innately comforting about being around someone who loved you for who you were rather than what you could become. Many loved the potential in others, whereas Liv loved the essence of a person. She didn't love the people in her life despite their flaws, but in many instances, because of them. They were all human, after all.

Liv might make light of her friends, but Sophia knew no one loved them more fiercely, and Sophia knew being loved by Liv Beaufont was like feeling sunshine on your cheeks on a winter day, or the stars breaking through a cloudy night sky. Liv's love was a cure to suffering most never knew they were enduring.

"All right," Rudolf began, pointing at the bed. "Firstly, you have to feed them."

"Every day?" Liv questioned, a serious expression on her face.

He nodded, rather seriously as well. "I'm afraid so. At least a few times every day. Each of them."

Liv pretended to be shocked. "No."

"Yeah, it's crazy but true," Rudolf complained.

"Okay, well, I will do my very best." Liv hid her laughter. "Feeding me is already a chore, so we will see how I do caring for other humans."

Sophia patted Liv on the shoulder. "Clarky will help."

Liv agreed with a nod. "He is an expert at keeping young ones alive and feeding them. Just look at you, Soph."

It was true. Sophia was alive because of her older brother. He had been her primary caregiver after their parent's death since Reese and Ian had to step up to replace their mother and father as Councilor and Warrior for the House of Fourteen.

Rudolf gave the children on Sophia's bed a look of longing.

"Are you okay?" Sophia asked, sympathetic for the man before her.

He sighed. "Yeah, I just forgot to tell them a ghost story before we left. Do you think we have time?"

Sophia grunted aloud. *And to think, I felt sorry for him for a moment,* she thought.

"I'm afraid we don't," she told him. "But if you want to offer them a quick kiss, I think we could make time for that."

He scoffed at her like she said something repulsive. "What are you thinking, you demonic woman? I want to return to my children. Do you know what a fae's kiss does if given at a departure?"

Sophia's eyes widened with alarm. "Obviously, I don't..."

From behind Rudolf's back, Liv shook her head and mouthed the words, "Absolutely nothing."

"Okay, is there something else you can offer them that can be given quickly? A high five? Fist bump, maybe? A salute since they are captains?" Sophia suggested, knowing they needed to get off soon.

Mother Nature's protection over the Gullington had ended. The giants were helping, but everyone knew it wasn't enough to protect the land of the Expanse entirely. Liv was there to help, but her attention would be divided as she needed to watch the triplets with Clark. That meant Sophia and Rudolf needed to be fast at the Fae's National History Museum. Then they could return, and hopefully, everything would go back to normal. That was the plan anyway.

"I'm just so worried about them," Rudolf mourned. "I have never left them alone before."

Liv gawked at him, an expression of disbelief on her face. "I'm sorry, but it's hard for me to believe that playboy fae boy, King Rudolf Sweetwater, hasn't parted from these babies since they were born."

He looked at his friend and smiled. "If they were yours, you wouldn't either. Just. You. Wait."

She shook her head. "Okay, what if I give you a way to keep an eye on them in a sense."

He clapped his hands, making Captain Silver squirm like she might wake up. "Yes, let's do it. What do you have in mind?"

Liv held a single finger to her lips, making the universal shush expression with her lips. "First off, let's shut our faces and our hands and be really quiet before godmother Liv is going to be in charge. I'm hoping these kids sleep until noon."

Rudolf eyed his wrist, which had no watch on it. "You have about another ten minutes until they demand nonstop attention. All three of them, at the same time. It's impossible to give them all what they want at the same time, and you will nearly kill yourself trying. You will lose your mind trying. You won't get any sleep and will go without showering and starve nearly to death trying to meet their needs."

Liv looked at her sister. "I want a puppy for Christmas. That is what you owe me for doing this."

Sophia pursed her lips, thinking she got the easy end of the deal. "Is that all?"

"Specifically, it's a puppy dog from Mars that pukes up gold and farts bitcoin currency," Liv told her. "I will settle for no less."

Sophia nodded. "Got it. I have made a note of the impossible creature I will have to get you to make up for this atrocious task I have assigned you."

"Good girl," Liv said, before returning her attention to Rudolf. "Now, I think I have a solution to your problem."

Relief flooded his eyes. "You do?"

"Yeah, well, you are understandably going to be worried about the Captains," Liv continued and held out her hand. "What if I offered you a way to check on them?"

She flicked her finger at her hand, and a small white bear appeared. It had large brown eyes and a blue bow.

"Oh, it's so cute!" Rudolf exclaimed, a bit too loudly. All three babies began to fidget as though they were seconds away from waking up.

Liv held up a finger to her mouth, silencing him. "Now this is Fluffy, and he will tell you what is happening with your babies." She pointed to the bear's smiling face. "Notice how he is smiling now?"

Rudolf nodded like a kindergarten learning the alphabet. "Yeah."

"Okay," Liv said, drawing out the word. "Well, if something isn't going right, it will be on Fluffy's face."

"And if they wet their pants?" Rudolf asked.

Liv shook her head. "Then, I will change their diapers. The bear will simply tell you about their moods, collectively. Not whether they are hungry or sleepy or whatever."

He nodded. "Okay, I like this." He grabbed the bear and held it in close for a moment before turning his attention to Sophia.

"Now," he pronounced, shaking his head at her. "The only remaining problem is you."

CHAPTER NINETY-FIVE

S ophia glanced down at her body. "What about me?"

She had remembered her sword, Inexorabilis, and the grappling hook Wilder had given her. She had on her armor and cloak. She couldn't fathom what else she could be forgetting. Maybe a snack?

"The biggest problem, Soph," Rudolf began good-naturedly, "is that you don't look like a fae, and there is zero way you are getting into the Fae National History Museum looking like a dumb, plain old magician."

Liv coughed rather loudly, making Captain Kirk move around.

"My apologies," Rudolf said to her, bowing slightly before looking back at Sophia. "Right now, you look like a smart but plain magician."

"Right," Sophia replied, realizing her error. "I don't know how to remedy that."

"But Soph," Liv encouraged. "You are the best at disguises. Just glamour your appearance. Fae can't see through glamour like giants. You should be fine."

Sophia's heart swelled with pride. It had been a long time since she'd had to rely on that skill. Before the Dragon Elite, she used to help Liv with disguises, helping her get ready for her warrior missions for the House of Fourteen.

Sophia had used the skill when she was younger and had little use for magic besides to turn herself or her stuffed animals into things. As a child, she had hidden in oil paintings or become stone statues in the garden, but since coming to the Dragon Elite, her skills had been about combat and riding and other things. The disguising spell she had perfected was going to come in handy, she realized. It would be how she would sneak into the Fae National History Museum.

The disguising spell wasn't an easy spell, but Sophia had learned it long ago and perfected it.

She pointed a finger at herself, pressed her eyes shut, and made a wish.

Sophia opened her eyes and looked at her sister and Rudolf with trepidation, waiting for their reactions.

They both gave her uncertain glares at first. Liv didn't seem to recognize her. Rudolf seemed in love. They both engulfed her with hugs.

"You are perfect," they both said in unison, hugging her tightly.

She allowed a smile to unfurl on her face before pulling away. Sophia chanced a glance in the mirror to spy the glamour she had created.

Sophia studied her reflection. She was a beautiful fae with perfect blonde hair arranged in ringlets down her back. Her cheekbones were high, and her face was framed by pointy ears. On her back were large blue wings and, on her face, a sneaky grin like she was hiding a devilishly fun secret. All the rest of her was perfect as well.

It wasn't that Sophia didn't think she was pretty in her normal body, but the fae were like gods and goddesses, like Queen Anastasia Crystal, pure works of art. They were instant love magnets, and it was almost impossible for anyone to resist them.

She would have no trouble waltzing into the Fae's National History Museum looking as she did. Breaking through the security of the place and stealing their most prized possession was going to be more challenging.

"Are you ready to go?" Rudolf asked excitedly like a Labrador retriever about to dive into the water after a bone.

Sophia pulled her eyes away from the beautiful figure that stared back at her in the mirror. "Yeah, right."

Sophia didn't know how they were going to steal the captain's hat. They would have to do a quick reconnaissance job before they crafted the strategy. The biggest problem was she had to pull off this mission with the most incompetent and most competent fae possible. How could those two people be the same person, she wondered, looking at King Rudolf Sweetwater.

"Okay, let's go," she commanded, encouraging him toward the door as she waved at Liv. Rudolf was looking back longingly at the three sleeping infants as Sophia ushered him to the door.

Her sister waved back, and just as they rounded out of her room, right on cue, all three babies started wailing like they were madder than hell.

CHAPTER NINETY-SIX

King Rudolf Sweetwater held tight to the stuffed animal as they left the Castle and down the steps onto the Expanse.

Sophia tried to tell herself the green of the grass hadn't dulled since the day before, but she wasn't buying it. Already the Gullington was degrading, as it had done before Mama Jamba saved it.

She tried to open a portal, and to her relief, it didn't work. That meant at least the Barrier was still in place. She hoped Rory and Bermuda Laurens were able to keep it intact.

At least until I return, she thought, looking back over her shoulder at the Castle. Her heart sank. It was starting to crumble. Not good.

"Sophia, what do you want to be when you grow up?" Rudolf asked, hugging Fluffy tightly as they walked to the Barrier, where he could portal them to wherever the Fae National History Museum was located.

She shook her head at him. "Rudolf, I'm a dragonrider for the Elite."

"I get you're stuck in this position," he said with a sympathetic smile. "But when you get free of this obligation, what do you want to be?"

Sophia couldn't help but laugh. "Well, although I'm young, I

411

consider myself pretty grown up. I think I'll stick around as a drag-onrider for what I hope is the rest of my long life."

They walked on in silence for a few minutes before Rudolf said, "Aren't you going to ask me the same question?"

Sophia tilted her head at him, although she realized it was the head of the fae she was impersonating. "Yeah, I guess. But you are the king of the fae. I don't think there is any upward mobility from there."

He nodded. "Yeah, it's sort of a dead-end job. But if I could choose a different position, well, I would like to be a window washer."

Sophia should have known by this point that she could expect strange stuff to come out of Rudolf's mouth. He constantly surprised her with the things he said. Maybe that was part of his charm. Even when one expected Rudolf to say something ridiculous, he pushed the boundary, saying something even weirder than one fathomed.

"Why a window washer?" Sophia asked, grateful for the conversation taking her mind off her worries about the Gullington.

"Well, because I like heights and having a nice view," he answered thoughtfully.

Sophia smiled. "That actually makes sense as a reason to choose the profession."

"Well and also," Rudolf went on, "I like the idea of making other's views of the world clearer, cleaner. Without window washers, when we looked out, what we see would be obstructed by dirt and grime. But window washers, they make everything clear."

Once again, he'd done it. King Rudolf Sweetwater had surprised Sophia. "Wow, that makes perfect sense. How very thoughtful of you."

He nodded. "I'm really thoughtful. Okay, so we need to figure out our story."

"What do you mean?" she asked. "What story?"

"Well, we need to have a backstory to tell the guards and museum staff when we do our investigations. I think we really need to flesh out our characters. You know, figure out their motivation, their fears, their dreams," Rudolf explained. It had been a while since he'd been to the Fae National History Museum, and he didn't know where the captain's hat was located or the security surrounding it, so they'd pretend to be patrons of the arts first to figure out their strategy.

"Um, Rudolf, you're the king of the fae," she told him. "I don't think you'll be able to pull off a disguise. You're probably the most recognizable fae in the world, especially to your own kind."

He let out a disappointed breath. "Fine, but you need a story. You can be my hand towel assistant."

"You're not actually referring to someone who gives you a towel after you wash your hands, are you?" she questioned.

He nodded. "I absolutely am. That would be my second-choice job if I was afforded such luxuries."

"Why would that person follow you around?" Sophia demanded. "Why wouldn't you just have bathroom attendants?"

"I can't trust every bathroom to have those, so I bring my own with me," he explained.

"Of course, you do," she said dryly.

"Of course, I don't trust the competency levels of just any bathroom attendant, so I bring my very skilled and expertly trained one," Rudolf pointed out. "You went to school for this and specialized in hand towels."

"How very ambitious of me," Sophia stated with no enthusiasm. "Is it bad that I'm a female? Shouldn't you have a male hand towel attendant?"

Rudolf let out a loud gasp. "Seriously, Sophia, sometimes I really doubt your judgment. Like I would want another man looking over my shoulder when I'm in the Whiz Palace."

"Did you just call it the 'Whiz Palace?'"

"I borrowed the term. But this is for your benefit," Rudolf promised. "Imagine you are the CEO of the Whiz Palace. That will really get you places."

"I can only imagine," she responded with no inflection.

"Okay, and your name can't be Sophia," Rudolf went on. "Your name is going to be Courtney Marie Annaliese Merriweather."

"I just wish it was longer," she joked.

He nodded. "We can give you a formal title. How about Hand

413

Towel Industries Chief Executive Officer Courtney Marie Annaliese Merriweather?"

"Cool," she agreed as they passed through the Barrier. "I'm ready for you to open the portal to this mystery location for the Fae National History Museum."

"You got it," Rudolf said, taking the lead. "Don't think that you can figure out the location of the museum. It is top secret."

She nodded. "Of course. I'm sure I won't figure it out."

CHAPTER NINETY-SEVEN

"Is that the Eiffel Tower over there?" Sophia asked after they stepped through the portal. They stood in front of a large stone building, but towering in the distance was undoubtedly one of the most recognizable structures in the world.

"Yeah, but that won't really tell you where we are," Rudolf answered, glancing over his shoulder at the building.

"We are in Paris," Sophia declared.

His mouth popped open as his eyes widened. "How do you know that?"

"Lucky guess," Sophia replied.

"Okay, well, don't tell anyone or everyone will find out about our secret location."

Sophia glanced at the large sign in front of the Fae National History Museum. "You're worried about me spoiling the secret?"

Plastered across the giant sign were the words: Secret Location for Old Fae Things.

"What?" Rudolf asked, looking between Sophia and the sign, his brow wrinkled.

"Don't you think the sign makes what this is a bit obvious?"

He frowned. "I don't think so. I mean, it says it's a secret. And it doesn't say it's a museum." Rudolf sighed. "Really, Sophia, you under-stand so very little about how things work."

"Yeah, I don't get it, obviously."

Sophia had always known the fae weren't the brightest magical race, but now she seriously wondered how they'd survived this long without falling into extinction. It looked like the trip to the Fae National History Museum would yield more than just a captain's hat. Hopefully, she'd learn how the airhead fae had survived when just about anything should have wiped them out.

When they were at the top of the stairs, Sophia was even more surprised to find a small sign on the front door that read, "Don't forget to give us a review on Yelp."

She pointed. "The Fae National History Museum is on Yelp, and you're worried about keeping the location a secret?"

Rudolf sighed like he was about to explain rudimentary math to a grown adult. "Sophia, it's listed on Yelp under Super Secret Fae Place with Old Things. Again, no one will know what that is."

"I think you just have to be glad I don't think anyone cares," she told him.

"Well, you care, which is why you're here," he argued. Rudolf lowered his voice. "Now remember you promised, you're just borrowing the captain's hat, right? Then you'll return it?"

She nodded. "Yeah, once I give it to Quiet, I'll give it back."

Rudolf shook his head. "To think, Captain Quiet, the gnome I named the girls after was dying in that castle where I was just hanging out. That is really cool."

Sophia gave him a murderous expression. "Hey, watch it. Quiet isn't dying. Even if he is, he won't. That's why I'm here. I'm going to save him. Or at least give him the motivation to want to save himself."

Rudolf opened the door to the Fae National History Museum, directing the way with a welcoming hand. "Okay, let's go and see some things, person who is a fae and not at all a magician."

Sophia shook her head at the well-meaning fae. "Thanks. Very subtle."

CHAPTER NINETY-EIGHT

S oft music filled the air of the museum, which was lit with pastel-colored lights. Even from the entryway, Sophia could tell the place would be beautiful. The walls were covered in gold, and the floors appeared to be made of diamond. The high ceilings were full of intricate designs.

At the front desk was a receptionist flanked by uniformed guards. She lowered her head as Rudolf and Sophia approached.

All three individuals were gorgeous. Sophia hadn't been around a lot of fae since Liv said going to Las Vegas would kill most of her brain cells. Mainly just King Rudolf Sweetwater.

It was hard for Sophia to not stare at them. All their features were in perfect symmetry and proportion. Their brightly colored wings framed their perfect bodies. They could have all been models with their perfect hair and skin.

"King Rudolf Sweetwater," the woman said, raising her head from bowing. "What an honor it is to have you here."

"Thank you, Rosephanye," Rudolf said after glancing at the woman's name tag.

Sophia muffled a laugh. The name tag didn't have a name. It simply said, "Receptionist."

He held out his hand and presented Sophia. "This is my hand towel attendant, Chief Officer Executive Courtney Marie Annaliese Merriweather."

The receptionist nodded at her. "It is nice to meet you, Chief Officer Executive Courtney Marie Annaliese Merriweather."

She pulled out a name tag and began to write Sophia's full name and title on it.

"Oh, you don't have to—"

The receptionist glanced up, her expression making Sophia halt.

"You don't have to use only one name tag," Sophia amended. The fae were very strange.

The receptionist handed two name tags over. "Now, here's a map of the Fae National History Museum. At the bottom, you'll see a box that tells you what the symbols represent. For instance, the restrooms are marked with a symbol of a man and woman."

Sophia nodded, taking the paper map. "Yeah, a key."

Rudolf jerked his head in her direction, giving her a scolding expression. "How would you know Chief Officer Executive Courtney Marie Annaliese Merriweather, since you only went to towel attendant college?"

"Oh..." Sophia sucked in a sudden breath, taking in the shocked expressions of the receptionist and guards. "I guessed."

"A key," the receptionist said like it was a brand new word to her. "That's a great term for it. Key. I'm going to start using that."

Sophia nodded. "Good idea."

"Now, is there any exhibit you're interested in?" the woman asked. "I can point you in that direction."

"Well, we are definitely not here to steal anything," Rudolf stated loudly.

Sophia covered her eyes with her hand and wondered if she should kill Rudolf now or wait until later when he ruined everything. She decided Liv would be peeved if she had to take on the responsibility of raising his children and decided against killing him.

"I believe," Sophia said, giving him a stern expression, "you said, you wanted to browse around today. Right, King Rudolf Sweetwater?"

He gave her a confused expression. "I thought you wanted to take the—"

Swiftly, and covered by the receptionist's desk, Sophia kicked the fae in the shin. He grabbed his leg and began jumping around.

"Ouch, that hurt," Rudolf exclaimed.

The guards jumped forward, checking the area over. "What is it?"

Rudolf gave Sophia an irritated expression, which she returned.

"Oh, right," he said, drawing out the words. "We are simply here to browse around. That is all."

The guards nodded and resumed their former positions. "Please let us know if you need anything, King Rudolf Sweetwater," one of them said.

Rudolf leaned forward, reading the man's name tag, which read: Guard.

"Well, Gavin, I'm really interested in upping my security measures at my palace," Rudolf began. "What can you tell me about the systems you use here to protect our treasures?"

"Systems?" Not-Gavin asked.

"How do I put this in a way you'll understand?" Rudolf thought for a moment.

Sophia couldn't believe she was around fae who were dumber than Rudolf Sweetwater.

"How about ways you protect your treasures?" Sophia supplied.

"Protect..." One guard looked at the other like he could define the word.

The second guard shrugged.

Rudolf read the other guard's name tag. "Oh, cool, you two have the same name. That makes things easy. Gavin and Gavin, what ways do you keep thieves from taking things in here?"

"Oh," both Not-Gavins said in unison, comprehension dawning.

"Well, we don't have alarms, lasers, or actual systems, to stop bad gnomes from stealing things," one of the guards supplied.

"Gnomes?" Sophia questioned.

"Well, everyone knows they are the ones who can't be trusted," Not-Gavin Number One said.

Not-Gavin Number Two nodded. "Yeah, really, we don't worry about any of the other magical races."

"Or fae, am I right?" Rudolf asked, elbowing Sophia, a wide victorious grin on his face. He leaned over. "This is going to be easy."

"Not if you keep talking out loud," she said through clenched teeth, a pleasant smile on her face.

The fae thankfully hadn't seemed to notice. They kept staring ahead blankly as if they were counting Pop-Tarts in their head.

"So, these systems?" Rudolf prompted.

"Yes, well, we just seek to confuse our would-be thieves," Not-Gavin Number One explained. "When the gnome enters—"

"Through an unlocked door?" Sophia queried.

He nodded. "Yes, we don't lock our doors. So, when the gnome enters, there's illusion magic that takes over. It makes it so all of the artifacts are duplicated to the letter of three."

"Three is actually a number..." Sophia trailed away as she caught the confused expression on all four of the fae's faces. "Please continue."

"Well, the illusion spell creates exact duplicates of the artifacts," Not-Gavin Number Two said. "That way, when the thief takes the object, they don't know if they have the right one or something that will disappear in a few hours when they leave here."

"Why wouldn't you just use that power to create a security system?" Sophia knew as soon as the question left her mouth, she should learn to be quiet. All the fae looked at her like she was from planet Mars.

"Oh, Chief Officer Executive Courtney Marie Annaliese Merriweather, you understand nothing," Rudolf taunted with a rude laugh. "That's why you are in charge of my hand towels."

He clapped her on the back hard, and she forced out a chuckle.

"That's right. I couldn't be trusted with complex systems such as this," she agreed, pretending to be good-natured.

"Well," Not-Gavin Number One began, holding up a finger. "If the thieves were smart, they'd know two things."

"For one," Not-Gavin Number Two began and leaned forward to

whisper, "the real object will have some sort of special marking that separates it from the illusions."

Sophia nodded, having witnessed Ainsley's shapeshifting abilities and was well acquainted with how illusions worked. They could never, ever be an exact replica. It was some strange rule of magic. There had to always be a way to identify the original. For Ainsley, it was the scar on her right temple. No matter who she shapeshifted into, the scar was always there. Sophia wondered what her defining characteristic could have been before the accident.

"What's the second thing?" Rudolf asked.

"Oh, well, we do have sirens that alert us if the real object is taken," Not-Gavin Number Two offered. "It's a weight system. I like that word. System."

Not-Gavin Number One nodded. "Yeah, it's a good word. The system makes it so if there's any change in weight the sirens go off."

"I thought you said there were no alarms?" Sophia asked, even as she realized trying to hash out semantics was ridiculous at this point.

"Well, we don't have anything if the place is broken into that alerts us," Not-Gavin Number One pronounced. "But if someone picks up an actual object, we get a message, and the siren is loud enough, it alerts the neighbors."

"Which are?" Sophia had to ask.

"Oh, a bunch of rowdy gnomes who run the bistros nearby." This was from Not-Gavin Number Two.

Sophia nodded. "Of course, they are."

"Okay, well, thanks for the help, Gavin and Gavin," Rudolf said, waving Sophia into the Fae National History Museum. "We'll just browse around at this point. Not heading straight for the main exhibit of the most prized fae possession."

Sophia shook her head at the king of the fae. She understood now why he had that position. With an IQ of under fifty, he was probably the smartest fae there ever was.

CHAPTER NINETY-NINE

"Okay, so what do you want to see first?" Rudolf asked, unfolding the map and glancing over it. "Do we want to head to the shrunken head exhibit of my ancestors who were punished by the elves for peeing in their springs or to the dinosaur exhibit that's actually just chicken bones according to the bold print here?"

"Or we can go find the captain's hat that belonged to Quiet's father and find out what it's identifying mark is," Sophia offered.

Rudolf yawned. "That sounds super boring." He looked back at the map. "Oh, there's this new exhibit about a king who had triplets with a mortal. I want to hear more about that. The story sounds familiar."

"Because it's you since you had three babies with Serena?" Sophia dared to ask because she apparently loved headaches.

Rudolf shook his head at her. "No, Soph. That can't be me. I had three babies, not triplets."

Sophia sucked in a calming breath. "Right. My bad. I'm so dumb."

"Maybe I'll pay to send you to hand towel college after all, so you'll have something to fall back on when this dragonrider thing falls through," he consoled.

"Thanks," Sophia muttered, pulling the map out of Rudolf's hands and locating the main exhibit. The captain's hat was located conveniently in the middle of the Fae National History Museum, through a labyrinth of stairs and displays. It would take them a good ten minutes to get there, and she was certain Rudolf would get distracted a thousand times before then.

Sophia guessed this was a thing about pretty people. They could be counted on to look nice and act nice, but when the time came to step up and be an actual member of a team, Rudolf often fell short.

"You're thinking about the guy you're dating right now," Rudolf said as they passed an exhibit about how the fae once froze and starved to death, but the magicians came in and gave them meat, rescuing them. It was from last year when the magicians literally dropped off a bunch of Subway sandwiches for fae who thought an ice-skating rink was their home and didn't know they could exit of their own free will. The magicians gave them sandwiches while they defrosted the rink so the fae would figure it out.

"I am thinking of people who irritate me," Sophia admitted.

"Why do you think he irritates you?" Rudolf asked, thoughtfully.

"Because he breathes," she answered quite seriously.

"And that's a problem because you're a necromancer who prefers the dead?"

Sophia was about to award Rudolf a hundred points for using such a big word correctly when they came to the place she was looking for. In the center of a large room was a single display platform. Sitting on a small platform was a single blue captain's hat. It appeared very much how she pictured the hat would look on display in Quiet's office.

Sophia thought there was something very sad about seeing the hat there. She wasn't sure why until she read the plaque sitting next to it.

The sign read:

The hat that belonged to the famed captain who sent his ship away, leaving him stranded, to save the race of the fae. This was his most prized possession and was later used to start the fortune of the fae. Thanks to Captain Quiet McAfee, the fae lived on, prospered, and built an empire.

Then Sophia got it. Quiet had given up everything. His ship. His father's hat. His life. And what did he get? Nothing.

He got the life of groundskeeper of the Gullington, and what was happening to him now? He was dying from some strange disease.

"I'm getting that hat for Quiet," Sophia said adamantly to herself.

"And returning it promptly like a library book," Rudolf finished on the heels of her statement.

"Yep," she replied, not really hearing him. She took a step forward, studying the simple hat. "Now, what is the identifying mark? We have to find that to determine how it's different from the duplicates that will later surround it."

"Maybe it's the rim," Rudolf offered because he had cantaloupe in his brain.

The captain's hat was blue and done in the old style with a high top and a round rim. Around the outside was gold trim, and on the top was a crest.

Sophia shook her head. "I don't think it will be a major characteristic of the hat. I think it's going to be something small."

She was thinking of Ainsley's scar on her temple. The identifying mark would be similar. It would be something that someone knew to look for to set the hat apart, but only slightly.

Sophia craned her head around at different angles, studying every inch of the hat. From where it was perched on the pedestal, she could see all of it except the inside.

I really hope the identifying mark isn't inside the hat, Sophia thought. Otherwise, I'm screwed.

Then she saw something on the underside of the bill that made her heart jump. On the bottom of the back of the rim were embroidered three letters. They were simple, but they made sense to Sophia, and she knew they had to be the defining mark. Or her instinct was not to be trusted ever again.

Sophia took a mental snapshot of the initials so she could remember them later: GQM

CHAPTER ONE HUNDRED

Once Rudolf and Sophia exited the museum, they had to find something to occupy their time until closing.

Sophia wanted to enchant all the dimwits inside the museum to think it was time to go home, but Rudolf wouldn't allow it. He said the theft had to be done naturally.

"But you want to return to the Gullington as fast as I do," she argued, watching him study Fluffy the bear for signs his triplets were in danger.

Sophia knew magic well enough to know the stuffed bear wasn't magical at all. Liv had given Rudolf a regular teddy bear and told him its emotions would emulate those of his children. The constant smile on its face wasn't going to change, and that was for the best.

Rudolf was already a distracted puppy on this mission, looking at strange exhibits and talking to strangers every five seconds. Sophia couldn't fathom what he'd be like if he had a stuffed bear that really showed the emotions of three infants. He thought it did, and it put his fears enough to rest that he could be sort of present with Sophia. Sophia knew Liv and Clark were taking good care of the Captains and ensuring they had everything they needed. It was a win-win for everyone as far as she was concerned.

"Do you want to go to the Louvre and steal back all the stuff that belongs to the fae?" Rudolf asked as they wandered the streets of Paris.

Sophia shook her head. "No, that sounds like a bigger mission than I'm ready for tonight and will definitely take me off task."

He shrugged. "Fine, then we will go into this bistro and eat cheese and drink wine."

Rudolf pushed open the door to a warm café, holding it for Sophia. She was invited in by the smells of freshly baked bread and pungent cheeses. Even though Sophia was worried about what was happening at the Gullington, she allowed herself to nestle into a corner booth and talked into enjoying a glass of wine. Lunis would let her know if anything happened.

Yes, she was on a mission, and things were tense, but there was nothing for her to do until the Fae National History Museum closed. Then she'd get the hat, which didn't seem like such a big problem, return to the Gullington, save the groundskeeper and return everything to normal. *Easy peasy,* she thought.

"You haven't touched your camembert," Rudolf said, getting her attention. "Can I have it?"

Sophia hadn't realized she had been staring off. "Yeah, go ahead."

Rudolf grabbed her cheese, taking it in one bite. "Do you want to talk about what's bothering you?"

Why was it everyone seemed to know she was dealing with something of a personal nature and wanted to comment on it? Mama Jamba, Mae Ling, Liv, and now Rudolf. As far as expert sources went, these were pretty good ones, but she was tired of advice. She just wanted to keep her head down, do her job, and forget she had a heart. Let the wind whirl uncontrollably around the Gullington. What did she care?

She shook her head at Rudolf. "Not with you."

Sophia covered her face after seeing Rudolf's reaction. He might not have a brain, but he had a heart. "I'm sorry. It's just that, I think... well, I think I have to rethink some things."

"Why would you need to do that?" Rudolf asked between bites.

"Because the heart is often wrong," Sophia said, feeling around in her cloak, and looking for that damn pocketknife. She must have misplaced it. The knife had to be on her. She didn't drop it. Even if she had... It was an accident, and accidents didn't mean feelings or anything else. They just meant she was a dumb klutz who needed to keep better control over her possessions.

"So how are we going to break into the Fae National History Museum?" Rudolf asked, finishing his glass of wine.

She shook her head at him and scooted her own glass in his direction, encouraging him to drink it. "We don't have to. Remember, there are no wards keeping us out. We just waltz in and figure out which hat is ours."

The fact the fae used illusions as a security device was smart and dumb. Safeguarding things with extra measures would have been brilliant. But not doing so meant the fae were...well not smart.

"Can I give you some advice?" Rudolf asked out of nowhere, pulling Sophia's focus from her thoughts.

She jerked her head up. She'd just hurt his feelings and didn't want to see that look on his face again. "Yeah, what's that?"

He finished her glass of wine and wiped his mouth. "Here's something it took me many hundreds of years to understand. The heart wants what the head doesn't. And vice versa."

She was right; no advice was for the best. Sophia deflated, not feeling as good as she thought she would after being given advice by a regal source. He was the king of the fae, and most people around the world would consider him knowledgeable. Sophia knew the truth, and maybe that's why his advice fell flat.

"Thanks," she said, wishing she had heard something that would make things right. Or easy. Or have it all go away.

"Oh, Soph." Rudolf sounded crestfallen. "Don't look so sad. I promised you long ago I'd never let you down—"

"You never promised me that," she interrupted him.

Rudolf nodded. "And I promised that any man who broke your heart—"

Sophia held up her hand, stopping him. "No, you didn't. And I don't want your help, or anyone else's with my personal matters. I don't know where everyone got the idea I needed help. What I really need is a friend." She looked around, suddenly lost. "Are there any friends who can help me out here?" she asked.

Rudolf lifted the tiny arm of Fluffy the bear, and in a small voice, he said, "I can help."

A smile cracked on Sophia's face. "Thanks. That's the kind of help I need."

CHAPTER ONE HUNDRED ONE

"Okay, friend," Rudolf said, looking at Sophia in the waning sunlight as Paris grew dark around them. "Ready to storm the Castle?"

She couldn't help but smile at him. He was silly and dumb, and so very sweet. She nodded. "Yeah, I'm ready."

They waited until the receptionist exited the Fae National History Museum, not locking up as she trotted down the stairs. When she was out of sight, Sophia and the king of the fae ran out of the shadows and straight for the doors.

It was still a shock to Sophia when they yanked back the doors to a national museum, and there was no alarm. She felt like someone needed to rescue the fae from themselves, but they'd lasted this long on their own, so she figured they knew more than the rest of them. At least they had survived with their good looks.

"Okay, you know where to go," Sophia said, looking back at Rudolf.

He nodded. "To the bathroom."

She shot him a murderous expression.

"What? I drank all that wine," he complained, doing a pee dance.

She shook her head and pointed to the bathrooms, figuring the slight detour couldn't hurt since there were literally no guards or real security measures in the place.

Rudolf ran for the bathrooms, and Sophia allowed her attention to be pulled forward.

At night, the beautiful building was a menagerie of colors. The lights strobed on the walls and floors, creating different patterns.

Sophia stopped in the middle of the main room. She was in an exhibit of how the first fae enchanted the first person who ever fell in love with them. The scene was of a party with elegantly dressed guests standing around. The music playing overhead was intoxicating, and the lights made it feel like a ballroom. On the walls were a spiral of party guests all staring at Sophia as if waiting for her to take her place at the dance.

She found herself bowing to the imaginary guests. "Why, yes, thank you. I'm happy to be here."

She curtseyed, realizing she'd never been an adult at a real party. What would that be like? she wondered, and wished she was wearing a real ball gown.

She turned to find a man's hand extended to her. Sophia brought her eyes up to find Rudolf looking at her with a handsome smile.

"Can I have this dance, princess?" he asked.

She found herself blushing. "I wasn't really..."

He shook his head. "Why do you think it's so wrong that you, a woman, would want a prince to ask you to dance?"

She didn't know what to say, so as usual, she said nothing.

He took her hand and continued to smile. "Now I'm not a prince and not available, but the question still remains. I have more advice you didn't want earlier, but that still remains true."

Rudolf, for being a dimwit with a head full of watermelon, was an incredible dancer. He led Sophia in dance, making her feel light as a feather on her feet. She forgot where she was or that the world was a crazy place, or the Gullington was in danger. It all fell away as the music rose up, and the beat swallowed her whole.

"Sophia," Rudolf continued a few minutes later as if no time had passed since he last spoke. "As I was saying. Only allow a real prince to take your hand. No matter what, you always get the choice. Even if you feel fate is directing your path, please remember that princesses always get to choose their prince. No matter what. You should never feel rushed into anything. Know that, my princess."

Rudolf spun her out, holding Sophia's hand and making her feel like she was the belle of a ball even though she was wearing a cloak and a sword and a disguise, in a museum where her kind wasn't allowed.

Sometimes, that's how fairytales were told in her world.

CHAPTER ONE HUNDRED TWO

Sophia found it hard to believe she'd rather dance all night with the king of the fae in a museum than do what a mission had dictated. It wasn't like her and went against her practical nature. But, she'd never danced with a king at a ball, so maybe she was more of a romantic than she thought.

Sophia knew she couldn't allow anything to totally override her practical side. She did as she was charged and let Rudolf's hand go, making for the main exhibit. He had once again proven to be more than she expected. He was her friend and trustworthy, and his advice was right and true. A princess always gets to have a choice. Fate wasn't dictating her path. Even if she dropped something, it didn't mean a prince would return it.

Sophia halted in the main room where they'd found Quiet's father's captain's hat. It appeared almost the same as before, except there were now three hats sitting on three pedestals in the middle of the room. They appeared identical.

"Okay, now let's ensure everything is all right," Rudolf said.

Sophia thought he would go to check on the hats, but instead, he pulled Fluffy from his jacket and looked the stuffed bear over. She shook her head at the fae and went over to the pedestals.

She craned her head down, looking underneath the hats for the embroidered initials. The first hat had nothing on it. The second one was the same. It wasn't until her eyes connected with the third that she spied the letters. Her heart rejoiced. She was about to grab for it when the hats did something unexpected.

They began to spin like cups in a magical act.

CHAPTER ONE HUNDRED THREE

Rudolf clapped a hand on her shoulder and tightened his grip as Sophia's eyes widened.

"Pay attention to that which you prize most," he instructed.

How had the fae been so wise, Sophia wondered as the hats rotated slowly at first then began gaining speed. She kept her eyes trained on the one she knew had the identifying mark, not wanting to lose track of it. The hats picked up speed, moving faster, switching places, rotating, and blurring in the air. Still, Sophia never took her eyes off the one she thought was the right hat.

They slowly stopped moving and came to rest on top of the pedestals where they'd been before. This time the bottoms were obstructed by the lip of the stands.

Rudolf tapped her on the back once more. It was time to choose, and they both knew it.

Sophia knew when she picked the right hat, it would change everything in many ways. Alarms could sound, fae could charge her, but more than anything, she didn't want to disappoint her own. Not now.

Sophia took another step forward, and Rudolf caught her hand.

She turned back to find him shaking his head, holding up the stuffed bear.

"It's all comes down to Fluffy," the king of the fae said.

Sophia scowled at him. "That's what it comes down to? The freaking stuffed bear?"

He giggled. "Remember the sensors? You need to replace the correct hat with the bear to displace the weight sensor, or it will trigger the alarm."

Sophia couldn't believe it. King Rudolf Sweetwater was a genius. She nodded.

"Yeah, that's right," she said and took the little white bear, which should weigh as much as the captain's hat. She held it in her shaking hand.

CHAPTER ONE HUNDRED FOUR

The exchange had to be perfect.

Sophia had to pick up the hat at the exact same time she replaced it with the stuffed bear. If she didn't, the alarms would sound, and who knew what would happen?

Sophia didn't want to find out. She suspected a bunch of fae could be just as menacing as a bunch of gnomes or giants or magicians if they wanted to be, even with their dim wits and pretty faces.

She held Fluffy in one hand, hovering it next to the pedestal. Her other hand shook next to the fabric of the hat. She flexed her fingers, ready to grab it but felt uncertain. What if the tradeoff wasn't perfect, and she didn't do it with precise timing?

Sophia quit worrying and made an impromptu decision. She shoved the stuffed bear over, trading places with the hat, as she scooted it out of the way.

Nothing happened.

The bear sat on the pedestal where the hat had been. Beside it sat the two illusions, looking as real as Quiet's father's hat in her hand.

Sophia turned it upside down and saw the initials. It was the real one, and the alarms hadn't sounded.

They had done it! Sophia was ready to rejoice when something familiar sounded in her head.

Hey Sophia, Lunis said, undeniable tension in his voice.

Yes, she answered, suddenly breathless.

The Gullington is under siege once more, her dragon informed her, his voice full of dread.

CHAPTER ONE HUNDRED FIVE

The Barrier was down.

It was the only explanation for why Sophia could portal straight into the Gullington from Paris.

Her heart sank at the sight around her. In the distance, there was fighting by the Nest. She spied dragons whirling, shooting fire at cyborg pirates running across the Expanse. There was way more than before—hundreds of them.

In front of the Nest, Hiker stood, flanked by his riders. They were defending the dragon eggs, but they appeared to be losing the battle, the pirates getting closer. On the ground below the cave, Sophia spied Liv slashing at the trespassers, Rory and Bermuda at her back

The area around the Cave was on fire, burning with a strange green and blue smoke.

But the worst was the Castle.

It was on fire and burning fast.

CHAPTER ONE HUNDRED SIX

How did they get in? Sophia asked Lunis in her head.

They set off a bomb on the back side of the Cave next to the Barrier, he explained, relief in his voice at knowing she was there.

Sophia spied the flood of pirates storming over the hills, a constant flow of steampunk cyborgs, screaming as they ran, their weapons overhead, and menace in every movement as they made their way to the Nest.

Of course, the pirates would have been able to see the Gullington. The giants were unable to shield it. All their efforts had focused on keeping up the Barrier, and that appeared to have failed.

The bomb, Sophia said, clenching the hat in her hands.

It was strange magitech, Lunis explained. *It cut a hole in the Barrier, and the giants can't get it back up.*

Sophia couldn't understand how Rory and Bermuda could do anything but fight. The giants were being overrun by pirates storming in their direction. They were doing their best, throwing their large fists in the air and knocking back the smaller magicians. Beside them, Liv was blocking attacks using magic.

They were outnumbered. This fight wouldn't last long.

She could tell that high on the hill, next to the Nest, the dragonriders were struggling to keep up with the pirates raging in their direction.

And the Castle. The fire on the roof rose higher, licking its way up to the stars.

"The Captains!" Rudolf screamed and sprinted for the Castle.

Clark would be taking care of them. He would get them through a portal to the safety of the House of Fourteen Sophia knew. Still, Rudolf needed to be with his triplets, and Sophia let him run off.

She pulled Inexorabilis, fury building in her as she had never felt before. She was about to take off, intent on killing as many of the thieves as possible when the voice of her dragon made her pause before her feet had started moving.

You can't help us, Lunis told her.

What? she questioned, confused.

Sophia, we will lose this battle, Lunis said. *We can only hold them off for a little longer. Rory and Bermuda can't get the Barrier back up. The only way to win this is to fix the Gullington. Go find Mother Nature. Beg for her help once more.*

CHAPTER ONE HUNDRED SEVEN

H iker had been in many a battle. Many.

But nothing like this. The attack had come so swiftly. They had been ready to defend and for the Barrier to come down. They had been ready to fight, but not anything like what they were facing.

He swung his sword, knocking down two cyborgs at once, sending them back down the hill. Beside him, Mahkah was using stunning spells to keep a slew of invaders from getting any closer.

Evan had his hands held out and was using a shielding spell to defend the top of the cave where the Nest was located. The pirates were coming from every direction now.

In the area in front of the Nest, Wilder threw axes that returned like boomerangs after they hacked into an enemy. They were all doing their very best, and it wasn't enough.

The magitech being launched at them was taking its toll. Hiker didn't know how much longer they had. Even with the dragons flying overhead, blasting fire at the thieves, they weren't making a dent in the numbers.

There was also the blimp that had dropped a bomb on the Castle, making it explode with fire. The blimp was now taking all the dragon's attention. There was a shield on the blimp that deflected all their attempts.

Another of those strategically placed bombs and the Gullington would be wiped out.

How had it all come down to this for Hiker Wallace? How could he lose his home after all these centuries like this?

He let out a scream as he pulled his sword again, slicing through men with wires covering their chests and strange eye patches.

Wilder spun around after catching one of his axes. "Hiker! Use it!"

"I am!" Hiker yelled, knowing what the young dragonrider was referring to. Wilder didn't think Hiker was embracing the power he inherited from his twin brother, Thad Reinhart. He thought he was holding back, and maybe he was, but he didn't know how to harness the power.

Something very deep in his spirit prevented him from fully trying.

Hiker had never felt a power like what lived in his blood and bones now. It was a power that, if he wasn't careful, would overwhelm him. It was the kind of power that could burn him up. It was Thad's power, and it corrupted, and Hiker would never allow that to happen.

As the Gullington was overwhelmed, he started to think he wouldn't have a choice anymore.

CHAPTER ONE HUNDRED EIGHT

L iv swung Bellator, never having faced so many enemies at once. They weren't normal magicians, sending normal combat spells at her and the giants.

These cyborgs threw lasers from their eyes and small missiles from guns on their arms. They came at them with attacks resistant to magic. They came with their mouths wide open and screams echoing from their lungs. There was angst in these men. And they were all men, which was weird since Hiker had said the leader was a woman by the name of Trin Currante.

So far, there had been no sign of her, but it would have been easy to miss her in the sea of attackers.

Liv was using every combat spell she could think of to keep a perimeter around the giants at her back. Rory wasn't a fighter. Bermuda, though, she was fierce in battle, throwing her arms wide and taking out multiple attackers at once.

Still, the shield wouldn't last long, to keep the cyborg's attacks at bay, and neither would Liv. That was a truth she didn't want to admit to herself. She'd come to the Gullington to help the Dragon Elite, and now it looked like she might go down with them.

CHAPTER ONE HUNDRED NINE

S ophia's feet blurred as she sprinted for the Castle. It was burning fast. The flames rose up into the night sky, sending strange green and blue smoke all around, the wind making the fire burn hotter.

The entire top story was engulfed.

Sophia pulled her cloak off her shoulders and wrapped it around her head when she entered the Castle.

She nearly ran into Ainsley pacing in the entryway.

"Ainsley!" she yelled. "You have to get out of here! Go to the southern border. There are no pirates there!"

The housekeeper shook her head. "Oh, no, S. Beaufont. I can't leave the Castle."

"Of course, you can," Sophia argued, the smoke burning her eyes.

"No, I must stay." Ainsley shook her head again. "I don't know why but if the Castle goes down, I have to go with it. It's a part of me, and I can't abandon it."

It was no good wasting time arguing with the shapeshifter, and in a way, Sophia knew she was right. She couldn't leave the Castle. It would be like abandoning a friend when they needed help or running when a loved one was dying.

"Fine, where's Mama Jamba?" Sophia asked, having to yell to be heard over the crackling of the flames.

"I don't know, S.," Ainsley said, her eyes brimming with tears. "I think she left."

Sophia shook her head. "No, she wouldn't have done that."

Ainsley nodded. "I watched her go. She walked straight through that door and said, 'If they survive, it's because they saved themselves. Only those worthy of protecting my Earth can do that. Otherwise, they were never right for the job.'"

Sophia spun around, searching the area in front of the Castle. She hadn't seen Mama Jamba out there, but there had been so many sights vying for her attention.

Ainsley's gaze darted to the hat in Sophia's hands. "What is that?"

It seemed silly now. She had a hat that was supposed to help save Quiet. What was the point if they were all going down? It was the only thing she had left, and the only hope remaining.

Maybe she couldn't get Ainsley to leave the Castle, and maybe the Dragon Elite couldn't win this battle. But she could save the groundskeeper, convince him to take the antidote, and get him to safety.

Sophia didn't hesitate another moment as she sped for the stairs, taking them two at a time, in the direction of the servant's wing.

CHAPTER ONE HUNDRED TEN

T hey couldn't hold them off much longer. Hiker could see that in the way his dragonriders were fighting. They were giving this battle everything they had, and it wasn't enough.

A blast from a cyborg hit Mahkah in the chest and sent him rolling down the hill. Wilder ran after him, slashing through enemies to help his fallen friend.

Evan sprinted after the pirates trying to come down the back side of the Nest, sending spell after spell at them. Hiker whipped his sword as fast as he could, and it didn't matter. There was always another enemy. They were like ants sent to attack, not caring they would be chopped down.

They were sacrificing themselves for this Trin Currante, but Hiker knew she had access to a kill switch in their heads. What choice did they have? Either they threw themselves at the Dragon Elite, or they died a different death. He wasn't sure what he'd do in their situation.

He figured if he had nothing left to lose, he'd do the right thing.

Something flipped in Hiker. He pulled in the power he'd been resisting. He let it flow into him and build in his veins. It made his eyes burn hot, and his blood boil. It made him feel he might explode embracing this power.

Just as he was about to unleash what he'd been resisting, a blast threw him forward. He had flown for most of his life on his dragon, Bell, but never ever like this.

At first, he thought the explosion had been him, and he'd been right not to use the power. As he was thrown to the ground a hundred yards from the Nest, he saw the area where he'd been moments prior in front of the cave opening had been bombed.

Green and blue smoke rose up from in front of the Nest. The bomb had cleared the area, sending all the dragon riders down the hill along with the pirates.

Hiker glanced up at the blimp overhead, knowing it had sent the attack, and now the Nest was unguarded. All the riders were too far away as a single woman slid over the front of the cave and slipped inside.

"NOOOO!" Hiker yelled, staggering to his feet and realizing his legs weren't operating after being at the epicenter of the explosion. If he hadn't been pooling power from within, he was certain he would have died. This was worse as he tried to crawl across the ground toward the Nest, where Trin Currante had just disappeared.

CHAPTER ONE HUNDRED ELEVEN

The explosion rocked the Gullington and sent everyone to their knees. Liv immediately tried to stand but found herself completely disoriented. There was something in the blue and green smoke.

She looked up and saw the dragons sending all their attacks at the blimp that had dropped the bomb. Still, their fire had no effect on the flying magitech device.

The blimp disappeared, portaling away.

A scream ripped through the air. Liv whipped her head in that direction, but it was hard to make out anything through the smoke and fire.

The Nest. The front of it had been bombed. Hiker Wallace had been blasted from his position at the front, defending the opening where the dragon eggs were.

Liv shook her head, trying to will her eyes to adjust.

Everyone, including the pirates, had all been laid out flat from the last explosion. She looked over her shoulder to see more cyborgs storming in their direction. She reached for Bellator that had flown from her hands. Her fingers shook. She was weak. The smoke was making her disoriented.

The pirates would be on them soon. They would defeat them. It would all be over.

CHAPTER ONE HUNDRED TWELVE

S ophia slid through the narrow opening that led to Quiet's room, covering her mouth from the smoke slipping down from the upper story. She'd have to carry him back down. She could do that. First, she had to get to him.

When she entered his room, she was surprised to find him sitting up. There were no windows in his modest room, but he was looking at the wall like he could see out to the Expanse where the deadly battle was ensuing.

"Quiet!" she yelled. "I need to get you out of here."

The stubborn gnome shook his head, keeping his eyes on the far wall.

"Come on!" she screamed. "You can't die here, and that's what's going to happen." She raced forward, pulling the antidote from her pocket.

"I know you don't want to do this, and I don't know why," she said rapidly. "But you have to tell me your real name."

He mouthed the word, "No." She didn't understand it.

"Fine, you want to die, then do it, but maybe you can remember what you have to live for." Sophia closed her eyes as she tried to remember the words from the letter Quiet's mother had sent him.

They came to her fast. Her eyes sprang open. She closed the distance between her and gnome. "May your father's captain hat house your soul on the days you need shelter. And on the days you don't, I hope it reminds you of your purpose. We all need a reminder of why we serve, and this one will be yours."

Sophia thrust the hat into the gnome's hands, and only then did he look at her, shock written across his face at the sight of the heirloom.

CHAPTER ONE HUNDRED THIRTEEN

Hiker had to get to the Nest.

He had to stop Trin Currante.

He promised to defend the dragon eggs.

Pressing up to his feet, he saw he was the only one in the vicinity standing. All his men were lying flat, trying to get up. Liv and the giants were alive but looked as bad as the riders.

With the blimp gone, the dragons flew to the edge of the Barrier, where more pirates continued to spill through the opening. It didn't matter. There were more on the way, and they couldn't stop them all. Soon the pirates would overrun them.

Hiker had to get to the Nest. He stumbled, and nearly fell back to his knees again.

Trin Currante appeared at the opening of the cave, her wire-like hair flowing in the wind and a bag strewn over her shoulder as she smiled down at Hiker.

It was the motivation he needed to push forward. He'd kill her. He'd make her pay.

He didn't get a chance, because the woman who had stolen their dragon's eggs opened a portal and disappeared.

CHAPTER ONE HUNDRED FOURTEEN

"Quiet," Sophia said, her voice urgent. "I need you to remember your purpose. I need you to want to live for that purpose. Whatever you lose by telling me your name will be worth it because we need you. The Dragon Elite can't lose you. Please."

She pulled the cork from the antidote and held it out to the sick gnome.

He brought his gaze up from the captain's hat. Sophia had never realized how blue his eyes were. They were the color of the Pond, and reflected in them was the green hills of the Expanse. Written all over the wrinkles lining his face were things that reminded her of the Castle.

He opened his mouth, pulling in a raspy breath.

Sophia was about to argue with him more, to point to the hat, and tell him he couldn't give up.

Before she could, he took the antidote from her shaking hands, and in a voice she could hear plainly, Quiet spoke.

"My name...is...Gullington."

CHAPTER ONE HUNDRED FIFTEEN

"NOOOOO!" Hiker yelled so loudly and furiously it shook the ground under his feet.

This had been his home for the last five hundred years. These were his riders. This was personal.

He turned at the pirates screaming as they sprinted in his direction, their weapons held over their heads and murder written on their faces.

Trin Currante had taken the dragon eggs, and yet the cyborgs weren't standing down. They were going to finish the Dragon Elite, or at least they were going to try.

The power that had been building in Hiker's veins pooled into his hand. He didn't resist it or worry it would corrupt him, and burn him from the inside out. It didn't matter even if it did.

He raised his hand and directed it at the storm of pirates yards away from attacking Liv Beaufont, the giants, and his riders.

With a scream, Hiker sent a wave of fury through his fingertips.

It was red as it sailed through the air, like the laser attacks the cyborgs had been sending using their magitech. There was no technology in the attack Hiker sent.

This was all magic. And it was all him.

The curse of red flew, knocking into every single trespasser who raced toward them and sent them flat to the ground, dead instantly.

In a matter of seconds, Hiker Wallace killed a hundred enemies with one assault.

Now that he had embraced his power, he was the most powerful magician in the world.

CHAPTER ONE HUNDRED SIXTEEN

S ophia sucked in a breath and let the truth wash over her.

Quiet was the Gullington.

He had always been here because he was the Expanse. He was the Cave. He was the Pond. Quiet McAfee was the Castle.

He was the one who made the flames rise in the chandeliers and the one who sent her strange messages. Who locked doors or made them disappear. He was Ainsley's best friend and the one who healed the riders when they were injured. The one who had almost died because he didn't want the Dragon Elite to know who he truly was.

Sophia had reminded him.

The gnome threw back his head and drank the potion in one big gulp.

The color in his face rose to the surface, making his cheeks and nose red. His eyes cleared. Strength took over as pure vengeance filled the gnome's every feature.

Sophia stepped back as he whipped the covers off his short legs and slid off the bed, his movements sharp and powerful.

He swept his arm to the side, and the wall in front of them he'd been looking at disappeared. Suddenly Sophia was standing on the edge of the Castle looking out at the grounds of the Expanse.

Green and blue smoke drifted in the air, and the Expanse was covered in bodies.

Her heart leapt to her throat, but she recognized her own friends moving beside the Nest. They were alive. Liv was standing and helping Bermuda and Rory up.

Wilder, Evan, and Mahkah went to stand next to Hiker, who was looking out at the bodies in the distance.

Above them, the flames on the top of the Castle cast a blinding light down on the grounds.

Quiet snapped his short fingers, and the flames disappeared from the roof. The smoke laced with poison evaporated from the air, and all the bodies of the trespassers were removed from the Expanse.

A piercing sound echoed over the Gullington as all the eyes of the Dragon Elite looked up at the Castle to see the gnome gazing at them powerfully.

Sophia was going to keep Quiet's secret and not tell anyone he was the Gullington, but she knew everyone had seen what she had. They would know the truth about the gnome.

Quiet clapped his hands together, making a booming sound that shook the entire Expanse. Everyone's chins jerked into the air as a dome shot over the top of the Gullington. It reflected a bright blue light before shimmering and disappearing.

The Barrier was back in place. The Dragon Elite's home was safe once more.

Quiet turned to Sophia, a grateful expression on his face. "Thank you. You didn't have to save me, especially since you didn't know my truth. Yet, you did because you always look out for others. A true dragonrider, you are, S. Beaufont, and it is a pleasure to serve you, which I hope to continue to have the honor of doing for a very long time."

The gnome bowed to Sophia, her friends and family on the Expanse witnessing the whole thing before the wall of the Castle reformed once more.

CHAPTER ONE HUNDRED
SEVENTEEN

L iv hugged Sophia for so long she had to finally encourage her
sister to let her go. When she peeled away, the sober expression
in her sister's eyes nearly made tears spill.

Clark stood beside them, unmistakable adoration on his face as he
stared at Sophia.

He pointed to the portal door. "Once we go through here…"

"You won't be able to return to the Gullington again," Sophia
finished, answering the question. "After you are through, only the
Dragon Elite and those who serve us can enter our grounds."

Liv nodded and ran her eyes over the walls of the Castle, amazement in her gaze. "I can't believe this is a person. Simply incredible."

It was incredible, and yet, it made so much sense when Sophia
thought of all the things she knew about the Gullington. The night
before, Sophia had curled up with *The Complete History of Dragonriders*
and randomly opened the book. That's when she'd read about how the
gnome known as Captain Gullington "Quiet" McAfee had sacrificed
himself to save his ship filled with refugee fae.

Just before the gnome was about to die, Mother Nature came to
him and made him an offer.

"Be the protector and home for my Dragon Elite and you, Gullington, will live on forever," Mama Jamba had said centuries prior.

That's how it had all come about. Sophia closed the book, her breath stolen away. When she went back to try and find that part of the text, she couldn't. That was the mystery of the book and the mystery of the Castle. Of the Gullington.

"Thank you for everything you both did to help," Sophia said, finding her voice scratchy. Clark had taken the triplets to the House of Fourteen, where they were now safe with their father once more. He had returned when the giants went through, informing him everyone was safe once more at the Gullington.

Liv shook her head. "We will always be here to help you, my love."

"Always," Clark repeated. "That's what family's for."

The tears broke through and began running down Sophia's cheeks. *"Familia Est Sempiternum."*

"Familia Est Sempiternum," her siblings repeated in unison before engulfing her in their arms and holding her tightly.

CHAPTER ONE HUNDRED EIGHTEEN

"What are you looking for, dear?" Mama Jamba asked Sophia, making her jump.

She knocked her head into the bottom of the dining room table where she was crouched, looking under the chairs for her pocketknife. "Nothing," she lied.

The old woman shook her head and gave Sophia a knowing look. "It's not there."

Sophia gulped. Of course, Mother Nature knew what she was searching for.

"You can have it back if you really want it," Mama Jamba continued, "but only if you want what it represents. That's the deal and the reason it was made. It's the only way you can have it back."

There was the question for Sophia, what this had all been building up to. "I think I do."

Mama Jamba smiled proudly. "Then, so be it."

The crazy, powerful entity had returned the night the Castle burned. She didn't say a word about walking out on her Dragon Elite or anything about making Quiet the Gullington. She did look up at Hiker Wallace and say three words. "Good work, son."

Liv had told Sophia about watching Hiker embrace his full power.

Sophia knew Liv had seen more than most when in battle, but the warrior for the House of Fourteen said there was nothing comparable to the power the leader of the Dragon Elite showed. He had killed one-hundred men at once with a single spell, and that wasn't even all his power. Hiker Wallace had been a formidable force before.

Now, he was as close to a god as any magician could become.

Evan, Mahkah, and Wilder entered the dining hall, all three men peering around speculatively.

"He's not in here," Mama Jamba sang to them, taking her normal seat.

"That's why he didn't want anyone to know the truth," Sophia said, shaking her head at the men. "He didn't want you to treat him differently, knowing he was the Castle, the Expanse, the Cave, the Pond, and now the Nest."

Mama Jamba nodded, unfolding her napkin. "He, as he was centuries ago as a captain, didn't want to be treated with favoritism based on his power. Quiet despises that sort of thing."

"How can I be mean to him now though, knowing he is the one who throws my belongings on the hills outside?" Evan complained, sitting down across from Sophia.

"How could you have been mean to him in the first place?" she argued.

He shook his head. "That was always our thing."

"That was your thing," Sophia spat.

Evan rolled his eyes. "Whatever suck up. You've always been his favorite."

"I'm his favorite, and that's how it should be." Ainsley came through from the kitchen, looking like her old self. She set a large tray of blueberry pancakes in front of Mama Jamba.

"Thank you, dear," Mother Nature said, taking a few off the top.

"Ains, did you know…" Sophia asked, not finishing her question.

The shapeshifter shook her head. "I didn't. Now it makes sense because I've always understood Quiet even though the lot of you couldn't."

Sophia's eyes drifted to the side as she thought. Quiet was what had kept Ainsley alive all these years. Maybe he would know how to save her.

Sophia made a mental note to investigate this more. She wanted to find out how to help the housekeeper. Ainsley may not have been willing to leave the Castle when it was burning to the ground, but what she didn't know was whether she stayed in the burning Castle or left, she would have died. There were no options for her. This Gullington was her entire life.

Sophia wanted to give her the option to leave and give her memories back. Ainsley should have the choice to leave the Gullington if she wanted.

Love was giving others the option to leave, knowing they may but hoping they didn't. Or at least hoping one day they would return. Real love couldn't be caged.

Every one of the dragon riders stood when Hiker Wallace came into the dining hall. He paused, a look of uncertainty in his eyes as he stared at the Dragon Elite, all giving him silent respect.

"At ease," Hiker said after a moment and continued forward.

Mama Jamba, who hadn't stood, snickered as she poured maple syrup over her pancakes.

"What's so funny?" Hiker asked, taking his chair at the head of the table.

"You're not used to it, and you nicked yourself shaving, didn't you, son?" Mama Jamba asked, putting a bite of fluffy pancakes in her mouth.

Hiker frowned, running his hands over his face. "Yes, apparently, the power I wield comes out when I'm in battle or shaving or even trying to fall asleep at night."

"You'll get used to it," Mama Jamba told him. "Or you won't, and you'll shave off that beard on accident. I've always liked your chin and wouldn't mind seeing it."

Hiker shook his head. "Real men have beards."

Evan looked between Mahkah and Wilder, his mouth open. "Are we going to be offended by that statement?"

Wilder laughed and combed his fingers over his smooth chin. "You can, but I don't think I'll be talking back to our leader anytime soon."

"Not until you've had too much whiskey," Mahkah said, making a rare joke.

Everyone at the table laughed.

When they were quiet once more, only the sounds of forks and knives scraping plates, Hiker cleared his throat.

Everyone paused and looked up.

"The eggs," Hiker said simply. "We're getting them back."

He looked at Sophia with conviction. A dozen eggs had been stolen by Trin Currante in her magical sack.

"I'm sorry she took them," Hiker apologized, regret filling his tone.

Sophia nodded, knowing he'd done everything to try and stop it from happening. There had been an explosion, but the magitech bombs didn't stand a chance of bringing down the Barrier now. Not with Quiet back in commission.

Sophia wondered how Trin had known how to bring the Barrier down. How had she known how to make the groundskeeper ill with the herbs? There were more questions that had to be answered.

"I hope you do get those dragon eggs back," Mama Jamba said, her eyes on her plate as she devoured the pancakes. "However, today, you all need to rest. Celebrate. Count your blessings. Tomorrow the battles outside the Gullington will demand your attention."

Evan raised his arms, stretching. "I'm going to make Quiet something special. Maybe a picture of the two of us together."

Mahkah shook his head but laughed.

Mama Jamba turned her attention to Sophia. "You should take a walk, my dear. The thistles are blooming by the Pond."

"You mean Quiet is making the thistles bloom," Hiker commented.

"I guess I do," Mama Jamba agreed.

"Why don't you think I want to see the thistles?" Evan asked, pretending to be offended.

Mama Jamba shook her head at the young dragonrider. "You stay off the Expanse. Hiker, you and I have a meeting in the dungeon after breakfast."

"Why the dungeon?" Hiker questioned.

Mama Jamba winked at Sophia. "Because there are no windows there."

Although Sophia had no idea what that was all about, she was certain Mother Nature was orchestrating something in her life, and she was okay with that.

CHAPTER ONE HUNDRED NINETEEN

The winds blew Sophia's hair back from her face as she hiked toward the Pond. The thistles dotted the Expanse with pink, contrasting nicely against the green hills.

Yes, Trin Currante had stolen more dragon eggs and figured out how to get into the Gullington. But out of everything, the Dragon Elite had gotten stronger. Sophia didn't regret any of it. Without hardship, it was impossible to get stronger.

The leader of the Dragon Elite had embraced his powers. The truth about the Gullington had been revealed. And the dragonriders knew that no matter what, they had each other's back. They were more a team than ever before.

Sophia glanced at the Cave, thinking fondly of Lunis resting in there with the other dragons. She knew they were all recovering after the epic battle. Dragons were like cats. They pounced hard and fast but needed a lot of recovery time after the fact.

The wind didn't let up when Sophia came to the edge of the cliff overlooking the Pond. She had only been standing there for a moment when she sensed him at her back.

Wilder moved faster than her. Quieter. His combat experience gave him that advantage, but also his age and experience.

She closed her eyes for a moment, considering her options, and chose one. She turned to face him, knowing what was coming next.

The dragonrider stood only a few feet away, a curious expression in his blue eyes, and his brown hair taking note of the wind that passed through it.

He had his hand extended. In it was her pocketknife.

"Why does it have a glass slipper on it?" Wilder asked, flicking open the blade with ease to show Cinderella's shoe etched into the silver.

Sophia reached out, her fingertips brushing his hand when she took her knife. "Because it's symbolic."

"I don't think I understand," Wilder said, scratching his head.

"It's got the glass slipper because Subner knew I would drop it, and you would find it and give it back to me," she explained, realizing that probably still didn't make much sense to him.

He smiled softly, his dimples surfacing. "That seems like a complex riddle."

She nodded. "That's how my life goes."

"Why did you drop it?" he queried.

"I didn't mean to, or at least I didn't think at the time I meant to," she answered. "I think the universe has a strange way of communicating with me sometimes. The real question I had to answer was whether I wanted it back."

"So, what does this mean?"

"It means although my head tells me to run, my heart wants me not to."

"What are you running from?"

"You mean who."

He tilted his head to the side and took a step forward. "Who are you running from?"

"You know," she said. She didn't think she could say it out loud. It was ridiculous to Sophia that she had fought seven-headed dragons and ogres and magitech, but standing in front of this guy made her feel weak.

"Why would you run from me?" he insisted.

Wilder knew. Of course, he did. There was no denying the obvious between them.

"We just don't make any sense together," she protested, finding her voice scratchy suddenly.

"Because…"

He wasn't letting her get away easy on this. He wanted her to say all the words, and not hide any of it.

"Because we are too different," she started, not wanting to state specifics.

"Because I have lived on the Earth for so much longer?"

Why did he have to say it out loud, she wondered with frustration. "We are just too different," she repeated.

"Age is a relative thing, especially when you are a dragonrider," Wilder argued. "The chi of the dragon changes us. It changed you."

"Hiker, he would…" she said and trailed away.

The laugh that spilled out of Wilder's mouth echoed over the Pond. "Oh, he will no doubt go ballistic. There will be yelling and destruction in his midst. But you know what?"

"Do I have to say what?" she muttered, a smile in her eyes.

"Well, you just did, so I will continue," he said with another laugh. "At the end of the day, it's our choice. No one gets to live our lives for us. If you want to make it work, regardless of our situation or age or whatever, then we will."

"And if I don't?" Sophia asked.

He shot her a challenging expression. "Then why did you drop the pocketknife? Why did you want it back?"

She didn't have an answer, so she stepped forward and looked up at him. "I guess we have a lot to figure out."

"Indeed," he said, the smile in his eyes making them dazzle. "But first things first…"

He lifted his calloused hand and brushed it across her cheek, a spark radiating from that first touch. It only intensified as Wilder laid his lips on hers, kissing her with gentle pressure and hungry thirst.

The winds around the two dragonriders whirled, wrapping around them before suddenly dying out completely. All at once, everything was calm, and the waters of the Pond were as placid as glass.

This wasn't a happily ever after for the two dragonriders, only a secret moment, stolen away. Tomorrow would come and bring more adventures. And tomorrow they would keep their secrets until the time was right to reveal them.

SARAH'S AUTHOR NOTES
FEBRUARY 26, 2020

Thank you so much for reading. Your support of the Liv Beaufont series and this one has been life changing. Thank you! Seriously! Thank you.

So wind was a pretty important part of this story. Here in LA, we have the Santa Ana winds and they've been blowing like crazy, keeping me up at night and distracting me while I work. When we have those windy days, I always say, "The winds of change are a blowin'."

I feel like wind represents change for me. In Sophia's case, I wanted it to symbolize her own internal struggles manifesting themselves outwardly. More on that later. Incidentally, as I write these notes, the winds are up again, howling through my old windows. I guess more change is on the way.

I don't know much about my own family history for various reasons. My father's side of the family I knew was mostly Cajun French. Anyway, imagine my surprise when I get back from Scotland and my parents inform me that we're Scottish. They sent me the family crest and reminded me that my father's middle name is McAfee, my grandmother's maiden name. And hence, that became the famous name of Quiet's ship. Incidentally, I got the name Quiet, for the very powerful gnome, because it's my dad's nickname for my step-mom. I always found it very endearing. She calls him "Bubs."

A big thank you to my awesome friends for all the ideas and inspiration they've contributed to this book. Martin, for instance, had the idea of Hiker getting roped into the Nigerian Prince scheme. There's something very entertaining about a 500-year-old Viking using technology for the first time.

Speaking of awesome friends, my friend Crystal and her wife inspired the Crying Cat Bakery scene. I think they are my favorite characters now. Crystal is often telling me of the funny things that happen between her and her wife. I finally was like, "You two are going into a book." And so we had the magical bakery run by an OCD baker and wanna-be assassin. When Crystal asked if her ski mask was clean, I totally was grateful that my friends are so awesomely weird and provide so much fodder.

There's a lot of bakery themes in this book between the Crying Cat Bakery and Fairy Godmother College. Happily Ever After was inspired by Zumbo's Just Desserts, a show Lydia and I watch together. Oh, and is there any interests in a spin off series about Fairy Godmother College? If so, let us know!

The bakery theme is also inspired by a strange thing I did in my mid-twenties. I had just graduated with my masters in management, moved across the country to a small hippie community in Oregon and taken a very stuffy job. I hated it! I was working for a very well known "Oprah Book Club" author. He was my idol. And he made me count paper... Anyway, I did what anyone with no savings and a ton of angst would do. I quit.

Then I went to the bakery down the street where I got my morning coffee and begged the sweet couple who ran it to give me a job. I had zero experience in the service industry or with baking in general. But I thought that running a bakery would be romantic in the poet-sort-of-sense. The couple took pity on me and gave me the early shift.

I had to be at the bakery at 5 in the morning to make, bake and stock the cases full of pastries for when the shop opened at 7. The oven was bigger than a normal sized kitchen and I couldn't reach the top racks without jumping. You can guess how smart of an idea that was.

Alone for hours each morning, I baked hundreds of pastries, sliced bread, made the coffee and also the pizza for the lunch crowd. I made $8 an hour and got more life experiences than in years at corporate America.

And I learned it *was* romantic working at a bakery. The smells of sour dough in the morning and flour on my cheeks and sore muscles at the end of the day... Well, it all stuck with me and although I didn't realize it at the time, those experiences would inspire parts of books. Seems pretty priceless thinking back.

Anyway, it was also freaking hard work. I lasted three months and then took a job for a government contractor that did secret reconnaissance work for foreign countries. I can say no more about that... but who knows if that fodder is in my books somewhere...

Speaking of fodder... Hold on. I've have to go hide under my sheets for a moment before I can tell this next reveal. I don't know why I do this to myself, but this is coming from the girl who wrote two books about her personal life. I blame MA.

After the release of those books, many LA guys wouldn't date me, so afraid they'd be put in a book and made fun of. One was like, "I'm glad you didn't put me in your freaking Asshole book." I was like, "Yeah, because the short guy who I called 'Adult Chris' totally isn't you..."

I've learned my lesson though. No more writing explicitly about my personal life. Oh no. Now I just do it covertly and then call myself out in my author notes.

So the Wilder romance storyline... Again, I'm casting the accusatory finger at Michael. Everyone has to have a good scapegoat and he's usually mine. Anyway, when we plotted out this series, he wanted the romance introduced in the beginning of this arc. If not for that then I could have avoided what happened next, hence the blame.

There might have been some influences from real life that influenced that whole romance storyline with Wilder. Like for Christmas,

I might have gotten a guy I'm seeing a fork. A single fork. It was based on a running joke. Since he's Scottish, I made a joke about forks when we first met. I was like, "Do Scotsmen even know how to use a fork?" Why yes, I am usually insulting to strangers at first meeting. It's how I keep the uptight jerks away. A screening process of sorts. A friend once asked me, "Don't you think being rude will scare people away?" I was like, "The hope is that it keeps the weaklings away." Anyway, the Scotsman admitted that he didn't know how to use a fork, so I got him one for Christmas with the promise that I'd teach him how to use it. Then for Valentines I got him a spoon. I'm a real romantic.

And hence we come to the Cinderella storyline in this book. Of course our Sophia couldn't drop a glass slipper. It had to be a pocket knife. Fork, spoon, knife. You get it now. 12 And remember that she gave Wilder a fork for Christmas when he unexpectedly gifted her with a grappling hook.

I probably shouldn't be sharing all this, but what the hell!

So the Wilder storyline is obviously inspired by parts of my own life. The complications and feelings that Sophia goes through are pretty close to my own. Fodder comes from reality.

In this book there was a story, inside of a story, inside of a story. I used the Cinderella metaphor for Sophia's situation which was loosely based on mine own. I knew like Cinderella that Sophia would run when the "ball" was over—after the King Arthur mission. Similar to Cinderella, she ran because her mind said it didn't make any sense. And I knew that she'd drop the proverbial "glass slipper" because of what was in her heart, as her fairy godmother foretold.

The question I haven't answered for myself is will I drop a glass slipper of sorts? Only time will tell. Or the next book will. PREORDER now to find out what Sarah does with her life! Lol Shameless, I am.

Okay, share time is over for you all.

Sincerely,

Tiny Ninja

MICHAEL'S AUTHOR NOTES
MARCH 7, 2020

THANK YOU for reading our story! We have a few of these planned, but we don't know if we should continue writing and publishing without your input. Options include leaving a review, reaching out on Facebook to let us know, and smoke signals.

Frankly, smoke signals might get misconstrued as low hanging clouds, so you might want to nix that idea.

Dammit, I don't know who the Scotsman is in Sarah's story. You know, the one she gave a fork to for Christmas.

First clue, it happened last year.

It's driving me nuts at the moment. I know of a FEW Scotsman it could be, but I don't know - and she hasn't been fessing up. Any comments about who she is seeing?

Is he an author? Is he the guy she went on the sight-seeing trip with (see other author notes.)

Is Sarah making this stuff up? She is a tiny ninja. It would be like her to throw up smoke screens.

Or just like. That's like her, too. Well, it's like all fiction authors. It's in our job description that we lie for a living.

I'm just hoping that her glass slipper isn't a knife. I'm not sure how the guy should accept that sort of gift.

Note: *The bakery oven really doesn't have to be much taller than...what, 5'6"?*

Ad Aeternitatem!

Michael Anderle

ACKNOWLEDGMENTS
SARAH NOFFKE

I feel like I'm on the stage at the Oscars, accepting an award when I write my acknowledgments. I stand there, holding this award, my hands shaking and my words racing around in my mind. I'm not an actress for a reason. I'm a writer and talking to people in "real life" is hard. Not to mention a ton of people all at once.

I picture looking out at the audience and being blinded by spot-lights and forgetting every word of the speech I memorized just in case I won. The speech would go like this and it's meant for all of you, not the guild. For the fans. The supporters. The people who are the reason I would ever stand on any stage, ever.

Okay, here we go. I clear my throat and smile, looking up at the camera, holding the little golden man. And then I begin:

This was never supposed to happen. I was never meant to publish a book and then another one. And then another. I was supposed to write in private and live a life that Henry David Thoreau called a life of "quiet desperation." I would always hope to share my books, but never bring myself to do it. And you would never read my words. But then, in a crazed moment of brashness, I did share my books and you all liked them. And because of that, I've never been the same. And here I am feeling grateful all just because…

That's why I'm here. Because of you. Thank you to my first readers. The ones who picked up those books that I didn't even outline and you still liked them. You messaged me and maybe you thought it was no big deal, but when your ego is new to the publishing world, it's a big deal.

I can't thank you readers enough. I've found that reading your reviews helps me to start a chapter when I'm stuck or lazy.

I really need to thank someone who has made this all possible and that's my father. I was going to quit. I can't tell you how many times I quit. But when I wasn't making it, he was the one who told me to not throw in the towel. "Give yourself a timeline," he suggested. If I didn't get to my goal by then, I'd quit. And apparently there was magic in that advice, because I'm still doing this. Dad, you're the pragmatic one, but when you believed in me enough to tell me to not quit, I knew I had to follow your advice.

And I thank all my friends who are constantly supporting me with thoughts of love and encouragement. Most don't read my books. I'm sort of self-deprecating, although I'm working on it and will be the first to tell my friends, "My books probably aren't for you." However, every now and then a friend surprises me and says, "I was up all night reading your books." It's always a total shock. But my point is, that even if they didn't read, I still have the best friends ever. Diane, you're my rock. And I love you, even though you will probably not read this.

Thank you to everyone at LMBPN. Those people are like family to me, although I'm not sure if they'll let me sleep on their couch. Well, who am I kidding? They totally will. Big thanks to Steve, Lynne, Mihaela, Kelly, Jen and the entire team. The JIT members are the best.

Huge thank you to the LMBPN Ladies group on Facebook. Micky, you're the best. And that group keeps me sane.

And a giant thank you to the betas for this series. Juergen you are my first reader and friend. Thanks for all the help. And thanks to Martin and Crystal for being some of the best people I know. What would I do without you? A huge thanks to the ARC team. Seriously, if it weren't for you all I might pass out before release day, wondering if anyone will like the book.

And with all my books, my final thank you goes to my lovely muse, Lydia. Oh sweet darling, I write these books for you, but ironically, I couldn't write them without you. You are my inspiration. My sounding board. And the reason that I want to succeed. I love you.

Thank you all! I'm sorry if I forgot anyone. Blame Michael. For no other reason than just because.

BOOKS BY SARAH NOFFKE

Sarah Noffke writes YA and NA science fiction, fantasy, paranormal and urban fantasy. In addition to being an author, she is a mother, podcaster and professor. Noffke holds a Masters of Management and teaches college business/writing courses. Most of her students have no idea that she toils away her hours crafting fictional characters. www.sarahnoffke.com

Check out other work by Sarah author here.

Ghost Squadron:

Formation #1:
   Kill the bad guys. Save the Galaxy. All in a hard day's work.
   After ten years of wandering the outer rim of the galaxy, Eddie Teach is a man without a purpose. He was one of the toughest pilots in the Federation, but now he's just a regular guy, getting into bar fights and making a difference wherever he can. It's not the same as flying a ship and saving colonies, but it'll have to do.
   That is, until General Lance Reynolds tracks Eddie down and offers him a job. There are bad people out there, plotting terrible

things, killing innocent people, and destroying entire colonies. **Someone has to stop them.**

Eddie, along with the genetically-enhanced combat pilot Julianna Fregin and her trusty E.I. named Pip, must recruit a diverse team of specialists, both human and alien. They'll need to master their new Q-Ship, one of the most powerful strike ships ever constructed. And finally, they'll have to stop a faceless enemy so powerful, it threatens to destroy the entire Federation.

All in a day's work, right?

Experience this exciting military sci-fi saga and the latest addition to the expanded Kurtherian Gambit Universe. If you're a fan of Mass Effect, Firefly, or Star Wars, you'll love this riveting new space opera.

NOTE: If cursing is a problem, then this might not be for you.

Check out the entire series here.

The Precious Galaxy Series:

Corruption #1

A new evil lurks in the darkness.

After an explosion, the crew of a battlecruiser mysteriously disappears.

Bailey and Lewis, complete strangers, find themselves suddenly onboard the damaged ship. Lewis hasn't worked a case in years, not since the final one broke his spirit and his bank account. The last thing Bailey remembers is preparing to take down a fugitive on Onyx Station.

Mysteries are harder to solve when there's no evidence left behind.

Bailey and Lewis don't know how they got onboard *Ricky Bobby* or why. However, they quickly learn that whatever was responsible for the explosion and disappearance of the crew is still on the ship.

Monsters are real and what this one can do changes everything.

The new team bands together to discover what happened and how to fight the monster lurking in the bottom of the battlecruiser.

Will they find the missing crew? Or will the monster end them all?

The Soul Stone Mage Series:

House of Enchanted #1:

The Kingdom of Virgo has lived in peace for thousands of years...until now.

The humans from Terran have always been real assholes to the witches of Virgo. Now a silent war is brewing, and the timing couldn't be worse. Princess Azure will soon be crowned queen of the Kingdom of Virgo.

In the Dark Forest a powerful potion-maker has been murdered.

Charmsgood was the only wizard who could stop a deadly virus plaguing Virgo. He also knew about the devastation the people from Terran had done to the forest.

Azure must protect her people. Mend the Dark Forest. Create alliances with savage beasts. No biggie, right?

But on coronation day everything changes. Princess Azure isn't who she thought she was and that's a big freaking problem.

Welcome to The Revelations of Oriceran. Check out the entire series here.

The Lucidites Series:

Awoken, #1:

Around the world humans are hallucinating after sleepless nights.

In a sterile, underground institute the forecasters keep reporting the same events.

And in the backwoods of Texas, a sixteen-year-old girl is about to be caught up in a fierce, ethereal battle.

Meet Roya Stark. She drowns every night in her dreams, spends her hours reading classic literature to avoid her family's ridicule, and is prone to premonitions—which are becoming more frequent. And now her dreams are filled with strangers offering to reveal what she has always wanted to know: Who is she? That's the question that haunts her, and she's about to find out. But will Roya live to regret learning the truth?

Stunned, #2

Revived, #3

The Reverians Series:

Defects, #1:

In the happy, clean community of Austin Valley, everything appears to be perfect. Seventeen-year-old Em Fuller, however, fears something is askew. Em is one of the new generation of Dream Travelers. For some reason, the gods have not seen fit to gift all of them with their expected special abilities. Em is a Defect—one of the unfortunate Dream Travelers not gifted with a psychic power. Desperate to do whatever it takes to earn her gift, she endures painful daily injections along with commands from her overbearing, loveless father. One of the few bright spots in her life is the return of a friend she had thought dead—but with his return comes the knowledge of a shocking, unforgivable truth. The society Em thought was protecting her has actually been betraying her, but she has no idea how to break away from its authority without hurting everyone she loves.

Rebels, #2

Warriors, #3

Vagabond Circus Series:

Suspended, #1:

When a stranger joins the cast of Vagabond Circus—a circus that is run by Dream Travelers and features real magic—mysterious events start happening. The once orderly grounds of the circus become riddled with hidden threats. And the ringmaster realizes not only are his circus and its magic at risk, but also his very life.

Vagabond Circus caters to the skeptics. Without skeptics, it would close its doors. This is because Vagabond Circus runs for two reasons and only two reasons: first and foremost to provide the lost and lonely Dream Travelers a place to be illustrious. And secondly, to show the nonbelievers that there's still magic in the world. If they believe, then they care, and if they care, then they don't destroy. They stop the small abuse that day-by-day breaks down humanity's spirit. If Vagabond Circus makes one skeptic believe in magic, then they halt the cycle, just a little bit. They allow a little more love into this world. That's Dr. Dave Raydon's mission. And that's why this ringmaster recruits. That's why he directs. That's why he puts on a show that makes people question their beliefs. He wants the world to believe in magic once again.

Paralyzed, #2
Released, #3

Ren Series:

Ren: The Man Behind the Monster, #1:
Born with the power to control minds, hypnotize others, and read thoughts, Ren Lewis, is certain of one thing: God made a mistake. No one should be born with so much power. A monster awoke in him the same year he received his gifts. At ten years old. A prepubescent boy with the ability to control others might merely abuse his powers, but Ren allowed it to corrupt him. And since he can have and do anything he wants, Ren should be happy. However, his journey teaches him that harboring so much power doesn't bring happiness, it steals it. Once this realization sets in, Ren makes up his mind to do the one thing that can bring his tortured soul some peace. He must kill the monster.

Note This book is NA and has strong language, violence and sexual references.

Ren: God's Little Monster, #2
Ren: The Monster Inside the Monster, #3
Ren: The Monster's Adventure, #3.5
Ren: The Monster's Death

Olento Research Series:

Alpha Wolf, #1:

Twelve men went missing.

Six months later they awake from drug-induced stupors to find themselves locked in a lab.

And on the night of a new moon, eleven of those men, possessed by new—and inhuman—powers, break out of their prison and race through the streets of Los Angeles until they disappear one by one into the night.

Olento Research wants its experiments back. Its CEO, Mika Lenna, will tear every city apart until he has his werewolves imprisoned once again. He didn't undertake a huge risk just to lose his would-be assassins.

However, the Lucidite Institute's main mission is to save the world from injustices. Now, it's Adelaide's job to find these mutated men and protect them and society, and fast. Already around the nation, wolflike men are being spotted. Attacks on innocent women are happening. And then, Adelaide realizes what her next step must be: She has to find the alpha wolf first. Only once she's located him can she stop whoever is behind this experiment to create wild beasts out of human beings.

Lone Wolf, #2

Rabid Wolf, #3

Bad Wolf, #4

BOOKS BY MICHAEL ANDERLE

For a complete list of books by Michael Anderle, please visit:

www.lmbpn.com/ma-books/

All LMBPN Audiobooks are Available at Audible.com and iTunes

To see all LMBPN audiobooks, including those written by Michael Anderle
please visit:

www.lmbpn.com/audible

CONNECT WITH THE AUTHORS

Connect with Sarah and sign up for her email list here:

http://www.sarahnoffke.com/connect/

You can catch her podcast, LA Chicks, here:

http://lachicks.libsyn.com/

Connect with Michael Anderle and sign up for his email list here:

Website: http://lmbpn.com

Email List: http://lmbpn.com/email/

Facebook:
www.facebook.com/TheKurtherianGambitBooks

Made in United States
Troutdale, OR
05/10/2025